Praise for
THE
Telling Pool

"A satisfying and well-crafted story that through Arthurian lore, brings a steadfast young boy to manhood and adult understanding." —*Booklist*

"An intriguing tale . . ." —*VOYA*

"Adds some new facets to Arthurian legend . . . An action-packed, suspenseful battle of wills . . ." —*BCCB*

"Clement-Davies draws you into his story and holds you there firmly with its constant intrigue and fantastic descriptions."
—*The Santa Fe New Mexican*

"Interweaving this historical fiction with a liberal dose of Arthurian legend, Clement-Davies creates a rich mixture of themes and metaphors." —*School Library Journal*

DAVID CLEMENT-DAVIES

THE Telling Pool

WITH DECORATIONS BY
RAND HUEBSCH

Amulet Books
New York

Artist's Note:

The illustrations at the start of each chapter were made by rubber stamps
that the artist carved with a linoleum cutter from soft polymer blocks, similar to
the material used for some erasers. The carved blocks were inked with a small
roller and then printed by hand. The resulting prints were then scanned and
incorporated into the finished book. The artist chose this image-making approach
because it echoes the two-thousand-year-old technique of woodcut printing that
was commonly used during the historial period in which the novel is set.

PUBLISHER'S NOTE: This is a work of fiction. Names, characters, places, and incidents are
either the product of the author's imagination or are used fictitiously, and any resemblance to
actual persons, living or dead, business establishments, events, or locales is entirely coincidental.

The Library of Congress has cataloged the hardcover edition as follows:
Clement-Davies, David, 1964–
The telling pool / by David Clement-Davies.
p. cm.
Summary: Relying on true courage and true love, as well as some surprising connections to
the Arthurian legends, a young Welsh teenager named Rhodri embarks on a quest to remove an
ancient curse from Great Britain during the reign of Richard the Lionheart.
ISBN 0-8109-5758-2
[1. Coming of age—Fiction. 2. Arthur, King—Fiction. 3. Magic—Fiction. 4. Adventure and
adventurers—Fiction. 5. Great Britain—History—Richard I, 1189–1199—Fiction.] I. Title.
PZ7.C59116Tel 2005
[Fic]—dc22
2005011796
Paperback ISBN 13: 978-0-8109-9257-3
Paperback ISBN 10: 0-8109-9257-4

Originally published in hardcover by Amulet Books in 2005
Text copyright © 2005 David Clement-Davies
Interior illustrations copyright © 2005 Rand Huebsch

Designed by Jay Colvin

Printed and bound in U.S.A.
10 9 8 7 6 5 4 3 2 1

HNA ■■■■■
harry n. abrams, inc.
a subsidiary of La Martinière Groupe
115 West 18th Street
New York, NY 10011
www.hnabooks.com

For Paul and Detta

Turning and turning in the widening gyre,
The falcon cannot hear the falconer;
Things fall apart; the centre cannot hold;
Mere anarchy is loosed upon the world,
The blood-dimmed tide is loosed, and everywhere
The ceremony of innocence is drowned

—W. B. Yeats, *The Second Coming*

Miri it is while sumer ilast
with fugheles song.
Oc nu necheth windes blast
and weder strong.
Ei, Ei! What this night is long!
And ich with well michel wrong
soregh and murne and fast.

—Old English Plaint

CONTENTS

1 ❖ THE TELLER AND THE SMITH

I caught this mornings morning's minion, king-
dom of daylight's dauphin, dapple-dawn-drawn Falcon . . .
—G. Manley Hopkins, "The Windhover"

White clouds, breaking into blue. Eyes, so sharp and piercing they seemed to cut the sky, moving at speed. Eyes that dropped suddenly and spied a vision of the earth; fields and rivers, mountains and valleys, then wattle-and-daub houses and, moving among them—humans. The old hunting bird extended its talons and then it was falling, straight toward its master and the village green.

As he saw the bird stoop from the clouds, a boy stopped and looked up. It was Glindor, his father's oldest but most skillful peregrine falcon, and he knew that somewhere his pa must be calling to summon him back.

For five days the little Saxon village, half a day's journey from the boy's farm, had been transformed by the arrival of an autumn fair. The air was thick with the scents of meat and mud, hay and animal dung, wood smoke and human sweat. Flutes, tambourines, and drums sang in his ears as he followed the noisy crowd down the lane. The shouts of stall holders came to tempt passersby to part with their coins, or to swap some vegetables or a loaf of bread for their wares.

The boy was desperately excited, and thankful that he was even here, for two days earlier there had been some doubt that his ma and da would take him on the difficult journey. With robbers haunting the edges of the forests, fear was rife in this countryside on the borders of Wales, where it was always dangerous to travel across open country. But his mother needed a new milk churn and his father another hunting bird from the trader Athulstan, for the coming feast day of St. Martin. Besides, neither of his parents had been willing to disappoint their son.

"Come," hissed a voice behind the boy, "come and look."

He swung round to see an old crone sitting at a table with a milking stool in front of it. Her face was more ravaged than anyone's he had ever seen before, and the boy gulped as she reached a leathery hand across the table and clasped him by the wrist.

"Hey. Let go of me," he snapped, pulling away. He noticed that her skin smelled strange and unpleasant.

"You want to know your fortune though, don't ye? We all want to know our fortune. Come, boy, don't be frightened."

The boy was repulsed by the hag. Her voice was like nothing he had heard before either, even with the many accents that mingled here on the border of Wales and England, whether Celtic or Saxon or Norman French.

"I'm not frightened," he lied.

The woman was already picking up the pack of cards, which the boy assumed she used to make her living, following these fairs and markets through the countryside. Her eyes sparkled evilly and seemed to carry a question as she glared at him.

"Such a pure and handsome face," she cried, through yellowed, broken teeth, "with a bold look, too. Like one of the heroes of old."

The boy stared back with distaste.

"Which brings both fortune and misfortune," added the crone, smiling. "Although I see you've your mother's manner and coloring."

The lad blinked in astonishment. How had she known? The locks of curly black hair about his shoulders were just like his mother Megan's. His dark Welsh skin and the freckled face were like hers, too, although his serious hazelnut eyes were like his father's. Many of the children he knew thought them strange, frightening eyes, for they were flecked with impurities, and the boy would stare at things for ages.

"How do you know that?" he demanded, sitting down abruptly on the stool in front of her.

The crone grinned and gave him the pack of cards to shuffle. She had him cut them, three times, before snatching them back again in her crabbed, witchlike fingers.

"What are they naming you, boy?" she asked, as she began to deal them out.

"Rhodri. Rhodri Falcon."

Rhodri opened his shoulders and sat up proudly. Few boys in the village, or the country around, would have dared give themselves anything as grand as a Sir-Name. Rhodri's father, Owen, was a master falconer though, who tended to a great Norman lord's hunting birds on the edge of his lands below the beech forest, so he had a right to the name. His father's real name wasn't Falcon at all, but Owen Ap Llewelyn, which means son of Llewelyn. Now that the family had come from Wales to settle among the English, Owen had changed it to draw less attention to themselves.

Many of the Saxon boys teased Rhodri about it and would try to bully him for giving himself airs and graces. But Rhodri didn't care much. Though a great dreamer, he was a feisty, energetic lad, far too impetuous his mother sometimes said, and he liked the name. Better than Cooper or Smith anyway, as the barrel maker and the blacksmith's sons sometimes called themselves.

"That pendant, boy," asked the old woman sharply, her eyes fixed now on Rhodri's chest, "where did you get it?"

Rhodri looked down at the thing. It was a strange shape, like some kind of animal's head, made of weathered bronze, with a swirling Celtic cross in its center. It was Rhodri's proudest possession. His father had once worn it, as his father and grandfather had done before him. The family heirloom had been passed faithfully from father to son, down the generations, and finally to Rhodri on his last birthing day.

"From my pa," answered Rhodri warily, remembering that thieves and pickpockets loved such fairs. The fortune-teller, just one of several who had set up their stalls on the edge of the village near the blacksmith's, nodded and smiled thinly.

"Very well then, boy." Wreaths of smoke drifted around the stalls from the forge, thickening the air of threat hanging like a pall over the weird women. The fortune-teller started to turn over the tattered cards.

Rhodri knew something of the pack, which was used to tell futures and would one day be known as the Tarot. It was still recent to Albion and was, as yet, called the Seeing Deck. He recognized first the King of Swords and then the World, a circle of gold and green and royal blue, a citadel depicted within it, held above the head of two winged children. Next came a man and a woman: the blindfolded Lovers. They were followed by the Hanged Man and the Fool, with feathers in his hair, and then a card that all children love to stare at for hours—Death.

"Don't be frightened," whispered the crone. "The card doesn't always mean what it seems to mean. Often it just tells of a journey, or a great change. Though death haunts us all."

Rhodri's attention was held fast now. The woman muttered to herself as she waved her hands over the cards and sucked in her breath. She had just turned over a card that showed a stone tower being struck by lightning.

"What can you see?" asked Rhodri, warming to the game.

"Destruction," answered the crone, "and great warfare. News comes of war, boy."

"The battle in the Norman lands?" asked Rhodri eagerly. "In France?"

The hag shook her head.

"A fight far older and far deeper. Once more the earth will drink human blood. Once more your realm shall be without a king. Word will come from Rome and place the Norman king in terrible danger."

The woman was looking strangely at Rhodri. The Norman king, he thought with glittering eyes, Richard Coeur de Lion—the Lionheart.

"And it will take a true hero to end the suffering that will grip us all. Only one with true courage and love in his heart may do it."

"When?" asked the boy. "When is the war coming?"

The crone turned over another card to reveal a figure in a cowl, standing quite alone. His back was hunched and he was leaning heavily on a wooden staff. In his hand the Hermit carried a tall hourglass. As soon as she saw him the fortune-teller looked about her and hissed angrily.

"Not you, you old meddler," she said as if she was talking of a real person.

"Who?" asked the boy, looking about, too.

The crone turned back to him sharply.

"Beware of him, child. Beware when he comes. But his hourglass shows that it will be soon. Now, let me see more."

Rhodri was trembling a little, frightened and equally fascinated, when he heard a voice behind him, addressing him in Welsh.

"What are you doing here, Rhodri?"

His father, Owen, stood there, holding Glindor on the heavy leather hawking glove that protected the falconer from its talons. Owen was a tall and powerful man, six foot two at least, with strong, vigorous hands and a prominent forehead. His eyes spoke of a natural authority. His hair, which flourished on his fine head, was beginning to turn from yellow to a glittering silver. At his belt was a bag of gold, his antler-handled dagger, and one of the long leather lures that he would swing to summon his birds.

"Come now," he cried irritably, "answer truly, son. What the heavens are you doing here? I've told you before not to talk . . ."

"Nothing, Pa," said Rhodri, dropping his eyes, "She made me watch."

"Then come away," said Owen sternly, speaking in English and glaring at the crone. "Ma will need some help and I still haven't found Athulstan yet. Besides, you don't want to be bothering with this foolery."

The hag looked up at Owen with interest, and Rhodri thought she gave him a sly look.

"You," she whispered, "the boy's father. You've strength in you, too. And a role in this."

"A role?" said Owen, "What on earth are you talking about?"

The fortune-teller turned over yet another card. It was the Enchantress, seated on a high-backed chair, like a throne, and behind her in the distance was a great, dark cave. Rhodri noticed the teller smile to herself.

"Wouldn't you like to know the boy's fate, too? He has a very great destiny."

Rhodri sat up.

"Does he now?" said Owen coldly, moving Glindor even closer to unnerve her. "If I covered your palm in gold, no doubt you'd tell me he'll serve the king himself and marry into a high family, have seven children, and live happily to a ripe old age."

"I tell you only what I see," answered the woman, scowling at Owen and the bird, "and I see you've both dreams in your eyes."

"Idle nonsense," snorted Owen. "The Holy Church teaches that magic is the devil's work. Come on, Rhodri, let's be going."

Owen turned and stalked away. The crone scooped the cross of cards back into the pack and addressed Rhodri as he got up.

"Parents are not always so right, boy," she hissed, "no matter how wise they seem. And, to their children, they always seem wiser than gods."

"I'm sorry, but I have to go," said Rhodri.

"I've more to tell you. Much more."

The hag turned over the last card. It showed another woman, holding a sword in her left hand and a golden scales in her right, backed by a fine, young knight on a white charger. The card was Justice and the crone seemed troubled by it.

Rhodri set off after his father down the muddy lane.

"Come back," called the fortune-teller, and her voice dwindled in the fair.

Rhodri was sorry that he hadn't had a chance to learn more of his great destiny, but he was soon caught up again in the sights all around him and his father. His heart began to race as they walked toward the center of the village, for it seemed that the whole of human life had descended on this wonderful place.

"You like it, *bach*?" asked Owen as they went, using one of the warmest words of affection in Wales, meaning "little one." He had already forgiven his son. Ahead a tumbler rolled along on a barrel, spinning forward in the air and landing perfectly on the moving stand.

"Oh yes, Pa. It's so much bigger than last year."

Owen waved to a man crossing the track, a common visitor to the Falcon home, Waylinn, who shod the horses. Two gigantic, sweating wrestlers were locked together in the mud, and a red-suited juggler, with a face like a moldy turnip, was throwing up batons, like those Rhodri had just seen on one of the cards in the fortune-telling pack.

"Yes indeed, Rhodri. Perhaps, with the wars in the Norman Lands that the Lionheart pursues so ruthlessly, more and more are running away to join such fairs."

Rhodri felt an odd tightening in his chest. The witch had mentioned the Lionheart.

"You'll not be sent over the channel to fight too though, will you, Pa?" Owen ruffled his son's hair.

"No, son. I'm a master falconer, Rhodri, not a soldier or mercenary, bless the good Lord. And the earthly lord we serve doesn't care to fight in the Frankish lands again. He's happy to watch his birds take their prey in the open air."

Rhodri wanted to take his father's hand and squeeze it tight, but he was too old for such gestures now.

"Besides, I'll never leave you or your mother alone and defenseless. But don't tell the other boys what I say, mind you," added Owen with a wink. "They might start to whisper that your father's a coward."

"I'll fight any that say it, and bloody their noses."

"Spoken like a true Welshman," cried Owen, smiling delightedly at his son. "And you were always hot tempered. I know that you'd fight like a lion. Your grandda would be proud. Think of how many brave scars he won himself in the Holy Lands."

Rhodri had never met his grandfather, who had fought in the first Holy War that took men to free the Eternal City, Jerusalem, from the infidel. The city where Christ was crucified for all men's sins. It had fallen to Christian soldiers a hundred years before, before being lost again almost as quickly to the Moselmen. Rhodri suddenly realized with a thrill that his own pendant must have journeyed with his grandda across the sea, like the rusting broadsword that hung over the hearth in their home. Owen had told him many glorious tales of the war, although he always said, too, that real glory is the happiness of hearth and home.

Nearby a minstrel began to strum on a lute and his voice rose in longing. It was an old Frankish song, about a wandering knight and his lost love, and it was so beautiful that even the tumbler stopped to listen. Then the minstrel sang another song in the English tongue.

"Merry it is while summer lasts, with wild birdsong, but now the naked winds do blast, and weathers strong . . ."

His voice faded as father and son came on a group of soldiers who served Owen's liege lord, Pierre De Brackenois. They were out of uniform, apart from the swords at their belts, and were passing round a flagon of strong mead, thoroughly enjoying the fair. The men seemed in good humor, although many of the locals looked at them darkly and muttered.

Well over a century after the Conquest, Norman lords, speaking the hated French tongue, still held the most powerful positions in England. But they no longer spoke the French quite so freely and many had mixed their own with Saxon blood. Owen's master, Lord De Brackenois, was such a man, for he had taken a Saxon bride. Yet there were still those who were deeply resentful of their rulers from across the channel, and of soldiers like these, who served them.

As Owen and Rhodri drew closer, another soldier ran up.

"Why are you loafing?" he cried angrily, "getting drunk when there's work to be done. Those serfs were spotted yesternight, they'll be long gone now."

"What are you chafing at?" growled the largest of them. "They only escaped three months back. There's time yet a plenty for the King's Law to work. We're enjoying the fair."

Rhodri knew the soldier was talking of the ancient law that allowed a serf, bound to the land and his lord for life, to go free if he ran away and remained on the loose for a year and a day. Soldiers were often hunting serfs down and showed little or no in mercy doing it.

"And what if they get into the forests?" growled the first. "Or cross the border into Wales? I'm not following them among those savages."

"They must escape to a town to become true freemen," said another. "That's the law."

"I know the damned law and I know your duty, too. Come on."

He grabbed the flagon and pushed the others away. Rhodri wanted to follow a while, but Owen had just seen the man he was looking for and hurried his son on toward the end of the track.

Here was an open green and a kind of village square. On the grass, among scruffy bullocks and squealing pigs, a man whom Rhodri had seen at last year's fair had set up a row of perches, where a line of young hunting birds sat. They were tethered by their feet with long jesses and were wearing little leather hoods. There were three goshawks, two falcons, and a tawny owl. Athulstan the bird trader was grinning proudly as he showed them to his clients, and Owen pulled out the pouch of coins and strode forward to inspect the birds.

Normally Rhodri would have been fascinated to watch his father pick the finest creature, for Owen had an almost infallible eye for hunting birds, but he was far too interested in exploring the fair on his own.

"Don't go too far now, Rhodri *bach*," cried Owen cheerfully, as his son drifted away again.

"No, Pa. I won't. I promise."

He wandered off and the noise from the fair rose loudly about him. A little boy was riding a wooden hobby horse around the green and a mother was scolding her daughter for getting mud on her new dress. Rhodri's head began to spin. There were faces all around him, laughing wildly, or scowling as the fair-goers bumped into one another, or parted reluctantly with a piece of coin. The shouts of approval or scorn, delight or disgust, rose like their own music and Rhodri found himself thinking of the fortune-teller and her prophecy.

He told himself not to be so foolish. Although only twelve, Rhodri was already very grown-up for his age. As Megan and Owen's only child, he had many responsibilities on their little farm. He was a caring and thoughtful lad, deeply loved by his mother and father, but there were few other houses round about them and so few children for Rhodri to play with, except perhaps pretty Sarah, the miller's daughter.

Rhodri would make up for his loneliness by inventing stories, day and night. Sometimes these waking dreams were so vivid, it was if he were actually there inside his reveries. He loved to listen, too, whenever traveling tinkers came through with their tales of old Angleland, lapping them up like a kitten would a bowl of fresh milk.

Rhodri had reached a raised platform where four men were dressed in lords' clothes. The traveling players were gesticulating wildly and mouthing their lines at the tops of their voices, as they tried to earn their supper.

The story they were telling was of King Arthur and his queen Guinevere, of her love for the loyal Lancelot, who betrayed his friend and king for Guinevere's heart, and so brought ruin to Albion. Of the great magician Merlin, too, who lived beyond time, and fought the wicked Morgana Le Fey. Of the final battle where Arthur had fallen asleep and been rowed across the waves, only to rise again when Albion needed him.

"Begone, Morgana," cried a man playing Merlin, in Saxon English, lifting a wooden staff like a wand and pointing it at a player in women's clothes. "Your evil is banished forever."

Merlin was rather short and fat and Rhodri didn't think he looked like a great wizard at all.

"No, Merlin," hissed the seeming maiden, "our battle goes on. For all eternity."

Rhodri suddenly felt a powerful longing inside him to go on a great journey. As he wandered on, he found that he had come back to the smithy's near the fortune-tellers. Through the open door he saw the blacksmith at work in front of the fire, hammering on a piece of metal. It would soon be alchemized by heat and the man's labor into a new sword. Great molten sparks flew into the air as the blacksmith hammered away, and Rhodri stepped back as he felt the blast of hot air against his cheeks.

The sight of the smith through the door thrilled him, for they were mysterious, even magical figures. Perhaps it was because their dangerous trade set them at the edge of the village, and away from the community, where stray sparks could not set light to the thatched roofs. Perhaps because, as well as making powerful weapons, the best blacksmiths were said to know of deeper mysteries, too, like the mixing of minerals and the nature of stones.

As he drew closer, Rhodri was surprised to see that this smith wasn't a strong young man, as was the case with the few smiths he had come across. This man had once been tall, but now he was beginning to stoop and his hair was completely white. He lifted a powerful arm and brought his hammer down sharply on the metal. Just then someone came running down the lane and almost bumped into Rhodri.

"Mind out," cried the hurrying man angrily, as he pushed passed.

Rhodri scowled. "Look out yourself."

"You like to watch blades being forged, lad?" said a voice through the doorway of the smithy. The smith did not look up as he spoke. His accent was rich and deep, but not Norman, Saxon, or Welsh. Rather a mixture of the three. Rhodri drew closer.

"Oh, yes, sir. I love the sparks and embers. The look of new metal, too."

The white-haired blacksmith nodded and seemed pleased, for he stopped working, wiped the sweat from his forehead, and invited the boy inside.

"I don't know, sir," said Rhodri, still hovering by the threshold. "Father always warns me of strangers. He was furious when I talked to a fortune-teller just now."

The smith cocked his head, but still he did not look up.

"Fire's a wondrous thing," he said instead, as the forge flared again. "For not only does it destroy, but it also creates. And it shows you things, too, does it not? Visions in its light."

The boy's keen eyes were already caught in the firelight, and he thought of the many times he had sat at home by the hearth with his parents and daydreamed happily to himself.

"Yes, sir."

"And would you not like to wield a sword yourself, boy?"

"I have done, sir," answered Rhodri. "Pa's sword. Though only when he's there."

"And not in anger, I hope. You're too young for real anger, yet."

The blacksmith suddenly turned to look straight at Rhodri and the boy gasped in blank astonishment. Not because of the smith's words, but his eyes. They were strangely dull and seemed to look beyond the boy, or straight through him.

"But you. You're . . ."

"Blind," said the smith softly.

"But how?" asked Rhodri fearfully.

"How do I ply my craft?" answered the man, turning the blade in his clever hand. "There are other senses than sight, boy. And senses just as strong. No doubt you think me too old, too, for such work. But then youth is the enemy of age, is it not? Come closer, lad."

As if drawn by his voice, Rhodri stepped through the door and right up to the blind smith, who had tilted his head and, although he could not see, seemed to be listening intently. He reached out and put a hand straight on Rhodri's shoulder. Rhodri didn't flinch, for the touch was very calm.

"You're a strong lad," said the smith, as the forge sparked and flared dangerously. "Though perhaps small for your age."

With that the smith moved his hand toward Rhodri's throat and, as if he had seen it, clasped the little amulet, rubbing it in his fingers, testing it with his touch.

"That's finely worked," he said approvingly, "finely indeed."

"Thank you, sir," said Rhodri, wondering how he had known it was there.

"Where did you get it?"

"It was my pa's," answered Rhodri, wondering why everyone was so interested in it. "And was once my grandfather's. It's been in my family for as long as anyone can remember."

The smith's blind eyes flickered as he let go.

"Has it now?" he whispered. "Yes indeed. And it's very old. Made by one of the great smiths, perhaps."

Rhodri clasped the thing proudly.

"So why do you want a sword?" the smith asked.

"I think it would be a fine thing to fight," answered Rhodri.

"Would it now?" said the man thoughtfully, lifting the blade he was working and turning it in the sparking light, as if he could see everything about him. "Well perhaps it would. But perhaps one day you'll learn of the true sword. The sword that brings only peace."

"Peace?" said Rhodri in surprise.

The smith seemed almost to be looking now, not into Rhodri's eyes, but straight at his forehead.

"There was a sword once, a sword forged in fire and legend, which dwelt inside a stone. A sword made for a high king who ruled then and forever, and protected all that wielded it with its magic."

Rhodri felt a shiver up his spine.

"Excalibur," he whispered, thinking of the players.

"Some call it Excalibur, indeed," said the blind man with a smile, "and others, Mythirion. Some know it as the blade of Ten Thousand Tears and others as Tintallor, the Hope Bringer."

Rhodri's heart beat faster.

"It was the sword whose edge cuts through lies, as a knife through butter, and whose true sheath is made of solid stone. The sword that the great sorcerer Merlin placed inside Bethganoth, the rock the roots of which go down to the very heart of the world."

Rhodri had heard nearly every story there was to hear of Excalibur, but this strange blacksmith was telling him things that he did not know. A rock called Bethganoth. The sword in the stone. As the boy stood there and gazed into the flames, for the briefest of moments he fancied that within the fire's heat he could see the great rock and at its top, the hilt of a magical sword.

"The sword that was cast back into the lake?" he said, not to seem ignorant, and shaking off the reverie. "When King Arthur passed away. The lake where the fair lady resided."

The smith thrust his handiwork back into the fire to temper it more.

"Was it now? Some say that it was not water into which Excalibur was cast, and that it will be redrawn again in a time of terrible danger to Albion. But that it can only be wielded by one with true courage and love in his heart."

Rhodri gulped. These were exactly the same words the old crone had spoken to him.

"Tell me, young man," said the smith, "do you believe in magic? Really believe, I mean, with all your heart and soul. Magic and miracles."

Rhodri didn't know what to say. He found himself aping his father's words. "Our Savior worked miracles, sir," he said, "but the Church teaches that magic is the devil's work."

The smith raised an eyebrow over one blind eye and now Rhodri saw that a thin scar ran right across both lids.

"And your Church teaches many strange things, to keep the ignorant under its yoke."

"My Church?" said Rhodri.

"There are many worlds," the blind man went on, and it was as if everything outside the forge had vanished and Rhodri could hear him alone, "and many people born into them. There are faiths far, far older than that taught by your holy Church."

"Faiths, Sir?"

"Oh, yes," said the smith, withdrawing the sword again. It was glowing bright red and Rhodri could feel its heat on his cheeks. "As for magic, some indeed use the Law to call on the dark forces of the world. But if black magic exists, must not white also?"

Rhodri did not know of this law, but the smith seemed to mean something other than the law of the king. Talk of black magic made him a little nervous, too, and he backed away.

"Wait," said the man and he pointed the tip of the sword straight at Rhodri, who blushed and stopped again.

"You said you were reading the cards earlier, lad, but wouldn't you like to see more than just pretty painted pictures? See something truly magical? You've a questing in you, and the air of one who really seeks. You're young yet, it's true, but maybe one day you'll be ready to look and see. To look into the deep, dark waters of the Telling Pool."

The smith was smiling at Rhodri and suddenly he plunged the blade into a bucket of water next to him. He had not reached out to find it at all. There was a furious hissing and a great cloud of steam billowed up around them both.

"The Telling Pool?" said Rhodri, wreathed in water vapor. "What's that?"

"An ancient spring, boy, deep within the heart of the forest," answered the smith gravely, "where some believe Excalibur itself was thrown. It's not a lake, but a forest pool that comes from within the belly of the living earth, fed constantly by the sacred spring. It gives life and power to the Telling Pool."

The man lifted the sword from the water once more and turned it in his hand.

"Why's it called that, sir?" asked Rhodri, wondering how a pool could have life.

"Because the pool can show you secrets that lie beneath the surface of things. Although it's dangerous to look, too."

"Where is it?" Rhodri asked. "Why are you telling . . ."

Before he could finish, he heard someone calling outside.

"My ma," he said. He hadn't seen his mother all morning. The old smith smiled and Rhodri was about to turn when the man spoke again.

"A darkness is coming, boy. When it touches the land, or those you love, seek it out. The Telling Pool. There's something special about you. You walk the Path of the Deer."

Rhodri hardly knew what to say, or what the man was talking about. His mother called more loudly.

"I'm sorry," he said, "I have to go."

Rhodri ran outside. The spell was broken instantly as the hectic, dancing noise of carnival broke over him again and from the smithy he heard the sound of hammering once more. Rhodri was sweating badly and he blinked and looked about him, wondering if he had just been daydreaming.

"Rhodri, my darling. I thought I saw you go in there."

Megan Falcon stood in the lane. A new clay milk churn was clutched to her breast and she was lifting her woollen skirts to keep the hem clear of the mud. Rhodri was pleased to see his mother. He noticed some of the men were staring at her also, for Megan was a very beautiful woman, with long, flowing tresses that tumbled down her back, clear chestnut brown eyes, and an open and generous smile.

On a little leather tawse about her neck hung another amulet, which Owen had bought for her that very morning. Though not as finely worked as Rhodri's, it was of beaten silver and formed the image of a man with a staff in a little circle—St. Christopher, the patron saint of travelers.

Megan beamed warmly as Rhodri ran up to her. He wanted to hug her, but thought better of doing so in full view of the village and any nearby boys, who might think him babyish.

"It's getting very late, *cariad*," she said, as she put down the churn and placed her hand on Rhodri's shoulder and looked at him. Megan spoke in English, although she used the Welsh word for darling—*cariad*. "Have you been having fun?"

"Oh yes, Ma. I met a fortune-teller and saw some players and just now . . ." Rhodri stopped. Something told him that he must not speak of the blind smith's words.

"Pa's on the green," he said instead, "buying the new bird for St. Martin's Day."

Rhodri had been disturbed by the smith and he felt at ease again at his mother's presence. But he pulled away when he saw some older boys he knew, and had once fought, too, walking toward them, striking out at the younger children with their stringed conkers and wooden swords.

Rhodri looked scornfully at the toys and stooped down to pick up his mother's milk churn and take charge.

Back on the green, Owen was paying the man called Athulstan two silver florins for a new rock falcon, a haggard which had just reached its first plumage. When Owen saw Megan with Rhodri, he strode up and took her in his powerful arms. He spun his wife round playfully, before leading them both over to look at the new falcon. It was a wonderful bird, with good, strong talons and powerful, angry eyes. Owen let Rhodri take it to carry back to their cart, but when they turned to go, Athulstan suddenly held up a jug of wine.

"What are you thinking, Falcon?" he cried. "To do a bargain without making a toast. A deal's a deal, and must be done well. You want bad luck for a lifetime? "

Owen smiled and drank a little, before saying farewell. As Rhodri waited, he held the new bird on his lifted hand and tried to calm his own breathing to settle the young creature. It was a trick his father had taught him with birds, to gain their trust.

Evening was coming in as the Falcons climbed on the cart that Owen had borrowed from Sarah's father, the miller, and set off at last for home. Rhodri was perched between his mother and father, and the new bird was tethered next to Glindor the peregrine falcon, in the back of the cart. The leaves on the trees at the edge of town had begun to fringe with gold and the path from the village was already thickly carpeted.

As their cart rattled along, they passed a single old woman trudging out of the village, carrying a woven bag over her shoulder. It was the ancient fortune-teller, and Rhodri wondered why she was leaving the fair. She looked up at the family as they passed, her greedy eyes sparkling wickedly.

"Ma," whispered Rhodri, suddenly feeling very tired, "do you believe in magic? That some folk can see things, I mean. Things that will come true."

Megan lifted her hand and stroked her son's cheek.

"No, my love. And even if I did I would turn away from it. Why do you ask?"

"That old woman, Ma," answered the boy, looking back warily, "She was reading the cards and she knew that I looked just like you."

Megan laughed.

"That's no magic, Rhodri. She saw us all coming into the village this morning. I recognize her. She was watching us and I think she was interested in your amulet."

Owen laughed, too. "There you are, Rhodri *bach*. Always trust your ma to show us foolish men the truth, see."

"But Ma," said Rhodri, "what's the Telling Pool?"

"The Telling Pool?" answered Megan. "I don't know, *bach*. I've never heard of such a thing."

"The lad's overexcited." Owen chuckled, spurring on the horse and thinking with sudden care of how dangerous the forests were at night. "He's been listening to the players."

The number of other travelers on the road, full of the chatter of the day and already beginning to sing, or light lanterns or torches, reassured Owen in the coming darkness, although he still wished he had brought along his father's broadsword and not just his dagger to protect them. Megan was humming to herself as she admired her amulet and Rhodri had already closed his eyes, rocked into sleep by the lilting of the cart and the tender, powerful rhythms of his parents' breathing.

As they galloped along, Rhodri Falcon was already dreaming, dreaming of a pool where the magical sword Excalibur had been thrown, a pool deep within the heart of the wild forests.

2 ❖ THE LISTS

Turning and turning in the widening gyre
—W. B. Yeats, "The Second Coming"

Higher, *bach*, swing the lure even higher."

Owen Falcon stood a way off in the big field, below the oak that Rhodri so loved to climb and look out on the world from, next to a wooden perch they had staked into the ground to launch the birds.

"Now, Rhodri, call to him now, son. If he goes too high, he'll no longer hear you, see, and then he'll be lost forever."

In the wintry sunlight Rhodri could just see the tiny speck wheeling in gyres, ever widening circles, high in the heavens above them.

"And don't let him fly too close to the trees," his father shouted, tracing the bird's looping flight with his own eyes. "Many a bird has gone wild again, lost in the wood. If we lose him at St. Martin's Day, it'll be to the family's shame."

"Come, bird," cried the boy as masterfully as he could, "come to me now."

"Use your shoulders and hands, too," Owen instructed. "A falconer must first master his bird with his voice, and then with every sinew of his being."

Rhodri opened his chest and gave a high-pitched whistle as he swung round the lure. He was desperately excited, not simply because they were out training the new falcon and had so little time if it was to appear at the coming feast, but because St. Martin's Day coincided with Rhodri's birthing day, too. He would be thirteen. He whistled again, longer and louder this time.

From the clouds, a shape came shooting toward him. The rock falcon missed the lure though and Rhodri drew it in, holding the dead field mouse tied to its end in his gloved fist and raising it slowly, so the bird could clearly see his reward. He whistled a third time.

"Come to me."

This time the beautiful creature turned in a perfect arc and sailed straight toward Rhodri. He thought it would miss again, but it landed right on his hand, gripping the rough leather glove tightly with its sharp talons, ruffling its feathers and dipping its head to taste the prize flesh with its beak, plucking at it like a musician plucks at a harp. Owen hooted with pure delight.

"Well done, truly, *cariad*," he bellowed, as he came running toward his son. It was nearly a month since they had bought the falcon at the fair, but this was the first time that it had come cleanly to the call.

"He'll be ready to show now, all right," said Owen as he reached Rhodri.

"The feast of St. Martin," said the boy, enjoying the bird's weight on his arm. "Can I take part this year, Pa? The other boys will be competing in the lists."

Owen regarded his son and the creature on his arm. Lord De Brackenois's boy, William, was only a year older than Rhodri, and Owen knew that he would certainly be there to test his own skills with the birds.

"Please, Pa, it's my birthing day."

The Master Falconer nodded.

"You're ready to compete, too. I'll let you fly him on your own this time. There'll be a prize among the children for the fastest kill and the surest return."

Rhodri's eyes grew wide, first with doubt but then pure delight.

"Hoorah," he cried, "I'll go and tell Mother straightaway."

"No need, Rhodri. Your mother's brought us our lunch."

Rhodri heard her now, too, for Megan was singing as she came up through the meadow, wrapped in her favorite green shawl. She was carrying a covered basket and a rug over her arm.

Megan smiled at her son as she reached them, but she did not make any remark or attempt to hug him, as she sometimes would in private. She knew that this was men's work and Rhodri would be annoyed if she treated him like a boy while he was falconing. Instead she kissed Owen and placed the basket like a trophy before them.

From under the cloth, Rhodri could smell the deliciously wholesome, yeasty scent of new baked bread. The falcon, who had just taken the last of the mouse down his gullet, dipped his beak inquiringly toward the basket, too.

"Husband. There's some ale for you there, and barley water for Rhodri."

"Thank you, my love," said Owen, "but the boy deserves a man's toast today. It was the first time the falcon came to the call, see. His call."

"And they've a bond," observed Megan with pleasure. "Look at them both."

The falcon swung its head toward Rhodri and snapped its beak and Rhodri swelled with pride.

"Mother, Pa says I can take part in the lists with the other boys at St. Martin's Day."

"Are you sure, Owen?" said Megan. "You know some of the older lads can get very rough now, and Rhodri is still small for his age."

"Oh, Ma."

"I'm sure," answered his father. "With skill like his the others won't touch him. It's time to prove himself."

Megan nodded. Rhodri carried the falcon over to the hunting stand and placed him on the perch with even more care than he had picked him up with that morning. Then he reached into his pocket and slipped out a plain little leather hood, which he popped over the falcon's tiny head to cover its eyes. This calmed the bird immediately, as was intended in hooding a bird of prey.

The family sat down together on the woven rug and soon they were all munching on thick slices of brown bread, smeared in creamy butter and layered with fat slices of cured ham from the pig that Owen had slaughtered two weeks before. Rhodri took his toast of ale straight from the clay jug. The thick, frothy liquid fizzed in his mouth and made his head woozy. The sun was shining brightly, and although winter was near, the day was unusually warm.

Rhodri lay back, thrilling inside at the thought of his coming birthing day and the lists. Megan and Owen were talking seriously about preparations for the winter, and as the boy listened to the reassuring sound of his parents' voices, above his head great mountains of white cloud rose in the blue. Somewhere a woodpecker hammered at a tree, making itself a winter home, and as Rhodri rolled on his side, he saw the fringes of the great forest, a flash of browns and reds and golds, shielding some impossible mystery.

He loved the forest, although even now he had only ever ventured to its edge. He knew too well the tales of danger and darkness associated with it, and although Lord De Brackenois's men made sure robbers and outlaws did not haunt these parts, you could never be certain that a stray cutthroat or a band of thieves would not appear suddenly, using its great green cloak to mask their villainy. Many wild animals lived in the woods, too: wild boars and bears and even wolves. As Rhodri lay there, he thought of what the blind smith at the fair had said of a sword called Mythirion and a mysterious pool. Of what he had whispered last, too, of his being special. What on earth had his strange words meant, about the Path of the Deer?

Rhodri was already starting to dose, imagining himself a wild and savage wolf padding fearlessly through the moonlit night, when an odd feeling came on him. Just for a moment it was as if the air itself had grown still and something had changed, although Rhodri couldn't say exactly what. He felt as if someone was watching him from the trees.

The boy was sure of it now and the rock falcon screeched furiously. Owen was already up and racing toward the bird, but as Rhodri jumped to his feet, too, he saw that his father did not make to calm the falcon, but instead grabbed for the antler dagger at the foot of the bird's perch.

"Don't worry, Ma," cried Rhodri. "There are men here to protect you."

Out of the forest came two horsemen, their sweating mounts tossing their heads and stamping their hooves. The riders turned the horses straight toward the family and came galloping furiously across the field. As they got closer, Owen let the dagger drop to his side again.

"Wolfrin," he cried angrily, "you startled us, man."

Rhodri recognized Lord De Brackenois's chief groom and behind him Wolfrin's son, Aelfric. Rhodri knew Aelfric well enough, as a spotty-faced bully who was rather too free with his tongue and his fists. They didn't like each other at all and Rhodri glared at him now.

"What goes, man?" cried Owen.

"Brigands, Falcon," answered Wolfrin from his horse, wrapping the reins tightly about his fists, "moving through the forest like wild dogs. They were spotted this morning and we're warning all the homesteads."

"We've little to fear then," said Owen, "if you're out in the wood, Wolfrin."

Rhodri's father raised an eyebrow. Long ago, when the chief groom had first arrived in the region, he had encountered outlaws on the borders of De Brackenois's manor—men who had stolen horses and stores of grain. Wolfrin, according to his own account anyway, had fought them off single-handedly. He had the battle wounds to prove it, too, a deep scar down his neck.

He was still a handsome man though, perhaps thirty-five years old, with arrogant English eyes. His blood and tongue were pure Saxon and there was something cruel in his face that Rhodri didn't like at all. The boy had met him a few times with Owen and always thought him as vain and boastful as his son. Wolfrin was often uncomfortable in Owen's presence, too, for he knew well that the master falconer doubted the tale of his courage against the bandits.

"Well, Falcon," he grunted, looking straight at Megan, "you may be right. But mind you don't drop your guard, for your wife and son's sake."

"I know how to protect my own, Wolfrin," said Owen.

Wolfrin pulled on the reins and his horse whinnied.

"Shall we see you at St. Martin's feast, Falcon? And your fair bride?"

"And my son, also. He'll fly a bird in the lists."

Rhodri fancied that something almost jealous flickered in Aelfric's eyes as he stared at the family.

"Shall he now?" asked Wolfrin, looking down his nose at Rhodri. "Then he'll meet my Aelfric here, though he's little chance against my lad's skill, let alone his bird. It's his own and I trained them both with my hand. I may be no master falconer, but I can handle a bird."

Rhodri and Aelfric stared at each other, but said nothing. Rhodri suddenly felt jealous himself that Aelfric had his own bird.

"We'll see," said Owen softly.

The groom rode off, followed by his son. The Falcon family quickly gathered their things and set off down the field toward their home and safety. Rhodri was excited by the thought of outlaws, but more consumed by thoughts of St. Martin's Day and the bond he was already forging with the bird.

The Falcon home lay beyond a copse of ash trees on the edge of the stream that snaked up toward the manor, before it joined the river on the edge of the Marches. The cottage was plain, mostly wattle-and-daub and thatched like the houses in the Saxon village had been.

The Falcons' spacious cottage was well stocked with wood from the forest, freshly chopped and piled high now against the western wall, a testament to Owen's care and hard work. The doorway was of half oak and above it Megan had hung a horseshoe to bring the family luck. The muddy courtyard was littered with the signs of farm life—wood chippings, goose and duck feathers, and wooden buckets and pails. Beyond was their patch of tilled land and Megan's little herb garden. In the distance, the green Welsh hills rose into the heavens.

As his parents went inside to prepare for the evening meal, Rhodri took the rock falcon up to the barn above the pond. Inside, one of their pigs squealed, and the smell of cow dung and dried hay came thickly to his nose. The family owned only one cow, but she gave them all the milk they needed. She was standing in her stall now, swinging her matted tail mournfully and chewing the cud.

Beyond was the birds' room, with a tiled floor, clean and lightly sprinkled with hay. Including the new falcon, Owen had five birds that, although they really belonged to Lord De Brackenois, he considered his own. The other four sat quietly on wooden perches in their mews, the wood and wire cages lined up against the long wall.

Glindor, the peregrine falcon, was at the far end, his great eyes looking as wise and circumspect as ever, and next to him was a large hawk named Karlor, then a saker falcon named Breeze and a fat, old eagle owl called Kalin. Rhodri greeted them all as he came in, with the low whistle he had learned from his father, to let them know it was him. He placed the new bird carefully on its own perch in the mew next to Glindor, and stroked its head to calm it as he tethered its jesses.

"Do you know what?" said Rhodri cheerfully to them all. "I'm going to compete in the lists on St. Martin's Day. Just think of that."

The birds looked back blinkingly and Rhodri smiled and went to find his parents.

In the house, a fire smoldered in the hearth and the air was scented with wood smoke that shimmered in the sunlight shafting through the single window. Megan had placed her basket carefully on the square oak table and was standing by the curtain at the side of the room. As Rhodri came in, she was just drawing it aside to reveal her and her husband's low-slung cot, then she opened the chest at the foot of the bed to replace the blanket she had used for the picnic.

Inside the chest were the Falcons' most valued possessions: Megan's fine lace bridal shawl and the embroidered tablecloth she worked on whenever the men were out falconing or hawking and she had finished the chores; two large pewter tankards she had inherited when her father died; several long waxen candles; and the rest of the linen for the house.

That evening, as they ate new bread with freshly boiled vegetables, the family talked eagerly of the coming feast, in just two days' time. Rhodri decided to rise even before sunup the next morning to fly and train the bird further. Since all the rhythms of the homestead were dictated by the movements of the sun, as soon as Rhodri saw that mighty fireball dipping in the west and the light outside beginning to pale to a steely gray, he said his good nights. He nearly bounded for the stair, trying to push time on as he went, toward his birthing day and the moment of his triumph at the meet.

The most peculiar aspect of the family's little home was that it had been built from the ruins of an old stone building in space cropped out of the riverbank, and although it wasn't exactly a mill house, part of the structure protruded out over the water, the little chamber at the top of the stair that allowed Rhodri, of all the children he knew, to have his own room. It was sometimes damp in winter, and it was small and often dark, but for Rhodri it was his own world, where he could sit and tell himself stories, or prepare lures for the birds, or just lie back and think and listen to the sounds of the stream and let them blend and mingle with his dreams.

His mother had brought up coals earlier to make up the little fire that glowed in the hearth at the end of his bed. Outside, a full moon had already risen, casting a cold, blue glow through the tiny window. Rhodri took off his shoes and lay down to close his eyes and listen to the stream churning and gurgling below him.

Whenever he listened, he could almost feel the coldness of the water, and imagined he could touch the reeds that clung like hair to the edges of the bank. In the daylight, Rhodri liked to look into the water and see his own reflection and experience that strange feeling, so common to children, that he wasn't at all the person looking back at him. Then he would wonder who and what he was and where he had come from.

But here above the water, Rhodri felt snug and safe. He sank deeper and deeper into the cot, down, too, into the murky, whispering stream below. He was thinking of those players at the fair, telling their tale of Arthur, and of Lancelot and Guinevere and how they had fled into the forest to seal their secret love and hide it from a king. In his mind's eye, a full moon hovered over a magical clearing. Guinevere was calling after Lancelot, but the knight was walking away from her.

"I may not, my love," he called back angrily, in Rhodri's reverie. "My oath is to him. Our King."

"I love him, too, Lancelot. But I love you also."

Lancelot was dressed in silver armor and Guinevere in a damask gown. They looked fine together, but suddenly Rhodri started and opened his eyes. The boy thought he had heard a voice in his room. He looked round.

"Rhodri. Rhodri Falcon."

Rhodri blinked and sat up. There it was again. The moon was still shining, sending long, pale shadows across the floor, but there was no one there. His sleepy eyes were casting toward the little fire and he gasped. A face was gazing out of the flames straight at him. It was proud and handsome, although it looked aged and sad, too, and on the man's head was a crown. His voice was talking to the boy.

"The oldest stories, boy, speak to us from the deepest places," it said. "For in stories lie great secrets. So listen well to them and to your heart and soul, and if you do, one day you may awake to your true destiny."

"My true destiny?" whispered the boy, rubbing his eyes in disbelief.

"You may wake to who you really are."

Rhodri thought of the smith's words about his walking the Path of the Deer.

"But who . . ."

"Rhodri, *bach*. Don't forget to do the milking tomorrow," cried another voice, calling from downstairs. It was his father. The face was gone and Rhodri shook himself, feeling foolish as he realized he must have been dreaming.

"No, Pa. I won't. I promise. Good night."

It was a good hour and a half before sunup when Rhodri woke. He dressed quickly and hurried downstairs, where Owen and Megan were still fast asleep in their cot. He quietly stoked up the embers of the dying fire and took some water and a crust of bread before going outside. As he walked across the yard, he could feel a new chill in the air, which added to the excitement bubbling up inside him.

It did not take him long to do the milking and turn to the room where the birds slept. The rock falcon looked as if it did not want to be disturbed. Rhodri stroked its head gently to rouse it, before slipping on its leather hood and lifting it from its perch and out of the mew. He took the bird to train in the big field, and as the sun began to climb over the eastern hills, shattering the skies with shards of brilliant red, he removed the blind and let the falcon fly free.

Soon Rhodri was whistling and calling, whirling the lure and raising his arm, while again and again the falcon swooped at its prey and returned to the boy's steady gloved fist.

By midday, Rhodri was so certain that he would win a prize in the lists that he ached for tomorrow to be with them already. He took the bird up the slope, closer to the trees. His father had said the forest would be a powerful temptation for the falcon, and Rhodri wanted to test the bird to its limit. He was recalling now what Owen had often taught him. "You know what they say a falconer really is, Rhodri?" he would ask. "Only one who offers a bird the chance of the best meal and one who can be a good guide in the hunt for his masters. Nothing more. For a bird of prey will always be wild, and someday he may choose to fly to a different aerie."

The falcon was not tempted by the trees, though, and with the bird there Rhodri felt little fear himself of the mysterious wood, despite Wolfrin's news of outlaws. Yet, as he stood there, the boy had the sensation again that something or somebody was watching him through the tangled branches.

• • •

The next day was St. Martin's Day. Rhodri was so excited that he could hardly speak as the family broke their fast. Megan and Owen watched him smilingly as he took his soup and ate his bread. They had wished him a happy birthing day of course, but Rhodri was disappointed that there had been no present waiting for him—a new knife, a jerkin, or perhaps a pair of shoes.

At last Owen nodded and Rhodri sprang from the table and raced up to the barn. They were to take two birds with them that day, Karlor and the new falcon, and Rhodri began to groom them carefully. The sun was mounting by the time the family gathered outside the house to walk up to the field below the manor. Owen was looking very fine, and had a brand-new hawking glove on. Megan had combed her beautiful hair, and Rhodri had bound the greaves about his legs with special care. Now he held the falcon proudly on his arm, as Owen carried Karlor.

"So," said Owen, grinning at his son, "I reckon you'll be wanting some token then. You'll ruin me, Rhodri, with all your birthing days."

The boy grinned, too.

"Well, *bach*. Do you like it then?"

"Like what, Pa?"

"Your present, boy. Who tests their skills at St. Martin's Day without their own hunting bird in the lists? Especially if you want to beat Aelfric, not to mention Pierre De Brackenois's son, William."

Rhodri's wide hazel eyes grew as round as cartwheels. "My own?" he whispered, hardly daring to believe what his father was saying, "But, you can't mean he's . . ."

"Yes, *bach*. By the way he's learning to respond to you, he's really yours already."

Rhodri gave a delighted whoop and the falcon screeched and flapped. For a moment Rhodri fancied it was signaling its approval of its new master by digging its claws even deeper into the boy's glove.

"What will you call him, Rhodri?" asked Megan. "Now you're becoming a master falconer, too."

Rhodri thought carefully awhile.

"Melanor," he answered at last, remembering a name he had heard in a tinker's story. "I'll call him Melanor."

"It's a fine, strong name, too," said Owen, "for a fine, strong bird."

"And Rhodri," said Megan, "I've this for you, too. I made it myself." She was holding up a tiny silver bell on a leather necklace. "For Melanor."

"Oh thank you, Ma."

He took the thing delightedly and tied it very carefully around Melanor's little feathered throat. It tinkled and Rhodri felt as if his heart might burst with happiness. This was the most wonderful birthing day he had ever had.

"But remember now, son," said Owen, "the first lesson of a master falconer . . ."

"I know, Pa . . . never to take him for granted."

They set off for the manor house and the big field where the neighborhood would gather for St. Martin's Day. As they walked, Rhodri found himself dropping behind his parents, thinking of his coming triumph. A voice behind him interrupted his reverie.

"Rhodri."

The boy swung round. Sarah, the miller's daughter, was coming along the lane toward him.

Rhodri was always glad to see Sarah. She was a lovely girl, of Saxon stock, with rich honey-colored hair and a sunny, friendly manner. Her face had filled out and she looked far prettier than he remembered her. As for Sarah, she noticed how much taller Rhodri had grown than when she had seen him last, perhaps three months before.

"Are you going to St. Martin's Day, Rhodri? Can I walk with you?"

"Of course, you can, Sarah."

The two hurried on together, but although they had often walked, or fished for minnows and tadpoles, or played Stay-in-the-Mud with some of the other children in the neighborhood, Rhodri now found himself at a loss for words. For the first time he felt awkward in the girl's presence, as if he didn't know her at all, and to hide the fact he kept stroking and petting the falcon.

"He's a fine bird, isn't he?" said Sarah, seeming just as awkward as Rhodri felt. "What is he?"

"A rock falcon. He's a haggard, which means he has his first plumage, see. And he's mine, Sarah."

"Yours?"

"My birthing day present. I'm going to fly him in the lists this morning."

"Happy birthing day then, Rhodri. I'll clasp a sprig of rosemary for you, to bring you luck."

Rhodri smiled. Sarah was always talking about charms to bring people luck. She liked collecting stones, too, and often spent time dreaming down at the little wishing well, along the path behind the church.

"I bet he eats a lot."

"A fair deal," said Rhodri a little stiffly, noticing Sarah's hair and the softness of the skin around her shoulders, "we sometimes give him bits of chicken, but mice and vole are his favorites."

"Uggh."

"I know," said the boy, grinning at her. "I have to catch them with bread in the barn and keep them alive until we hunt. He'll only have the fresh ones. I have to break their necks, too."

His eyes sparkled mischievously and Sarah shivered, only partly from cold.

"Stop it, Rhodri."

"I'm sorry. I mean no harm."

Sarah smiled and flicked her hair with the sudden naturalness of a girl. Rhodri felt an odd feeling in his stomach. They were walking close, their hands almost touching, and although his parents were just up ahead, Rhodri had the urge to slip his hand into Sarah's. He had never kissed a girl, although he had seen some of the village boys do so and he had always wondered what it would feel like. But instead Rhodri lifted Melanor on his arm and began to walk even faster.

"I don't want to be late, Sarah. Pa will need help making lures."

The girl looked at Megan and Owen up ahead.

"You're good to your parents, Rhodri," she said warmly. "It's one of the things I've always liked in you."

Rhodri felt strangely threatened by the remark. They walked on in silence for a while, pretending to admire the day or look out across the trees. But both were intensely aware of the rhythm of each other's breathing and the pace at which they moved side by side. At last they saw the manor in the distance.

The field near it had been transformed. A great white tent had been erected where Lord De Brackenois and the other nobles of the region would feast, although there was no sign of the lord, only his stewards and retainers and another local noble, a tall, black-haired man named Treffusis. He was giving orders and getting things ready. All around, simple folk of the district were here, too, to celebrate, and had set up food stalls and little shops. At one end of the field, a horse race was already under way and there were plenty of animals on sale. Rhodri suddenly wondered, a little naively perhaps, if it was all for him on his birthday.

"There's my pa, Rhodri," cried Sarah, interrupting his daydream. "God's luck in the lists."

As she ran off to join her father, Rhodri watched his old friend for a long time. She was thirteen and nearly as tall as his mother, but there was something new and unfamiliar in her tread. Something he felt powerfully drawn to.

Just then, a horse come trotting across the crowded field and distracted the boy. Riding high on it was an extraordinary man in a black satin robe and a hood that dangled down from his neck. He was very well fed and his ruddy cheeks were lightly veined from too much mead and Burgundian wine. He had an expensive pair of leather shoes on, pointed wildly at the tips, and Rhodri knew that he was somebody of importance. A kind of quiver was strung about his chest, but inside were not arrows, like the ones Owen sometimes launched to take a deer or a rabbit on the edge of the forest, but scrolls of new parchment.

"Come," he cried, in a loud English voice, "come and read of the certain way into paradise."

Rhodri stepped forward. He had always wanted to read, but there was no such schooling on the estate, except for that given to Lord De Brackenois's son. He felt a shiver of frustration as he watched others line up to buy. His father and mother joined him.

"Who is he, Pa?" Rhodri asked.

"A pardoner who brings indulgences," explained Owen, scowling at the man, just as he had done at the crone at the fair. "Pardon and the official forgiveness of sin, from the Holy Father himself in Rome, written on those parchments."

"Cures for the soul," added Megan with a laugh.

Rhodri shivered a little. He always felt peculiar when the priest in the church near De Brackenois's manor talked to them of sin. The pardoner had already begun to call out to the sinners all around him, loudly and cheerfully, plucking another one of the scrolls from his pouch and waving it tantalizingly in the air, as all around the merrymakers crowded in.

"They just want gold from the trade," said Owen, shaking his head. "Lord De Brackenois argues that you cannot buy forgiveness of sin, or less time in purgatory. For did not Christ drive the moneylenders out of the Temple?"

"And Pierre De Brackenois is a truly educated man," said Megan.

A plump woman who had overheard them shook her head and made a sharp tutting.

"Shame on you, Master Falconer," she chided. "A holy pardoner deserves real respect, and who are we to argue with the will of the Pope, the ruler of Christendom?"

Owen muttered something that Rhodri had often heard him say. "I respect what I respect."

"Sign here," cried the pardoner, looking down at an old farmer from his horse, "and for a new piece of gold, your soul will be freed from torment far sooner than it might. And you'll have the document to prove it."

The pardoner dismounted and told the farmer to make his mark, since he couldn't write. Then he began to make a kind of impromptu sermon, although in truth it was well rehearsed. But another man stepped up in front of the crowd. He was a young apothecary who was offering cures for the body, not the soul, in little bottles of liquid that looked as green and slimy as the scum on the pond when the tadpoles came and which he claimed healed anything from the ague to rheumatic fever.

"And make you fart silently at night, I hope," called a Saxon yeoman, nudging the friend at his side heavily in the ribs, "even after a stew of buttered beans and broiled ox tongue. So your wife don't kick you out of bed in winter."

"Peasant." The apothecary snorted.

The yeoman's companion blew out his lips like a horse, and they both laughed as the apothecary blushed and turned up his nose. Owen led his family away, with Rhodri wondering if a liquid really could do such miraculous things as cure the body. They settled under a copse of beech trees and Megan began to lay out the food she had prepared for the day.

"Come on, Rhodri," cried Owen, "the men will compete first, but the boys will be waiting for their turn."

Rhodri was rather nervous as he followed his father to the fence beyond which the falconry field lay. The field sloped straight up to the forest and beaters with sticks were disappearing into the trees. They would soon begin bashing the undergrowth to send up prey for the hunting birds. The men were already preparing themselves to compete, but Rhodri was more interested in the group of lads gathering nearby with their own birds. In the middle he spotted Lord De Brackenois's son, William, in a fine set of St. Martin's Day clothes.

Rhodri had not seen much of William, since the young noble had spent years being tutored away from home, but he had passed close to him two months back in church and had spotted him many times about the neighborhood recently. Although Rhodri had often wanted to, he had never spoken actual words to the older boy. Their homes were close, but to a humble yeoman boy like Rhodri Falcon, and a Welsh one, too—their worlds were so far apart that William seemed like a cardinal of the holy city to a mere priest, or a high courtier to a burgher of London.

Next to William, dressed more humbly, stood Aelfric. Although Aelfric was only a groom and of Saxon not Norman blood, he and William were the same age and as young children had almost grown up together, so they were friends. Perhaps because of the easier mingling of bloods on the Welsh borders, the ties between the social ranks were somewhat freer on De Brackenois's estate than they might have been elsewhere.

There were several other boys Rhodri recognized too, all the sons of local squires, and the boy tightened his belt and set off boldly toward them. Owen was about to call something encouraging, but he stopped himself. He understood that his son wanted to be separate from him now, especially in front of the other children.

The boys had their birds perched on wooden stands, and there was a space for Melanor at the far end, so Rhodri settled him carefully, and turned to size up the competition. Aelfric gave Rhodri a sneering look, but William seemed to smile back openly enough. He was surrounded by six other boys, all laughing and joking together. William and Aelfric had fine birds, too, a peregrine and a laner falcon, but, by the look of them, the other boys' birds seemed little real competition. Rhodri wondered what the boys were saying and if they were talking about him, but he pretended not to care and reached down into his bag instead to take out some lures. He began to rub them with walnut oil to make them spin faster and then set to cutting off any frays with his knife. He straightened Melanor's jesses, too.

They heard a shout. The men were beginning their competition. Rhodri was far too nervous though to think about anything but his own coming event. At last he plucked up the courage to join the other boys. As he drew closer, he wondered if they were discussing their tactics for the day.

They weren't talking about falconry at all. One of them, a lad called

Simon, was describing a fight he had had at the fair with two other boys, and was growing more and more heated. A debate began about what kind of sword the boys would all like to own, and there was much ragging and showing off.

"I've already used my father's sword," said Aelfric boastfully, shaking out his red locks, "and he lets me sharpen it, too."

"Good for you, Aelfric," said William de Brackenois. He spoke in English but his voice was threaded with the quick, lilting song of a Norman child, who spoke French, too, in the home.

"I want a sword," said another boy. "I want one like our blacksmith forged last spring for Lord Treffusis."

Rhodri felt it a privilege to listen. But as they talked excitedly, no one was paying him much attention and suddenly he wanted to join in and impress them all.

"Well, I'd like Mythirion, see," he interrupted loudly, "which some call Excalibur, and others Tintallor, the Hope Bringer."

The boys stared back at the odd little Welsh lad in surprise, and Rhodri couldn't help blushing. One of them laughed and Rhodri lifted his chin.

"It lay in the great stone Bethganoth," he insisted, "where the sorcerer Merlin placed it, with a spell, so that only the High King Arthur could draw it forth. For it may only be wielded by one . . ."

He paused.

"Well?" said Aelfric.

"By one with courage and truth in his heart," finished Rhodri, dropping his eyes. "It will come again at a time of peril to the land."

The boys all grinned and Aelfric's look had grown particularly mocking. Rhodri had already overreached himself, but there was no turning back.

"At the fair last month," he said, "a fortune-teller read the Seeing cards for me. She told me that news of warfare comes to our land from Rome. That the earth will drink human blood."

Some of the boys seemed impressed by this.

"But not the war in the Frankish realms. King Richard shall be in danger and it shall take a great hero to end the anguish. Perhaps, too, the sword that brings only peace."

With the boys staring at him as if he were some rather ridiculous new beast, Rhodri wished he could draw the words back into his mouth, but Aelfric stepped up and pushed his face straight into Rhodri's.

"A great hero?" he sneered. "Like you perhaps, little Falcon? The size of a stile gate, with goose feathers in your head. A useless haggard. And what do you mean our land, Waelas?" Aelfric continued, using the rudest word he could think of for the Welsh. "The Waelas have no land, except the bogs across the border, and we'll take those from you soon enough."

The others laughed loudly, all except William, who was watching Rhodri keenly and stroking his bird, a beautiful creature called Shadowfell. Rhodri's face turned bright red and he clenched a fist, ready to fight.

"Unless you go about stealing and thieving land, see," Aelfric went on, in a mock Welsh voice, "as is your want, look you."

"Shut up, Aelfric."

Aelfric bridled but he saw Rhodri's fist and, although he was a lot bigger than Rhodri, it made him pause.

"It's true what my father says of you, Falcon," he snorted, covering his own nervousness with a loud contempt, "spending all your time moping and dozing and daydreaming. And I'd like to see a pipsqueak like you wield Excalibur. Even a fable would pull you flat on your face."

"I could wield it," snapped Rhodri, and he remembered that face in the firelight, talking to him in his room. "Perhaps it's my destiny."

"Your destiny?" The boy laughed loudly and the others, except William De Brackenois, joined in. "I'll tell you your destiny, Waelas. To serve your betters dutifully and keep your mouth shut. Besides, I've never heard of a sword that brings peace. What childish rubbish."

Rhodri was going to answer when again they heard a great shout behind them and a burst of applause. The men had just finished their competition. Rhodri knew what had happened from the smile on Owen's face. The master falconer, who always competed himself at St. Martin's Day, before attending to his lord's own hunting needs, strode toward them with Karlor on his arm. Wolfrin was just behind, looking angry and jealous. The groom didn't spend much time with the others, but instead mounted his horse and rode off in the direction of the manor. Aelfric had seen his father's anger, and his own look became really evil, but before he could say anything more to Rhodri, one of the stewards addressed the boys.

"Come, young men, it's time."

In an instant, the lads were all at their perches preparing their birds excitedly. As Aelfric began to tend to his own laner falcon, a hard-eyed creature called Mordrin, he looked at Melanor and scowled.

"What's a peasant doing with a bird like that?" he said, so the others could overhear him. "A knave like you might own a kestrel, but not a rock falcon. It's not right."

Rhodri was still smarting from his earlier humiliation, but he could hardly argue. As the falconer's son, he knew the clear rules stating who in the social order could own certain types of birds: from the merlins and golden eagles that someone as lofty as an emperor might fly, to the gyrefalcons of a king, the saker falcons of a knight, the female sparrowhawks of a priest, and the humble kestrels reserved strictly for servants, knaves, and yeomen.

"Leave him be, Aelfric," said a voice. William De Brackenois was separating Shadowfell's jesses. "He's the master falconer's boy, so he's as good a right as any to the bird, if he can fly it. As does a groom's son, Aelfric my friend."

Aelfric blushed and Rhodri felt grateful to the young lord. But he would still show them all.

The competition between the children was divided into three parts. The first involved grooming and care, and Rhodri and Melanor had done especially well by the time the second round arrived. This was to fly the birds with lures in the open field. Again the two of them fared well, although William and his peregrine falcon won this section of the contest.

With points added together from both rounds, only five of the children could go on to the next stage, to take live prey, beaten up from the wood. Rhodri came through with William and Aelfric, Simon and another boy called Basil. So they stood, the five of them, Rhodri between William and Aelfric, waiting for the most thrilling part of the lists. The steward raised a gauntlet, preparing to time the contest.

The grown-ups had all gathered round to cheer their children on, and Sarah was there, too. Owen and Megan were looking on proudly as Rhodri stood waiting for the beaters. There was a cry from the wood. Rhodri, distracted by Sarah, was slow to release Melanor. Already William's bird, Shadowfell, was streaking through the sky toward the woodcock and Melanor was quick to follow. They reached it together, but Shadowfell's talons snatched it from the skies and made the kill.

"Five points," cried the steward.

William De Brackenois turned to smile at Rhodri, dipping his head in acknowledgment of Melanor's skill and grace.

Ten more game birds came up in quick succession and several of the children took one, although by the end of it William and Aelfric had taken three birds to Rhodri's two. Aelfric looked smugger than ever and Rhodri knew that if he didn't make the next kill he would be out of the running.

"So, Falcon, how could you wield Excalibur if you can't even wield a bird?" sneered Aelfric.

Just then Rhodri noticed a fluttering of wings far to the right.

"Take it, Melanor, take it for me. Fly, bird, as fast as the wind."

Rhodri threw his arm out and Melanor shot forward and struck in an instant, taking the partridge in his lifted claws and beating his beautiful wings even harder as he compensated to take the weight. Rhodri loved Melanor in that moment. He whistled and the falcon turned to see him holding up the lure to tempt him back again. The graceful bird swooped in hungrily and the steward dropped his gauntlet to a huge burst of applause.

"Thank you, Melanor."

The steward called to Rhodri, William, and Aelfric, who had tied with three birds each, and they advanced proudly to compete in the final round.

Rhodri could feel the anger coming from Aelfric, but he kept calm and steady, and soon he and William were in the lead. The steward held up his arm and a servant picked up a little wooden cage with a grouse in it and began to march down to the end of the field.

"You've all done well, boys," he cried, looking at William, "but it is between my lord De Brackenois and the falconer's boy now."

Aelfric scowled.

"To end it we will release just one quarry. Whoever takes it, wins."

As a mark of respect, the steward had not told Aelfric to stand down from the lists, so when the grouse went up he was still on the field of battle. Just as Melanor flew past Aelfric's line of sight, Aelfric threw out his arm angrily and released Mordrin, too.

Melanor and Shadowfell were flying fast but Mordrin was on their tails, his jesses streaking in the wind. The grouse was rising fast, and all the birds curved upward, but Melanor was the fastest. He would have taken the prey and won the competition for Rhodri if, just as he was about to hit, he hadn't been knocked sideways. Mordrin had struck him from behind and Shadowfell took the grouse instead, to more delighted applause. The other two falcons turned in the skies for a moment, fighting in the air with their talons, but they broke free of each other almost as quickly and curved away.

Rhodri wanted to run at Aelfric and punch him, but Melanor was rising higher rather than turning back toward the field. Rhodri began to call and whistle to him desperately. If he didn't master him quickly he could lose the frightened bird altogether. He pulled out one of the lures and began to whirl it frantically in the air.

"Melanor!"

The grown-ups had already surrounded William and were congratulating the young lord on his victory, while Mordrin had just landed on Aelfric's fist.

"Melanor. Come back, Melanor."

Rhodri believed he had lost the bird, and all thought of the contest vanished into bitterness, when suddenly the speck in the heavens turned and began to descend. The falcon had taken Rhodri's call. There was the bird again, landing on his fist and screeching angrily as it flapped its wings.

Aelfric scowled as he hooded his own bird, while Owen and Megan ran up to console their son. Owen put a hand on Rhodri's shaking arm. The boy noticed the cut on Melanor's belly where one of Mordrin's talons had caught him. Owen examined the wound and said it wasn't deep, as Rhodri slipped the hood back over his bird.

There was loud cheering for William De Brackenois. Megan took the falcon from Rhodri, and the family walked over to join the crowd around the young lord. Rhodri looked jealously at the prize that William had just won. It was an exquisite little falconry hood, not plain leather, but worked in the finest hide and woven with gold braid. Rhodri felt sick and glared at Aelfric.

"What are you looking at, Waelas?"

"You're a filthy cheat, Aelfric," cried Rhodri.

"Cheat? What do you mean, dolt? You think I can talk to animals and order Mordrin to . . ."

"No. But you waited until Melanor was passing him. If you hadn't cheated . . ."

"Say another word, Waelas, and you'll feel my fist."

Rhodri couldn't hold himself in any longer. He hurled himself at Aelfric with a shout of fury and, grabbing him round the waist, knocked him to the ground. Megan cried out as fists flailed and a ring of children formed around the boys, whooping and cheering and goading them on.

"Hit him, Aelfric. Punch him in the face."

"Stop it, Rhodri." The boy felt a fist strike his jaw as Sarah shouted from the crowd, and a sting of intense pain. He saw Sarah's face contorted with distress and let fly at Aelfric. His fist struck the boy's nose and he felt a thrill as he heard Aelfric groan. He felt his being move by instinct, delighting in the tussle and proud at his obvious courage in fighting a boy so much larger than himself.

But suddenly there was a louder cry from across the field. A man's cry. Aelfric's father, Wolfrin, was galloping toward them, waving his arm furiously, and next to him rode a nobleman on a fine black steed. It was Pierre De Brackenois himself. As the chief groom and his master wielded in their horses, the fight broke up immediately. Aelfric and Rhodri got to their feet, dusting themselves down and glaring at each other, as they wondered what was happening.

"Our lord wants all bonded men to come up to the manor," cried Wolfrin, dipping his head in deference to the older man. "There's grave news."

"News?" said Owen, stepping forward and bowing to De Brackenois, too, but looking hard at Wolfrin. "What news?"

"A call has come, Master Falconer," answered Wolfrin, from the saddle. "From Londinium and the king himself. King Richard the Lionheart."

3 ❖ THE DECISION

Ancestral voices, prophesying war!
—Samuel Taylor Coleridge, "Kubla Khan"

The children, whether Norman, Saxon, or Welsh, high or low born, had grown silent and deathly still. The pardoner looked rather put out and the apothecary put down his bottle.

"And when a king calls," said Owen gravely, "even the freest falcons answer. What call, my lord?"

"Holy war," cried Pierre De Brackenois. "The Pope in Rome has called another Holy War, Owen Falcon, and the Lionheart answers. Men go from all over Albion to free the Holy City once more. The banner of Christ is on the march again."

The pardoner seemed to stand up straighter and Megan clasped her husband's hand. Rhodri looked at William, who had gone white. The crowd was beginning to murmur nervously, some speaking in Norman French, others in Saxon English. But several of the boys had turned to look at Rhodri in astonishment. Even Aelfric's eyes were frightened. A call from Rome. It was just as Rhodri had foretold.

"Lords and serfs already journey from across the lands of Albion," said old De Brackenois, turning in his saddle to address them all, "bonded and freemen, vassals and villains. The Lionheart is raising a great tax to pay for his armies, and the southern ports swell. It's still-ing the conflict in the Norman lands, too, for Norman lords go to fight for the Cross and the French King Philip shall join Richard in leading them."

The chatter around the lord grew even more frantic.

"The Pope has again offered plenary indulgences to kill the Saracen. Total and complete forgiveness of sin. If we slaughter the murderous Moselmen in this Holy War, we shall all go straight to paradise."

Some of the men in the crowd grunted approvingly and the pardoner started putting away his parchments, but Megan looked desperately at Owen. The falconer seemed measured and calm, although his eyes had grown very somber.

"And you, my lord?" cried Owen, pulling out a kerchief to rub the sweat off his neck. "Will you go?"

"His lordship is not decided yet, Falcon," said Wolfrin, though his eyes were twinkling darkly, "hence he calls this meet."

"I want you there, Falcon," said the old lord, smiling fondly at the falconer, "for you know how I value your counsel."

Rhodri saw something jealous flicker in Wolfrin's face.

"Come with me now, Falcon," said the groom irritably, "ride at my back and I'll return you home by sunset. All the stewards are to come to the house, too. St. Martin's Day is at an end."

Owen stepped up and quickly swung himself onto the horse behind Wolfrin. The two men looked hostile sitting so close. Pierre De Brackenois had already turned and ridden away.

"Rhodri," Owen called, "take your mother and the birds back to the house straightaway and wait for me there. I must obey his lordship."

The boy nodded at his father, his jaw too hurt to speak, although the news had robbed him of words anyway.

"And tell our good lord," whispered Megan, coming forward to touch her husband's knee, "not to do anything so foolish as go to war, even for the living Christ. Please, husband."

Rhodri was embarrassed by his mother's soft words, especially after all he had boasted of Mythirion to the other boys. But he noticed that Wolfrin was looking down almost cruelly at Megan, as if he was pleased by her distress, and he felt a knot of anger in his stomach toward the man who had brought such black news. Wolfrin spat and spurred his horse away toward the manor house at breakneck speed.

All around them the St. Martin's Day party was coming to an end. Rhodri and Megan stood watching Owen's retreating form, and the boy wondered now what Owen would tell them when he came home to them with the sunset.

Sarah was watching him, and she shook her head as she recalled how he had lashed out at Aelfric, but she felt his worry, too.

"It'll be all right, Rhodri," she called, as the miller dragged her away, too.

Rhodri smiled thinly. Through this worry, though, Rhodri also felt a wild excitement, bordering on anger, as he remembered Lord De Brackenois's words of the southern ports swelling and Norman knights joining with nobles from Albion. Lost in these thoughts, Rhodri started when he heard a voice.

"Falcon." William was standing right behind him, holding up the intricate little hood he had just won in the lists. "This belongs to you, I think."

Rhodri stepped back in surprise and shook is head. "No, my lord. You won it fairly and Shadowfell . . ."

"Take it, Rhodri," the young lord insisted. "I've many and the day was really yours."

Rhodri didn't raise his hand to take the hood though, and just stood there before the young nobleman. He realized how like his father he looked.

"You would honor me by taking it," William insisted.

Rhodri made up his mind. He clasped the beautiful thing.

"Thank you, my lord."

"But you frightened us all back there," added William, "with your talk of fortune-tellers."

Rhodri blushed.

"You've strange eyes, Rhodri Falcon," said the older boy, "and a special manner about you. You were brave to speak up among us like that, but be careful of the things you tell others. People are frightened of such talk. Not to mention such keen fists." William grinned. "And I know we'll be friends," he continued, "and I'd be proud to call anyone a friend who can handle a bird like that."

Rhodri felt a rush of pride.

"But now I must hurry. With this news, I want to be at Father's side. Who knows, perhaps I will be raising a sword sooner than I thought."

It was as if Rhodri could hear a voice in his head again. *Can you wake, Rhodri Falcon, wake to your destiny?*

Rhodri smiled back warmly, and the young lord hurried up toward the manor, after his father. Megan already had Karlor on her arm, and Rhodri put the prize hood proudly in his pocket as he fetched Melanor. As they set off together back toward home, Rhodri took Megan's other arm. His mother was trembling violently.

"It'll be all right, Ma. Pa promised he'd never leave us."

"If your father was free to choose, *cariad*," Megan whispered, "if any of the humbler people were free to choose."

"What do you mean, Ma?"

"Though we are no serfs, we've sworn an oath to our Lord De Brackenois, like all the Saxons on his land. De Brackenois is bonded to the Coeur de Lion. If he sets out for Jerusalem, then he'll take retainers with him."

Rhodri thought of what Owen had said of even the freest birds having to come when the king called and how the Lionheart could reach down through this chain of duties as easily as sighing, and pull at the life of a humble Welsh boy. Everything was somehow bonded to everything else and it suddenly made him angry, though he thought of the excitement of the war, too.

"Where's Jerusalem, Ma?" he asked.

"Beyond the known seas, at the very center of the world. Where the Jews live. The Christ killers."

Rhodri shivered. Just as he always did in the church when the priest spoke of the Jews. As if he had suddenly been touched by the devil's hand. The tales he had heard of Jews were filled with dark and terrible acts, of their turning the milk sour or poisoning the streams and wells, of dabbling in the black arts and even eating children alive.

"Come on then, Rhodri. We'd better get home and wait for your pa."

The sun was beginning to fall, seeming to melt in the sky, as they reached home. Rhodri returned Melanor and Karlor to their mews in the barn. As he entered the house, he looked up hopefully at the great sword hanging above the hearth.

Megan was seated quietly at the table, waiting for him.

"Do they go to fight the Jews then, Ma?" Rhodri asked, closing the door.

"No, *bach*. Now the Saracen rule in the Holy Lands. The black-skinned Moselmen. Christian knights have fought with them for many years, they say, to secure their lands and keep open the pilgrimage routes. Like the Jews, the Saracen have their own faith. In a great prophet, who came to them four hundred years ago."

Rhodri thought of the blind blacksmith, who had talked of other worlds and other faiths.

"I'd like to see Jerusalem, Ma."

"And fight in the burning heat," whispered Megan cheerlessly, "and watch your dearest friends die of pestilence or hunger, or cut down in cold blood by the Saracen?"

The boy fell silent and his mother saw the worry and confusion in his eyes.

"I'm frightening you, *cariad*," she said softly, getting to her feet. "Owen won't leave us, as you said. Come, there's some broth warming over the hearth. I'll fetch some wood and draw some water, then we'll eat together."

Megan touched her son's cheek tenderly, and went outside into the yard. Rhodri looked around their home. The firelight was dim, but everything was so familiar to him that he could have found his way about this place even in darkness. He went over to the table and drew one of the chairs across the floor back toward the hearth. Although he knew that what he had in mind was forbidden, he stood on the chair and, reaching up, unhooked the sword hanging on the wall. It was sheathed in a long leather scabbard and strung there on a leather cord.

He jumped down again excitedly and walked back to the table, laying the sword flat. Rhodri grasped the hilt and drew it carefully from its sheath.

"Mythirion," Rhodri whispered, with sparkling eyes, "the blade of Ten Thousand Tears."

Although he had a good swing, his arms began to ache badly and he grew flushed in the firelight. The sword seemed to grow heavier and heavier and Rhodri was almost relieved when he heard his mother returning. He sheathed the blade again quickly and climbed up on the chair to replace it on its hooks. By the time Megan had come in, the chair was back at the table and Rhodri was laying out some wooden platters for supper. His mother didn't notice the old blade swinging gently above the hearth.

Mother and son sat down at the table to eat and await Owen's return. But by the time the sun had sunk beyond the forests, blazing the skies in great scars of bruised purple, and darkness had crept in about them like a pall, they were still sitting there, waiting nervously and hardly talking.

"Come, *cariad*, it's best you get to your bed now."

"No, Ma. I'll wait with you here until word comes."

"No, Rhodri. I want to think and pray, see. Go up to bed now, there's a good boy. I'll wake you as soon as there's any real news."

The boy respected his mother's words almost as much as his father's, and he could see that it was best to leave her be. He looked back at the sword and Megan sitting quietly in the firelight and, blessing her in his heart, went upstairs. But as soon as he entered his room, Rhodri heard it again, that voice.

"So it comes, boy. Be ready."

The boy rushed to the fire that his mother had laid that morning, but there was no one there in the dimming coals. He waited for the voice to speak again but heard only the rush of water from the stream below.

He peered through the window, down at the small river, and noticed an otter he had often seen playing with its mate on the banks shaking its glistening coat and sliding once more into the chilly waters. Outside, their bantam cock crowed loudly, while somewhere in the forests a dog, or perhaps even a wild wolf, had begun to howl mournfully through the trees. Rhodri shivered as he listened to the chilling song.

Tomorrow, he thought, tomorrow I will go down to the stream and gather some stones and dig a channel and dam it up. His father had taught him to do it, and it was a kind of playful ritual every year. But as Rhodri thought of it, he suddenly felt that such games were beneath his years, and a strange loneliness surrounded him.

He got into bed, and as he lay on his cot, his feet sticking over the end now, he wondered what his father was saying to the lord of the manor. Rhodri could always picture his father's face, silver headed and strongly lined on his prominent brow. It was a proud Welsh face, quick to anger if insulted, but kind, too, and at times full of laughter. Rhodri had often watched him at work around the house, chopping the wood with those powerful hands, or in the fields setting snares for rabbit and hare or working the birds, and he had wondered, as sons and daughters always wonder when they first recognize a parent's movement or gesture as like their own, what part of Owen lived in him.

Rhodri opened his eyes and realized he had fallen asleep. The moon had risen even higher, and he stirred and sat up. He could hear a noise now from downstairs. He had a lump in his throat as he crept out of his room and stopped at the top of the stairs to listen.

"I have to go with this army, Megan," came his father's voice. "It's my bonded duty and De Brackenois will not defy the king. He's old now and I think he wants a shot at paradise."

Megan was sitting on the bed with her head in her hands and Owen was seated at the table. The boy felt a twinge of resentment that they hadn't woken him. The fire was blazing, sending gloomy shadows about the walls, and the boy trembled as he caught sight of the sword in his father's hands. The master falconer was polishing it with a rough cloth, and as he removed the layers of rust, it flashed brilliantly in the firelight.

"You want to go," said Megan coldly.

"Want? . . . I . . . No, wife. But think of the honor it'll bring us among the villagers, when I return."

"If you return."

On the stair, Rhodri clutched the amulet at his throat. His heart was beating fast.

"And what use is honor in the tomb?" asked Megan angrily.

"They say there's great wealth to be had in the cities of Tyre and Acre," her husband said, ignoring the remark. "We may pass the noble city of Byzantium, too, and I'll win enough to buy myself several horses and become more than a master falconer. Perhaps become a gentile-homme, like the Norman lords. And you and Rhodri shall live in a large house, with fine . . ."

Megan stood up and tossed back her head. "Do you think me a fool, man?" she cried, her voice shaking with anger. "Besides, I don't want to live in a big house. I'm happy here, with you and Rhodri. You always say the only true happiness lies at home."

Rhodri felt ashamed of his mother. Owen stopped polishing the sword.

"Come, my love," he said gently, "where's the courage I married in my young bride? I'm as good with a sword as a hawk, or a peregrine falcon, and I'll not take any risks out there. It shall be no more than a year."

"No, husband?"

"No. My love for you and Rhodri will bear me safely to the Temple of the Mount, and back again. But I need you to be strong for me. Please, my love."

Megan's eyes pierced the mysterious shadows. Her face was suddenly resolute.

"You swear you'll come back to us?"

"Of course. By the Savior, and my father's sword."

"I love you so much, Owen."

Rhodri's eyes grew moist as he listened and watched Owen get up and take Megan in his arms. Then Owen held her away again and looked straight into her eyes.

"Thank you, wife."

"I'll pray for God's speed then, husband," whispered Megan cheerlessly.

"And with you in here," said the falconer, touching his chest and heart with a flattened hand, "I'll never give up hope."

"With me at your side, too, Pa."

Rhodri was standing boldly at the bottom of the stairs.

"Rhodri—" said Megan.

"I'm decided, Pa," the boy said eagerly, striding forward. His face was hot with the fire and his proud blushes. "I'm coming with you."

It was not unheard of for boys even younger than Rhodri Falcon to accompany men to war, but he was small and, although bold, knew nothing of real fighting, or even the arts of a camp boy or a groom. Owen smiled at his son, but he was deeply touched, too. He would never have contemplated taking the boy with him, but Owen didn't want to hurt his feelings.

"Spoken like a king yourself, Rhodri," he cried, striding forward and gripping his son by the shoulders like a man, "and it'd be fine to have such a brave companion at my side. But as a man you'll have just as important work here, while I'm away."

"But, Pa," said Rhodri, flushing.

"You must stay and look after your mother, Rhodri," Owen insisted softly, "the farm and the birds, too. Think of what it would mean for your mother if we both left her."

"But, Father, please," begged the boy. "If I don't come with you, then I'll never see the world, or journey to strange and far-off places." Rhodri was almost on the point of tears. "Besides, the king. I've got to . . ."

Rhodri stopped. How could he tell his parents of the fortune-teller? How could he make them believe that he knew King Richard was in danger and that somehow Rhodri had to warn him? That he had heard a strange voice in the flames, too, talking of destiny?

"You've time," said Owen quietly. "You're just a boy now, see. There'll be other journeys. Great journeys. Now I need you here to protect your mother. Besides, you'll be master of the house now."

Rhodri looked at each of his parents in turn. The boy felt two warring emotions, for the thought of being master of the house and protecting Megan made him feel proud, but the sword was still glinting on the edge of the chair and he felt as if something were struggling to get out of his body.

"But I've got to come. I've got to see the king. And to tell the Lionheart . . ."

"Listen to me, *bach*," said Owen, crouching down in front of his son. "I'm sure the king would be proud of your fealty, but you must do as I say, with a glad heart. If you love and honor us both."

Rhodri's heart was pounding like a drum. "But, Father, you don't understand."

"Rhodri, don't be foolish now."

The boy dropped his eyes. He knew his mother was staring at him, too, and at last he sighed and nodded bitterly. "Very well then, Pa."

"Good lad, Rhodri," cried Owen, standing up again and slapping him on the back. "Now come, son. Help me clean up my sword and we'll talk of my journey and what I need. You must have as much courage as I, Rhodri, while I'm away."

* * *

As the little family waited for Owen to leave, Megan pretended to be merry, for she wanted to send her husband on his journey with all the love and reassurance she had, but her tread was bitterly heavy around their homestead. Rhodri dreamed only of adventure in the holy lands.

It was the eve of the Mass of Christ when the final call came. The next morning, Christmas Day, a sheet of frost lay like glass across the mud in the yard and Rhodri had to drop a stone to break the ice on the well before drawing the water. The air was like forged steel, but the day was bright, too, and the heavens a brilliant blue.

The family said their prayers together as they always did on the Lord's birthing day and then took a special meal—new bread, a plump woodcock taken by Glindor, and honeyed apples. Neither Megan nor Rhodri could enjoy it much though and both of them kept looking up at Owen. He chatted or told them jokes, regaled them with stories or gave Rhodri another piece of advice about the birds, or tending to the farm.

"And remember, *cariad*, fly the birds as often as you may. For hunting birds are always wild creatures and long to be free. But never let them stray too close to the trees. There the danger lies."

Different feelings stirred in mother and son as they listened.

Megan wondered how she could bear to see her husband go and how cold the nights would be without him in her bed. But Rhodri's heart was like stone. All the boy saw ahead of him was an endless round of work and care, as he took on his duties in the farm.

The little family said good-bye that day on the edge of the track above the barn. Owen was dressed in winter clothes, a heavy tunic and a coat lined with fox fur, which the winter before Lord De Brackenois had rewarded him with. Thick woollen trousers, too, cross-bound down to his boots with strips of leather. On both wrists he wore the long leather arm gauntlets he often used in falconry, and his antler-handled hunting dagger was lodged prominently in his studded belt.

His silver hair had grown and Rhodri thought how fine his father looked. Like a warrior indeed, and the hero that Owen had always been to his son. Owen's bag was at his feet, filled with clothes and a sack of coin, and his own father's great broadsword was across his back, as bright and sharp now in its sheath as if it had been newly forged.

Owen and Megan held hands together for a good while. They were renewing, as they had done almost every day of their lives, the secret pact that had brought them together, first as lovers, and then as lawful husband and wife. But at last it was time for them to part.

"I'll bring you back such tales from the East, Rhodri *bach*," cried Owen as merrily as he could, "to make those keen eyes pop from your head, see. And treasures and mysteries, too."

"Yes, Pa," said Rhodri sullenly, wondering sadly about all the wonderful things he would never see.

Owen looked at Megan. He ruffled his son's black hair and tried to cheer him.

"It'll be a great journey, Rhodri, boy. But an even greater return."

"Father," said Rhodri, with as much gravity as he could summon. "The king. Will you look after him?"

Owen smiled. "Look after the Lionheart? Why, I'll be lucky to even see him."

Rhodri wanted to say more, to make his father really listen, but Owen had already begun to gather up his bag, and it was Megan who caught hold of his arm.

"Wait, husband," she said. "I've something for you." She took off the pendant of St. Christopher he had given her at the fair. Megan kissed it gently and gave it to Owen. "Wear it for me. For the safety of travelers."

Owen took the thing and kissed it, too, then strung it about his neck. "Always, Megan. Against my heart."

"And take this, too," said Megan, reaching into the large pocket of her skirts. She pulled out one of the pewter tankards—the largest and most valuable things in their chest.

"But wife," said Owen softly, "you may have need of it in the times to come. With De Brackenois gone there'll be no falconing, and it'll be harder for you, though you have the animals and the land."

"Use it, husband," said Megan, pressing the cup on him. "To buy yourself a horse. That'll give you prominence in this host, and bring you back to us all the swifter."

Owen smiled sadly, and touching his hand to his lips, he took the thing and put it in his pack. "I've a very special gift for you, Rhodri," he said. Owen pulled the antler-handled dagger from his belt and held it out it to his son. "To protect your mother with. But not too much fighting, eh."

Rhodri's frustration and anxiety for his father and the king was stilled for a moment, as he accepted the weapon eagerly, his very first.

"No, Pa. Thank you."

There was so much more Owen Falcon could have said, but there is no real way for lovers or families to part. So, stiffening his back and pulling in his stomach, Owen turned and walked away toward the manor, without once looking back. As Rhodri stood by his mother, he felt, as a falconer knows the temper of a bird, that her body was straining to run after her husband, to throw herself on his neck and beg him not to go. But Megan had the strength and pride in her of a Welshwoman, and instead she put her arm warmly round her son.

"He'll come back to us soon, Rhodri. I know he will."

Though a part of Rhodri was glad that he was with her and safe at home, when Owen was almost out of sight, Rhodri broke free of his mother's grip, jammed the antler dagger into his belt, and began to run, as fast as he could. He felt the cold winter air slapping his cheeks. He did not chase his father. Instead he broke from the track and ran up to the stile and the field where Melanor had first come to his call.

As soon as he reached the big oak, the boy began to climb furiously, breaking branch and tearing bark. He knew several routes up the tree by pure instinct and was quickly up to his usual spot. But he went on climbing, pulling himself up by the sheer strength of his arms, careless of the growing drop below him.

At last, high in the oak, the dark-haired lad pushed his head out through the branches. Behind him he could see his house, a thin plume of gray smoke rising above the thatch, and Megan walking slowly across the yard. His mother's head was bowed and it had started to drizzle. Her lovely hair was already wet with rain.

Rhodri turned and saw what he was looking for. There in the distance was the great manor house, partly obscured by the trees. He knew the sight well: the stone church, where the priest spoke to them and where Rhodri had sometimes wandered to look at the graves of the De Brackenois family; the fine fortified Norman manor house, too, and the stables beyond it.

It was the unfamiliar now that drew Rhodri's gaze. A great number of armed men were gathered in the yard by the stables. Some were on horseback, though most of the retainers were on foot. Men and boys had come from all parts of Western England to travel south to join the great fight in the Holy Lands. Some as retainers in the retinues of their lords, others freemen keen to join the fight, or serve their God, or seek their fortune in distant lands. Singly they had come, or in newly bonded fighting groups. Some carried nothing but the humble scythes they used in the fields, while others bore newly forged swords and glittering armor. They carried colored banners at their backs, and their shields were stamped with the proud crests of their lineage. Rhodri ached that he would not be a part of the great pageant.

The gathering was already moving off toward the southeast and, although at this distance there was little detail, Rhodri fancied he saw a flutter of red and green, the colors of De Brackenois's arms.

Rhodri felt as if something were tearing inside him and he wondered where his father was and if the falconer would journey in the lord's private retinue to the southern ports. The boy watched for ages as the body of brave fighting men moved out, the riders leading the party and the others beginning to straggle and trail behind, as they found their natural pace. The leaders had soon reached the river beyond, but Rhodri got no sight of Owen, as he had hoped. They were all leaving him behind.

"Good-bye, Pa," he whispered.

The air had grown colder and Rhodri felt his shoulders stiffen. Behind him now the sun was sinking rapidly and the light seemed to be draining into the ground.

"Come back soon," Rhodri said desperately among the trees. He remembered the blessing the priest sometimes used after his sermons. "And may the Savior himself protect you."

The light had gone altogether and the Holy Warriors had vanished into the returning shadows. Rhodri's thoughts were already journeying with them, out into the wide and dangerous world. As he perched there, again that feeling came over Rhodri, the feeling that someone was watching him from the forests. His eyes scanned the dark trees, which seemed arrayed like a rank of guards, protecting a great secret. A face formed in Rhodri's mind, that of the blind blacksmith. Rhodri heard his words now, as if he were there with him. "A darkness is coming, boy. When it touches the land, or those you love, then seek it out. The Telling Pool."

4 ❖ THE HERMIT

Things fall apart; the centre cannot hold;
Mere anarchy is loosed upon the world
—W. B. Yeats, "The Second Coming"

Where do you think Pa is now?" said Rhodri gloomily to Melanor as the bird sat on his arm, ruffling its chilly, brown feathers. It looked fine in the golden hood William had given Rhodri, but the boy was feeling too distracted and lonely to care as he trudged with his bird down the lane in the snow, toward the stone church on the outskirts of the manor. A hare dangled limply from his belt, which Melanor had just taken in the big field.

"Do you think they've taken Jerusalem yet, with the Lionheart?"

Ten long months had passed since the men had set out, and Rhodri was almost fourteen. He was taller and somehow more confident. It had been a hard time, full of labor and worry, and with so many gone to the holy wars, there was more work to do than hands to do it. Much of the burden had fallen on the children of the district.

Rhodri had not seen much of other children of his age, with all there was to do about the farm. He had only seen William De Brackenois four or five times around the estate, riding on the path. Each time they had waved cheerfully to each other and both had wanted to stop and talk about their birds and all that was happening. But William had never been alone, for Aelfric seemed to shadow him now wherever he went, and that promise of friendship at St. Martin's Day had not really blossomed.

Rhodri had set about his duties with will and care, and very quickly had become a master of his little world. There had indeed been no more falconing at the manor since his father and De Brackenois's warriors had left, and Megan had already begun to run short of coin. But at least, with Rhodri's and Melanor's growing hunting skills, there was always the bounty of the land and air to keep them from starvation, even with winter come so early. Rhodri felt confident now as he looked back at his home and saw the healthy banner of smoke rising from the roof.

There was already much talk of lawlessness and discontent in the region. With so many knights and soldiers gone from the land, there was no one to oppose the anarchy and brigandage, and in the North there was rumor of a Saxon revolt. But as yet little of the unrest had penetrated the forests around Rhodri's home.

It was his mother, Megan, who filled Rhodri with the most care. Although she never said anything, after Owen had gone there were times when the boy thought his mother might die of the pain of it. At first she had been positive and resolute, but Rhodri could see that she was turning in on herself, growing sadder and more brooding. At night, as Rhodri lay in his little room above the stream, he often heard her talking, although there was no one there, and sometimes crying, too.

It made Rhodri even lonelier, and sometimes he would go down to visit Sarah and her father. They were pleasant enough visits, and Rhodri realized how much he liked Sarah, although the miller drank too much and Sarah's mother had little to say for herself. Yet it was never the same as talking to his father. Girls were different somehow, and the strange feelings Rhodri sometimes had when he was with Sarah seemed to put a barrier between them.

It was a barrier that had got stronger on the day when Rhodri had gone to the miller's to fetch some flour for his mother. There he had been surprised to see Sarah and William De Brackenois at the gate, talking and laughing loudly, like old friends. Although he had not approached, the sight had set something secretive in Rhodri's heart.

Rhodri stroked Melanor now. He felt foolish talking to him and a little guilty, too, for he knew he should be hunting the other birds to keep them alert and in trim, but Melanor was naturally his favorite and he spent most time with him. The falcon swiveled his head beneath his hood again, but Rhodri could feel that he was calm, for those angry eyes, which kept him connected to the living world, were covered and the blind bird was at peace.

"What could you really know of the world?" Rhodri sighed. "You're just a bird, and the priest says animals don't have minds and souls like ours."

Rhodri walked on through the snow, and after a while reached the church. Down the path he could see that the wooden door was open. He shivered, for there was something about the church that always made him nervous. Even so, he placed Melanor on the fence outside, tethered his jesses, and walked to the door, wondering if the priest was there, and ready to run if he was.

There was nobody inside. The air was colder than without, and Rhodri's breath began to smoke as he walked down the aisles where the villagers sat or knelt, past the carved-backed wooden seats of the De Brackenois family. The boy felt dizzy as he looked at the high wooden ceiling and the strange font, filled with holy water. It had frozen over in the cold.

The building was said to be at least a hundred and fifty years old, and in the corner he could see the tomb of the second Lord De Brackenois, who had died in the first wars to free the Holy City. His effigy was carved there next to his lady wife. The newly wrought stone figures lay side by side, on top of the tomb, forever seized together in stone, reminding Rhodri of that card he had seen at the fair—Death. Rhodri thought of his father again and missed him all the more bitterly. He wished he was here to answer questions, for so much that Rhodri had learned, Owen had taught him. Owen had taken him hunting or falconing and taught him to fish and shown him the secrets of the land. He had told him the names of things and shown him how to plow and plant, to cut wood safely and listen to the animals. Only now did Rhodri realize that Owen had been his friend, as much as his father. But now Rhodri had no one at all to ask advice of, or to tell his worries to.

He looked at the carvings all about him and thought of that crowned face in the fire. Had it been nothing but a silly dream? Now Rhodri's head filled with tales of Arthur's brave knights, standing vigil before setting out on their grave quests across Albion, to defeat dragons and save damsels, to fight wars and return the Holy Grail to Camelot. As Rhodri passed the font, he let his hand touch the ice, then he walked closer to the end of the church, where the great rood screen barred the way to the altar. He noticed that one of the doorways through the screen was ajar. Rhodri pushed it and peered beyond.

There was nobody here, either. Only the great effigy of the Christ, pinned in suffering to a wooden crucifix, looking down on him with sad and weary eyes. There were unlit candles on the altar and beside them a book. Rhodri's heart fluttered. It was the huge bible that he had often wondered about when they came to pray. He walked up to it, and slowly he opened the cover.

From the occasional reading that the priest gave in church he knew that the symbols did not make words in Welsh, Norman, or English, but in the sacred language of Latin. Even if he had been able to read or write, he would not have understood what was scribed there. Rhodri clutched the edges of the sacred book and ached to know what it said. It was the same longing and frustration he felt at not being able to travel out with his father to the wars and see the world.

Rhodri felt something else, too, quite natural to the young, especially standing here in the church. A heavy weight of responsibility for everything about him. As he stood there, Rhodri suddenly felt, as strongly as anything he had ever felt before in his short life, that he had to believe and have faith. That somehow it was his own love and faith alone that would bring his father home safely again, and that his belief in it was something he must never betray, as Judas had betrayed Christ in the garden.

His hand was moving across the page, and he saw now that marked there were not only symbols, but intertwining with them, beautiful colored pictures. They showed scenes of men and angels, of demons and devils, of lords and ladies, and of the stories that he had heard so often as a young child. They were quite beautiful and Rhodri found himself slipping into one of his reveries, when he suddenly heard someone address him.

"What are you doing in here, Waelas?"

His stomach lurched as he turned and saw Aelfric staring at him coldly through the door to the rood screen, his red hair curling like snakes about his head. Rhodri closed the Bible fast.

"None of your business, Aelfric."

"And is it your destiny to steal from a church?" said the big lad, stepping forward. "If the priest caught you, he'd thrash you soundly. And my father has taught me how to deal with robbers."

"I wasn't stealing," cried Rhodri indignantly, stepping away from the book with a clenched fist and remembering angrily how Aelfric had cheated at St. Martin's Day. "Don't say it. I just wanted . . . I wanted to read, see."

"A falconer's son read? I don't believe it. First you fly a bird far beyond your rank and now you want to read. You'll want to be a knight next. Or is it a fortune-teller?"

Aelfric burst out laughing, which made Rhodri hate him even more.

"The land is at war and villains and thieves roam the wilds," hissed Aelfric, "while murder stalks the forests. Just as you prophesied they would, little Falcon, at St. Martin's Day, with your strange eyes."

His voice was hard and suspicious.

"They say witches have power to foretell such evil things," he went on loudly, his words echoing about the stony church and seeming to frighten the very statues, "and you know what the Holy Church sets to witches? The fire, Waelas. Or worse."

"Peace, Aelfric."

William De Brackenois stepped into the gloom behind the red-haired boy. He was dressed in a green cloak and he, too, had grown. His handsome blue eyes were glittering.

"My lord?" said Aelfric.

"Rhodri said a fortune-teller told him, that's all. It's not his fault what he hears. And maybe she had heard the news before it reached us and there was no magic at all."

William smiled at Rhodri.

"And we have to stick together at times like these," said William. "My uncle says many Saxons are restless, too, now our Norman king is abroad, but you would wish no harm on me, I hope, Aelfric, just for my Norman blood?"

"Of course not, my lord. But a Waelas—"

"I believe Rhodri wasn't stealing, but trying to read," interrupted William coldly. "A fine ambition, too, Father always says."

Rhodri smiled gratefully at William, but Aelfric was suddenly pointing at Rhodri's belt.

"What's that then?"

Rhodri looked down.

"A hare. Melanor took it."

"Well, I call it poaching to take game so near the manor," said Aelfric coldly.

William saw the hare, too, and for a moment something serious flickered across his intelligent young face. Although he was hardly more than a boy, as De Brackenois's heir he knew it was his duty to protect his father's lands and rights while he was away.

"But Pa has always been allowed to hunt around here," said Rhodri indignantly.

"Your father perhaps," grunted Aelfric, "but you're no master falconer, Waelas, no matter how impudent you are."

Another thought had come to William though, which seemed to please him.

"Well, Rhodri," he said, "our fathers fight together in the Holy Lands, so I'm sure two comrades in arms would not begrudge a hunter his wild bounty. Times grow hard. You're welcome to a fair kill."

Aelfric bit his lip.

"We should see more of each other," William went on. "We're truly bonded you and I, by our fathers' journey. With the wars, none should be strangers. Norman or Saxon, Welsh or Angle. For do we not all serve Christendom?"

Although the remark about fighting side by side had been innocent enough, Rhodri could see that Aelfric thought it was directed at him. By no means had all the men set out with De Brackenois's retinue, for William and the children and women of the manor had to be cared for.

Aelfric's father, Wolfrin, was one of those who had been left behind. Although Rhodri didn't know it, it had been on Wolfrin's own pleading and now, with most of the other grooms gone, he had gained a new authority in the district, if not quite a respect. Rhodri had often seen him riding about the estate like a lord himself. Aelfric was much teased for the fact that his father had not gone off to fight though, and now Rhodri felt a secret satisfaction at Aelfric's shame.

"Yes, my lord," said Rhodri carefully. "I wanted to go, too, and see the world. To fight bravely at their side, and to meet the king."

"Ambitious as always, Waelas," snapped Aelfric. "Perhaps you could advise him yourself as how to lead the army, or take back the Holy City?"

The big boy's tone was utterly mocking, and although Rhodri would not respond to his taunts, he felt ashamed in front of William. He knew how absurd it was that one of his rank should dream of meeting the king and being a part of his high plans.

"Enough, Aelfric," said William. "You're right though. We shouldn't let the priest catch us in here. Come on."

He led them back through the rood screen, past the grand pews, and Rhodri was very relieved to come out into the sunlight.

"Well, Rhodri," said William merrily as they stood in the sunshine, "how is the hood? I see Melanor is wearing it."

"Oh, fine indeed. Melanor feels very comfortable in it."

"I'm glad. We should hunt together soon."

"Oh, yes, I'd like that, too. Melanor has grown so strong."

"And Shadowfell. We'll race them again."

Rhodri was delighted and his young heart went out to William. Aelfric just stood sullenly watching them.

"How about tomorrow?" said William suddenly.

"Well, I've much to do. But why not."

As Rhodri looked about him in the snow though, another idea crossed his mind.

"My lord," he said.

"William, Rhodri."

"William. Before we race, if you meet me at the top of the slope in the big field, I'll show you the best winter game I know. My pa taught it me."

William hesitated, for he wondered if he was too old for games, but then he grinned.

"All right then. We've a bargain."

They shook hands and agreed to meet early the next morning. As Rhodri set off with Melanor, there was a huge smile on his face. That night he went up to the barn and broke off an old plank of wood from some spare cuttings and began to cover the bottom in pig grease.

When William De Brackenois arrived in the field the next morning, Rhodri was waiting with it at the top of the snowy slope. William tethered Shadowfell next to Melanor on a nearby tree—they looked very splendid side by side—then wandered over, with Aelfric at his heels. The red-haired boy looked hatefully at Rhodri and contemptuously at the plank of wood.

"What is it?" asked William.

Rhodri laughed and threw the plank down onto the snow.

"Watch this, William."

Rhodri sprang forward and threw himself onto the board and William and Aelfric were amazed as it shot off down the snowy incline, carrying Rhodri with it. He gave a delighted whoop as he rode the thing through the snow and then tumbled into a laughing heap at the bottom. Aelfric stood back haughtily as William had the next turn. At first he didn't go as fast as Rhodri, because he let his heels dangle in the snow too much, but after a few goes they were both hurtling down the slope.

"Oh come on, Aelfric," cried William. "Join in."

They were having so much fun that Aelfric couldn't resist, and soon all three of them were taking their turns, or going in pairs on the wonderful thing. Rhodri and William were trying it together when the young lord said, "I've never had so much fun, Rhodri. I bet Sarah would like this, too."

Rhodri felt something cold in him.

"Yes," he whispered, "I suppose she would."

William blushed and fell silent.

On their last run all three of them clambered onto the board and went so fast they thought they might take off and fly. But as they came to a crashing halt, they saw a horse coming toward them. Aelfric got up hurriedly and began to dust off the snow. It was Wolfrin and he was staring disapprovingly at all of them, though he addressed just William.

"I'm glad I've found you," he said. "Your mother wants you at the manor. Don't you think you are a little old for such foolery?"

William's eyes flickered to Rhodri, who realized that the young man was embarrassed.

"Tell her I'll come when I may, Wolfrin," he said, getting up, too. "We are going to fly . . ."

"Now," the groom said firmly. He paused and smiled. "My lord."

William blushed, but Rhodri could see that he did not know how to stand up to the man.

"Very well then, Wolfrin," said William curtly. "Tell her I'll be there straight."

There was something both cruel and mocking in Wolfrin's smile.

"Yes, my lord. And Aelfric, get up to the stables, sharpish."

"Good-bye then, Rhodri," said William, as Wolfrin rode away and Aelfric set off toward the stables, too. "Thank you for the game."

"I hope I haven't got you into trouble, William," said Rhodri.

"Not at all. Wolfrin gets too big for his boots. He's hardly my father. Let's meet tomorrow. We'll fly the birds then."

"I'll try and get away. When the chores are done."

They made the pact, and the next morning found them together once more, but this time for a more serious purpose.

They raced their fine birds, with none of the sense of the competitiveness of St. Martins Day, only the mutual delight of two growing boys sharing their knowledge and growing skills.

After about an hour Aelfric joined them, too, and he was clearly in an angry mood again. He obviously resented the renewed friendship, and when Rhodri made some remark about Shadowfell, he tried to remind Rhodri of the difference between him and William.

"You talk like a lord, Falcon," he said. "Perhaps when you learn to honor your betters and to pay them vassalage, as is your bonded duty, you'll remember who you are."

William and Rhodri looked at each other very uncomfortably. The boys had not thought of it before, but if Rhodri wished to stay on the land, one day, when he was grown and Pierre De Brackenois was gone, he, too, would have to swear fealty to William himself, as his father had done to William's father before. The thought made Rhodri embarrassed, and angry in his heart, too.

Just then the three boys spotted Sarah and the miller coming down the track on their way to market. Sarah saw Rhodri first and waved warmly. Rhodri was delighted to see her and was going to wave back, when he saw her catch sight of William. Her pretty cheeks turned bright scarlet and she began to straighten her clothes.

"A fine, crisp morning, my lord," said her father, bowing to the young noble as they came past.

"Indeed it is," answered William cheerfully, acknowledging the miller's bow. "And a fine day to walk abroad. Hello, Sarah."

"Good day, my lord," said Sarah and again she blushed.

Rhodri could see that Sarah was nervous, and he felt a violent knot of jealousy in his stomach.

"Shall you be walking in the meadow tomorrow, Sarah?" asked William.

"Yes, indeed."

"Then maybe we shall walk together."

"I would like that very much."

Sarah looked almost guiltily at Rhodri as she and her father passed on, and William turned to his friend.

"Is anything wrong, Rhodri?"

"No, my lord," lied the boy, trying to conceal his feelings.

"Well, let's try the birds again."

"Not now," said Rhodri. "I have to be going."

"Going. But why?"

"There's much to do, my lord."

Rhodri lifted Melanor on his arm, and turned abruptly for the wood. He walked fast, with a straight back to the other boys.

Although Rhodri normally had better sense than to hunt Melanor so close to the forest, he was soon on the edge of the trees, crunching through the snow, his feet as cold as blocks of ice. In the distance, a black rabbit darted from its warren, and with the speed of a river otter, Rhodri pulled the hood from the falcon's head. Melanor took wing toward the prey, but the falcon missed, and when a flock of birds suddenly flew up, Melanor swerved toward them instead.

"No, Melanor, don't."

The falcon was dangerously close to the wood and, in its excitement, did not hear Rhodri. In an instant the bird had vanished into the trees.

"Melanor. Come back!"

Rhodri ran frantically after the bird, cursing its stupidity and himself for forgetting his father's advice. He stopped instinctively as he reached the border of the forest, but, determined not to lose the bird, he plunged into the trees.

At first it was dark, but as Rhodri's eyes grew accustomed to the gloom, he saw before him a great sweep of mystery. Here the snow had penetrated the canopy and great pools of dappled light were falling everywhere among the branches. But as Rhodri began to walk, he noticed that the branches grew more tangled above his head and the snow beneath him became less and less thick, until he was walking on twigs and moss and leaf mold. The air was warmer among the trees, and a strange, impenetrable silence was deepening all about him.

"*Mel-an-or.*"

As the sound came echoing back at him, Rhodri shivered nervously. Something moved high above and Rhodri followed the shape. His tread was easier now, for he had come on a deer track. As he looked for his falcon, the wintry sun flashed and sparked all about, and as the trees soared above him, he grew dizzy with light and shadow.

"Oh, where are you, Melanor?"

Rhodri kept calling, as much to reassure himself as anything else, but after half an hour there was no sign of Melanor at all and the boy stopped and looked about him. The deer track had disappeared under his feet and Rhodri had no idea where he was at all. He turned back on himself, or thought he did, because after another half hour Rhodri realized that he was actually deeper within the forest. Owen may have taught him many things in their time together, but he had never taught him how to read the sun in a wood. Now Rhodri had no idea in which direction he was going. He was lost and all alone. His lips felt dry, too, and he was very thirsty.

Rhodri pressed on regardless, his heart plunging as he thought that he could never be a master falconer if he couldn't even find his way in the forest. But he reassured himself that it was still early. Melanor would soon turn back for the lure, and finding Rhodri gone he would fly to the barn and settle with the others.

Suddenly something flashed in the trees. It was not something as small as a bird though, and not high up, either. Rhodri thought of outlaws and robbers. He put his hand nervously to the antler dagger at his belt. Even as he touched it, he knew that the something was close by. The boy's heart was pounding furiously now and he drew the little knife as a shape darted by him to the right. Rhodri was preparing to stand his ground and fight, when he saw what it was that was haunting him in the forest. There, in a little clearing, stood a beautiful, wild stag.

The creature was perhaps five years old, for its tines rose like great branches above its elegant head. It had its winter coat and its throat was thick with fur. Its huge, nervous eyes were staring straight at Rhodri, and little clouds of hot air wreathed out of its flaring nostrils, as it sniffed at the wind and explored the human's strange, unfamiliar scent.

Rhodri had often seen deer in the fields and on the edge of the forest, and he had even hunted a roebuck kid with Melanor that year, but he had never seen one so close as this. He could see everything in such detail. Its fine legs and the muscles about its belly were braced, ready to spring away at any moment. As Rhodri returned its gaze, he remembered the story the priest had told them once in the church. The story of St. Hubert, a great Norman huntsman and pleasure seeker who had lived across the channel, but had been converted to faith in the Savior after seeing a stag in the forest with a golden cross in its antlers.

In another mood Rhodri would have wanted to chase the thing with a bow, for such a prize would have brought him and his mother fresh meat for two whole months, with enough left over to barter in the village. But as Rhodri stood there, so close to the creature that he fancied he could almost feel the beating of its heart, something different came on the boy. A sense of wonder and privilege and mystery that had often gripped him when he walked alone, or when the others had left the church and he had sat there, thinking and dreaming to himself of the Holy Lands.

Very gently Rhodri lowered the antler dagger. The stag, as though released from some spell, dropped its head to graze. It was as if it knew there was no danger, and it drifted slowly away, as it nosed through the leaves. Then, startled by a sound in the wood, the beautiful deer lifted its head and sprang away. In an instant it was lost again in the forest.

Rhodri slipped his dagger back in his belt, but as he walked on he had the sense that he was still not alone and that something else was watching him, something shadowing him through the trees. The light was changing and it was already growing late. His mother would be beginning to worry. Just then Rhodri heard the hard snap of a branch behind him and saw a flash of gray.

He swung round and drew his dagger again, feeling the grip of cold fear about his throat as he saw a man standing there in the trees, facing in his direction. A great bundle of twigs was lifted on his stooped back and he was dressed all in gray. His head was dropped slightly in his hood, like a monk's, and Rhodri could not see his face. He looked like a ghost.

"Welcome," said the stranger softly, slowly putting down his burden. "You're far from your home. No doubt you're nervous of the spirits of the forest."

"Spirits of the forest? Who are you?"

The stranger cocked his cowled head, as if listening. Although Rhodri could not see the man's face under the hood, his hands, thin and almost blue with cold, trembled like autumn leaves.

"I am a hermit," answered the stranger, "and though many might do, in these times of sorrow, I wish you no harm, boy. Trust me. For does not the law tell us to harm none?"

A hermit, thought Rhodri, and a distant memory of the fair came back to him.

"What law?" asked Rhodri, thinking of De Brackenois and the manor and wondering if the man was really an outlaw or cutthroat.

"The Craft," answered the old man quietly, "the Wiccan Law. I've been out collecting wood to warm old bones in the winter. What does a young man do so deep in the winter forest?"

"I got lost, sir," answered Rhodri, putting back his dagger a second time. "I was hunting my falcon too close to the trees and I'm looking for him."

He paused and blushed. The strange old man raised his head slightly in his cowl.

"You're not used to the forest then, boy?"

"No, sir. I suppose I'm not. Pa always warned me against it."

Rhodri felt how strange was this meeting among the trees. All about them great shafts of light were slanting through the branches like arrows. A ray caught the pendant around Rhodri's neck and made the metal gleam. The man tilted his head slightly again and then plunged his hands into his robes to keep them warm.

"Is the forest not beautiful in winter?" he said more cheerfully, "Although it seems dead, it holds the promise of things to come. Like all life. It changes, too. As all is change, and these are changing times indeed. But you. I've been watching you a long time from the wood, boy. Watching you change, and grow up with the land."

"Me?" said Rhodri in astonishment, but feeling a little angry, too.

"When out collecting mushrooms, or lichen or berries close to that manor . . ."

The man paused.

"You've a skill with that bird. It's a good sign to know of animals. The forest will welcome you."

"Welcome me?" said Rhodri.

He thought the man must be a little mad talking about the forest like this, as if it were a person. The priest had often warned them of the travelers who lived in the forest and dabbled in the ancient arts. Evil tales of witchcraft and magic and druidical sacrifice, and Rhodri suddenly felt very nervous indeed.

"It already knows of your care," said the old man, "and of your heart. As the land knows all things. So yes, it will welcome you."

"Then I'm glad to meet you, sir," said Rhodri stiffly. "But now I must be getting back home. My ma will be worrying about me."

"But what of your bird?" asked the man, seeming to want to stop him.

"Melanor will be safe enough. He's probably home already."

"No, he's not," said the man. "Melanor is wild. Like you, I think."

Rhodri was startled by the certainty that rung in his voice, but the stranger shrugged, too. "Yet if you're decided, then take this track to the right, walk until you reach a split oak and turn to the left. You'll be home soon enough."

Rhodri was deeply impressed that somebody could so easily know their way about the wood, which, to his inexperienced eyes, looked all the same.

"Thank you, sir. Perhaps I'll see you again."

"Perhaps you shall."

The old man had turned and was stooping to lift the bundle. Rhodri moved off down the path, but as he looked back he saw the old man straining painfully, his icy hands hardly able to grasp the burden. The boy hesitated and then he was back by the stranger's side.

"I'll help you," said Rhodri, resigning himself. "To carry your wood, see. If your home's not too far off, that is."

He fancied he saw a smile on that old face within the hood.

"That would be kind, boy. It's not far."

The old man seemed very pleased, and as Rhodri shouldered the great bundle of wood, he was startled and rather suspicious to see the stranger move off down the path with a spring in his step that belied his years, or his inability to bear his load. Though he walked with a strange tread, too, as if at each step he was testing the ground with his feet.

"It's this way," he called cheerfully, as Rhodri turned to follow.

The boy caught up with him, sweating and straining with the wood and wondering how on earth the old man had managed to carry it in the first place. Rhodri could not help worrying about his mother and Melanor, but he was glad, too, to be helping the funny old man, and suddenly, inexplicably, he felt a piercing pang for his father that made him slow his pace.

"Your heart's heavy,," said the stranger immediately. "Something makes you very sad."

"Sad . . . What do you mean?"

"I've been listening to your tread," answered the old man. "For are not all the secrets of the heart and soul carried within the body? Tell me what's wrong, boy."

Rhodri was irritated that this man was prying into his affairs, and yet there was something so gentle in the way he had asked it that the boy could hardly be offended.

"Well, if you must know," he answered, "it's my pa. He left us to fight the heathen in the Holy Lands, in the name of our Savior and I get . . . well . . . I miss him."

"The Savior," whispered the old man. "And his is a tale that has haunted the world indeed."

"A tale?" said Rhodri in surprise. "But the story of the Christ is the living truth."

"Perhaps it is, boy," said the man, "and perhaps we all need to hear it, even if it isn't. For stories dwell deep inside us all, to tell us of great secrets."

Rhodri felt strange. He remembered that voice in the fire again, that had spoken of old stories and great secrets. Or had it just been in his young dreams?

"Like tales of the land long ago," the old man went on, "and of the souls that dwelt amongst its living magic. They, too, were made by stories, and they, too, in their battles, quested for the truth of the Savior, who came to teach us above all to love. Does it not seem odd though that men should rise up and kill and slaughter, in the name of love?"

Rhodri said nothing. It was a thought that had not entered his head before.

"And because of a Holy War," said the old man almost angrily, "the land is deprived of its king and so begins to bleed. The nobles turn on one another as readily as lesser men, while Saxons stir against their Norman overlords. The blood and hearts of men are troubled indeed, as they were long, long ago in Albion. When the high king was shorn of his power, by the weakness and treachery of his queen and his finest knight. A knight who broke faith."

Was this stranger really talking of Lancelot and Guinevere? Rhodri wondered. But the old man was silent now and, bending down, he reached out with his hand. He broke off a toadstool, sprouting among the cold lichen. It was bright red, flecked with white.

"It's a very powerful fungus, boy," he said merrily, as if he had forgotten his recent words. "Used well, it can bring on visions. What's your name?"

"Rhodri Falcon."

The stranger nodded and put the fungus into his robes.

"They call me Tantallon, Rhodri Falcon," he said. "I live in these parts, among the trees and the birds and the wild animals. As a kind of hermit, although not a hermit of your Holy Church," he added, chuckling to himself, "and although I earn coin by offering my skills in the villages in these parts from time to time, I don't care much for the company of men anymore. Your father. He marched out with the others. A year ago?"

Rhodri felt an odd confidence in this stranger, and he realized how long it had been since he had talked properly to a man, as he had often talked to his father. He felt something welling up inside him, and then it was as if the little dam had burst on the stream. It all came out at once.

"I so wanted to go with him," said the boy, "to fight at Pa's side and help him clean his sword and saddle his horse. To drive back the Saracen and save the Holy City like one of our heroes. Perhaps to meet the king himself and serve him, too."

"Yes."

"But to see. The world, I mean, sir. The great Southern ports and maybe even the city of Londinium. To sail the wide waters and see the monsters of the deep. To touch distant shores and know of other places. But now I never shall."

He sighed heavily. The burden was growing painful.

"Now you speak from your heart," said the old man warmly. "It is good and perhaps you're ready. To look."

They had stopped on the edge of a clearing and just up ahead was the stranger's home. As they stood there, the old man lifted his hands and removed his hood entirely.

"Don't you remember me, Rhodri Falcon?" he asked.

Rhodri gasped in utter astonishment as he saw that face again. Those eyes. Those blind but searching eyes. It was the blacksmith, who had first spoken to him of the Telling Pool.

Tantallon was older than he had seemed at the fair, with wisps of pure white hair that hung loosely about his leathery chin. His hair had once been blond, Rhodri imagined, and his large, blind eyes were a kind of green, ringed by chestnut. The boy felt frightened again at this apparition, for he had just remembered the fortune-teller again and what she had said when she turned up the card of the Hermit with the hourglass. "Beware of him, child. Beware if he comes."

"But how?" stammered Rhodri.

"How can I find my way?" said Tantallon. "I'm well used to the wood, Rhodri. My memories guide me."

"But the toadstool?"

"I know the smell of fly ageric. Come."

Rhodri stepped away from the old smith, but when Tantallon turned to his homestead and beckoned to the boy, he was far too inquisitive not to follow, although he clutched his dagger firmly.

He was surprised, almost ashamed, at the poverty of Tantallon's house. It was nothing like Rhodri's own home. It was more like a hovel, tumbled down and disheveled. The door was cracked and the shutters on the window hung from their hinges. The mud roof was heavily mossed over, and all about the doorway were cluttered branches and bark. To one side stood what seemed to be a mud-brick oven, strewn about with stones and broken clay molds.

A cockerel was strutting about outside, and two cats, one black and one gray, were stretching themselves and arching their sleek backs in the shadows. A rowan tree stood to the right, in full winter berry. Everywhere Rhodri noticed cuttings of other plants, eyebright and dried lavender, stalks of dried rosemary, nightshade, and plants that Rhodri had no name for at all. Tantallon stopped again, as one of the cats rubbed herself against his old legs and purred happily.

"Hello, Reagan," he said, closing his eyes, "I'm home."

"But I thought I'd dreamt it," said Rhodri. "How you spoke to me in the forge."

"It was no dream," said the old man, grinning and opening his eyes again, "and as I said, I've been watching you."

"But you're blind, Tantallon."

Tantallon chuckled, just as he had done by the fire.

"Ah yes. Perhaps, it's my manner of speaking. But I learn much of these parts in the forests, with these old ears. So I've been listening and waiting, until you were ready. As a sword is tempered by time. Ready to . . ."

Tantallon paused and put his hand out and placed it on Rhodri's shoulder.

"You have grown indeed," he said approvingly. Then, once more, he moved his hand and grasped the pendant at Rhodri's neck. "And you still have your amulet."

The boy looked down.

"Yes."

"Good. Keep it safe. But now, Rhodri. Don't you wish to see your father?"

"See my father!"

"Of course. And something more of the wide world, too, as you've dreamed for so long. You've done me a kindness, and one unasked, which is the only sort that really matters. Now may not an old man do something in return? Come then, boy."

Tantallon almost kicked the cat aside, but rather than walking into his hovel as Rhodri expected, he turned toward the rowan tree. Rhodri was amazed at how well the old man moved, just as he had two years before in the forge. Tantallon seemed to know exactly what was in front of him. Beyond the hovel, the land banked downward steeply and the forest thickened again, and as Rhodri followed, he heard a strange gurgling and gushing sound from among the bushes and trees below.

The old man's pace had slowed, for he had come to the top of a steeply sloping track, where Rhodri saw that rough stone steps had been laid. As Tantallon lifted the skirt of his robe and began to pad down the steps, Rhodri noticed, as the bushes and branches opened around them, that they were wet and mossy and running with water.

"Don't slip, boy," cried the blind man, "for the pool is deep indeed."

Tantallon dipped his head to pass under a little archway of stone, covered in ivy and calloused with tiny limestone crystals. In the center of it hung a thick bunch of mistletoe. Despite the old man's warning, as Rhodri stepped under the arch he lost his footing and fell heavily against the stair. He felt something jar beneath him and heard a snap. When he picked himself up, he saw that his father's knife had broken clean in two. He was bitterly upset but Tantallon was already back at his side.

"Are you all right?"

"My pa's dagger," said Rhodri bitterly. "It broke."

"No matter, Rhodri," the old man said kindly, taking the broken pieces, "perhaps we shall find you a better weapon. But my craft will restore it."

He put the pieces inside the folds of his robe and led Rhodri on down, until the stairway stopped and the ground flattened to reveal a sight that took Rhodri's breath away. Under a kind of half lip of earth and stone, formed by the rise of the hill on the far bank to make an open grotto, and surrounded by trees, was a wide, smooth pool.

At first sight its waters were as black as a raven's wing and as flat as glass, except when a droplet of water plashed from the covering above and sent circles of water arcing over its surface, the air echoing with the hollow plop. The first impression of blackness changed as Rhodri saw the fading sunlight from the trees and bushes, sparking and dancing everywhere.

"They say it has no bottom," said Tantallon, his blind eyes looking out and his voice echoing all about them, "but plunges down forever and ever. Through great chasms of rock and stone, formed when the world was young. Like the stone, the stone whose roots reach into the center of the earth."

Rhodri remembered what Tantallon had said of a sword long ago at the fair, and the great stone Bethganoth. Was this really where the fabled sword Excalibur had been thrown? Mythirion. He was shaking furiously with excitement.

Just as he was drawn to the stream outside their home, Rhodri was immediately drawn to the water. He stepped to its edge and noticed that there were rowanberries scattered all about. Laid out in a line, too, were three rough purple crystals, like the one Rhodri had once seen Sarah give to her father for his birthing day, and several shards of greenish rock.

The boy looked into the water at the edge, and for a moment caught his own reflection, but then through the surface he saw a bed of white limestone. He fancied two pieces of coin glinted among the stones, as he had seen once in the wishing well near the manor. But as he looked farther out toward the center of the pool, the ground shelved away and the waters grew dark and impenetrable. Rhodri shivered and stepped back, for he felt as if something sinister were whispering to him from the very heart of the pool.

Tantallon had crouched down, too, and was reaching out, until he touched one of the lumps of green rock. He picked it up and turned the half perfect, half ragged shape in his hand.

"Malachite," said the blind man, "taken from the earth and used in the fire to forge the magic of men. For it holds raw copper inside it, and when it is blended with flame and tin, you can make bronze."

Rhodri wasn't listening. He was still looking at the water.

"It really does exist," he whispered. "And you knew where it was all along. You said it can show me things."

Tantallon dropped the lump of malachite.

"Yes, boy. Great secrets."

Tantallon was stooping to pick up another stone when Rhodri, who felt very thirsty, knelt down to drink. Tantallon cried out to stop him, and the startled boy let the silky water he had cupped in his hands fall back again with a splash.

"You must never drink of the Telling Pool," cried the blind man hotly, rounding on Rhodri with those dead eyes. "Its waters would be as fatal to a boy as the strongest poison. As deadly to you as the nightshade, or the sharpest henbane."

The hermit had become very sinister, just as the fortune-teller had warned Rhodri. Was he safe here?

"Is that what you meant then, Tantallon? When you said it's dangerous?"

The blind man rose.

"In part. But the real danger comes when you look. Who knows what one may see, or how the visions may affect him. For the world is made by what lies both without and within. The power of the mystery is both grave and very sacred. Some men are sent blind. Others mad."

Rhodri gulped and wondered if this was why Tantallon had lost his sight.

"There," whispered Tantallon, pointing to a little rock on the edge of the Telling Pool, without even looking at it. It was lightly furred with lichen and set deep into the ground in a bed of twisted roots that reached out like fingers from the slope.

"That is the Seeing Place, Rhodri Falcon. If you dare to, sit there and look. Some who come to look see nothing at all, while others see the whole world. So we shall find out if you have the power, as I thought when I first . . . when I first met you and knew you walked the Path of the Deer."

Rhodri was frightened, but he sat down on the stone anyway. He felt the rock move under him, but it settled. Though damp, it was soft and comfortable, too.

"And if you do look, know that this is your choice and yours alone," said Tantallon gravely, "and after, when the world is dark again or you are alone and you recall what you have seen this day, you must not blame the Telling Pool, or a foolish, blind old man, for showing you the truth."

Rhodri felt dizzy with fear now, but he nodded. The boy did dare. Before him, like some strange window, lay the calm, still waters. He sat quietly and the blind old man lifted his hand from his shoulder and stood back. Rhodri noticed that the air had grown stiller and twilight was coming in the forest.

"Very well then, Rhodri Falcon. Your fate has brought you to this sacred place. So behold at last—the secrets of the Telling Pool."

5 ❖ THE TELLING POOL

Then saw they how there hove a dusky barge,
Dark as a funeral scarf from stem to stern
Alfred, Lord Tennyson, "Morte d'Arthur"

Fingers of light came shooting up from the deep, like little fishes swimming and darting upward, and swirled and coalesced in the middle of the Telling Pool. The boy gasped in utter astonishment. Now, before his eager young eyes, a picture appeared.

There was the most beautiful woman. She was dressed in gauzy white robes as she lay suspended there, but her clothes seemed dry in the water and blown by an invisible breeze. She had a crown of gold about her head, and on her forehead a jewel that flashed like a star. She looked very sad and she was holding out her hands to Rhodri, as if pleading with him. The boy felt a strange lightness in him, and a rush of warmth through his whole body, as if he had just woken and stretched and was lying safe at home in bed. Then suddenly the boy realized that he was hearing things. This woman was speaking to him.

"Find it, boy," called her lovely, haunted voice. "Find it for me again. For all of us. The time comes once more. Fulfill your destiny."

Rhodri felt as if he were being pulled toward the woman in the water. He felt a yawning longing in him and wondered if he could fall, down through its waters, down through those chasms of darkness and if he did, where he would finally lie.

The image faded and now Rhodri saw a group of robed figures on the shore. All were men, apart from the beautiful woman with the crown, who now wore a fine sable cloak with a strange animal emblem on its back, and stood there weeping. There was a black boat on the water and in it lay a man on a bed of ferns. He, too, was crowned, and from his closed eyes Rhodri could not tell if he was dead or just sleeping. Candles burned all about him, and as he lay there, the woman in the cloak and the figures on the shore pushed the boat out onto the lake and the current seemed to take it immediately. Rhodri sat up as that face drifted by. It was the man he had seen in the fire. Now another voice was around Rhodri, echoing like a sigh, or a breath of distant wind.

"Arthyre."

"King Arthur," whispered Rhodri.

Then Rhodri was looking at a knight. He walked alone and his head was bowed. He was surrounded by wild sedge and there was a great heaviness in his tread. He came to a strange mound and there, in weathered stone, stood a Celtic cross. The knight dropped to his knees before it and began to pray.

Once more the scene changed, and one of the hooded men was holding up a sword in the pool. Its size seemed magnified in the water and it was finer than anything in the world. Its blade seemed to be made of molten sunlight, although it flashed with blues and greens, too, and golden red runes were worked all along the shaft.

"Excalibur," said the boy.

The hilt was made of yellow gold and the handle of the finest folded silver. The man lifted it and turned toward the lake, but before he did anything, the Telling Pool faded again and there was Tantallon standing calmly at Rhodri's side, smiling at him.

"You saw things, didn't you, Rhodri Falcon?"

As soon as the boy told him of the sword and the people he had seen and the things he had heard, the old man's face lit up delightedly and he began to nod and ring his hands. A smile had spread out across his lips. As Rhodri described the lady and the man in the black boat, Tantallon looked as if he was recalling old friends.

"I'm never mistaken," said the hermit warmly. "You've the power indeed. You've seen things that have been, long before. Ancient things, that are at the heart of the Mystery. Part of the stories, too, that forge us all."

"Stories?" said Rhodri. "At the fair, you spoke of Excalibur. Of Mythirion. And in my home, in the fire, the same face that I have just seen in the pool. He spoke to me, too. He talked of destiny, just as the lady did."

"And now your destiny brings you to sit where Arthur himself once sat as a boy," whispered Tantallon, "as he wondered about his rightful place in the world."

Rhodri looked at the old man in awe. His heart was thundering.

"The high king sat here. It can't be."

Could the man speaking to him in the fire really have been King Arthur, too?

"You don't believe it?" asked Tantallon. "And because in these days the young do not believe such things anymore, their ancient powers and magic have faded from the land. Because men have no faith, the stories of the great ones fade like tears shed in the rain."

"The woman in the water," said Rhodri, "who was she? The Lady of the Lake?"

"By the sounds of her, the Lady Guinevere."

"Arthur's queen. Then is this where Excalibur was thrown?" asked the boy, trying to peer into the depths. Tantallon tilted his head and sighed.

"No, boy. The secrets of Mythyrion's hiding place were lost long ago. Or kept hidden."

"But the pool . . . Why is it showing me these things?"

"The Telling Pool holds memories within it, of the things that have been," said Tantallon. "Just as it can show things of the living present, and of the future, too. A boy is also more open to the visions, for it is often as we grow that we lose contact with the powers that made us. Lose our sensitivity and forget the Miracle."

"Memories," whispered Rhodri wonderingly, thinking of how Tantallon remembered the things about him to find his way, "but Guinevere looked so very sad. Was it because he was dead? Arthur."

"Her wound was far deeper than that made by Arthur's passing," answered Tantallon tenderly, again appearing almost to reminisce. "It was made even before Arthur's death, by her own fair hand. Her hurt was the wound of betrayed love, when she gave herself to Lancelot and brought a curse on the land."

Rhodri looked up.

"A curse? Guinevere said that the time comes again, and that old woman at the fair, who read the cards for me, she told me that the king was in danger. Our king."

Tantallon's face seemed to darken, but he nodded gravely.

"And so he is. So are we all, perhaps."

"But I don't understand," said Rhodri. "What's it got to do with me? You said I . . . I was special."

Tantallon was listening silently with his blind eyes.

"You walk the Path of the Deer, but too many questions, too soon, are a bad thing, Rhodri. Come. Is it not special to touch the power of the Telling Pool, more quickly than anyone I've ever known?"

"Truly?"

"What happens to you when you look into a smithy, or sit at the hearth and gaze deep and long into the firelight?"

"I suppose I see things. And hear them, too."

"Just as you do in dreams, for fire, as ancient as the need to eat, calls to your inner mind. As do all natural things. Earth and air, fire and water. So it is with the deep, dark waters of the Telling Pool."

"But what makes it happen?" asked the boy, wondering what else he might behold in these waters.

"How does a tree grow a hundred feet tall, or the salmon know its way back to die in the waters that spawned its birth? It is part of the Miracle."

"And can I really see my pa there, too?" asked Rhodri, looking hopefully into the glassy water.

"Perhaps. Though you may not control what the pool shows you. But look again, boy, and perhaps the pool shall grant you your heart's desire."

Rhodri leaned forward.

"But beware," added the blind old man sternly. "It is good to see many things in life, if they don't harm and hurt your mind and heart, but other things are not so good. So, as you look again, be sure to keep a light heart and know that the visions can only touch you if you let them."

As Rhodri gazed out thinking of his father, the waters began to move again. This time everything about Rhodri seemed to go dark and shadowy, as if Rhodri's vision was narrowing to the corridor of sight known only to the hawk or the falcon.

The vision came this time with a single drip of water from the half ceiling, like a pearl that caught the sunlight as it fell and landed right in the middle of the Telling Pool. It sent out a ripple that seemed to move faster and faster toward the boy, and in that moment Rhodri's heart thundered. There, in the middle of the Telling Pool, was Owen Falcon.

His father was riding a dark brown horse and had his own father's sword slung over his shoulder. His skin was much darker than it had been when he had set out from their home, weathered now by wind and sun, and his silver hair had grown even longer about his shoulders.

"You're alive, Pa," cried Rhodri.

A warning voice was whispering to the boy from the shadows. It was Tantallon.

"Beware, Rhodri, for although the pool tells only the truth, these things may already have passed away."

Rhodri wondered if what he was looking at was in the present, but even as he did so the scene on the water seemed to widen and grow clearer and clearer. Rhodri noticed that whereas the vision of Arthur and the Lady Guinevere had been strangely shadowy and wrapped in mist, like something seen in dream or candlelight, the things he was looking on now had the hard, cold clarity of daylight. Rhodri could see where his father was. He was riding down a rough, dusty track and all about him came soldiers, on foot and horseback.

They were hard men, as weathered and worn by the furious sun that beat down on them as the rocks on the path. Strange trees grew on the roadside about them, with giant green leaves that sprouted only from their tops. Near Owen a monk was walking wearily through the dirt, in a black cassock that looked oddly out of place in such bright sunlight, swaying a censor before him. Behind the monk came two boys holding up white banners, each of which had been painted with a single red cross.

"The Holy Army," said Rhodri. "Can it really be the Holy Lands, Tantallon? Do you know this place?"

Rhodri blushed as he remembered that Tantallon was blind, but the old hermit seemed to read his thoughts.

"These are your visions, Rhodri," he answered. "Only one who sits in the Seeing Place may behold. But look deeper. Only then may you truly see."

"It's so strange," said Rhodri, peering at the desert that stretched all about the straggling army, like a field of coastal sand, but with no waves or water to break its cruel monotony. Now the boy felt the wonderful feeling that he had not been left behind at all.

A horseman was forcing his way through the soldiers on a white steed, far finer than Owen's. He was dressed in full armor and visor, and over his coat of metal was a cloth with a red cross on it, just like the banners. He carried a lance in his right hand, and as the templar knight came on, he kicked aside one of the foot soldiers with his metal boot and the man staggered and fell into the dust.

"But why?" whispered Rhodri.

The sound of hoof beat and drum, of groaning animals and of angry voices, was all about the boy, too. It was as if Rhodri were actually there.

"Bastard," grunted the soldier loudly from the pool, pulling himself up from the dust. "If he wasn't wearing that old tin suit, I'd teach him. One sun, when this is over, he'd better watch his back. A dagger in the ribs makes all things equal."

The soldier's bearded face was flushed with anger and now Owen was talking from his horse, too. Rhodri's heart thrilled at his father's voice. It sounded almost the same as that day he had kissed them good-bye, although it was hoarse and dry, as if Owen had not drunk in a while.

"Silence, Hellard. If one of the lords hears you, you know the price a common soldier'll pay."

"I know it, Falcon," said the soldier, waving away a fly buzzing about his head, "and I'll hold my tongue all right. But it's easy for you, comfortable and safe on your grand horse, like a lord yourself . . . if a Waelas lord."

Hellard laughed at the thought of a Waelas lord.

"Perhaps I spend my pay more wisely," said Owen, refusing to be offended. "But camp comes soon. They say we reach the Crack de Chevalier tonight. Then we can all rest, see."

Owen was already reaching down to the side of his saddle and unstringing a leather water bottle that hung there like a ham. He slowed his horse and gave it to the soldier.

"You're a good man, Falcon," grunted Hellard, taking it gratefully and drinking deep. "Not like most of these filthy scum. They'd cut your throat, as soon as look at you."

Rhodri stirred proudly.

"And goodness and the love of Christ's charity will ease all our paths to paradise."

The voice was different now. The monk Rhodri had spied before had stepped into view, and his leathery face was beaming up at Owen. The bald patch on his head was burned and peeling and his lips were badly cracked. Rhodri was so amazed by the unbelievable things he was seeing that he crouched forward and poked a finger into the water. Immediately the images seemed to quiver and begin to break up, until Rhodri quickly withdrew his hand.

"Ease you straight into the grave, you mean, Father," said Hellard, taking another deep draft of water and wiping his mouth roughly with his filthy sleeve. "To be buried alone and leagues from home."

"And if you're laid to rest out here," said the monk piously, "then you'll go straight to heaven, cleaned of your sins by papal indulgence. Even a wicked sinner like you, Hellard. We go to free Jerusalem once more. Where our Lord God himself was crucified for our sins, and rose again on the third day, to bring us all the gift of eternal life."

An animated light had lit in the monk's eyes and he crossed himself. So did Hellard, almost despite himself it seemed, for he was still shaking his head and scowling.

"If you think half these swine give a silver coin for the Holy City, old man," said the soldier, "you've spent too long pawing over your pretty books. You know how many died of that sickness. And how many have deserted."

"Our faith shall sustain us all," said the monk, crossing himself again.

"Oh, you think they came for the Christ, Father, but in truth half of them came because they were so poor back home," Hellard responded contemptuously, "they'd give their right arm for a chance at something better. And many of them already have. Given their arms, I mean. I saw two hacked off yesterday."

He chuckled at the joke and then spat angrily in the dirt.

"Christ, most of us are here because if we stayed back home, or in the great cities, we'd get nothing but the same old dung heap."

Rhodri sat back, surprised and angry at what he was hearing from a soldier in this Holy Army. Didn't the man believe?

"And you, Falcon, what's in your heart?" asked the monk, looking up at Owen hopefully. "What faith sustains a soldier in the armies of the Lord?"

Rhodri strained forward to hear his father's answer. For a while Owen was silent, but when he did reply, he was neither fervent nor angry. He was as measured as he always was when he called home the birds. A master falconer.

"I come to fight because I must," he answered quietly, "and as for life and what really sustains me . . ."

Owen clutched the amulet that Megan had given him and Rhodri put his hand to his own talisman. Suddenly the images in the Telling Pool began to change, to swirl and move and there in the middle of the water were Megan and Rhodri themselves, sitting together at their hearth. The pool was showing Rhodri Owen's very thoughts.

"Ma," cried Rhodri, craning forward from the Seeing Place. "It's me and Ma. Then Pa does think of us. And misses us, too."

Rhodri's heart swelled to overflowing but the visions faded and once more the pool was dark. Around the boy, the air had lightened and there was Tantallon standing at his side, as firm and real as a tree.

"What do you think of my pool, lad?" he asked. "Is it not a miracle?"

Rhodri paused. Some of the things he had seen had been shocking, and yet he had seen his father, and the power was indeed miraculous.

"It's wonderful," the boy answered, rubbing his eyes and peering all about at the grotto.

Tantallon was standing above him, his old head, wrought with age and care, framed by the night sky and a million little stars twinkling and glittering in the wintry heavens. Rhodri was amazed, for when he had first looked in the pool it was only twilight, and now it was deep into the night.

"How long have I looked?"

The old man chuckled.

"Time is as nothing," he answered, "when you gaze into the Telling Pool."

Rhodri blinked and nodded.

"But this you must swear," said the hermit, putting his hand on Rhodri's shoulder again. "Not to reveal to any what you have seen this night. Not even to your dearest loved ones. For this place is a secret as deep as the root of the oldest tree in the forest, and as sacred as the ribs of the most delicate leaf."

Rhodri thought of Aelfric accusing him of witchcraft, and what the church might do if they knew of it.

Tantallon, once again seeming to know his thoughts, said, "While there are those, especially your priests, who if they heard of it would not only shrive you, but seek to find it, too, and destroy it, though perhaps the Miracle can never be destroyed."

"I swear it. But who are you, Tantallon?"

The old man turned his blind eyes hard on Rhodri. He paused.

"I've told you already. No more than a humble hermit, who sometimes sells his skills in the smithies around these parts, to earn a crust of bread. But now I'm the guardian of the pool."

"The guardian?"

"It's a sacred duty, that only those with knowledge of the Law may inherit."

Rhodri suddenly felt very weary and yawned and stretched himself.

"Your visions have made you tired, boy," said Tantallon. "Come, I've brought some bread and meat from my cottage."

The old man was holding up a beaker and a wooden bowl, and the boy realized that he must have left him alone at the Seeing Place at some point during his visions. There were strips of cured venison in the bowl and a hunk of dry bread that looked delicious. Rhodri had a sense of his own body again and he was as hungry in his belly as he was weary in his limbs. Tantallon handed him the beaker, but the boy paused before eating. He thought of the warning the old woman had given to beware of the hermit. The blind man cocked his head, as if listening once more.

"It's only wine, Rhodri," he said, chuckling again, "mixed with a little rainwater. Trust me."

Rhodri smiled and took it. He drank gratefully, but before Tantallon handed him the bowl, the old man held up his hand over it and bowed his head slightly.

"We should bless the meal, especially beside the sacred Telling Pool."

Rhodri expected a Christian prayer, as Megan spoke in their home, thanking God and Christ for the food, so what Tantallon whispered next shocked him.

"Oh, Goddess within, Oh, God within. Oh, Goddess of the Moon, the Waters, and the Earth."

A wind seemed to rise and stir the forest around the Telling Pool, as, with closed eyes, Tantallon intoned.

"Oh, God of the Forests and the Mountains. Thank you for this gift of food taken from the living world. Bless it, and in eating it, may it bless us, too, and fill us with your power."

He gave the boy the food and Rhodri began to wolf it down, for he was desperately hungry. The ache he felt in his whole being had begun to lessen, and as the venison touched his stomach, he sensed strength returning and began to relax a little. Tantallon sensed it, too.

"That's better," he whispered. "If you're not used to the pool, you can take it too much into yourself, into your body and heart, and there its danger lies. Men can grow sick with the sights they behold. So be careful, Rhodri. For although you may never affect the Telling Pool, it may affect you. When you look too long into it, it may look back into you."

Rhodri shivered.

"Tantallon," he said, "your eyes. Is it because of the pool that you're . . ."

The hermit shook his head. "No. I . . . I'm old and my eyes grew weary with the endless years. As sometimes my memories fail me."

There was something in his face that told Rhodri he was hiding the truth from him, and Rhodri noticed that scar again.

"Tell me then, what is this craft, the Wiccan Law?"

Tantallon's eyes flickered.

"The foolish and ignorant call it witchcraft, but the wise, who look beyond fear and prejudice, know of it as the ancient faith. It's the pagan law, of the God and Goddess, whose spirit and force we believe abide and live in all things, though their shapes change constantly."

"Their shapes change?"

"Do not all things change their shapes," said Tantallon, "as a tadpole turns into a frog, or a boy into a man? In the ancient faiths they believed that men could even live as animals in the forest. Shamans, which they sometimes call magicians in Albion, know of special herbs and plants that can help them travel from their bodies and inhabit the wild creatures of the land."

Rhodri looked at Tantallon in astonishment and the old man smiled wryly.

"You're beginning to learn," he said, "which pleases my heart. For there is so much to learn. If you wish it, I shall teach you."

"Teach me?" said Rhodri delightedly.

"First of the animals and the forest, of the arts of the smith. Then of the Mystery. Perhaps one day we may need another guardian."

Rhodri could not believe his ears.

"Close your eyes, Rhodri," the old man said.

Rhodri looked at him in surprise, but did as he asked.

"Now calm your breathing. You may not see with your eyes now, but there are other ways of seeing, as I said. With your ears and your nose. With the very air on your skin. But above all with your spirit. So listen, Rhodri Falcon. Listen to the living world and breathe in its power."

As Rhodri sat there listening, at first he heard an owl hooting mournfully in some distant tree and the wind stirring the darkness through the branches. He felt the breeze lightly on his face and the stone beneath him. Then he became aware of the dripping in the pool, and as he sat there he began to hear more and more. The gentle creaking of wood and soft rustlings in the undergrowth. The night cries of different animals and the song of the air in the forest. His nose was filled with the odors of fern, and moss and leaf, and the wind seemed to be stroking his hands and face.

Although his eyes were closed, it was as if Rhodri could see everything around him. Tantallon and the trees, the pool and even himself, sitting there. Not see as he saw every day, or as he had seen in the Telling Pool, but with some other part of his being, some part where sight and sound, touch and smells were not separate things at all, but all connected to each other, and to the things around him, too. Rhodri felt dizzy, and it was if he could sense the very stars above them, and for a moment as brief as a sigh, he thought he saw two shapes moving together through the wonderful trees. He opened his eyes and blinked with pleasure.

"Did you sense them?" whispered Tantallon. "The God and Goddess? The power of the Miracle."

"I . . . I think so. The pool," asked Rhodri, looking at the water again. "How long has it been here, Tantallon?"

The old man laughed.

"Not even I know that secret, boy, even if I could remember it. For it's more ancient than even I can see. And I see far."

The boy shivered. Who was this blind, forgetful hermit that could see so far, and what did he really want from him?

"Now lead me up to my home," said the old man, "and you shall rest. It'll be morning soon and the images are harder to see in the daylight."

"No, Tantallon. There's so much more I want to know. When it happened. Where my pa was. Do you know what it is? The Crack de Chevalier."

"No," answered the hermit, "but you are keen indeed."

Tantallon fell silent and seemed to be trying to make up his mind. At last he nodded.

"Very well then. Though it's dangerous, you've more strength in you than these tired old limbs. If you're sure, then neither I nor the Telling Pool shall deny you. If you really want to know then, in your inner mind, ask the pool to tell you."

6 ❖ THE LIONHEART

The blood-dimmed tide is loosed, and everywhere
The ceremony of innocence is drowned
—W. B. Yeats, "The Second Coming"

Again Rhodri leaned forward from the Seeing Place. He was so amazed by what he saw now that his whole body broke into a sweat. A desert stretched before him, toward a mighty castle. So huge and forbidding was the place that it might have been a city that he was seeing in the Telling Pool. It was built into a mountainside, and it soared above monumental slabs of stone, turreted in the clear blue sky, with a gigantic ramp running up to its gates. Knights and archers and foot soldiers were streaming up it, like a column of tiny ants. Once more Rhodri had the feeling that, after all, he had become a part of this great adventure.

Flags and banners and pendants fluttered like wings from those monumental walls, and everywhere in the sun flashed the hard, bright edges of weaponry. Rhodri knew that the Telling Pool was showing him the Crack de Chevalier, for in his heart that is what he had ached to see. That heart stirred, and he wanted to be there in the pool in this place of warfare and amazement. He wanted to climb on a horse and robe himself in armor, and draw a sword for the Cross, like a man. Even as he thought it, another sword gleamed in the water. His grandfather's sword.

Owen was holding it, sitting in a kind of manger, running a sharpening stone up and down its edge, surrounded by filthy soldiers slumped over their weapons. Rhodri started immediately as he noticed the fresh scar on his father's cheek. He had been wounded.

"For the Christ's sake, Falcon," said Hellard, appearing next to Owen, "why won't they tell us when it will come, damn you? You know more than the others."

"Be patient now. All things visit those who wait."

"But I want to be done with it," growled the soldier bitterly. "Look at us, Master Falconer. You know the Saracen have cut the supply routes. Hardly enough food gets in now to feed us all."

"I know it, man," said Rhodri's father quietly.

"Though the Coeur de Lion and his lord lieutenants fair well enough," grunted Hellard, "eating their rich French foods and fattening themselves on our plunder."

The Lionheart, thought Rhodri excitedly, and he suddenly wanted to see the king, too. Even as he thought it, the pool seemed to quiver and the surface move. The boy felt that his own thoughts were affecting what he was seeing there. His desperate worry for his father returned and the image stayed.

"Why are you so keen to fight, Hellard?" asked Owen. He stopped polishing his sword and looked hard at his wretched companion. "We need as much rest as we can get, before we march out again."

"I hate this damned waiting, Falcon. If we break this army, then the route to Jerusalem itself will be open. It's the waiting I can't stand, even if I'm to die like a desert dog out here."

"The Saracen are close and the battle will be in two or three suns' time, no more," said Owen softly. "A battle the like of which none of us have encountered before."

Rhodri sat up. A battle. This is what he longed to see.

"Then we'd better pray with all our hearts," said Hellard, "and at least you'll be in the thick of it with us, Falcon. We can thank that Saracen arrow for that, and for a week's good horseflesh, eh?"

Some of the soldiers laughed, but Owen's face darkened. Rhodri realized that his father's horse had been killed and the hungry soldiers had been forced to eat it as they ran short of food.

"And on foot you, too, are just a pawn in the Lionheart's great chess game," added the soldier, "like the rest of us miserable sinners. To be moved about and sacrificed at his will."

"Richard leads us well, man," said Rhodri's father. "The king cares for the men. Last week you know I saw him help a simple . . ."

"You're such an innocent, Falcon," sneered Hellard, and Rhodri was reminded of Aelfric. "King Richard cares for nothing but glory and blood and warfare. Can't you see that he'd sacrifice us at the drop of a lady's favor to save his blasted knights?"

Knights, thought Rhodri wonderingly. The king. He wanted to see them all. But the boy felt ashamed of Hellard for speaking like this. It seemed like sacrilege and a betrayal of the very thing his own father was fighting for. For the holy cause of Christianity and the freedom of Jerusalem. For the king of Albion, too.

Owen did not argue with Hellard, and the lights were swirling again. Rhodri gasped as, beneath the terrible Crack de Chevalier, he saw a range of great white tents, fluttering with noble banners. Young grooms ran about everywhere, and through the dust, knights were on the move. Some were being helped to mount their horses, others were being fitted with helmets or bucklers. Rhodri felt a pang of envy toward the lads aiding the adults to go to war.

A group of armored knights was standing outside the largest of the tents now, and in their center, taller and far more powerful than the rest, was a bearded man in the finest armor of all. Next to him stood the very same lord Rhodri had seen outside the tent at St. Martin's Day—Treffusis. He was talking.

"Sire," he cried, "we await your orders."

Rhodri sat bolt upright. Treffusis had called the man "Sire." Rhodri Falcon was looking on the Coeur de Lion himself—Richard the Lionheart. He was gazing at a king, from a place where another king, the high king himself, had sat. Richard turned his proud head and he seemed to be looking back straight at the boy, though his gaze registered nothing but the dusty plain about him.

"God's teeth," he growled in the water, "it's hot enough under this sun to roast a heathen. Let's be done with it soon, before the sun reaches its anvil."

Richard spat in the dirt and turned again to address one of his nobles. Rhodri could not understand a word this time, and realized that the king was speaking in French. Then the king turned back to Treffusis and spoke English again.

"So then, do you think we've brought enough men and equipment with us?"

"I pray so, sire."

"The taxes I raised in England emptied our coffers, Treffusis," said the king. "But it's worth the gamble. To win Jerusalem I'd have sold London itself, if I could have found a buyer."

Treffusis laughed.

"And what news of home?" asked the king.

For a moment the lord dropped his eyes. "There's trouble, sire. Much unrest and villainy. And you know the rumor that Philip of France himself plots with powerful Englishmen against you."

"My ally the French king woos powerful Englishmen?" said Richard coldly. "John, I think you mean? My dear, loyal brother was ever ambitious for my throne. And he'll pay for his treachery on my return. But are we ready, Treffusis?"

"Yes, sire. If we can tempt the Moselmen onto the field."

"Then we'll send in your contingent first. They've rested enough and there are some good ones among them. Like that big Welshman. Let them prod the filthy heathen in the guts first and make 'em chase them into the open, where we can slaughter them like camp curs."

It felt strange to be watching Richard himself in counsel, and with a jolt of satisfaction Rhodri thought of Aelfric's mocking words about Rhodri advising the king.

"Our knights will charge them," grunted Richard, "hit them as hard as we can with full horse, and I shall lead them into battle myself."

Rhodri wondered if this battle was the great danger to the king that the fortune-teller had foreseen. The boy wanted to warn King Richard now, but he knew that it was useless.

"But we must call my men back first," said Treffusis.

"Of course, man. Let the heralds do that. And in the meantime tell the priests to bless the Holy Army. That'll reassure them and fill them with a touch of nobility. If such a miracle were possible among these villains. Our army may not frighten the enemy, but I tell you this, they scare the hell out of me."

The king laughed and slapped one of his knights on the back, and they all laughed with him. Rhodri was a little angry at what the Lionheart had said about his own men. Yet, in that place, there had been something perfectly natural about the remark. Something true. Rhodri supposed this was soldier's talk.

As the boy sat and the waters swirled again, a desperate excitement came over him. Owen was marching on foot with Hellard and many of the other soldiers Rhodri had seen before. Behind them the rest of the army was ranged up in front of the tents, and a line of over a hundred knights, plumes swaying like colored birds on their helms, waited on their stamping horses. Hellard was cursing furiously, but Owen's eyes were set straight and clear. Rhodri felt the sting of pride at the sight, for courage and determination shone in his father's strong face.

But what was Rhodri seeing now in the Telling Pool? Other soldiers were on the march. Rather than plate or buckler, they wore leather armor and their round helmets were like studded pudding bowls. Their drawn swords were strange indeed, for their scimitars were curved like the new moon, and their skin was dark as a devil's. Black faces, some bearded, others clean shaven, some filled with fear, others with cold hate. The heathen were on the march.

The waters churned, and Owen was reaching his arm over his shoulder and drawing his sword, the blade his own father had once wielded in the Holy Lands when Jerusalem had first fallen to Christian Knights. The sword flashed brilliantly.

"Fight, Pa," cried Rhodri, clenching his fists. "Fight like a lion."

"Calm yourself, Rhodri," said Tantallon at the edge of the pool, "for you may not alter what is, has been, or is to come."

Rhodri looked again and saw that something new had come upon his father's face, something that terrified the boy, and as if shaking the voice out of his body, his father gave a bloodcurdling scream. The air around the Seeing Place was suddenly filled with shouts and the hard clatter and clash of metal on metal. Owen slashed left and right as the two forces locked.

At first Rhodri's heart thrilled as Owen struck down a Saracen in his path. He turned to another and they engaged, too, and in an instant his father had cut him down as well. Rhodri wanted to shout out triumphantly, but found he couldn't speak, just watch, mesmerized as an entirely contrary feeling washed over him.

It began with the sight of Hellard. The soldier had just lifted his sword to strike, when those angry eyes filled with the blankness of incomprehension. An arrow had passed straight through his throat, just above his Adam's apple. Rhodri blinked in horror as the soldier slumped to his knees, and, as he did so, a curve of metal flicked toward him, there was a slash of red, and Hellard's head fell from his shoulders, like a stone tumbling off a wall.

Rhodri tried to sit back, but he felt as if something were gripping his body in a vise, and it was as if a force were churning through his being, making his heart thunder and his head ache. Now all Rhodri saw in the Telling Pool was metal cutting into flesh, as the shouts turned to screams of agony and pain.

"No. Don't."

A Moselman scimitar opened a human cheek like a soft cheese, an arm was hacked clean off, and a blade cut into a shoulder and was lodged there like a sword in a stone. Rhodri felt sick and tried to pull away, but the Telling Pool held him fast. Horror began to swamp the boy, not only at the ghastly vision, but because he realized as he looked on that De Brackenois's contingent was being overrun by the swarming Saracens.

But like a rush of hope came the sound of blaring trumpets, distantly, and Rhodri remembered what the Lionheart had said in the Telling Pool. The knights. The king's knights were coming to their aid.

"Hooray," cried the boy.

There rode King Richard himself, looking like a god in his fine armor, and Rhodri saw terror in the faces of the Saracen. Richard had his sword arm raised, and there was such boldness and courage in his eyes that Rhodri wanted to bend his knee and serve him.

The knights at his side kept looking toward their king, for his fearlessness and certainty was bearing them forward. Yet as Rhodri watched helplessly, he realized that in the terrible melee there was no way that his father and his comrades could hear the approaching trumpets. All in the battle was mayhem and confusion. All was dust and dirt and blood.

"Pa," cried Rhodri, his voice echoing impotently about the pool. "Look out, Pa."

Rhodri saw a Christian turn in terror and slash at one of the very soldiers who had been fighting at his side. His father was still there, on his feet, but the Saracen were all about him. Then the ground was rocked with the sound of thunder. The king's charge broke on the foot soldiers like a wave of hoof and metal, trampling or hacking down men in their path.

Rhodri was appalled, for although the king tried to control the charge, the knights were riding down not only the heathen, but their own soldiers, too. It was as if the boy's head were bursting with the thunder and the screams and the terrible vision was whirling and blending, limbs and men and horses, turning and swirling and the light was going out and the Telling Pool was growing darker and darker. Deeper and deeper.

But this darkness was not the blackness it had been before, but a thick, sickly crimson red, and suddenly the waters were not waters at all, but a huge pool of human blood, surging and whirling and pumping up from the depths. Rhodri bent forward again and reached out a hand, half to stop the vision, half in a desire to help, but as it touched the water it grew warm, and when Rhodri lifted it he saw that it was dripping not with water, but with blood, too. The boy screamed and he was falling. His hands flailed out, and as they touched dry earth and crumpled beneath him, everything vanished.

7 ❖ THE CAVE

Ha! ha! the caverns of my hollow mountains,
My cloven fire-crags, sound-exulting fountains,
Laugh with a vast and inextinguishable laughter.
Percy Bysshe Shelley, "Prometheus Unbound"

"Ho, don't. Stop it. Please."

"Open your eyes now, Rhodri Falcon."

The boy opened his hazelnut eyes. Above his head he saw a wooden ceiling and he felt something soft beneath him. He was lying on a simple cot.

"Where am I?" he whispered faintly.

"In my home," said the kindly voice.

Tantallon was wiping his fevered head with a cloth, and as Rhodri groaned and struggled in the cot, the blind old man lifted another beaker and put it carefully to his lips. The liquor was sweet on his tongue, and Rhodri, as though parched by a terrible journey, drank it all in gratefully. "Now try to sit up."

The boy lifted himself on his elbows and looked about. He expected the cottage to be even more disheveled inside than outside, but although the place was poor indeed, with hardly a stick of furniture and only the straw mattress he lay on for a bed, Tantallon's home was clean and neat and proud. The hovel comprised just one room, in the far corner of which hung drying plants, and mushrooms and fungi curling into wild, woodland shapes. There was a small hearth where a peat fire glowed dimly, and next to it Rhodri saw an hourglass. It made him think of the card of the hermit at the fair.

"How long have I been here?"

"Two days."

"Two days!"

"Your visions put a fever in you, Rhodri, and for a time I thought you might . . ." The hermit shook his head. "But I used my skill to wrestle with it. The sickness has broken now. You will be well."

Rhodri propped himself up painfully.

"I shouldn't have let you look so long," said Tantallon, shaking his head guiltily, "and you forgot what I told you, too. To see with a light heart, for the visions may only reach you if you let them in. And you must not touch the water."

Rhodri stirred guiltily. Had Tantallon seen him touch the surface?

"A light heart?" whispered the boy, shuddering with the memory, but looking at his hand, too, and seeing no stain of any kind. "It was horrible, Tantallon. Our knights and King Richard tried to help, but they cut down our own men."

Tantallon sat on the edge of the cot.

"Then you are learning quickly," he whispered. "A boy thinks swords and warfare fine and noble, does he not, like the tales of ancient heroes? But in truth war is a cruel, uncertain business. So it often is in life, if you look deeper. So it is as a boy begins to grow up."

"And the king. King Richard, I mean. He seemed so fine and strong. Yet in the battle, once the charge had got out of control, he did not seem to care much about the foot soldiers."

"A king's can be a hard way," said Tantallon, nodding. "Especially in time of war."

Rhodri thought of Arthur and King Richard. How were they connected?

"But tell me now, Rhodri, tell me all you saw this time. Be my eyes."

Rhodri described precisely everything he had seen and heard in the Telling Pool, but when he had finished Tantallon just shook his head, as though disappointed.

"There was nothing else? Are you certain of it? Absolutely certain?"

"Yes. Why do you ask?"

Tantallon sighed and was silent and thoughtful. He seemed to be trying to remember something. He got up slowly.

"I must be tending to the animals and light my fire to remake your dagger. Lie here and rest and we shall talk some more. As I said, you've much to learn."

"No," said Rhodri, struggling on the cot. "I have to look again."

"It's too dangerous this soon."

"I don't care. My pa was in a terrible battle, but I didn't see what happened to him."

"Patience, boy," smiled the old man. "All things visit those who wait."

Rhodri shivered, for it was just what his father had said in the water.

"Please," he whispered faintly, but as he struggled he felt a terrible weariness in him and sank back on the cot. His brow was sweating and he felt hopelessly weak. He wanted to shut out the ghastly memories from the pool.

"And my ma," he groaned. "If I've been gone so long, she will be worried sick."

"She is fine," said Tantallon gently, his blind eyes looking down kindly into the boy's face. "Worried yes, but safe at home. Now sleep."

As Rhodri heard the hermit's certain, reassuring voice and closed his eyes, fearful that those horrible visions would return, only for an instant did he wonder how the blind man could know this of his home that was so far away, before dreams took him once more. He dreamt of Lancelot and of Guinevere as they walked together in the forest, but this time he saw that Guinevere had on that cloak she had worn by the seashore, and now he could see that crest embroidered on its back. It was the head of a beautiful animal, the shape of a deer.

When he woke again, he felt much better, and Tantallon was humming to himself as he crouched over the peat fire in the hovel and stirred a pot of bubbling soup. He immediately sensed the boy's waking and turned his head and smiled.

"I'm glad to see your strength coming back. Lunch will be ready soon."

The old man reached out and picked up some herbs and other plants and popped them into the cauldron.

"Rosemary and basil, Rhodri. Some plants are sought out for their power to heal, to stop blood and cure toothache and ease pain. While others are sought for their poison, which in small quantities may heal, too."

Tantallon put a sprig to his nose.

"Still others are sought, though, because they make things taste so good."

The old man laughed to himself happily.

"It is good to have you here, you know, Rhodri," said the hermit warmly. "I have been alone for too long."

The soup tasted very good, as did the fresh hunk of bread and cow's milk cheese, and soon Rhodri felt completely restored. They sat there in the hovel talking like old friends, and Rhodri told Tantallon all about his mother and the homestead, about Aelfric and William, Sarah and Wolfrin. The old man's blind eyes flickered with interest and care, and every now and then he would interject with a wise observation or a piece of advice. They talked about Rhodri's work on the farm, too, and Tantallon told him the best way to make an oil to rub on the birds' wings to keep them healthy and shiny, and the surest poison for rats in the barn. He told him how to name flies on the river, too, that come at different times of the year to tempt the fish, and how best to thread a hook, so that the line didn't come loose.

For the first time in nearly a year Rhodri felt really happy. It was so good to have someone there like his father to learn things from and talk to. To ask advice from a man, even a blind old man like Tantallon.

"Tantallon," he said as they sat there, "Excalibur—you said that it was hidden. By who?"

The old hermit smiled.

"The great sorcerer Merlin."

Rhodri shivered excitedly.

"But why?"

"Because in its very forging, Mythirion represented a promise—a promise that was broken."

"By Guinevere and Lancelot?"

Tantallon swung his head, and those blind eyes seemed to be searching the boy's face intently, although such a thing was impossible.

"Yes. But they were not wicked, Rhodri," he said almost sadly, in a strange, fatherly way, "they just could not fight their love. But in their betrayal they broke faith and Arthur's heart, too. He and the land began to sicken and then the real evil came."

Rhodri was straining to remember the stories.

"A curse fell on the whole land," said Tantallon, "from the witch Morgana and Arthur's half-son, Mordred. They wrought a terrible evil, but above all they wanted the sword Mythirion, to bring them even greater power. So Merlin hid Excalibur again."

"Hid it? Where?"

A strange look came over Tantallon's ancient face.

"That secret was forgotten. For even Merlin's power began to fade with the curse, and his own memories, too."

"You talk, Tantallon, as if you . . ."

"I've looked long into the pool," said the hermit, getting up quickly. "And have seen much of the ancient ways. But we talk of things past. Come. There are more secrets I'd show you of the present. Lead me outside."

Rhodri took Tantallon's arm and led him outside, over to a clay oven set among the trees, where a fire was burning brilliantly. Lumps of malachite lay all about, and within the heart of the fire was a stone crucible. It was filled with a glowing, molten liquid.

"I've been stoking it all morning," said the old smith, crouching before it. "The fire is ready to remake your dagger. So let me teach you something of my arts."

As the flames flickered over his face, Tantallon reached out and picked up two metal rods that lay on the ground. He used them to move the crucible out of the fire. Then he stooped down and picked up what looked like a hollowed out rock. It was long and thin, almost in the shape of a dagger.

"For common blades I use ordinary clay molds," said Tantallon, "but for you, Rhodri, it must be stone."

The old man worked with extraordinary dexterity as he balanced the stone receptacle between two more rocks and, mumbling something to himself, tipped the crucible toward it. Rhodri leaned in to watch.

"Careful, boy, it can burn."

Rhodri pulled back, but Tantallon seemed perfectly in control of all his movements as the fiery metal poured out.

"The magic in the heat has bled the rocks of their raw copper and tin, to make the greatest of metals—bronze. A metal to make high kings among men indeed."

Tantallon was still pouring the molten metal, and when the stone mold was full, he took the broken antler handle from his pocket and slid its point into the top.

"It shall rest here to cool and bind," said the old man, "and then we'll break the stone and release the newly forged blade. You should feel privileged, Rhodri, for such things are great secrets of ancient magic."

Rhodri nodded, but he was thinking of his father.

"Tantallon," he said, "I feel better now and I must look again."

The hermit shook his head and sighed.

"So impatient and impetuous. Even after you saw how dangerous it can be."

"I don't care how dangerous it is," said Rhodri fiercely. "My father. I must know what happened to him."

"Very well, Rhodri," said Tantallon, getting up wearily. "I must try to remember that a boy's heart is not a man's, and perhaps a teacher must learn from his pupil, too, eh?"

They went back through the arch with its mistletoe and down the stairs to the magic pool. Rhodri sat down again at the Seeing Place, but as he looked and the pictures appeared, he saw not his father nor the Holy Wars but the entrance to a huge, dark cave. The ground before the cave was thick with heavy green moss that looked soft and pleasant to walk on, but the cave entrance was hung with spears of stone, stalactites, that looked like the tresses of a witch's hair. It looked like an entrance to another world.

Rhodri was startled by a memory. The memory was of another card on the fortune-teller's table. He felt a sharp pain in his guts and sensed—no, knew—with all the certainty of his young being, that something dwelt inside that cave that was just as dangerous as anything he had witnessed in the Holy Wars. He noticed a bird, too, sitting on the bank by the entrance. It was a flint-black raven. Its eyes seemed to be looking out of the water, and suddenly it opened its wings and flew straight inside the cave.

As he watched, it was as if Rhodri himself were following it. He was passing under those tresses of stone, and the cave opened before him. It revealed a long stone tunnel, the walls of which glinted and sparked with the sheen of wet crystal. The cave was oddly ribbed, too, with the weathering work of water on limestone, like folds of human skin. It was both beautiful and sinister. As Rhodri looked closer, he saw that among the sparking yellow and white crystals, the walls of the cave were studded with colored stones, glinting with reds and greens and blues, things of great and rare value in the world of men.

Rhodri leaned forward and reached out again, despite what Tantallon had warned him about the water, and scooped some up in his palm. This time when he looked he saw that a ruby was lying there, until the water trickled away through his fingers and it vanished.

In the cave, a woman appeared before him. Rhodri hardly understood the feelings that flowed through him now as he looked into the Telling Pool. She was dressed all in black, and was the loveliest person he had ever seen in his life, even more beautiful than the Lady Guinevere. Her skin was almost the color of the Saracen, and great wild ringlets of thick raven-black hair fell all around her delicate head.

Her eyes were huge and dark and filled with a cunning light, and her feet were bare on the cold stone.

The woman turned and swept away, and it was as if she had vanished into a mist. Rhodri realized that she hadn't vanished at all. The end of the tunnel was veiled with a curtain of smoke, and she had simply passed through it. On the ground were little wooden tapers, the tops of which glowed orange and red, and from them the smoke was rising.

The vision paused at the smoke veil, for something seemed to be holding it back. Rhodri realized that not only could he hear from the Telling Pool, but that he could smell, too. His nostrils were thick with the scent of the tapers, rich and cloying, and his head grew dizzy and he felt sick. As though an unseen hand were drawing aside the smoke curtain, the veil parted and a voice seemed to beckon Rhodri inside.

The cave was huge, and all about burned candles, glittering like captured stars. In the ceiling and the walls, rounded by time and water, the boy saw the most wondrous rock formations. Stalactites fell from the ceiling like daggers, and stalagmites rose from the ground like stone candles. In the walls were strange shapes like bodies and faces that seemed for an instant to be pulling free of the stone, until Rhodri realized that they were nothing but the cave itself and the shadows of the candles.

Yet it was the decoration of the cave that most amazed Rhodri. Everywhere there lay rich tapestries and cushions, silken scarves hung from the ceiling; a rich oak wood table stood covered in food and glittering cutlery. There were ornaments, curious-looking figurines, an astrolabe, a globe, and furniture that had turned this wild place into a home of rich and rare device.

Rhodri could see no fire in the cave, except a flickering red to the right, but somehow he knew that it was very warm, for a kind of filmy steam hung in the air. To one edge of the stone chamber, above some carved steps, was a raised area where a bed lay, rich with silken cushion and soft white sheets. The Telling Pool began to quiver and ripple, and the images were suddenly gone. A fish darted through the water, but as it did so, Rhodri heard a sound echoing from the water that chilled his blood. It was laughter.

"What did you see, Rhodri?" asked a voice behind him.

"A cave, Tantallon. And a strange and beautiful woman."

The old man knelt at his side. His face had an urgency he had not shown before, and again he seemed to be trying to remember something.

"A cave? Tell me quickly, Rhodri. Tell me everything, and leave nothing out."

The boy was surprised by his vehemence. He told Tantallon, and the blind old man nodded gravely.

"She's an enchantress of very great power."

The card. The Enchantress.

"An enchantress? You know her?"

Tantallon dropped his gaze. "I . . . I have heard word of her, yes. You must look again. Look and tell me all. Be my eyes."

Rhodri felt very nervous as he strained forward once more from the Seeing Place. The scene returned, but it had changed. There, set back in a kind of recess, Rhodri saw a sort of hearth, although it was made entirely of the stone floor of the cave. The woman was standing over it looking down. It looked like a low well, and Rhodri saw what was inside. At first he thought it was water, for it was moving and bubbling, and yet it was as red as fire, although here and there hard and dark, too, like cracked earth.

The enchantress raised her hand and cast something into the lava. A flame leapt up from it, although it seemed more than an ordinary fire, for amidst the red tongues of light were other colors, yellows and blues and greens, like the gems in the walls of the cave.

Then the lava was swirling, and pictures seemed to arise inside the fire, too. To Rhodri looking down from the Seeing Place into the Telling Pool, showing him another surface of image or dream, it was as if he had suddenly slipped, although he was still seated, as a sleeper dreams of the chair he is on and finds himself falling, only to wake to find himself still in his chair.

In the lava there appeared a huge domed temple of pure lapis blue and a turret that soared into the heavens. From its circular balcony a bearded figure, dressed in the manner of the East, was lifting his head to the evening skies and calling.

His call was so strange and haunting, so full of longing and mystery, that it made Rhodri tremble, and the glowing fire rock was filled with the scenes of a busy city, crowded with people. But they were not the people Rhodri had often dreamt of in the streets of Londinium, for these people were as dark as the enchantress. The men at least, for the women who moved among them like shadows were covered from head to foot in black robes that hid their faces and showed only their dark, lovely eyes.

They were moving through such strange and wonderful alleyways that Rhodri wished himself there, too, for the finely carved wooden balconies that hung out over the streets, the patterned doorways, the fountains that played among stalls laden with wondrous tapestries and rare carpets, exotic fruits and rich spices, were a world to the boy that seemed to answer some ancient longing in him.

Then Rhodri saw a figure walking through the bazaar that made him catch his breath. At first he could easily have been mistaken for a Christian knight in the Holy Army, with his pale skin and a lord's bearing and wealth. He wore trousers and boots like Owen's and was helmeted like a Templar knight. Yet this was all that was of Albion about him, for over his helm he wore a shawl in the manner of the Saracen and the fine, silken cloak that hung about his shoulders was of an intricate design. He stopped, as several figures greeted him warmly and touched their hands to their chest, lips, and forehead, in the manner of a Moselman greeting.

The picture faded. Rhodri reached out again, and through the water he plunged his hand toward the lava pool to try and touch it. He felt nothing but cold, yet as he withdrew it again, he was amazed. Though he felt no heat, liquid fire seemed for a moment to be dripping from his hand.

The enchantress in the cave had picked up a metal hammer from the edge of the hearth, and next to it was a pile of sand. She picked something else up that glinted in the firelight. A clear shard, like crystal, which she placed on the edge of the pool. She lifted the hammer as Tantallon had done in the forge, and brought it down on a strip of metal.

She worked for a while and then turned. Hanging down from the wall of the cave was a little silken curtain, which she pulled back. There, in a stone alcove, stood a box. It was the oddest casket Rhodri had ever seen. The box shone and sparked in the light, like some brilliant jewel. Its glass seemed to have many colors in it, too, and on the metal edges that held the glass in place it was encrusted with rubies and emeralds and sapphires from the cave. At the corners, the casket was finished in the finest carved wood.

Rhodri desperately wanted to know what was inside that box but as the woman reached up and added a pane of glass to it, Rhodri realized that whatever she was making was not yet finished and that the box was empty.

She turned away again, and now the boy looked on in horror. In the ceiling above the casket the boy could clearly see a face, looking back at him. It was a man's, and the lips seemed to be curling in pain, and the eyes held terrible anguish in them. Rhodri blinked and shook his head as the light shimmered and he realized he was just looking at the roof of the cave where, in the play of shadows, an outcrop of rock had made him think there was a face.

Then everything was gone.

"Well, Rhodri?"

"It was so strange."

"The woman," asked the old man, "how old is . . . this woman?"

"I don't know. My mother's age. Perhaps thirty years. She has a well that shows her things, like the Telling Pool. Only this is made of fire and stone."

Tantallon stepped back a little. Rhodri noticed that his hands were shaking, but he was nodding to himself, too.

"Lava rock. It rises from the belly of the world."

"It's hot," said the boy, "and when I touched it . . ."

"You touched it?"

"Yes," admitted Rhodri, feeling ashamed. "Like I did during the battle."

When Rhodri described these moments, Tantallon shook his head and seemed very disturbed.

"The enchantress," said Rhodri, "she makes a small casket at the well."

"Makes something in the fire?"

"Yes. It is made to hold something, but as yet is empty."

"Tell me."

Rhodri did so, in great detail, and when he came to the moment when he had thought he had seen a face locked in the stone, Tantallon's mouth pursed immediately, though he did not speak.

"But what does it mean?" asked the boy. "What has she to do with Pa or the Holy Wars?"

Tantallon shook his head.

"Then I must see more."

Rhodri leaned forward over the water and looked, but this time only a single image appeared. It was of a man, dressed in a great black cloak. He stood on a huge rock, and on his head was the most amazing headpiece in the world. It was tall and pointed, like some wizard's hat, and was made of beaten gold. All around its metal were circles and half globes, also beaten out in rough gold, so many in fact that Rhodri could hardly count them. Then the image shimmered and faded, like some distant memory drifting away.

Rhodri waited, but now nothing happened at all. The waters lay flat and still.

"What's wrong?" asked the boy in exasperation, wanting to know more of his father.

"Perhaps the pool has shown you all it will for now," said Tantallon. "For it knows when to give up its secrets. And there's an art to seeing, too. Few may really control the Mystery."

"But my father and King Richard, how can I find out . . ."

"Patience," said the old man firmly. "We must start by teaching you patience, boy. For you could not hope to make a beautiful harness, nor a fine, strong weapon in just one morning. And your mother, Rhodri, is it not time to look to her?"

The boy stood up immediately.

"I had forgotten." The stone moved slightly at his feet. "I've been away far too long already, and it'll be even longer if I can't find Melanor."

Almost as he said it they heard a jangling and a fluttering above them. Tantallon swung round and looked up. On the branch of the tree to their right sat Melanor, the silver bell tinkling about his throat and the rock falcon's piercing eyes watching the boy and the blind old man, as it jerked its little head up and down. Rhodri was amazed, but Tantallon laughed.

"It seems that Melanor has found you, instead," he cried, smiling up at the bird. "He must trust you very much, Rhodri. It's good indeed that you make this bond with animals. Especially such a fine bird. Never break it."

Rhodri raised his arm and made a clicking sound, and Melanor took sudden wing and sailed down to land on his master's hand. Rhodri was not wearing his hawking glove, but so lightly did Melanor land and so gently did his clawed feet rest there, that he hardly felt anything at all. He pulled the hood from his pocket and placed it on the falcon's tiny head. With Melanor on one arm and Tantallon clasping the other, together they went back up the steps.

At the little forge where Rhodri's dagger lay half remade, the boy thought of the beautiful woman and her lava pool, as Tantallon tested the stone sheath with his hands and then plunged it into a bowl of water. He laid it flat on the earth and then took a large rock and began to bash hard at the stone. Each blow was as precise as the blows had been in the forge. At last the stone cracked and fell apart to reveal the new dagger. It's dull, green patina was not very fine and the edges were rough and ragged, but it was a blade nonetheless.

"We must smooth it, Rhodri," said Tantallon, testing the blade with his fingers, "and sharpen it for you."

Tantallon picked up a kind of file and began to work on it, and soon the dagger was sparkling and its edges were as sharp as glass.

"There."

"Thank you, Tantallon."

"And when you return, I shall polish the hilt for you."

"When I return?" said Rhodri excitedly. "Yes, Tantallon. When can I look again?"

Tantallon was thoughtful for a while.

"Soon perhaps, but first tend to your duty and gather all your strength. I'll send you a sign."

"What sign?"

Tantallon chuckled. "You'll know it when it comes."

"But when?"

"Patience, boy. Rome was not built in a day. Now off with you, young man. At your age you don't want to spend all your days talking to a foolish old man."

Rhodri smiled. He could think of nothing he would rather do.

"But you must be careful," added the hermit. "Other eyes watch the forests, and these are dangerous days. So remember to say nothing of this place. On your sacred oath."

"I promise."

Rhodri turned, delighted to share this secret, but he stopped again. "Please tell me, Tantallon. Why did you show this to me?"

The old man seemed to look back at Rhodri and at the amulet tied to his throat. Rhodri felt he wanted to speak, but Tantallon dropped his eyes.

"I told you long ago. You've the air of one who quests and one who might understand . . . the Miracle. As Arthur himself came to understand. He was a simple country lad, like you, Rhodri Falcon. It took work to make him into a king. Now go."

As Rhodri carried Melanor down the path the hermit set him on, he felt almost like a king himself, and the trees seemed to hold no dread to him now. The boy had tasted of a deep magic in the wood and it seemed to him as he went that all the animals of the forest and all the creatures that lived within its secret places knew of it and, because of that knowledge, were friends. But Rhodri had another friend now, and a teacher, too.

As he went, the boy did not see the blind man turn hurriedly and rush down those steps toward the Telling Pool, without once stumbling. He did not see him sit in the Seeing Place and, leaning forward, wave his old, wrinkled hand across the waters and look out with those sightless eyes. He did not see that beautiful, mournful lady with the jewel like a star on her head, arising from the depths, nor hear Tantallon talking softly to Guinevere.

"I almost told the boy," he whispered, "who he is. But it is too soon. He walks the path, but the beauty and hardship of those who do is that they must find their own way, if they are to truly grow."

The lady in the water nodded.

"But his power is great. Several times he touched the water with no harm, and now he has found it. The forge. Let us pray he can help us. But first he must grow and deepen and I must watch him."

Rhodri hurried on in the forest. After a couple of hours the trees began to thin and he saw the open fields. As he left the wood he heard a fluttering in the trees behind him and turned to look up. A bird was sitting there, watching him calmly. Rhodri was startled to see such a rare creature in these parts, for he knew how highly prized such a bird could be, worth perhaps a king's ransom. It was a fine specimen, although too old to train for the chase. It was a male merlin.

8 ❖ OLD FRIENDS

You did not come,
And marching Time drew on, and wore me numb.
Thomas Hardy, "A Broken Appointment"

Megan was overjoyed at Rhodri's return. She questioned her son keenly, for he had spent three whole nights and half a day in the forest. But as Tantallon had instructed him, Rhodri said nothing of the Telling Pool and the place where the boy King Arthur had sat. Instead he told his mother simply of Melanor's loss, and nights spent searching for him and sleeping in the open.

His birthing day came again, and every morning Rhodri woke, wondering when he could return to the pool. But a lethargy had fallen over Megan that was growing deeper, and Rhodri had many labors on the farm to distract him. Besides, Tantallon had told him to wait for a sign and gather all his strength. Weeks passed. The mass of the Savior's birth was a solemn day in the Falcon home that year. All Megan could do was talk of Owen and where he might be, and Rhodri blushed as he thought of what he had seen, but could not speak of. Then mother and son prayed together for his safe return.

That evening they walked together to the church, where the priest was already addressing the flock.

"My breathen," he said loudly, as they settled in their pew, "let me talk once more of the need for faith."

The priest gave them black news of what was happening in Albion. Of how outlaws openly defied edicts, now that the king was gone from the land, and that murder and blasphemy were rife.

"But if life is a vale of tears," he went on piously, casting his eyes over his flock, "filled with pain and sorrow and sin, with disease and hunger and the certainty of death, while we live we must carry on with courage and love in our hearts, as the Lord God Christ himself did."

For the final part of his sermon he took the theme of the sins of the fathers, but Rhodri wasn't really listening anymore. He had noticed William sitting in the De Brackenois pew and nearby, Sarah sat next to the ruddy-faced miller. Rhodri felt sad as he saw the two friends casting fond glances at each other, but guilty, too, that he had such feelings in church. He ached to share his new secret with someone—Sarah or William perhaps, but he knew it was his secret alone.

Outside the church he lingered for a while as Megan went on

ahead, but a gloom had got into him and at last he set off down the track.

"Rhodri. Hold on awhile."

Sarah was running after him. The boy was tongue-tied as she reached him, and he stood there blinking and thinking that she had grown even prettier.

"What's wrong, Rhodri? You never come to see me anymore. Aren't we friends?"

"Of course, Sarah. It's just, well, with so much to do and worry about . . . You know how it is."

"Yes, of course. But I miss your visits."

"Do you?" Rhodri dropped his gaze.

"Of course, Rhodri. Come and see me soon. You know what day it is next Tuesday?"

"No."

"My birthing day."

Rhodri promised to visit Sarah, and his heart felt as light as Melanor riding the air as he set off home. He had begun to believe Sarah was only interested in William, but now he knew she cared about him, too. Rhodri was hatching a plan as he walked. To make her a wonderful present for her birthing day.

That night, Rhodri lay in his room, and as soon as he closed his eyes found himself dreaming. Not of his father or the Telling Pool or the enchantress, but of Sarah. She was walking in front of him through a field of poppies. She was dressed all in white and her hair was sparkling in the sunlight. About her head was a wreath of spring flowers, like the girls wore to dance around the maypole, and her pretty feet were bare.

She turned and looked back at him and smiled sweetly, as she slipped from the path and entered the wood.

Rhodri found himself following, his body hot with fire, but as he went the air was alive with birdsong and the rich scent of flowers. The sun streamed through the trees in pools of hot warmth, and Rhodri found his clothes clinging all about him. He had a wonderful feeling and opened his shirt to touch his chest and found it glistening with sweat. The warmth and moisture of the wood was all about him, as spring flowers rose and opened their sticky buds to the sunlight and filled the air with perfume.

The next morning when Rhodri came down to break his fast, Megan was at the hearth, working on her tapestry. She looked up and smiled, but Rhodri noticed immediately that she had been crying. Her eyes were red and puffy.

"Are you all right, Ma?"

Rhodri noticed the needle shaking in her hand as she worked the tapestry.

"Yes, Rhodri."

"But you've been crying."

Rhodri suddenly felt angry at his mother. He was trying so hard himself.

"Please, Ma. Father said we must have courage. He needs it of us as he fights the Saracen."

Rhodri saw the needle move and slip toward Megan's thumb. It pricked her and a bead of blood swelled on her fingertip. Megan jumped up and her eyes flashed at him.

"Silly boy," she snapped. "Because you catch a few hares with your bird, you think you're a man?"

Rhodri felt the words like a knife in his gut. He was horrified by the change in his mother. Megan's beautiful eyes were still blazing.

"I'm sorry, Mother. I didn't mean . . ."

Megan glared at him, but then she gave a sigh and her look softened to pain and sorrow.

"Oh, Rhodri. I'm sorry, too, *cariad*. It's hard, that's all. Every day I wonder where he is and what he's doing. What new danger or hardship he has to bear. If he's alive even. It's terrible not knowing."

Rhodri felt a great rush of tenderness.

"Come," the young man cried, as cheerfully as he could, "it's a year since he went away. Pa will be home by spring, I'm sure of it. Let me make the morning meal and then we'll play at domino together, like you and Pa used to."

As he took charge, Rhodri felt better. He made his mother sit at the table while he bustled around her, laying out the wooden plates. He cut up some fresh bread and salted it, before covering it in butter. He tried to be as attentive to Megan as he had often seen his father being. His mother seemed grateful and later sang one of Rhodri's favorite songs, but she could not mask a sadness that the very climate seemed to magnify.

On the Tuesday, Rhodri got up well before dawn and it was all he could do to stop himself rushing over to the miller's. But he waited until breakfast to wish his friend a happy birthing day.

"And Sarah," he said fondly, as she gave him a jug of hot, frothy milk straight from their cow, "this is for you."

He handed her his special present, which he had made in secret in the barn. It was Melanor's old falconing hood, which Rhodri had attached to a new piece of leather so Sarah could hang it about her neck. As she looked at it, she saw that, very delicately, Rhodri had scored a swirling S into the leather with his father's dagger. It was a humble gift, it is true, but deeply felt.

"Rhodri," said Sarah softly, "your letters are coming on."

There was a teasing note in Sarah's voice and Rhodri blushed.

"Thank you, Rhodri," said Sarah warmly. "It's lovely. I'll treasure it, always."

With that she leaned forward and kissed him lightly on the cheek. At her gentle touch, Rhodri felt a warmth like fire run through his whole body. Later they wandered down to the church and took the path to the wishing well. It was only a crumbling stone well, with a wooden canopy, and Rhodri looked at it rather scornfully as he compared it in his mind to the Telling Pool. There were local legends about it, which Rhodri thought even more silly and fanciful now, for it was said that here you could see your future husband or wife. But it was Sarah's favorite place, and they sat together on the edge, dropping stones into it and delighting in the echoing plops.

"You miss your father badly, don't you Rhodri?" said Sarah after a while.

Rhodri looked down mournfully into the well.

"I should be with him," answered the boy, "fighting at his side."

"Fighting," said Sarah scornfully, shaking out her hair. "Is that all boys can think of?"

"What do you mean?"

"On St. Martin's Day, I hated it when you attacked Aelfric. It was horrid."

Rhodri felt a twinge of resentment at his friend. "He deserved it. He cheated and he's always throwing his weight around."

"Perhaps," said Sarah softly, "but you must try to forgive him. It's been hard for him since his mother died of the sickness two years ago." Rhodri turned to look at Sarah in astonishment. He hadn't known this, and he suddenly felt rather sorry for the groom's boy, despite his deep dislike for him.

"Well, he should act less like his father, and as for fighting, it's a man's way. William thinks so, too."

Rhodri hardly knew why he had mentioned William, but both of them blushed. Rhodri could see Sarah's evident embarrassment, and it made him garrulous. Although he said nothing of the Telling Pool, he began to talk of the wars abroad, and even the Crack de Chevalier. He claimed he had dreamt the things he told Sarah, but he really described the battle he had witnessed in the waters.

"Well, Rhodri," Sarah said rather disapprovingly as he finished, "you do have a strong imagination."

"It's not imagination," said Rhodri, hurt. "It's real. And any true man needs to know how to fight like that."

"Oh, why," said Sarah angrily, holding up a sprig of rowan berries. "Life's so beautiful and we could all be so happy here, if it wasn't for the horrid wars. Animals aren't like that. I don't understand it."

Rhodri smiled sympathetically, but what Sarah had said of animals gave him a vision of Melanor, streaking through the skies at his prey. Just then, they saw a hare bolt from the copse nearby. Even as they did, another shape, a sumdge of moving red, came bounding after it. It was a fox and it pounced. There was a squeal of pain as it took the hare. The children looked at each other silently, and suddenly the world seemed bigger than either could understand.

Rhodri felt oddly guilty in his heart as he left for home, for he realized that he had been showing off about the wars and that he was really competing with William. But though he felt annoyed that Sarah could not understand his natural desire to go and fight, he put it down to the fact that she was just a girl, and he was delighted with how the day had gone. Rhodri did not wash his cheek for nearly a whole week.

Even winter cannot last, and with the second spring new hope came to Megan and Rhodri. The breath of renewal and expectation was everywhere, and they could not help but feel their hearts swelling with the land. For a while Rhodri forgot all the horrors he had seen in the Telling Pool and the fear he had felt at seeing the enchantress. All he remembered was the wonder.

Tantallon's sign must come soon now, he knew it, and then he should see his father again and bring his mother real news, however he might share it with her. Several times Rhodri wandered on the edges of the forest and thought about trying to find the pool again, yet something held him back. Not a fear of the wood, but what the hermit had said of patience. Perhaps Rhodri had something yet to learn before the hermit would call on him.

There was news, though, from a group of mendicants that men and knights had been seen returning to the Southern ports. Megan began to sing more often and made the house spick and span in preparation. She even laid out her wedding shawl expectantly. But Owen Falcon did not return home with spring, nor with the summer, either.

Nor did any sign come from Tantallon. Rhodri began to grow bitterly disappointed with his friend. At the fair, Tantallon had told him to seek out the Telling Pool and then had led him to see it. He had cared for him and told him wonderful secrets. He had hinted at the unfolding of some great destiny. Yet now Tantallon appeared to have abandoned him entirely.

It made Rhodri especially sullen, even when he was with William or Sarah, for new emotions were working in the growing boy, too. Often Rhodri dreamt of Sarah, yet after the day by the wishing well, he remembered her scolding him for fighting and grew awkward again. Sometimes he found himself so unsettled in her company that he would have to make an excuse of some work and leave. Sarah could see it in him, too, which only made matters worse.

Then one hot day Rhodri was walking along the river toward the manor when he saw Sarah. She was going the opposite way, and when Rhodri walked on he spotted William, too, sitting bare-chested in the sunshine, on a rock that jutted out into the water. William had been swimming. He looked well and healthy and Rhodri was delighted to see him. There was no sign of Aelfric or Wolfrin, either, who seemed to cling to him now like hounds to a hare. Rhodri quickened his pace, keen to talk to him without Aelfric around, and share all their news.

As he drew nearer, Rhodri thought how fine and strong his noble friend looked. Water still glistened on his chest from the river as he shook his wet, blond head and leaned up to drink in the sunlight. Rhodri thought how splendid it would be to swim by his side, or stand again in a field and challenge him to another contest with their two growing birds.

But as Rhodri approached, William suddenly reached into his pocket and pulled out something that made Rhodri sick to his stomach. It was the very hood that Rhodri had given Sarah for her birthing day. He turned it fondly in his hand and threw it in the air, before catching it again and putting it safely back in his pocket with a laugh.

Rhodri turned and ran. The sunlight beat down, but inside the boy felt as if a true fire were burning, and he hardly knew what to do with himself. He was furious and hurt that Sarah could have given away his gift. In that moment he felt like drawing a sword and lashing out at anything in his path. How could she have betrayed him? What he had seen had felt like a betrayal indeed, yet Rhodri could not decide what he was more jealous of, his bond with Sarah or with William.

On he ran, and he thought angrily of Tantallon. The old man had shown him great mysteries and promised to call on him, but he had broken his promise to the boy. In Rhodri's fury he directed all his feelings toward the blind old man.

He would find the pool, with or without Tantallon's blessing, and look for himself. But as he reached the trees, Rhodri realized that the contours of the forest had changed completely with the summer, and although he stumbled around for hours in the thick branches and tangled undergrowth, calling his friend's name, he could no more find his way than fly across the lands to find his father in Jerusalem. At last, thoroughly exhausted with all he had felt that day, Rhodri turned glumly for home.

The autumn followed that hot summer, as surely as night follows day, bringing with it Rhodri's own birthing day once more. Over a year had passed since Rhodri had looked into the wonderful pool and now he was fifteen and nearly as tall as William. But since that day by the river, he had avoided his friend almost completely.

The leaves began to change and fall, and autumn blew through the land, the west wind shaking the air once more in a riot of whirling colors. Wild, heavy rains swelled the ford to a river, and then winter stretched out its hand and gripped the earth in its hard, unforgiving grasp. With it, something cold and dead seemed to enter Megan Falcon's heart, too. She lost her color and moved about the farm like a ghost, or a sick animal pining for its own kind.

The winter grew colder and colder about them, and the animals of forest and field began to grow more and more desperate for food. One bitterly cold morning, as Rhodri was walking up to the barn, his heart began to race, for a section of wood had been torn away.

He could already hear the cow lowing in distress and the pigs squealing in terror. He rushed inside. The larger animals were unharmed, but as soon as Rhodri went into the bird's quarter he stopped in horror. The straw on the tiled floor was splattered with blood and there were feathers everywhere. A sickly, sweet smell was on the air. Breeze and Glindor sat on their perches still, safely in their mews, but the other three cages were torn open. Karlor, Kalin, and Melanor had all vanished.

"No," gasped Rhodri, looking around helplessly. His foot struck an object on the ground and he bent down and turned the carcass. It was Kalin. The old eagle owl was striped with blood, and there was a hole in its breast where the fox had done its hungry work.

"Melanor," cried Rhodri bitterly, turning the dead thing helplessly in his hands and looking around the room for his falcon. He felt sick and wanted to cry. He cursed himself, for he had seen the loose panel before and meant to mend it, but there were so many other things to worry about on the farm now.

"Oh, Melanor. Where are you?"

Rhodri looked everywhere, and ran outside to scan the skies, but there was no sign of the falcon. Later that day, when his chores were done and the barn repaired, Rhodri cut a hard hole in the earth by Megan's herb garden. He noticed how few herbs were growing there, even winter herbs, and where once the air would have been rich with their scents, there was now the only smell of mud. He shivered as he laid the dead eagle owl in the grave. The priest said that animals had no souls and so they couldn't go to paradise, but wherever they were, Kalin, Karlor, and Melanor had gone for good. Rhodri went up to his room and sobbed his heart out.

The Savior's birthing day came again.

The priest told the parable of the fig tree that the Savior had cursed for not sharing its bounty. Rhodri had the strange feeling as they sat there that he was directing his words toward Megan. As they left the church, Rhodri overheard the priest speaking quietly with Wolfrin and touching his arm, as Wolfrin looked at Megan.

"Talk to her, man," he was saying. "My sermon will have helped. She can't grieve the falconer forever."

"But is it right," said Wolfrin, "in the neighborhood's eyes?"

"Leave that to me. And perhaps you can make a donation to the church."

Wolfrin paid them several visits over the coming days and although Rhodri was unfailingly cold with him, Megan was always careful to be polite. Wolfrin even brought her some pepper, from across the seas, which was a rare gift indeed. Megan kept talking of Owen's return, but she took the valuable gift nonetheless and was never openly hostile.

Rhodri scolded her for it one morning after another visit, and his mother rounded on him.

"Don't be such an innocent. Your pa may have gone to war, but don't you know life at home can be just as dangerous here as across the seas? That man Wolfrin has real power now, with his lordship gone, and the boy in his charge, and one day we may have need of it."

"We need nothing, Mother," said Rhodri angrily. "Our home is safe enough and we have the land."

Rhodri knew in his heart, though, that his mother had resigned herself to the thought that Owen might indeed be dead. Tantallon, Wolfrin, William, and Sarah, even his own mother, they all seemed somehow to be betraying the boy.

January brought heavy snow, heaping the fields in white, and for a moment Rhodri's heart sang again as he looked out of his little window and saw the riverbank laden with snow, and the trees heavy with a glittering brilliance. Through the window the solemn, sacred quietness of snowfall whispered to the boy of wonder and childhood.

That day, Megan and he lit a great fire in the hearth and warmed themselves by it, and Megan heated some ale over the flames. There was no question now that the boy was old enough to drink it, and as he sipped in the hot, nourishing liquid and told his mother that soon he must go out to chop more wood and set some lures, he looked about the room and felt for the first time the sense that he had indeed become the man of the household. But it was a mournful feeling. He wanted to grow, it was certain, and be the master of all about him, but it was not right that Owen was absent.

The fire crackled and sparked cheerfully though, and mother and son felt as if some great, joyful presence were in the room with them. Although the priest might have scowled at it and crossed himself in fear, they felt as those of older faiths had felt, that the great god Janus had visited them, the Roman god who sits smiling at the gates of the New Year, and looks back into the past and forward into the future.

The very next morning, Rhodri was chopping wood in the yard when he saw his mother come out of their house. As Megan walked, she tripped and stumbled at the well.

"Ma," cried Rhodri, throwing down his axe and rushing over to help her. As soon as he reached his mother and put an arm round her, he realized that she was desperately hot.

"What is it, Ma? What's wrong with you?"

"I must be sickening with something, Rhodri *bach*," answered Megan faintly, trying to get up, but staggering again. He lifted her in his arms and helped her to the house. Inside he sat her down carefully on her cot, but as soon as he did so, his mother burst into furious tears.

"Oh, Rhodri, I don't think I can bear it anymore. Your father, I must know what has happened to him. I can't live like this anymore."

"Hush, Mother. Rest awhile."

Megan lay down and slept, and just then Rhodri heard a gentle tapping at the window. He swung his head and there, to his amazement, sat a bird, knocking with its beak. It was a merlin.

Rhodri ran outside, and just as he did so it took wing and flew toward the forest. Rhodri watched it glide away with all the admiration of a falconer, but thinking longingly of Melanor, too. But then something flashed in Rhodri's mind.

"The sign," he cried. Pausing for only an instant to wonder if he should leave Megan, he raced after it. If his ma was sick, he told himself, then the one thing she had to know was if Owen was alive. Only the Telling Pool could reveal that now.

The bird had entered the wood, and this time the weather and the forest aided Rhodri, for the trees were bare once more, and after a while the boy thought he recognized the place where he had first lost Melanor. He plunged into the wood, too, but he was soon lost again and stumbling about fruitlessly.

He was cursing himself, but then he heard a piercing cry. Sitting on a branch above him was the merlin again. It ruffled its feathers and looked about, then took wing. Three times the merlin settled above the boy, as it led him into the forest, and three times it took flight, and the boy knew now that it must be the sign. On the third time it landed, Rhodri gasped. There, in middle of the forest, was the little clearing and the outline of Tantallon's hovel. The merlin rose into the air and was gone.

"Tantallon, are you still here?"

Reagan the cat slunk passed him and hissed, and Rhodri pushed open the door with a loud creak.

There was no one inside, but as Rhodri looked at the hourglass he heard the wind moan in the forest and rustle the trees. In that moment he knew he wasn't alone. Rhodri turned and saw Tantallon standing behind him, framed in the doorway, his sightless eyes locked on the boy.

"Welcome back, Rhodri Falcon."

"Tantallon. You are here, after all."

"You sound angry. What's wrong? Did you think a foolish old man had forgotten all about you?"

"You startled me, that's all," said the boy, trying to keep the resentment he felt for his friend out of his voice.

The old man smiled, but his look was furtive, too. "I'm sorry, Rhodri. With all the eyes in the forest, I must be careful. Besides, now you have tasted more of life, have you not? You've come back to find out about your father, I think. The enchantress, too, perhaps."

"Yes, sir. I couldn't find my way at first, but a merlin . . ."

Tantallon's lips broke into a smile. "The birds know of my clearing, for there's always food here," he said. "But tell me, how have you faired? I'm sorry I didn't come for you sooner, but these are grave days and I've been traveling."

Rhodri looked at him in surprise.

"Traveling? Then you weren't here at all?"

"Not for a while. My cats were on guard. You've grown, my boy."

"Grown? How do you . . ."

Tantallon chuckled.

"It's in your voice, Rhodri."

The hermit stoked the fire as Rhodri told him all that had happened that year. While he talked, the boy looked around at the old man's neat home. Everything seemed just as he remembered it, as if he had hardly been away for more than a day. They ate some broth, and Tantallon closed his eyes as he listened to all Rhodri had to say. He cocked his head and nodded, particularly when the boy mentioned Melanor and then William and Sarah. Although Rhodri said nothing of his jealousy, or his sense of betrayal, he could not keep his emotions out of his voice.

"Well, you are growing indeed," said Tantallon, "learning of the heart perhaps, and of death and loss, too. So my sign came to you. And do you still want to go off to war and fight, Rhodri Falcon?"

The boy looked up.

"If I could help, Pa. Yes, of course."

"But the things the pool taught you of war. Did you remember any of them?

"Of course. And I was thinking, in the church," answered Rhodri, "of what you said of the Christ and it being a story."

The old man nodded slowly.

"Is it not a blasphemy to say it?"

Tantallon smiled. "Rhodri, belief is important, but if you'd been born in the land of the Moselman or the Jew, and listened to your friends and parents, would not you believe what they said of their gods?"

The boy thought hard for a while. "I suppose so. But the priest says Jesus was crucified, for our sins. The son of God."

"Or the son of Man, Rhodri. They called him that, too. The Church says Christ was God and persecutes any who deny it, but there are those who believe that Christ, though great and holy indeed, was a man. A man who married and, before he was murdered for his goodness and his love, fathered children."

"Children," said Rhodri in amazement.

Tantallon was nodding again.

"Some believe that he married Mary Magdalen and that she fled into France with their family after . . . after it happened. There are those among the Templar Knights, who fight now in the Holy Land, who believe that and guard it as a great secret."

Rhodri felt a deep confusion in him.

"It's strange, no?" said the hermit. "But I'll tell you why the Church hates such a story. Because many in the Church hate the things of this world. In their desperation to prove that there is a world of spirit, and in their fear of death, they try to drive out what is natural. For does not the Church talk above all of sin?"

Rhodri thought of the priest again and then oddly of Sarah and William.

"But other faiths hold that what is natural," said Tantallon, "in the birds and the flowers, in the animals, in man and woman, is the greatest law. Why should God make such a wondrous Miracle, if that God really hates his own creation?"

Rhodri shook his head.

"But these are difficult thoughts for a boy, perhaps," Tantallon said, getting up and moving swiftly across the room. "Rhodri, would you like to see something very special? Where did I put it last?"

First the old man knelt by the cot and, reaching under the bed, began to search among a host of cluttered objects. But he got up and shook his head.

"You old fool," he grumbled irritably to himself, "try and remember. Now, let me see. Ah yes."

He walked to the wall and, stretching out his hand, reached toward a rickety little cupboard in the corner of the hovel.

"Most men would call me poor and despise me for it," he said with amusement, as his hand pulled back the latch and opened the cupboard door. "But quite apart from the animals and the forest and the pool, I have my treasures, too."

Rhodri nearly fell off his stool. Inside was a vision of gold, but not ingots or a cup or jewelry, as he had sometimes glimpsed in the villages about. What the boy saw was the strange gold headpiece he had seen in the pool, worn by a man standing on a rock.

"It's fine, no?" said Tantallon, drawing it forth and holding it up toward Rhodri in the firelight. "Although I've not seen it in an age."

"Yes, indeed, Tantallon."

"Only the guardians may wear such an ancient thing," said the old man, stroking it fondly, "for this, too, keeps great secrets and knowledge."

"Knowledge?" said Rhodri, wondering how the golden hat could do such a thing.

"These markings," whispered the hermit, exploring the bumps and ridges along the circle rim with his clever fingers, "they help one recall the shape of the heavens and the reappearance of certain stars in the skies. For then one may foretell the solstices, and so know when the weather changes. For what greater power is there than to know when to plow and harvest the land, and so share in the bounty of the living Miracle?"

Rhodri wanted to try it on.

"And the number of these globes have great power, too," Tantallon continued. "One day perhaps, you shall learn of the power of numbers. One day, too, perhaps I shall teach you how to read."

Rhodri's heart was pounding; he had forgiven this forgetful old hermit already. He was so glad to be back. He thought if only he could live here with his friend for a while and learn all he could teach . . . But just as this happy idea entered his mind, another appeared, too, of his mother, sick with uncertainty and fading hope.

"But first, Tantallon," said Rhodri, "I must look into the pool again. Ma grows ill and I must bring her some real news of my father, to help her."

The old man got up.

"It's been nearly a year. Come then. What you seek still awaits."

9 ❖ THE STORM

Come away, O human child!
To the waters and the wild
With a faery, hand in hand,
For the world's more full of weeping than you can understand.
—W. B. Yeats, "The Stolen Child"

Evening had come as Rhodri sat down nervously once more under the giant canopy of branches and stars. It wasn't just fear of the magical pool shimmering before him he felt, but terror of what it might show him in its waters—what he had secretly feared all year—his father's body, torn and broken, lying dead on that distant battlefield.

As soon as Rhodri leaned forward to see, the waters rippled and the boy knew that he had not lost the power. There he saw not his father, but Lord Treffusis, and next to him, on an even finer horse, sat an old man. It was Pierre De Brackenois. His hair was grayer and his face worn and wrinkled. As he rode down that dusty track, there seemed to be a feeling of peace in him.

There was a sudden cry and Treffusis's horse reared. Rhodri's heart began to race as he saw Treffusis draw his sword and De Brackenois draw his own. There was a swishing sound and De Brackenois was knocked back in his saddle. He slumped on his horse and then slipped and crashed to the ground. Treffusis jumped down, and Rhodri saw an arrow shaft sticking from the old man's chest, close to his heart. Soldiers had come from everywhere and formed a circle to protect the fallen nobleman from the ambush. Treffusis gently lifted the old man's head.

"My Lord De Brackenois."

He gave a groan. "Treffusis, the devils have got me at last."

Treffusis reached down to clasp the arrow, but his eyes darkened as soon as he touched it, and he let go.

"The wound is deep. I must not disturb it."

"Fatal you mean," whispered De Brackenois faintly. "I feel it. Deep enough in me to bury me in the earth forever."

"No."

"You could never lie to me, my friend," whispered the old man sadly, "and your eyes do not lie now."

Treffusis dropped his head.

"Tell me," said De Brackenois urgently, grasping his friend's hand, "do you think me an old fool to bring you all out here?"

"No, Pierre. Be still."

"If it's true what the Holy Father promises," said De Brackenois, smiling faintly, "then paradise is close for me, Treffusis. And because of this journey my sins are lifted. And my sins have been deep indeed. I have killed many."

"Hush."

"No. Listen to me. Tell my son, William. Tell him that I was always proud of him, and that I love him with all my heart and soul. Please do that for me."

De Brackenois's old body stiffened.

"My lord."

"Promise me."

"I promise."

It was no good. The Saracen arrow had been deep and its tip had scraped De Brackenois's heart. With a last furious shudder, old Pierre De Brackenois gave up his spirit. Rhodri sat there shaking and thinking of poor William. Even his friendship with Sarah, his betrayal of Rhodri, did not make William deserving of this bitter news. In that moment, Rhodri felt resentful of the Telling Pool.

"But what of my pa?" he cried, as the old warrior's image faded.

"Seek, Rhodri," said Tantallon behind him. "Seek with your heart and mind."

The water rippled again, but still Rhodri did not see his father. Instead he saw that face he had seen by the tents on the battlefield. King Richard the Lionheart. The king was riding in a contingent and though he looked hardened and brutalized by war, he still carried himself with the noble bearing that Rhodri had seen during the battle. The men who rode with him, whose eyes seemed filled with sadness, would brighten when they looked up at their leader, and the fear that surrounded them seemed dispelled by a new courage.

Just then, horsemen came galloping toward them from the trees. They drew their swords as they surrounded Richard.

"The king," cried Rhodri.

The waters rippled, and the Lionheart now looked anything but a king, for he sat on a stone bench in a filthy prison cell and his royal robes were torn and bloody. His hands were manacled, too, and there was a great anger in that proud face.

"What's happened?" whispered Rhodri as the waters began to change again. "And what has become of Pa? Are you dead, Father? Tell me."

A ship, heavy hulled and with white sails lightly bound to its masts, now appeared before Rhodri Falcon. It was out to sea, licked by white horses and shadowed by the darting, spiraling bodies of dolphins, bracing the dangerous waves. But as it sailed on, Rhodri saw the clouds darken and a terrible storm begin, and then something occurred that was the strangest thing that had happened to him yet. Rhodri was there, on board the ship. Or at least he seemed to be, for although he knew he was still sitting on the rock, he found himself standing, too, on the deck. Everything was moving about him, sailors running to take in the sails as the storm struck, boys climbing the masts, the captain struggling with the rudder. Rhodri could feel the wind and taste the salt sea on his lips, could feel the ship rising and falling as it began to ride the churning waters.

Rhodri was flabbergasted, as great waves began to break over the churning craft, and then he saw him.

"Pa. You didn't die, Pa."

It was his father. Owen had just emerged from below and was now rushing about, helping the other sailors and bellowing orders. His skin was so tanned that it looked liked hide, his silvery hair long and disheveled, a broadsword strung across his back. Rhdori saw the scar on his right cheek.

"Father, it's me, Rhodri."

His father didn't turn or hear the boy, and when he swung round once in his direction, seemed to see nothing but the terrified sailors about him. Rhodri realized that his presence aboard must be a trick of the pool and even as he appeared to stand there near his father, he reached down and felt the rock at his sides. A wave struck and Owen was knocked to the ground but he caught hold of a rope and, reaching out his arm, stopped another sailor being washed clean overboard.

For hours Rhodri seemed to stand there as the terrible storm raged about his father, but at last it broke and as the lurching of the ship calmed, he seemed to withdraw from the scene and was looking down on it once more. The ship was anchored in a port now, at a stone dock laden with rope and barrel and lobster pot. Men in jerkin or rough sailor's habit were laboring and cursing there, and a great wooden plank bound the ship for a while to this haven. There, walking down the gangplank, too, was Owen.

"Pa," cried Rhodri from the Seeing Place, realizing that this shore was Albion. "You're coming home to us."

Rhodri wanted to jump up and dance with blind old Tantallon under the stars. But the vision was so real and powerful that the boy was held in its thrall. The people who milled about looked nervously, not just at Owen and his sword, but also at all the other soldiers who were coming up from the belly of the ship. The odd little village where the boat had landed was in a bay so wild and rocky it looked like something from legend. Surely not one of the great Southern ports where the soldiers had embarked on their perilous journey, but somewhere far humbler on the coasts near their home.

The water rippled again and Owen was sitting in a wooden cart, rattling through hilly countryside. A man and woman, dressed like peasants, drove the cart and its thin, dappled horse, and they kept looking back at him. But it was not in fear, for the woman was smiling and nodding and nudging her husband. It was clear that they were delighted to have such a man to protect them on the road, in return for their help in bringing him closer to his home.

"Tell me, friend," asked the yeoman in the cart. "You're Welsh, are you not?"

"Indeed I am, man," answered Owen proudly.

"But if you've returned from the Holy Lands, you should have sailed from the South. Why did your ship land to the west?"

"We were blown off course by a terrible storm. We lost many. Lord Treffusis, who led us in the end, and three of our priests."

Lord Treffusis, thought Rhodri sadly. Dead, too. Then who would tell William of his father's dying words?

"And you really saw the Holy City?" asked the woman, "as they did in the days of the first wars, when it fell to our noble knights?"

Owen shook his head sadly.

"We never took back the Holy Citadel," he answered. "But as for seeing Jerusalem, yes. We came within twelve miles of its great walls, but by then we were so short of men and supplies, there was no hope of taking it. For the Lionheart that was a bitter day indeed, to give up that ambition, and he turned away his brave eyes rather than gaze on it. No. That journey is over for us now."

"And what of the king?" asked the woman. "Is he safe?"

"They say he's a prisoner," answered Owen gravely.

"And the kingdom bleeds for it," grunted the peasant.

"I have heard it. So I hurry home."

Rhodri felt as if the visions he was seeing were growing clearer and realer, and as he peered at his father's face, he saw that beneath that scar and the weather-beaten skin Owen was just the same as his son remembered him. There was care in those eyes, it is true, and a constant seriousness, like that of one who is taken by a bitter memory and is trying to grapple with it. But as he rode, Owen would reach up to the St. Christopher medal at his throat and clasp it like a talisman. Then his face would lighten and his eyes start to flicker brightly and a smile would break out on his lips, with the memories that came.

Owen said good-bye to the couple, who turned away to the east, and set out on his own across open countryside. The sun shone down and the rains fell. The days and nights passed in ripples on the pool, but still Owen tramped, camping in the shade of a bush or by a stream, lighting a stone circle of fire at night, or setting traps to snare hare and rabbit, just as he had taught Rhodri to do. The boy felt sad as he thought how lonely his poor father looked, but he seemed to feel every sensation his father felt and suffered, too, from the wind and the bitter air as he watched the pool.

Then Owen was crossing a wide, barren moor, heavy with peat

earth and boulders and coming down on a lake, its waters as dark and mysterious as the Telling Pool. Behind it the skies lowered with heavy rain clouds that looked like they brooded with the anger of heaven. The rains came once more, as heavy as anything Rhodri had ever seen and his father was drenched in the deluge. In the cold the boy could see his father's skin and it was wet, not just with rainwater, but with sweat that was breaking out across his brow. He had a fever and Rhodri realized that his own forehead was sweating, too.

Owen passed the lake and came to a strange stone circle like a solid wheel set in the ground, and Rhodri felt a premonition of terrible foreboding. His father began to climb a slope, at the top of which stretched a little forest. It was of hawthorn and ash, and the trees were wide and easy to pass. But suddenly Owen stopped. He had come to a patch of open ground, a clearing fenced in by wooden posts, and inside a small herd of horses was grazing. There were so many of them feeding in the corral that Rhodri wondered if some great homestead stood nearby.

It was strange to see them here in such wild country. The trees had reached the rise of a larger hill and among them, set about with boulders and thickets, was something Rhodri had seen before.

"The cave," he gasped fearfully. "The enchantress's cave."

He wanted to shout and warn his father, just as he had wanted to warn the king, but he knew it was foolish and he could see that what Owen needed now was somewhere to shelter from the storm. There was the raven again, watching Owen beadily, and as it flew into the cave, his father began to follow it.

"No, Pa. Don't go in. Not there. There's an enchant—"

"Peace, Rhodri," whispered Tantallon. "Whatever you are seeing was meant to be."

A desperate fear crept over Rhodri Falcon, but Tantallon's words came back to the boy as he watched. *You may affect nothing in the pool, though it may affect you.*

As soon as Owen stepped inside, there was the beautiful enchantress. She smiled at his father and then, with the grace of a girl, lifted both her hands toward him and turned up her palms.

"Come," she said. "You're wet and cold from the storm. Come into my cave and shelter awhile from the tempest."

Her voice was deep and strong and its tones seemed ribbed with laughter. But it was a voice not of England, or of Wales either, not Norman or Saxon, but of some foreign land.

"Who are you?" asked Owen warily, as if in a dream. "You're not of Albion. What is this place?"

The woman smiled slyly. "I come from a land close to those parts where you have wrestled, Owen Falcon," she answered softly, and her voice sounded like music as it echoed about them, "a distant land we call Persia."

"Persia," said Rhodri's father in surprise, "but how . . . who . . ."

The woman laughed.

"Homeira they call me. I traveled to your country with the knights returning from your Holy Wars. But come."

The woman turned and swept away through that smoke veil, which parted as Owen followed her. His eyes opened in astonishment as great as Rhodri's had been on first seeing that magical place.

"Now this cave is my home," said Homeira, as she drew him in. "It's in a wild enough place for me not to be troubled by . . . by intruders. For one of my kind is rare indeed in your land."

Owen was looking at all those myriad candles, and those fine objects. His eyes fell on the bed in the corner. Homeira smiled as he noticed it and tilted her pretty head slightly.

"You're amazed at such luxuries?"

"It's strange to find such a home in the heart of the mountain."

"Do not your monks, your anchorites, and druids go to seek their God in caves?" Homeira said with amusement.

"Not with such ease and comfort, perhaps," answered Owen, smiling as he looked about him. "The air, it's almost hot."

"My cave sits above a maze of ancient, underground springs," said the enchantress, "that bubble from the earth and heat it naturally from the cold. The rock in places is as hot as a bread oven."

As Owen walked toward the wall to touch the rock, Homeira did something extraordinary. "No," she cried, just as Tantallon had done when Rhodri had made to drink the water of the Telling Pool. Owen turned again and Homeira smiled oddly.

"It might burn you," she explained softly, "and it's hot enough to dry a soldier's clothes. You're soaked to the bone."

"Yes," whispered Owen, and Rhodri saw that he was shivering terribly and sweat was pouring from his father's brow, "I've a fever. I . . ."

Suddenly Owen slumped forward and collapsed on the cave floor. "Father."

The Telling Pool began to ripple and the images were gone. Rhodri felt as if something had been wrenched from his very being.

"Tell me your vision, Rhodri," said Tantallon by the Seeing Place. "Be my eyes again."

"Her name is Homeira, Tantallon. The enchantress. She comes from the East."

The old man nodded. "Then your father's in terrible danger. You must look again. Miss nothing."

Rhodri strained forward once more. The scene returned, but it had changed. Owen was lying across the silken bed, asleep, and Homeira was standing beside him, holding up a silver goblet. She lifted some leaves or herbs in her hand, crushed them, and dropped them into the goblet. Then she stepped forward and gently lifted Owen's head and put the cup to his lips.

The thought crossed Rhodri's mind that it might be poison, but the woman's manner seemed tender and caring enough. His father drank in his sleep and groaned slightly, but he did not open his eyes. Then Homeira was kneeling beside him and putting a wet cloth to his fevered brow.

Once more the waters rippled, and Homeira was at the table crushing up more leaves to make a powder. Rhodri noticed that her lips, which had been plain before, were now colored bright red, and he saw something sitting at the edge of the table that reminded him of another of the fortune-teller's cards: Death. It was a human skull, blackened with grime and smoke. Now Owen was standing behind her. He no longer had his soaking tunic on, but a clean white shirt that he fingered uncertainly. The shirt was the finest Rhodri had ever seen, and he noticed that his father's fever had broken.

"How long have I been asleep?" asked Owen faintly in the water.

"Seven days," answered Homeira, turning and smiling at him. "But my craft has made you well again."

"Thank you . . . I did not expect . . ."

The enchantress stepped closer to Owen in her bare feet, and now the man and woman were standing face to face. She flicked her hair from her beautiful eyes and smiled sweetly at him. Rhodri blushed.

"It'll be good to have company for a while," she said softly. "And such handsome company, too."

She lifted her hand slowly and placed it flat on Owen's chest. As Rhodri watched, it was as if he could feel her touch himself and it made his heart pound furiously. There was something strong and powerful in it. Her slim, dark arm was downed with black hairs and her fingers were long and tapering. He noticed a beautiful red ruby ring on her slender forefinger, that must have been made from one of the gems in the cave. Owen flinched and Homeira withdrew her palm.

"I made the shirt myself," she said sweetly. "Those wet clothes would have killed you, had you kept them on. And they were filthy indeed. I've washed them. And darned them also."

She lifted her hand, and in it was a long silver needle that curved at the tip. It was like one of the needles Rhodri's mother used to work her tapestry, although much finer.

"Would I not make someone a fine wife?" she laughed.

"You dressed me?"

Homeira nodded.

"You're weathered with war, but still so strong," she said, and there was admiration in her voice, "Now you must be hungry and thirsty after your battle with the fever."

"My sword," said Owen, looking round anxiously, "where's my sword?"

"It's safe, Owen Falcon. Look."

Homeira pointed to the wall of the cave, and there Owen saw his father's sword. But it was not alone. It stood among other blades, and bows, and all manner of weaponry. Rhodri remembered the horses corralled outside the cave.

"It's a fine weapon," said Homeira, "though I have known one far finer."

Rhodri sat up immediately as she said it, and the stone moved beneath him, but the enchantress said nothing more and instead walked back to the table and lifted a great silver jug. As she tipped it into a goblet, the liquid that flowed from it was as red as the blood Rhodri had seen in the pool.

"Drink."

Like a servant, she held up the goblet to Owen Falcon. He drank deep, and when he had finished, his son fancied that a new health and vigor shone in his father's skin and face.

"That's better, is it not?" said Homeira softly. "There's nothing to fear from me. To suffer so hard and long is a man's way perhaps, but does it not deserve the ease and softness and love of a woman's care?"

Owen smiled gratefully.

"Tell me, Homeira, how did you know of my journey from the Holy Lands? Of my name, too?"

Those brilliant, eager eyes flickered with secret knowledge and cunning, as she turned and led Owen over to her pool. "Come."

"Fire rock," she whispered at its edge, "the lava comes up from the belly of the world."

She raised her hand and cast something into the lava. A flame leapt up from it instantly.

"The power of the Four is mysterious indeed, is it not? Water, earth, air, and fire. Are not all things made of the elements, Owen? Are not all secrets contained within them, too?"

Just then pictures came. Deep within the lava appeared a row of soldiers dressed as the Saracen had been in the terrible battle. They were all kneeling in the burning sunlight and their hands were bound behind their backs. A monk was walking among them, blessing them, and Owen leaned forward, for it was the same monk that had accompanied him on the road and talked with Hellard. Rhodri could see that his father's eyes had grown glassy with fear and pure astonishment.

Then there were knights, too, in the lava and the Lionheart, who lifted his hand, and as one his men began to draw their swords. The heathen looked up pleadingly, but the Christians began to hack at their helpless prisoners. There were distant cries, but as the blood came, as red as liquid fire, Homeira swept her lovely hand angrily across the well, and the hard earth sheen of cooling lava came again.

"This was the holiness of your Christian knights," cried Homeira coldly. "Seven thousand lives were slain that day, even though your good King Richard had made a pact with the Saracen Lord Saladin to spill no blood at all. Still they cut them down."

Rhodri felt a confusion within him at the sight. The king was hard, yet he filled his men with courage, too. But how could a king do this terrible thing?

"War is cruel," whispered Owen, and he dropped his eyes sadly. He looked almost ashamed of his king.

"It was murder, Owen Falcon. You call us devils and barbarians, yet is it not you who are the true barbarians? Yet maybe you can learn. Maybe your king can learn."

Homeira moved her hand again, and now the very same image appeared that Rhodri had seen before, of the man calling from the turret and those women with their veiled eyes in that strange city.

"My homeland," she said. "Often I haunted the bazaars in my youth."

"But dressed in the manner of their women," whispered Owen, smiling to himself. "You have changed much, Homeira, since you came into Christendom."

A hard look came to Homeira's beautiful face.

"The girls are covered only when they begin to come to womanhood and the blood flows from their bodies," she whispered. "But my father would always say that I must never cover my beauty. The faith of the Prophet and his laws were never for my heart, Owen Falcon, nor your Christian God, either."

"Then what do you believe in, Homeira?"

The enchantress smiled. "Many things perhaps incomprehensible to your world. But mine is the belief of the ancient Persian lands before the Moselman ways changed the world again. The faith of the Fire God Ahura Mazda and the spirits of power, which all in their ignorance fear."

Owen was hardly listening. Instead he leaned closer to the lava well. He had spotted that Christian knight whom Rhodri had seen a year ago in the pool, walking through the Persian streets. Homeira followed his gaze and the look on his face.

"You're surprised, perhaps, that one of your kind and faith should find peace and friendship so far from home? Among my kind."

"I've heard of it before," said Owen softly, "of Christians settling in the lands we went to conquer. Of their taking on, too, the customs and the ways they encounter there. They say the Holy Father frowns on it as a betrayal and a terrible sin."

"Sin?" cried the enchantress scornfully. "Men wrestle with their gods, Owen Falcon, and fight and murder each other for beliefs they can never really touch. But when they stop to think and feel again, they find that life is short and they are just people. Would you have the whole world live in hate in the name of your God? Or ours?"

"No, Homeira. I would not. I have seen too much killing in the wars and know that men who talk too readily of evil are sometimes evil themselves."

"And you would never harm a woman, I think. Even one with magic in her."

Owen shook his head.

"Good. Perhaps this man found the subtle ways of the East more to his liking. Perhaps you may, too."

She smiled and again swept her hand across the fire. Suddenly there stood Owen himself, on the dock of the little port, just as Rhodri had seen his father before in the Telling Pool.

"This is how I knew of you and your journey," said the enchantress, though she seemed to be looking away, so that he would not see her eyes, "and how I followed the progress of your king back from the Holy Land, too, before he fell into the clutches of the Austrian duke. How I knew you would come to me."

The picture faded, and Owen turned to look around the cave. He noticed the little alcove, for the curtain was drawn back and he had seen that odd casket.

"What does it hold?" asked Rhodri's father. "Some relic of Persia perhaps? Like a finger of our blessed virgin, or the shroud of the living Christ."

"Or one of the pieces of the True Cross," answered the enchantress as scornfully as when she had spoken of sin, "sold so many times over to the gullible that they could build a whole fleet of ships with the wood."

She turned and her eyes flashed darkly. "Some believe a casket made in this fire could hold the whole world," she said, "but as yet it is empty, for it is not yet completed."

In that moment Rhodri saw something he had not noticed before. Beside the casket was a dagger, curved like the moon or the Saracens' swords and as sharp a falcon's claw, hilted with gold and studded with jewels like the cave. It made him frightened for Owen.

"Come," said the enchantress, closing the curtain on the box and the knife, "let's eat and talk more together."

As they turned away, Rhodri looked on in horror. In the ceiling above the casket the boy could clearly see that face again, looking straight back at him, pleadingly. It seemed to be alive, and yet then, once more, it was nothing more than the walls of the cave.

In the stone chamber, Homeira seated Owen at the head of the table, and then the beautiful woman began to tend to him like a king. Wines she laid before him, and rare meats, bowls of thick honeycomb and quince, sweetmeats and plump fruits. Rhodri longed himself to try that meal. The candles burned down as the two adults talked and drank and ate. Even Rhodri could not help thinking how fine they looked together as they sat at that enchanted table, in that enchanted place. He felt strangely heavy, though, as if an enchantment were surrounding him, too.

"Tell me of your home, Owen," said Homeira, while her guest drank more and more wine, "and of your family."

The master falconer spoke then with such pride that Rhodri's own heart swelled with love for his father. But the boy noticed, too, that, as his father spoke, Homeira had placed her hand on the skull on the table and gripped it hard. When Owen finished, the two were silent for a while.

"When did you come into our lands?" asked Owen at last.

"After your Holy Wars came and I saw Jerusalem fall with my own eyes."

Owen seemed to be in a kind of dream, but Rhodri had stirred. The woman must be lying to her father, thought the boy, for Jerusalem had fallen only in the first wars in the Holy Lands and Homeira was far too young to have seen such a thing.

"Then I dressed as a boy," she said, "and journeyed across the seas into Christendom. I used my powers to find this place, Owen Falcon, and here my arts have grown stronger and I've fashioned my magic casket."

"But what's it for?"

The enchantress sprang up abruptly and walked down the table toward Owen.

"What do you think of my little kingdom?"

"It's wonderful," he said, looking all about the cave.

He stood up, too, and again the man and woman were face to face.

"But I've known such loneliness here, Owen," said Homeira tenderly, "such longing. The longing of a woman. Not for the fools who came to my cave, and thought they could win my love, but . . ."

Her head had turned and she was looking toward the weapons stacked at the side of the cave. Rhodri suddenly wondered how many men had been in this place and what had happened to them.

"But for one such as you," said the enchantress softly, "one with a heart that knows real love, one with the strength of a true warrior."

Owen had touched his hand to the amulet at his neck and his face had furrowed. He pulled back, but Homeira was looking up at him with such fire and longing, it was as if something unseen were pulling them toward each other.

"Why do you fight me, Owen Falcon?" said the enchantress, "why do you resist what you may not resist? Come to me."

"But, Homeira. I . . ."

"You're worried about betraying your wife perhaps."

Owen dropped his gaze.

"But who can ever be certain of the faith in another heart? And she has been without you for a long while. The body is weak and even your own myths tell of the greatest hearts being less than perfect."

Rhodri stirred angrily, but he thought of Wolfrin and his visits to Megan.

"Think of Arthur and his love for Guinevere. And of Guinevere's love for a knight who swore truth to his lord, before he broke it. Fools say that was a wickedness, but was not their love brave and true enough to defy a king? Come to me."

Rhodri drew back as he saw his father step forward and drop his head toward those bright red lips to kiss Homeira. They were as red as the blood that had stained Kalin's chest in the barn, and the boy remembered yet another card the fortune-teller had shown him that day at the fair: The Lovers.

Rhodri did not want to see. He suddenly felt in his stomach a terrible anger for his father. In his young heart he felt that an act of sacrilege was about to take place, and that it would be sacrilege, too, to witness it. He was remembering the little church, one cold autumn morning, and the priest telling them the story of how Eve had tempted Adam in the first garden of the world, and how God had made them ashamed in their nakedness and cast them out of paradise.

A word was echoing through the boy's mind that had always made him shiver, but want to know too, and the word was "sin." The waters of the Telling Pool were flat and still and empty again and, as Rhodri Falcon got up, he saw Tantallon listening to him silently.

10 ❖ THE BARGAIN

No villain need be! Passions spin the plot:
We are betray'd by what is false within.
—George Meredith, "Modern Love"

Something you've seen hurts you, Rhodri," said the blind old hermit in the shadows.

"My father, he . . ."

Rhodri looked down.

"I'm sorry," said Tantallon kindly. "Some secrets, even given up by the Telling Pool, perhaps they're better left dark."

The boy raised his head. It was still night, and even cooler than before. The air in the forest seemed alive with mystery and threat.

"My father's back in England, Tantallon, but in thrall to the enchantress. Homeira."

Tantallon's sightless eyes seemed to shimmer as he spoke.

"And so in grave danger, as I said."

"Tell me," asked Rhodri, "is there nothing I may do to change what I see in the pool? Or to help my father. When the storm came, it was as if I was really there."

Tantallon listened hard to the boy, and when Rhodri told him all that had seemed to happen during the storm, the old man shook his head in bewilderment.

"Well," he said wonderingly, "you have a deep connection with the pool. But as for changing what happened in the past, how could that be?"

Rhodri looked angrily at the water. "What heavenly use is it then?"

"As I said," answered Tantallon slowly, "the Miracle is ancient. As ancient as it is new. I'm just a foolish old man, who's spent a life guarding the secrets of the law and the magic of the forest. But even I do not know all the pool's mysteries. Perhaps a boy may teach me. As children must always teach adults. To remind them of their faith."

Rhodri nodded, but as he looked at those waters and knew that he must gaze once more, he was even more fearful at what was happening in the cave than he had been after that terrible battle . . .

"I must know, see," he said, trying to convince himself.

Tantallon made no objection. "But these are things deeply felt," he said, "and I will leave you for a while. Call me if you need me. Be careful."

The waters moved once more as Tantallon wandered away. In the enchantress's cave everything was even firmer and clearer now. There sat Owen in fine new clothes at the table and Homeira in that carved chair. She was wearing a purple gown and her brow was crowned with a strange headdress. It was made of metal and jewels and looked like the helmets the Saracens had worn into battle. She lifted her goblet to Owen and spoke, but for a while Rhodri could hear nothing. At first she smiled, but then saw that Owen was holding the amulet at his neck, and dashed her goblet to the ground.

Then voices came to Rhodri. Angry, adult voices.

"You feeble fool. You think you can just leave?" Homeira cried and she began to laugh. The sound was so mad and horrible Rhodri wanted to cover his ears.

What had happened?

"If you tried, the smoke veil at the mouth of the cave would blind you and make you choke," she snarled savagely. "What has your wife, a humble peasant on a filthy, miserable little farmstead, to offer you that I cannot give you?"

Rhodri waited for his father's angry reply, but Owen's head was bowed and he did not answer her.

"And if you did leave me, Owen," snarled Homeira, "if I let you, I mean, then the memory of me would burn you up like the fires of the earth, or the lava in my pool. In the womb of being I was made, and men were made to worship me."

There was something terrible in Homeira's look, as though a great greed had come on her beautiful body and being. In the Seeing Place Rhodri clenched his fist. What was this woman saying? Was she trying to hold his father prisoner?

"Tell her, Pa. Fight her. We love you. We need you."

Owen looked up. He seemed helpless in front of the enchantress. Defeated.

Rhodri sprang up and knelt at the edge of the water. He was thinking suddenly of what Tantallon had said of the pool's mysteries. He paused though as he remembered the old man's words about the water, too—as fatal to a boy as the strongest poison. *As deadly to you as the nightshade, or the sharpest henbane.* But Rhodri had to help his father. He held his breath and plunged both his hands and head into the pool. At first his eyes stung, but then the watery film cleared and Rhodri felt a kind of fire rippling through his whole body. Suddenly he didn't know where he was at all, or rather found that he was everywhere. It was as though he had become a part of everything in the cave. The walls and the furniture, the very objects on the table. It was as though Rhodri had become pure mind. Strange bubbles of red and blue rippled up as Rhodri spoke beneath the surface.

"Father. I'm with you, Father. It's me."

He felt a profound wonder as he saw his father tilt his head slightly.

"Father. We need you."

Rhodri was gasping for air, and as he pulled up again, with a gulp, water poured from his soaking hair and he wondered if Owen had heard him.

He saw now in the Telling Pool that courage and strength had entered Owen's eyes, that though these things seemed to have already happened, it was as if his father had truly heard him calling to him.

"Others may worship you, Homeira," said Owen coldly, as if some spell had already been broken, "but I'm a master falconer, and love to roam the open fields and watch the birds flying in the free air. And what is love, real love, if not given freely? Is that what you want of me, Homeira, a prisoner?"

"Yes, Father. Tell her."

The enchantress screamed and stamped her foot, but as she looked to the alcove where the casket lay, her body relaxed. She turned slowly back to Owen Falcon. Once more she was smiling and beauty had returned to her ravishing face.

"You're right," she whispered, "you must be no prisoner, Owen. So you're free to go. To leave me and return to Megan and your son and the love that you say they bring you. Even though I could make you love me. Even though I could enchant you now, for my casket is finished."

Her casket. What could it mean? Rhodri fancied that a doubt, even a regret, flickered in Owen's eyes.

"And yet," said Homeira, "you've tasted of my world, so we've made a pact already, have we not? You do not seem the kind of man who breaks his word lightly."

"No," said Owen.

"Then I'll make another bargain with you."

"Another bargain?"

"You talk of prisoners. In Christendom is not the serf bound to his master by the law of king and God? Yet if he leaves the land and escapes for a year and a day to the city, then he becomes a freeman."

"It is so, Homeira," said Owen, wondering what she was saying.

"So it will be with you, Owen Falcon," the enchantress cried scornfully. "For if you can really go from my cave and be happy and stay from me of your own free will, for that year and that one day, then you'll be free in truth and shall never think of me or these enchantments again."

Rhodri's heart was racing, but Owen looked back at the beautiful witch and gave her a look the boy had often seen him give Megan. In that moment Rhodri knew that his father wanted to hold her. That he was still wrestling with himself and his own deep desire for Homeira.

"Very well," Owen whispered, "we've our bargain then. But I warn you, Homeira, when I return to them, I shall never leave Megan and Rhodri again."

Rhodri stirred happily, but was still again when he saw that Homeira was smiling confidently.

"Spoken like a king," she mocked, "like King Arthur himself."

She laughed pleasantly though, and now her mood was as light as gossamer.

"Don't look so serious, Owen," the woman said, stepping toward him and taking his hand gently. "Come, tomorrow is the eve of your Christ's mass and we're friends at least, so let us eat and drink and laugh together. Then, in the morning, I'll give you your sword again and send you safely on your way. Back to your loving wife and your son."

She turned and walked toward the jug of wine. She hovered over it for a moment and when she turned back she was holding up a glass.

"Drink. To seal our bargain."

"One year and one day, Homeira," said Owen, taking the cup. "No more."

Homeira smiled like a girl. "No more, Owen Falcon."

Owen looked at her firmly and drank. Then he followed her, and as Rhodri watched them he saw that Homeira was looking over his father's shoulder. Although her manner was light and easy, her sly black eyes were set as hard as stone on that crystal casket in the recess.

The image faded and the surface of the Telling Pool was water again, reflecting that lip of stone. Rhodri blinked and sat up. All about him light was coming, streaming with the excited brilliance of dawn through the trees, and somewhere a bird was singing happily in the forest. The boy turned and there was Tantallon, standing with his back to him, shivering slightly in his long gray robes.

"My father's safe," said Rhodri simply. "He's coming home."

The old man swung round and the boy was startled. Just for a moment, in the half-light that marks the coming of morning, the boy thought that Tantallon's face was subtly changed. Perhaps his blind eyes were brighter, or there were fewer lines on his ancient cheeks. But as he drew closer, Rhodri realized it must have been a trick of the light, for the hermit was just the same.

The old man's expression was grave.

"What's wrong, Tantallon?" asked Rhodri.

"This is fine news, boy," answered the hermit quietly, "and I'm glad for you, indeed. But Rhodri . . ."

Tantallon paused.

"But?"

"Your father may be returning to you, Rhodri, and bringing happiness once more to your home. But what of the other things the Telling Pool showed you?"

"Other things?"

"Others are in danger from Homeira's enchantments. Terrible danger.

I told you that seeing is an art, and did you not see? The walls of the cave, those weapons, and the horses."

"What of them?"

"They belong to living men. Men who are still in her cave."

Rhodri stood up in astonishment. "Still in her cave? What do you mean?"

"Brave knights from the Holy Army," answered Tantallon, his unseeing eyes searching the forest floor, "have vanished on their way back to their homes. I've heard more and more of it in my traveling. Even as King Richard languishes in prison and the kingdom suffers from his loss, so on each of their estates men miss their lords and vie for power, while all things feel an anguish. For are not all things bound together?"

"Did Homeira murder them?" whispered the boy.

"Something far, far worse. For their bodies and very souls, Rhodri, are sealed in Homeira's cave. Encased in stone."

The boy looked at his friend in horror and remembered that pleading face in the wall above the casket.

"The enchantress has many tricks and many powers," said Tantallon. "In the myths of this land, such times would bring a quest among the braver hearts. If the beliefs had not faded and memories failed us."

"A quest?" asked Rhodri, thinking not of his father but of King Arthur.

"Yes, Rhodri. An ancient quest."

The boy thought of that sad and beautiful queen in the pool, with the star on her head, and of Guinevere's words. *Find it. Find it for all of us.*

"Can you mean for the Grail?" he asked nervously, remembering that lesson in church. "The Holy Grail? Is that what she meant when she told me to find it? Is that the quest?"

Tantallon tilted his head and smiled and Rhodri suddenly felt angry with him.

"Why are you so mysterious, Tantallon?"

"I . . ." The old man paused. "You've heard things in church of your Savior perhaps, and so you speak of a Holy Grail into which Christ dipped the sop he gave to Judas. But King Arthur and Guinevere, they lived in a time before the Church controlled the land. And stamped its mark and beliefs on men."

"I don't understand," said the boy, with frustration. "You tell me about Christ sometimes as if it were a story, and Arthur and Guinevere as if they are real. Yet did not the high king and his knights go out to seek the Grail?"

"But what is the true Grail?" said Tantallon. "Did not the legends of Arthur mingle with that of Christ himself? They were Christian men, Rhodri, but pagan men, too."

"Pagan?"

"Yes. Yet did not the pagan Arthur share something with your Savior? Whether Christ was the son of God, or just a man, were not both the Savior and Arthur full of love and betrayed?"

Rhodri nodded and he thought of Guinevere's lovely face, wrought with pain. But then he thought of William and Sarah, too, and it made him angry and weak.

"Such betrayals go deep, as deep as the waters of the Telling Pool, perhaps," said Tantallon, and his eyes flickered. "Such curses go deep."

"Curses? What are you talking about?"

"With Guinevere's betrayal, an ancient curse gripped the heart of men, and the land, too. For the ancient ones had a deep bond with the land. And now the curse comes again. To heal that ancient wound, perhaps another king must be freed and those poor souls released from stone."

"But how, Tantallon? Why are you telling me this?"

All Rhodri wanted to do now was to return home to his mother and tell her the wonderful news of Owen.

"How, Rhodri?" said Tantallon. "That I cannot see."

The boy stepped away from the pool. He knew that Tantallon was asking something of him, and thoughts of a great destiny rose in his mind, but he was not sure what the old man wanted. For now he must think of his mother and father.

"I must get home, Tantallon," he said.

The hermit turned his head and seemed to look at the boy deeply for a while, but at last he nodded. There was neither criticism nor praise in his voice when he spoke.

"You're a loving boy and have your duties there. Duties I would never impede. So come."

Rhodri led Tantallon silently up to the house, and the old man seemed to lean more heavily on the boy's arm than before. As they went, Tantallon spoke. "Rhodri, I have a surprise for you."

"A surprise?"

Tantallon gave a long whistle and Rhodri heard a jingling and swung round. From a branch above his head there was a fluttering of wings, and a familiar shape came sailing straight toward him. At first the boy thought it was the merlin, but then he realized it was a more familiar shape. The boy could hardly believe his burning eyes, or his racing heart.

"Melanor," cried Rhodri joyfully. "You're alive, Melanor."

The bird landed on the boy's lifted arm, the broken jesses about its talon dangling freely, the rock falcon's furious eyes like needles, as he blinked and looked about.

"Oh, Melanor, I thought you were dead."

There were tears in Rhodri's eyes as he stroked the bird's head.

"How, Tantallon?" he asked.

"He came to me on his own," answered the old man. "I would have sent him home, but he was badly ruffled by what happened in the barn and I thought he might go wild. So I have tended to him until you came."

Rhodri was too grateful for words. His heart felt as if it might overflow with joy.

"And he carries another lesson on his wings, Rhodri. Not to give up hope and to know that often things are not as they seem. That things may be restored to us, too, as well as taken away. Now you must go."

"Good-bye, Tantallon," said Rhodri on the edge of the hovel.

"Good-bye, my young friend. I'll be here if you need me, or if you wish to sit once more by the Telling Pool and see the enchantress."

"No," said Rhodri firmly, now deeply wary of the pool and just wanting everything to be back to normal. "It'll be all right now."

"Will it, Rhodri? I will pray so. To the God and Goddess."

"Melanor and I must tell my ma that Father's almost home. That'll make her well again."

The old man smiled softly.

"Yes. Of all the magic in the forest, Rhodri Falcon, of all the powers of stone and wood and stream, perhaps none is as great as the power of the heart. Of love. Remember that." He smiled again into Rhodri's eyes. "But be sure to know what love and duty really are. And the difference between the two. Go well and harm none."

As Rhodri walked away, he was sorrowful, and he thought of his father and Homeira and an anger stirred in him that Owen could have done such a thing as lie with the enchantress. But then the boy reminded himself of the power of that woman to seal beings in her cave, and that when Owen came home, he must help him, with all the strength in his young being, to stay away from her for a year and a day.

He came out of the forest and saw William and Aelfric hawking in the lower field near the manor. He wondered what they would think if they knew of the Telling Pool and all he had seen of King Richard and the wars in the Holy Land. All he had seen of the witch and her magical cave. He wondered how Aelfric would look at him if he told him that he, Rhodri Falcon, a mere Waelas, had sat where King Arthur himself had sat and seen such visions.

They spotted him, too, and William waved, but Rhodri's heart hardened. He was still resentful of William because of Sarah. Yet he had also seen William's father's death in those waters and felt a dreadful pity for the older boy. He pondered for a moment telling William of it, but the thought so saddened him that he changed his mind. Rhodri raised his arm in guilty acknowledgment, but quickly turned for home.

The fire was smoldering to almost nothing as Rhodri opened the door to the house, after returning Melanor to his mew, and he felt the sting of worry. His mother was lying on the cot asleep and Rhodri saw that the fever had worsened. Her dark hair was wet, and water beaded across her trembling forehead.

"Ma. wake up, Ma."

Megan groaned and opened her eyes. They were flecked with tiny veins of blood.

"Rhodri, where have you been?"

"Hunting in the forest, Ma."

She tried to sit up.

"Forgive me, Rhodri. I should rise and cook for you, *cariad*. But there's no strength left in me. I cannot bear it longer. Without him. I'm dying, boy."

Rhodri gripped her hand.

"No, Ma."

"Your father's gone, Rhodri, gone forever," said Megan bitterly, "Cut down in the Holy Lands. And now I must follow him. I'm sorry."

"No, Ma. Melanor's come back and father's alive, too, I know it."

Megan's eyes seemed to clear a little. "Know it? What are you saying, *bach*, you've seen him at the ford?"

Rhodri hesitated. He had to keep the secret. Yet there was a blessing in that secret, too, for he knew that because of it he would never have to tell Megan of Homeira and what he had seen of his father's betrayal. He was glad of it, for the knowledge would surely break his mother's heart.

"I just do, Ma," Rhodri insisted. "He's coming home to us. I swear it. On my life."

Megan's eyes flickered, and very faintly she squeezed his hand.

"You're a wonderful son, Rhodri," she whispered, "and you always had faith. You always believed he'd come back to us. But the world can be cruel and we must face it clearly. I'm glad that when I'm gone you'll have this home and all there is in it and enough knowledge of the birds to make a living on your own. You'll find somebody, little Sarah perhaps, and then . . ."

"What are you saying?" cried Rhodri. "You must believe me, Ma. Father's alive and in Albion. He's on his way back to us, now."

Megan smiled, and although she believed it a lie, the very thought seemed to relax her fevered body.

"You'll get better, Ma," said Rhodri tenderly, "and Pa will come back to us and be a master falconer and we'll be happy again together."

His mother had fallen back into her reverie. A chill stole over Rhodri as he held her clammy hand and looked down helplessly. He knew instinctively that the sickness was deep and that he must do something soon. But he had no idea what to do. At first he thought of running back to Tantallon, but what if he couldn't find him? Then he thought of the manor, but would Wolfrin allow William to help?

He dismissed the idea immediately and thought of Sarah. His memory of his gift so rankled though that he dismissed that, too. Perhaps he should journey out and find one of the traveling apothecaries to buy some potion. But he couldn't leave Megan alone, and besides, there were no coins with which to pay for medicine.

He must help his mother alone. Rhodri got up and looked about, and then, remembering Homeira in the Telling Pool, the young man began to busy himself. First he plumped up the pillow and laid Megan more carefully on the bed, as Homeira had done for his father, pulling the blankets up around her. Then he fetched wood from the side of the house and fed the hearth. After that, he set some broth over the flame to boil and went out to draw a bucket from the well.

When he got back, Megan was turning and groaning and the fever had worsened still. Her forehead was so hot to the touch that Rhodri pulled away his hand in surprise, and it was the memory of Homeira that told him he must do something to counteract this heat. So he dipped a cloth in the bucket and laid it across her brow. He could see immediately that it felt pleasant to her and she seemed to relax.

He sat there, bathing her forehead to cool the fires in her, drawing the blankets about her when she shivered furiously and holding her hand all the while. He tried to give her some broth, but she would not take it. He managed to make her drink some water, but it was little. He wiped her forehead and smoothed her hair. Rhodri whispered to her, too, again and again.

"He's coming back to us, Ma. You must believe me."

Perhaps, in the great cities of Albion, or in the Norman lands to the south, perhaps in the streets of Rome or the mysterious bazaars of Persia and the East, there were learned men who could have helped Megan Falcon. Apothecaries might have come to purge or bleed her with leeches, to set hot vials on her skin to suck out the evil humors, or to make her drink strange potions. Perhaps doctors of the Church, more concerned with the secrets of the soul than the body might have prayed over her cot, or mixed old spells with the new words of scripture, trusting to their God to do the work. But there was no power so healing as the love that Rhodri showed his mother in those long hours that he tended to her.

Animals of the forest, unthinking in the ways of men and unaware of books or schools of medical learning, know immediately how to heal themselves. When a dog sickens, it knows to eat grass and so expel the poison. Wolf and bear when hurt or wounded know to retreat into the bosom of some secret place, a cave perhaps, away from the dangers of the world, and sleep and wait. For in man and animal the body is its own healer, if we will only trust its own power.

But man, in his searching, in his reasoning and thinking, has something that is both a great boon and danger to him. The power of his mind. For that power can sometimes step like a wall between him and his own being. And Megan Falcon's will, like an unseen hand choking her own breath, was fighting her. For in her heart she had lost hope and had pined for Owen for too long. She loved her son with all her heart, but it was not the same desperate love that she had for her mate, to touch him and lie with him and feel his strength. A love so natural it is like eating and breathing.

A sickness was inside her, too, a sickness that men in far-off days to come would set glass and microscope to witness and see, where before they had only dreamt of its being and called it bad humors, or demons, or evil spirits. A sickness that the body itself could fight, if only Megan's will, her desire to live and feel, had not grown so faint. Which is why, as Rhodri sat there, holding her hand or stroking her brow, his words were like an elixir.

"He's coming home to us, Ma. Believe."

To Megan, lost in the country of the sick, it was as if those words were calling her back, summoning her from the distant, shadowy place to fight.

"We both love you, Mother. We need you."

"Owen," groaned Megan. "Where are you, Owen?"

"Close, Ma. It will be soon now."

For two days and two nights the young man sat there by that sickbed. It was near to midnight of the second day when the fever broke. Megan shuddered and opened her eyes, and gave a great sigh. Then she lay back more gently on the pillow and slept. Her forehead was cooler and the sweating had stopped. Her body had conquered the invasion.

Rhodri didn't wake her. He was so exhausted himself, he lay down in front of the hearth with his jerkin over him and plunged into dreams. He dreamt of Melanor and Tantallon and the Telling Pool. Of Homeira and his father and the magic casket in a cave made of souls, wondering all the while what it was made to hold. He dreamt of a curse. But above all he dreamt of his mother.

When he woke, Megan was sitting at the table, smiling at him. She was wrapped in a blanket, but her color had returned and there on the table sat two bowls of steaming vegetable soup. Rhodri sat down without saying a word to her, but smiling, too, and she took his hand in hers. Her grip was weak, but her palm was not clammy as it had been before.

"You brought me back, Rhodri," she whispered tenderly. "You alone, my darling boy."

That day, Rhodri went for a walk on his own. He felt much better, and he was very proud at what he had done. Near the church he met William. The young lord had Shadowfell on his arm and his face was very cheerful.

"Where are you going, Rhodri?" he cried.

"Nowhere, my lord. I wanted to think"

William regarded Rhodri carefully. "What's this? You call me 'my lord,' Rhodri. We are friends, no?"

Rhodri dropped his gaze.

"Do you want to fly Shadowfell with me?" William asked. "He's wild today, and two voices would be better than one."

"Perhaps another time."

William smiled.

"It's been hard for you, hasn't it Rhodri, without your father I mean? It's been hard for me, too. There are so many people about to look after me. I've Wolfrin and Aelfric and the household. But none of them really understand me. As my father would."

"I . . ."

"Don't worry, Rhodri," said William cheerfully, "they'll both be home soon. And when Father returns, he'll hold a great feast, for Norman and Saxon and Welshman. There'll be much falconing again, and you and your family shall come to the house. Who knows, perhaps the king himself will . . ."

Rhodri's heart went out to the older boy, but how could he tell William what he had seen? What he knew already. That poor William's father was dead.

"What's wrong, Rhodri?"

"Oh, William."

"Don't you believe it? Oh you must, Rhodri," cried the young lord cheerfully. "Have faith. King Richard will return and then my father . . ."

"My Lord. Your father. He's not . . ."

William's face grew cold and Shadowfell fluttered on his arm. "Not?"

"He isn't coming home, William," whispered Rhodri sadly. "And the king is a prisoner. In Austria."

William's eyes flashed like steel. "What do you mean not coming home, Falcon?"

"A Saracen arrow. It struck your father in the heart."

"Liar," snarled William. "How do you know this?"

Rhodri so wanted to tell his friend, but still he couldn't break his promise to Tantallon.

"I'm sorry, William."

William De Brackenois wouldn't hear of it. He lifted Shadowfell higher on his arms and for a moment looked as if he wanted to launch the bird at Rhodri's throat.

"Aelfric's right," he cried, his eyes burning, "I was a fool to ever give you the time of day, with your moping eyes and your strange, secretive ways. Fortune-tellers and prophecies, and all your talk of the king. All you do is show off. You're mad."

"I'm not," said Rhodri angrily.

"Yes you are, Waelas. Everyone thinks so."

"And you're just too foolish to see what you don't want to see," answered Rhodri, hurt by William's insult. "Like being friends with Aelfric."

"Mind your tongue, Waelas," said William icily, "and remember your place. Or perhaps you want me to throw you and your mother off the estate."

Rhodri blanched.

"What," said Rhodri, "and put the miller and Sarah in our home instead?"

Now William blushed, but he straightened his back, too.

"One day," he said coldly, "one day you'll learn some respect, Falcon. Learn, too, to bend your knee and pay the vassalage you owe me, or there'll be no place for you here. But, as Aelfric says, perhaps the fire's the only thing good for the likes of you."

William De Brackenois turned and stalked angrily away.

• • •

A month passed and Megan had just noticed the first crocuses pushing through the spring earth by her herb garden when she saw the shadow appear at the end of the track. At first she was too frightened to dare believe it. She felt her stomach move and then hold itself in against the hope, for she knew that if she was wrong it might kill her. But as the figure came closer, her brown eyes grew brighter and brighter. That firm, certain gait, that pack strung over his shoulder, the outline of the sword across his back.

"Rhodri. Rhodri, *cariad*. Come quickly."

Rhodri was in his room when he heard his mother's joyous cry and he knew what it meant immediately. He came tearing down the stairs. Megan was already running as fast as she could across the yard. The young man saw her reach his father, he saw her throw herself on his neck and Owen wrap her in his still strong arms. Then the master falconer was clasping her, lifting her, and turning her around and around. It was if they were there, all together, back on the green at the fair and no sadness had touched the family at all.

Owen was kissing Megan now and putting her down and smoothing the dark hair from her lovely, tearstained face. Rhodri's walk got faster, but still he held himself back. His father turned, and Rhodri noticed two things immediately: the surprise in his eyes as he saw how much his son had grown and changed, and the scar on his cheek.

The scar. So all he had seen in the Telling Pool, it had all been true. Rhodri felt a jolt of fear and then anger and resentment, but Owen was laughing and beaming so broadly it was as if the sun had come out and then Rhodri was running again toward his mother and father. They both took him in their arms and they were all together again, hugging one another and weeping and laughing for joy.

11 ❖ MEMORIES

Memory, hither come,
And tune your merry notes
—William Blake, "Song"

W as it truly terrible, Father?" Rhodri asked, as Owen Falcon and his son sat by the stream below their little home. "In the Holy Lands, I mean."

Father and son were fishing quietly together in the bright, hot sunshine and the remains of delicious food and drink lay beside them on the grassy bank. Owen had been back two whole months.

"Sometimes, Rhodri," answered the master falconer, "But it's best not to speak of such darkness."

The air was full of the languid movements of summer, and they had both stuffed themselves on the picnic Megan had made for them. Megan was truly transformed with Owen's return from the wars, and once again the little home was filled with her happy song and her lovely, merry laughter. She had set to work on her tapestry again, and the house was as clean and neat as it had ever been.

"You swore you'd come back to us," said Rhodri cheerfully, as his father threaded a fishing hook in his powerful hands, "and you did, right enough. You kept your promise."

Owen peered into the stream as he strung the line, wound about a long stick. Since his arrival, the little family could not have been happier, and the past weeks had been like a joyful dream. The entire neighborhood had heard of Owen's return, too, and many had come down to the farm to offer their blessing, or bring food and to see a Holy Warrior with their own eyes. No others had returned as yet, and Owen had told them that Lord Treffusis and De Brackenois never would. Rhodri had pretended to be as surprised as the others.

The very first day of his arrival, the falconer had marked how well his son had looked after the farm, and had forgiven Rhodri for the fox and Karlor and Kalin. Owen had taken up the reins of care himself again, and Rhodri was delighted to have time to himself once more. He almost felt like a boy again, with all the lightness of a boy growing up in the bosom of health and home, and he had pushed away the thoughts that Tantallon and the pool had placed in his mind, of an ancient curse creeping through the land.

Over the past weeks, Rhodri had often taken Melanor out hunting, not with the grave concern of the falconer who knows that he must kill or go hungry, but with the freedom and wonder of one living creature watching another glorying in the power and mystery of flight and sun and air. Yet he had noticed, too, that his father had begun to brood, and wondering if he was thinking of Homeira, Rhodri determined to keep his eye on him.

Now, as he watched his father's sure hands threading the hook, something made him ask a question that he regretted.

"Did you ever doubt, Father? That you'd return to us?"

Owen's brow darkened a little. "Sometimes, in the thick of battle, I wondered if the Lord God would spare me, Rhodri. It was a gamble out there and he took many others. A host. De Brackenois himself. I've seen his poor boy, to tell him."

Rhodri thought sadly of William, and their last meeting. What was his friend feeling in his heart now, and had his own father really returned for good?

"But back in England, I mean. Nothing could keep you from us, could it?" Rhodri felt his hands shake as he asked it.

Owen paused and looked deeply into the stream. "No, Rhodri, *bach*. I came as fast as I could."

Rhodri smiled, but anger stirred in his gut and suddenly he realized just what had caused it. His father had never lied to him before, at least not that he knew of. Rhodri pushed away the emotion and told himself that Owen had at least told half the truth, for not even the power of the beautiful enchantress had prevented him from coming home to them.

"Who gave you that scar, Pa?" he asked, shrugging off the thoughts.

"Rhodri," smiled Owen, "It's too lovely a day. Why should a boy want to know of such dark things?"

"I'm not such a boy, Pa."

Owen turned and looked at his handsome young son. Rhodri had grown so much and filled out indeed. The master falconer realized he hardly knew his boy.

"No," he said, smiling, and putting a hand on his shoulder, "perhaps you're not. It happened on the road, Rhodri, when a Saracen archer felled my horse, which I bought for myself with your mother's pewter cup."

"Tell me."

"We were attacked by the heathen," said Owen somberly, "hiding among the rocks, and one of them gave me this with his blade. But I gave him a deeper cut with my sword. One that he never recovered from."

"You should have had me with you though," said the boy, smiling at his father, "to watch your back."

Owen looked at his son and smiled again. "And sometimes I wished I had, *cariad*. Now I'll truly teach you to use a sword, if you like. But I'm glad you didn't see what I saw."

Rhodri flushed a little, and Owen stood up and cast the line into the stream, which gave a lovely plop. The sunshine gleamed on the water and he sighed contentedly.

"It's so good to be home, my boy. You know, I think I've seen enough of the world for a lifetime. There's much danger in the land, but at least we're safe and happy. Perhaps it's selfish to say it now, but I no longer care for what happens elsewhere."

There was a quick movement in the water and the line went taut.

"Here," cried Owen happily. "You take it, now."

Rhodri played the fish confidently, pulling it up gradually onto the bank. Its scales glittered like quicksilver and it was dotted with little specks of red. The boy was delighted. But as he looked over at his father, he noticed that his expression had changed. He was looking down at the rainbow trout and his lips had curled into a kind of angry sneer. So concentrated was his face that he seemed mesmerized, and suddenly he clutched his hand to his chest, as if in pain.

"What is it?"

Owen stood staring down at the fish and the hook. He was trembling furiously and it was as if he couldn't look away.

"You're scaring me, Father. What's wrong?"

"Damn it, boy," snapped Owen, breaking from the trance and looking up at the sun. "Why didn't you tell me how late it grows? I forgot to check the mews. We can't afford any more mishaps."

Rhodri was amazed by the change in his father.

"But it's Sunday."

"Boys," snapped Owen, glaring at his son. "All you think of is play and fun. There's work to be done, see. There's always work to be done. Would you let the world go to rack and ruin?"

The master falconer turned and strode away up to the barn. Rhodri was deeply shaken. He took the hook from the fish's gills and went mournfully up to the house.

That same night, lying in his little room, the boy was woken by a shout. It was his father, crying out in his sleep.

"No, please. Don't."

Rhodri ran to the top of the stair and looked down. The curtain was drawn in front of his parents' cot, but the voices were clear enough and now Megan was speaking.

"Owen. Wake up, Owen."

Behind the curtain Rhodri heard his father stir at his mother's words and groan painfully again.

"No, please."

Rhodri had a horrible feeling that Homeira was in the room with them.

"Owen. My love."

"What?" cried Owen, waking suddenly. "What's wrong, damn you, woman?"

Rhodri stepped back from the stair. It was his father's voice, but it was changed, and so rough and angry and unkind that Rhodri hardly recognized him.

"You were dreaming, husband," said Megan tenderly, behind the curtain. "Some dark dream of the Holy Lands. A nightmare, see."

"Dreaming?"

"Lie back, my love. Your memories of war hurt you. You're home with us now. Nothing can touch you here, my darling. You're safe again."

"Fool," shouted Owen. "Why do you trouble me so, or talk like a woman always of safety? Now get some sleep and let me rest, for the Christ's sake."

"But Owen . . ."

"Silence. Or perhaps you'd care to bed down alone. Or go up to the stables. That's where Wolfrin sleeps. Unless he's moved into the manor by now."

"Owen," said Megan indignantly, "why do you speak so? Why do you talk of Wolfrin?"

"He's become a fine one now, hasn't he, getting his hooks into that boy William?" said Owen harshly. "And do you think me a dolt that I don't know the truth of people's hearts. It must have been lonely with your husband off to the wars for so long. Even the purest hearts are tempted."

Rhodri felt a wave of anger. What was his father saying? He had never spoken to Megan like this before. The boy wanted to go downstairs and speak up for his mother, but he heard his father turn in bed and then a sound came to him that tore at his own heart. It was a sound he had heard before, though for different reasons. His mother sobbing.

Rhodri crept back to his own cot and lay down, but he could hardly sleep that night and his thoughts were full of sadness. But toward morning he had a dream. There was his father, standing before him, looking up at the sky and reaching out his hand helplessly to the bird that was wheeling high overhead. Then he looked down and his face was hard and wary. He kept whispering, again and again, "Help me, Rhodri, help me."

Another dream followed, even deeper and darker. Homeira was before Rhodri and she seemed to be beckoning to him and whispering his name. "Rhodri. Rhodri Falcon." She was close to him and placing her hand on his chest and pushing him back against a stone wall. The boy's limbs were heavy, and it was as if he himself was becoming part of the stone. He was unable to move or cry out, unable to do anything at all. A terrible, leaden sadness was inside him and then, all about him, there were skulls.

Suddenly the boy was standing before a great rock. It lay deep in a forest and its sides were covered in moss and lichen. Arthur stood on the rock, and on his head was the crown of gold.

"The land," he cried, "the land bleeds, Rhodri Falcon, and only true hearts can heal it. Such a one must find it again. So can you wake, boy, wake to your destiny? Wake to who you really are."

"No," groaned Rhodri, kicking and turning in his sleep, "leave me be."

"You must help us. Find it, boy. For all of us. The sword."

Rhodri woke with a start. His face was pouring with sweat.

"Excalibur," he cried. "They mean the great sword Excalibur."

As Rhodri lay there, he felt a great sense of mystery surround him, and a breathless excitement, mixed with pure terror. He found his hand was gripping the amulet at his throat.

• • •

The sun was streaming through the window when he came down to breakfast. His father's mood seemed quite restored. Owen was sitting at the table, chatting merrily to Megan, as she busied about the fire. Rhodri noticed that Owen had slung his father's broadsword above the hearth again. Rhodri smiled at them both as he sat down at the table.

For a while they talked happily and Rhodri grew excited, for Owen had decided to fly the hunting birds that day, close to the manor. But when Megan walked to the table with the broth, Owen glared at the bowl she had put before him and, with a sweep of his arm, dashed it to the floor.

"What's this muck, wench? Am I a common villain, to put up with weak water and stale bread? Haven't I suffered enough, without coming home to a peasant's fare?"

Megan looked at Owen in amazement, but he just got up and strode out of the door, slamming it behind him.

"What is it, Rhodri?" said Megan. "What's got into him? I thought he was happy to be home. But he's so changed."

"Perhaps he's tired," Rhodri said cheerlessly. "He's been through so much."

"You're right," his mother agreed, collecting herself. "We must be kind and loving to him."

"That's right, Ma. We must love him as hard as we can. And be understanding if he loses his temper. We must remind him of his home."

Rhodri remembered Tantallon's words about love. *For a year and a day,* added the young man in his thoughts, *just a year and a day.* Then the bargain will be done.

"It will be all right, Mother, believe me."

That night, Owen showed no sign that he remembered anything of what had happened at breakfast. He was as tender with Megan as if they were newlyweds, and he joked and laughed loudly at the table. Megan kept looking nervously at Rhodri, but she was glad at least that the mood seemed to have passed.

●   ●   ●

Two days later, Waylinn the blacksmith came through on his fat gray horse. Since the Falcons had no mount to shoe, he knew that he would earn no food or coins, but he liked the family and he, too, had heard the rumor of Owen's homecoming from the East. He stood for a while talking to Megan and Rhodri by the well.

"It's bad news abroad," said Waylinn as he leaned there. "Everywhere you go, villages flame and the people suffer. They should never have gone to fight."

Rhodri looked down.

"Last week I passed a village where a group of our own soldiers, short of pay, had raided the common people's homes. It was terrible what they did."

Owen had just come out of the house and walked up to Waylinn's horse to stroke its head. Almost immediately the animal set back its ears and began to throw up its snout and stamp.

"Calm yourself, damn it," growled Owen.

The horse seemed to become even more distressed and started to snort and whinny at Owen.

"Damn stupid beast," cried Owen furiously, "what devil has got in you? I'll take a whip to your back."

The words had an even worse effect on the animal. It reared, sending some of the smith's tools clattering to the ground. Rhodri gasped as his father raised a hand to strike the horse, a thing he would never normally do, but the blacksmith went running over and grabbed the stallion by the reins.

"There, there, Carradon, peace now."

Waylinn managed to calm his horse, but Owen noticed that all three of them were looking at him and he turned with a scowl and went back inside.

That very afternoon, Rhodri and his father went falconing together. They took both Melanor and Glindor, but as they walked up to the big field and staked the perch, Rhodri noticed that Glindor was already very distressed, and kept flapping his wings and trying to take off.

They flew the birds, but every time Owen called, Glindor and Melanor failed to come to him. It was to Rhodri's firm arms alone that the birds would return. On Melanor's last dive Owen grew so furious that he gave the lure an extra jolt and hurled it through the air straight at the falcon. Rhodri gasped as it tipped Melanor's wing and nearly knocked his bird from the sky. The boy was angry and frightened, but as they walked home he told himself again that's his father's moods would surely pass, if they only kept faith.

Though as the days came and turned into weeks, Owen's strange moods grew worse. Often Rhodri would see his father stop, as if gripped by a terrible memory, and clutch his chest, and then a haunted look would come into his eyes. Rhodri knew that somehow Homeira was calling to him. His father would gaze out longingly across the fields, or take out his dagger and run his thumb across its edge. Rhodri learned in those times never to cross him or ask him questions, for if he did so his father's eyes would blaze and he would shout at his son and tell him to get on with his chores, or mind his business.

• • •

It was a cold, windy day when Rhodri met Sarah walking toward the wishing well.

"Hello, Rhodri. It's good to see you."

Rhodri just shrugged.

"I'm so pleased for you, Rhodri. That your pa's back and safe, I mean. It must make you all very happy."

"Yes." Again the boy shrugged and thought angrily of his gift.

"Not like poor William," Sarah said warmly. "The news has made him so sad. Though he bears it wonderfully."

A wistful look had come into Sarah's lovely eyes, and Rhodri felt an anguish deep in his heart. De Brackenois's death had brought Sarah and William even closer together, and in that moment Rhodri had a thought that made him ashamed immediately. A tiny part of him suddenly wished, if it would have made Sarah look on him with greater favor, that Owen had suffered De Brackenois's fate that day instead. But the boy pushed it from his mind.

"You're always talking about William," he said resentfully.

"What if I am?"

Rhodri remembered how Aelfric had reminded him of his station in life.

"Do you really think a miller's daughter should let herself look so fondly on such a one?"

Sarah looked at Rhodri in astonishment. "How could you say such a thing?"

"But is that why you think he's so special? Just because he lives up at the manor."

Sarah was really furious now. "I think he's special," she answered sharply, "because he's kind and gentle and doesn't spend all his time talking about war and fighting, like a child."

Sarah turned and stalked away, and Rhodri felt so miserable that he could have laid down and cried. On the way home, though, he saw William. At first he thought his old friend would not acknowledge him, but the young lord strode straight up to him.

"Rhodri."

Rhodri turned warily.

"Yes, my lord."

"Don't call me that," said William. "I'm sorry for what I said. I was angry and frightened. Can you forgive me?"

Rhodri thought of William's father. He nodded.

"I want to speak with you, Rhodri. About my father," the older boy said softly. "Please tell me how you knew that he'd been killed. It was true, just like what you said of the king and the wars. Your father told me. But how did you know? Was it this fortune-teller?"

"You swear, William," Rhodri whispered, looking around, "you swear not to tell anyone else—not Wolfrin or Aelfric or even Sarah?"

Rhodri couldn't keep the secret anymore. Not if he could ease William's pain. The young man nodded.

"Oh, yes."

"Very well then."

So at last Rhodri told William of the magical pool, of Tantallon, and all he had seen. When he had finished he knew that his friend believed him.

"But William," added Rhodri warmly, "it's all right. Your father was at peace. I saw it. He believed that his soul had been saved by the war in the Holy Lands. And he asked Lord Treffusis to tell you. To tell you that he loves you more than anything in the world."

The young lord smiled, but there were tears in his blue eyes. "Thank you, Rhodri Falcon. For telling me the truth. I must go into the church now and pray and think."

The younger boy nodded. The new Lord Brackenois turned to enter the church, then stopped.

"Rhodri," he cried, "with all that's been happening, I quite forgot." He reached into his pocket and pulled something out. "Forgot to give this back to you. I've been carrying it with me. I found it by the river last year and recognized it from St. Martin's Day, although you must have made it into a pendant . . ."

As William handed him the little falconing hood, Rhodri felt sick and guilty.

"Rhodri," William added, "there's some great mystery about you, and these things that you see. But the fortune-teller and this pool, you must be careful what you say of them. For if any learn of it—Wolfrin for one—there'll be grave trouble."

William smiled sadly and went inside.

Rhodri was glad of what he had told William, and that they were friends again, and ashamed now of what he had believed of Sarah. She must have lost his gift and been too embarrassed to tell him. His heart felt a little lighter, though, as he turned for home.

As he walked, he did not notice the figure step out from the side of the church. It was Aelfric, and his mischievous, jealous eyes were sparking. He had heard everything the boys had said.

· · ·

At home things worsened still. The next evening they were eating together, and Owen was scowling at the food Megan had just laid out, when suddenly Rhodri's mother, stinging with hurt pride, rounded on her husband.

"Falcon," cried Megan fiercely, "has Satan himself got into you? Or is my humble home not good enough for you now you have been to the East?"

Owen's hand clenched on his goblet, but he was silent and sullen.

"Speak to me, Owen," said Megan more gently. "I beg of you, husband. Is it what you saw out there that makes you so angry? Why don't you tell me?"

"You dare to talk to me thus," her husband cried, slamming down the cup and knocking it from the table as he jumped up, "in my own household? Am I not master of my house? Without me you would be nothing, Megan Falcon. You would be living as a scull in the manor, or . . ."

"Owen, please."

"Silence, woman."

"No," cried Megan. "How dare you talk to me so. I'm your wife, husband, who loves and honors you. But I will not be . . ."

"*You* will not?" bellowed Owen, banging down his fist on the table. "Have you forgotten the law? Under the king's rule a man owns his wife and may do with her as he pleases. You'll do as I tell you. You're no more than chattel, to be disposed of as I will."

Megan looked at Owen with such fury that Rhodri was really afraid. Megan knew she could not fight her husband physically, so she tried to hurt him with her tongue instead.

"You're changed, Owen. Even the birds resist your call now, and animals know what's really in a man. Perhaps the wars broke you, husband. Others, too, whisper that a devil has got into you."

Owen's face had grown puce with rage. He advanced on his wife with clenched fists and seemed about to hit her.

"Damn you, wench."

"Pa, stop it," cried Rhodri, stepping between them.

"Silence, boy."

"No, Father, I won't be quiet."

"Get out of my way, boy, or by God . . ."

Rhodri knew that his father could knock him aside with relative ease, but he did not get out of the way. He felt a rush of anger that turned to courage. He was determined not to allow his father to lay a hand on his mother.

"Pa, stop it now."

"I'll teach you, boy," thundered Owen.

The energy that came out of Rhodri seemed to meet Owen's and block it. He stood his ground, and Owen, wanting to strike out, but holding back, too, put his hand to the back of his son's neck. As Owen gripped him there, the boy felt a horrible, angry sickness inside him. He wanted to punch his father, but he was afraid to. He felt dizzy and choked and suddenly very small. Owen let go and turned and stormed from the house. Rhodri's shoulders slumped. He was shaking terribly and he wanted to cry, to cry all the pain out of his body. But he would not cry.

Another terrible thing happened that day. After what Megan had said of the birds, Owen went straight up to the barn. He took tools and wood, and all day Rhodri heard him at work, sawing and hammering. When at last he had finished, he emerged with a new mew, larger than all the others, and inside he placed Melanor, Glindor, and Breeze. He sealed the cage fast, then nailed it shut. That night Rhodri pleaded with him, but Owen sat there at the head of the table like a stone.

"You spend too much time with the damned birds anyway," he said coldly, "and there's more important work to do on the farm than falconry."

"But Pa, you always told me that birds like that, hunting birds I mean, need to fly free."

"Free," said Owen, and a bitter melancholy came into his look. Rhodri knew he was thinking of Homeira. "Nothing is free. Is a king free, when he follows a pope? Or a lord free when he follows a king? Is a Welshman free when he must serve the English, Norman, or

Saxon? Are any of us really free in the end? For are we not all born to die? Besides, what use are hunting birds when there's no hunt?"

Rhodri ran upstairs and threw himself down on his bed. Ten months had passed since he had seen his father in the Telling Pool and wished with all his might for him to come home. But now Rhodri felt as if a great tragedy was facing them all. As if a curse had come on them.

As he fell asleep, he heard a voice. Homeira's voice. "Now do you see, boy? The world is hard and cruel," she was whispering. "And to conquer it takes not goodness or purity or faith, not the love of home but strength and knowledge and cunning."

A terrible sadness swamped the boy, and the dreams gave way to the dark. But not the darkness of night, the thick, sickly darkness of human blood, pumping up from the Telling Pool. The pool was welling up, overflowing its banks, and had become a river, swelling the ford, turning to a torrent in the stream, a torrent of blood that was sweeping his home, the barn, his parents, and everything away.

Dawn was coming as Rhodri crept down to the barn to see Melanor. The bird was sitting there in the mew and his eyes seemed angrier than before.

"Oh, Melanor," whispered Rhodri bitterly. "I'm sorry, Melanor. But I'll fly you again soon. I promise I will."

He walked back to the house, but in the mounting light he stopped. His father was at the well. His shirt was off and he had drawn up the bucket with fresh water to wash. Rhodri drew closer, for Owen seemed at peace again and was whistling cheerfully to himself.

He turned, and the lad was relieved to see a smile on his father's face. Rhodri came closer to him, but then stopped and stifled a gasp. He was looking at his father's bare chest. There, right in the middle, was a livid red scar in the shape of a sword. Rhodri had not seen it before. Not in the Telling Pool. Not since his father's return either.

"What are you looking at?" said Owen.

"Your chest, Pa."

Owen looked down, and his eyes seemed to mist over with incomprehension, as if he was startled to see the thing there himself.

"Father. Why didn't you tell us that you'd been wounded so badly?"

Owen touched the scar, so red it was almost like an open wound, but the feel seemed unfamiliar, even to himself.

"You got it in battle, Pa? In the Holy Lands?"

"Yes . . . I think . . . I must . . ."

Rhodri was face to face with his father now. "It must have been hard for you, Pa," said Rhodri kindly, desperately wanting to ease his pain, "so hard. That's why you . . . you're so changed."

The boy had no time to defend himself. Owen's hand came out and struck his son full across the mouth, and Rhodri was flung backward into the mud. He was so startled, there was no time for any emotion but shock. He just felt the numbing pain in his lip, and when he touched his hand to it, it was wet with blood.

"You talk like a foolish woman," said Owen savagely, "like your damned mother. You'll show your father some respect, or you'll feel my fist again."

The young man got up, his eyes on the edge of tears, but blazing defiantly. "I'll respect what I respect," he said through gritted teeth.

"I'm your father, damn you. Respect me."

Then Rhodri was running. Away from his home. Up, across the field toward the wood.

"Rhodri, come back, Rhodri. I'm sorry."

A storm had broken inside Rhodri, and now, as he ran, his being was like thunder and he hated his father with all his soul. He could hardly breathe as he ran, and it was as though something were forcing him on, pounding through his whole body and being. He stumbled and got up, the tears of anguish and indignation and betrayal stinging his cheeks.

All he had meant to do was to help his father and his mother, and his father had struck him, knocked him to the ground. Perhaps some dark enchantment was working inside Owen, but it was not the boy's fault that he had betrayed his family to a witch. That he was somehow under her spell.

For a moment the furious boy wanted to turn back. To find his mother and tell Megan all he had seen in the Telling Pool. To tell her that this man, whom they had loved so long, had broken faith. Had been tempted with pleasure and wine and enchantments. Rhodri wanted to step between them and use one against the other to take revenge. But as the boy ran on, the idea faded in him. Even in his raging anguish there was purpose in Rhodri's flight. He needed now to find a friend. Somebody he could trust and who would understand. Somebody who knew the secret of the pool. He needed to find Tantallon.

Rhodri stopped. He had heard a noise in the wood and he swung round. There was no one to be seen and Rhodri ran on again. He was sure he knew the way now, but as he drew closer to the hovel and the trees opened, high above him he saw a bird wheeling in the air.

"TAN-TAL-LON."

The clearing was still. Only Reagan the cat nosed about the shack. The shadows fell through the slanting branches and light glowed through the trees. Rhodri drew nearer and saw that the door to the hovel was wide open.

"Tantallon, are you here? Please, Tantallon."

He dipped his head and walked inside. An air of expectancy hung about the room as though someone had just left it, but would soon return. Rhodri noticed something by the fireplace. The hourglass. He sat down on the straw mattress and waited, trying to still his throbbing mind, trying to calm the burning hatred he felt for his father. But no one came. The cat meowed mournfully and Rhodri got up and wandered outside.

Perhaps Tantallon was at the pool, thought Rhodri, looking down the slope toward those weathered steps and the stone arch. He was calmer now and he had another thought. The rage that had gripped his father and the anger and hate that seemed to overcome him—surely it could not just be the memory of the beautiful Homeira that was eating at his soul? Surely there had been something else, something that Rhodri had not seen in the Telling Pool. He had to look deeper still.

Somehow it was even more thrilling and magical approaching that pool on his own. The steady echoing drip of water and that silken surface seemed to be beckoning to him and him alone. But as he stood there, at the water's edge, it was not like standing by a pool at all, but as if he were tottering on the edge of a mighty cliff and could never see to its bottom. It felt like facing the future or becoming an adult.

Tantallon was nowhere to be seen, so Rhodri turned toward the Seeing Place. He sat down quietly on the mossy stone and swung his head to look. Thoughts and memories were racing through his mind. Suddenly the darting fishes of light and shadow came once more. But there before him was not Megan, or Owen, or Homeira, but a young man, sitting on a stone. But not just any stone. It was the Seeing Place.

He could have been no more than Rhodri's age, and he had thick black hair and bright, searching eyes. He was dressed as simply as Aelfric had been at St. Martin's Day, but his face was as strong and open as William's. He was leaning forward and gazing into the water before him, and Rhodri suddenly realized, with a thrill through his whole being, who he was. It was Arthur, as a young man like Rhodri.

The picture faded, and then before Rhodri was a girl. She was smiling back warmly at him. Her lovely face was quite dark, almost like Homeira's, but there was none of the cruel cunning in her rose red lips that he had seen in the enchantress's, although there seemed a sadness in her glittering eyes, too. Her jet black hair fell straight about her delicate cheeks. The Telling Pool rippled again and there was Wolfrin.

He looked much younger, much like his son Aelfric, and he was walking down the track that ran toward the ford. Suddenly there were men all about him. They were on horseback and had drawn their swords and Rhodri could see the pure terror in Wolfrin's cruel face. It must be the time Wolfrin met robbers on the road, thought Rhodri, and single-handed, drove them off. But Wolfrin did nothing of the sort. He had already dropped to his knees and was pleading with the men. They began to laugh as he begged, and a clever light came into the groom's eyes.

"Look," he cried, "don't harm me and I'll reward you well."

"Reward us," sneered one of the men in a Welsh voice. "What could a mere stable boy reward us with, Saxon scum?"

"Spare my life," pleaded Wolfrin, "and I'll tell you of riches at the manor. Where grain can be found and how to get into the stables unseen and carry away a decent horse."

Rhodri was amazed, and as he heard Wolfrin make the bargain, he thought how full the world was of secrets and darkness and trickery.

"So be it," said one of the men.

After the men rode away, Wolfrin sat and thought for a while. A crafty smile came to his face, and he got to his feet and took out his dagger. He clasped the hilt and then cut into his own neck. As the blood came, he reached down and began to rub dirt over his face and to tear his own clothes. Rhodri shook his head and thought of what Homeira had said of the world being a dark and dangerous place. The waters rippled again, and there was the beautiful enchantress standing with Owen again, just as she had done before.

"Don't look so serious, Owen," she was saying, once more, "Come, tomorrow is the eve of your Christ's mass and we're friends at least, so let us eat and drink and laugh together. Then, in the morning, I will give you your sword again and send you safely on your way back to your loving wife and son."

She had turned toward the table and the jug of wine, but now Rhodri saw more. Saw what had happened. As she bent over it now in the Telling Pool and poured the wine, she lifted her right hand and touched her beautiful ruby ring. She pulled at the jewel and the ring itself opened. Homeira turned her hand gently, and a white powder came falling from it into the goblet like snow.

The water rippled and again Rhodri saw his father lying in that silken bed. But as he watched and night thickened in the cave, the witch rose from his side. At first her movements were as stealthy as a cat's, but then she turned toward Owen and began to shake him. He did not wake and Homeira smiled delightedly.

"Leave me, would you?" she said. "And scorn my love. Well, Falcon, we'll see. Now you shall taste my love, forever. And you shall taste my fury, too."

Homeira swung round and walked away to the recess by the lava. When she returned, she held the glittering glass casket in her hand, which she placed carefully on the table and opened the lid. Then Homeira turned back toward the bed.

"It's finished," she whispered, "and ready to hold its true prize."

She advanced on Owen. There was something in the way that dark-eyed beauty approached the sleeper that made Rhodri shudder to his bones. She looked like a thief, or a murderer. She hovered over his father and then slipped her hand inside her robes and drew something forth. When the boy saw what was hanging there above Owen, he cried out. It was the curved dagger he had seen by the casket.

"Pa. Wake up, Pa," shouted Rhodri.

But before he could plunge his head into the pool to warn his father, down the enchantress plunged the blade, down into Owen's chest and she laughed as she did so and pulled it low, like a man cutting open a sack of grain. Owen did not cry out or wake, but instead lay there like one drugged. The bloodied knife came up and Homeira dropped it on the bed. Her sleeves fell about her elbows as she lifted her arms and now she was kneeling over Owen, as if reaching inside his very being. Homeira struggled for a moment and then, rising with an exultant cry, turned back toward the casket.

When Rhodri saw what the smiling enchantress held, a horror so ghastly crept over him that he felt as if the blood were draining out of his own body. There in the witch's hands, as she approached the crystal casket, was Owen Falcon's beating heart.

It was as if Homeira had put on crimson gloves to carry it, for her hands dripped with his warm blood, and so carefully did she bear the thing in her stained fingers and place it in the casket, Rhodri thought of Owen holding a new owlet chick, its little body quivering in his palm.

"So, Owen Falcon," hissed the enchantress, closing the box with a snap, "with this enchantment you shall really feel the wounds of love. Feel them for the rest of your days."

She had picked up that long silver needle she had used to darn Owen's clothes, and licking the blood from her fingers, she began to thread some cotton. Then she was kneeling over Owen again and with the care of a seamstress stitching a magical dress, she started to sew shut his open chest.

The waters rippled, and there was Homeira standing with the heart in her hand, squeezing it. As she did so, Rhodri saw his father at home again in the yard. Pain and anger had gripped his features, just as Rhodri had seen in real life. Tighter and tighter she squeezed Owen's pumping heart in her slender fingers, and images swam up from the core of the Telling Pool.

Rhodri knew that he was looking on Owen's very thoughts and memories again. Megan as a young bride, radiant and lovely in her bridal gown; a child in a cot—Rhodri; Owen tasting a fig and kissing Homeira's bloodred lips. Then his memories became a barren desert. A horse lay dead on the track, an arrow through its eye. Then men were screaming and crying out and Christian and Saracen were there, side by side, begging for a mercy that never came.

"See," came Homeira's hissing voice, echoing around the grotto, "see all we do in life and despair. For you, Falcon, you too have done these things. And so you shall never escape my clutches."

It was as if Homeira were there at the edge of the Telling Pool, and Rhodri knew that she was squeezing the heart harder and harder. Rhodri shuddered and looked about him, but there was no one there. Only Homeira's haunting voice.

"Your heart," gloated the witch, "it can never be young and pure again. For you've tasted the bitter truth of the world, and its pleasures and sadness, too. But you can have love still. My love. Not the foolish love of hearth and home, but a love that burns the world."

She was leaning forward and whispering to Owen's heart, and it was as though in that moment she loved the very thing that she clutched there.

"Remember, my darling," Homeira said. "Remember the pleasures we tasted together. Remember my food and wine and the taste of my lips."

She raised her eyes, and now she was looking out of the waters of the Telling Pool, straight at Rhodri. The young man sat back in revulsion, and the stone where Arthur had once looked moved under him. For a moment he thought she had actually seen him, but then she leaned forward and did something so disgusting that Rhodri turned aside. She kissed that beating heart and put it away, safely in her casket, like a child's toy.

"A year and a day," she hissed, "and you were fool enough to think my bargain would be so easy. A year and a day it shall be, Falcon. But not as you think it. Not with you resisting my call, but with your heart trapped inside my magic casket. For if it stays locked inside for that time, then you shall be my slave forever and ever."

Homeira began to laugh.

"No," cried Rhodri. "No."

The boy felt cold sweat run down his neck as the witch screamed laughter. He jumped up from the Seeing Place and ran up those steps to Tantallon's house. He went inside, but still no one was there. As he waited, he felt a great weariness overcome him again and sat on the cot. He lay back, and in no time at all he had fallen fast asleep. Homeira was there in his dream, and now the young man felt truly appalled by her. She was coming closer and closer and there was blood on her lips. Rhodri woke with a jolt. There, in the doorway, stood Tantallon.

"You've found what you seek, Rhodri Falcon?" the hermit asked as he came inside. Rhodri blushed.

"Yes, Tantallon. I searched for you. But you were not here."

The old man smiled. "I . . . I was collecting herbs. But I told you that you are always welcome to use your power at the Telling Pool. Tell me what you saw."

"The witch," said Rhodri, "she's a liar. Her bargain was false."

The old man crouched down and listened gravely.

"I feared it," he said, as Rhodri finished, "the casket and that dagger were forged in the heat of . . . of her enchanted well. It is a mighty spell."

"How my father lives," wondered Rhodri, "I don't understand."

"What are you going to do, Rhodri?" asked Tantallon.

"I don't know. Talk to him."

"He doesn't know what has really happened to him," said the old man, "he'll not listen. And if you tell him all you know and have seen, that you know his secret, how will he take it? Not well, I think."

Rhodri nodded again and got up. He looked about him and suddenly felt a great fear in his stomach for what he was about to say.

"I must go then."

"Go?"

Rhodri thought of his home and then the dangerous world beyond the forest. Of traveling out and alone into a land racked with pain and sorrow. But life at home seemed hardly better now.

"Yes, Tantallon. To rescue my father's heart."

The hermit was silent.

"But there's something else," the boy said.

Tantallon raised his head immediately.

"This curse, Tantallon. Arthur and Guinevere. The land and all that happens. I tried to ignore it and my dreams. But all the while I felt guilty and I can't hide anymore. Though I don't know why, my fate is somehow bound up with this strange magic. So if I can help these souls in the cave, I will."

Tantallon's eyes seemed to be sparking with fire.

"I knew it," he said delightedly, "even when I first met you at the forge, boy. I knew I was not wrong about you. You have courage, and not all may sit where Arthur sat. So know this, Rhodri, Homeira's magic is powerful indeed, but with courage and faith and a true heart, a soul may defeat even the mightiest enchantments."

"In the pool," said Rhodri, "the Lady Guinevere told me to find it again. For all of us. But she didn't mean the Grail at all. She meant Mythyrion, didn't she? The sword, Excalibur."

There was something veiled in Tantallon's expression, but he nodded slowly.

"Forged in the fires that made the world. Worked with runes of the deepest magic. I told you that it represented a promise. And it has always waited, for a time of great danger to Albion. With Mythirion at your back, Homeira could not touch a hair on your head."

Rhodri shivered. "But where is the sword?"

"Its whereabouts were lost long ago, as I said, and even Merlin forgot the secret. That you must discover for yourself on your journey, if you can. The time grows short. It's been ten months since your father's return. Her wicked bargain will be up all too soon."

"Then I have only two months to find her, two months and a day."

"Yes, Rhodri. You've little time left, and from what you told me, the cave is far to the west. You must find it if you are to help the knights and your father."

"Then I must fly. Like a falcon."

"Wait," said the blind old man. Tantallon groped over to the end of the hovel, and when he returned he was holding a little skin satchel, with a leather strap, something like the bag Rhodri had seen Waylinn the blacksmith carry, although its edges seemed bound not with hemp but with vines.

"This is for you," said Tantallon softly, "I made it myself and it has power and health in it."

Rhodri hardly understood, but he took the thing gratefully nonetheless and put it over his shoulder.

"Tantallon. Will you not come with me?"

The old man smiled, but he shook his head.

"A blind old man would just slow you down," he answered. "This is your time, Rhodri Falcon. But I . . . My thoughts will be with you on your quest. And Rhodri, you think from what you've seen that the road may be hard. But remember, there'll always be friends on the way, if you know how to recognize them. Remember the art of seeing. I have something else for you, too."

Now Tantallon hobbled over to the cupboard where the golden headpiece lay, and from inside he withdrew a little glass bottle. It looked like one of the vials the apothecary had been carrying, but the liquid inside was completely clear.

"What is it?" asked Rhodri as Tantallon held it out to him.

"Water," whispered the hermit, "from the Telling Pool. Take it, lad. It, too, may aid you in your quest."

Rhodri took the thing and slipped it inside his tunic.

"But remember, never drink of it. And see well," said Tantallon. "But remember, too, whatever you do, watch everything that happens. Miss nothing. Your life and your very soul may depend on it. For if you find her, she will surely try to enchant you, too."

Rhodri turned toward the door. As he left, he did not see Tantallon walk over to the corner of the hut, to that hourglass. He did not see the old hermit stoop and upend the thing, or the sand begin to run down within the globe.

"Time," whispered the old man. "All things are revealed in time. All of us are part of its mystery."

Nor as he hurried away did Rhodri see the figure in the wood, watching the hovel from the trees. A figure who had been watching and following Rhodri since that day outside the church. Aelfric.

It was night by the time Rhodri reached home, carrying the pouch Tantallon had given him. His parents were in bed, and as soon as the boy opened the door, he saw that his father was deep in anguished dreams. He padded upstairs, and as quickly as he could, he packed his bag. He stopped at the window and, for a moment, looked down fondly on the stream that had been the friend of his dreams for so long. Then he went downstairs again, and drawing a chair toward the hearth, he reached up and unhooked the broadsword that had seen so much suffering in the Holy Lands. His reflection flickered on the blade. It was lighter than it had been, for Rhodri had grown much. The young man slung it across his back, and after making up a pack of food from the larder, he headed straight for the door.

"Rhodri. Where are you going, Rhodri *bach*?"

Megan had woken, but Owen was still deep in sleep. Rhodri turned.

"Hush, Ma. I'm going on a journey. And when I return, all will be well again, I promise you that. Pa will know us once more and you will be happy. We will all be happy again."

"Oh, Rhodri."

"Ma, I'm sorry I cannot tell you more, but you must trust me. Now sleep."

Megan's fine eyes were sad. Mother and son had grown close in the time Owen was away, and Megan had great faith in her son, in the brave and loyal man he was becoming. Now she nodded.

With that, Rhodri turned and walked through the door of their home and closed it behind him. He went straight up to the barn, where Melanor screeched in his sealed cage. Rhodri bent down and took out his dagger. He thrust it between the bars and began to pull angrily at the wood. There was a crack, and one of the nailed wooden bars snapped in two.

"You think I'd go without you, Melanor?" said Rhodri as he reached inside. "I go on a great quest and I need any friends I can get. But friends I can trust. Perhaps your eyes and your talons will help us."

The bird stepped onto his fist as if he had understood, and Rhodri drew out the rock falcon carefully.

"I'm sorry I can't take you, too," said Rhodri, looking at Glindor and Breeze. He used some twine to replace the wooden bar, locking them in the mew once more.

Rhodri crossed the yard and made for the big field. A morning dew was already on the ground, beading the quivering grass with the sheen of crystal, and everything around the boy and the bird—the stream and the earth, the fields and trees, the air and the very stars themselves—seemed to be whispering to them with the passion and power and glory of life. Rhodri looked across the fields and caught sight of the miller's little house and he fancied he saw Sarah in the yard. His heart ached, and he wanted to go to her and tell her that he had been unkind in his thoughts and believed wrongly that she had given away his gift. He wanted to stand with her, too, and have her hold his hand and wish him God's speed on his quest, but he turned away.

Rhodri Falcon knew what he had to do. That he had to journey out, out into the wild and dangerous world, and find Mythirion and face the witch. That he had to smash that horrible casket and free his father and the knights from the cave. He knew now, too, what Tantallon's first gift had been for. It was to carry back his father's beating heart.

12 ❖ QUEST

Swift as a spirit hastening to his task
Of glory and of good, the Sun sprang forth
Rejoicing in his splendour
—Percy Bysshe Shelley, "The Triumph of Life"

Rhodri and Melanor took the path along the forest that the Falcons had taken long ago on the day of the fair. By the time the great sun rose, flecking the clouds with pink and giving the night's gloomy shadows shape and form and color, they had passed the ford and were already a long way from home.

As Rhodri had passed the ford, as far as he had ever traveled on his own before, the very limits of his experience, the sun blazed brilliantly and a sudden rush of excitement and possibility had overtaken him. He felt his chest swell with pride at what he was setting out to face, and he had the feeling, too, that, although he had never been allowed to go to the Holy Lands, now he faced a quest far graver.

For two whole days, Rhodri and Melanor met no one on the road. In the distance they saw many serfs working in the fields, for it was the end of the harvest and all hands were set to garnering the fruits of sunlight and earth, but they stayed clear of them.

It was the afternoon of the third day when Rhodri saw three horsemen coming round a bend in the track. He did not have time to make for cover and instead reached up and pulled off Melanor's hood. Melanor screeched and opened his wings, just as Rhodri had intended, and the young man lifted his head and pushed out his chest and kept walking.

The strangers' horses were in a poor condition and the men were dressed roughly. Their faces looked as if they had spent a long time in the open, and two had daggers at their belts. Rhodri didn't like the look of them at all, but they seemed put off by the bird and the young man's sword and passed him by.

Rhodri sighed with relief, but for a good while he kept looking back to see if they had changed their minds. When twilight came again, a deeper doubt stirred in him and rather than make a bed among the leaves, he climbed high into a tree and lodged himself and Melanor there to sleep. Darkness fell quickly, but Rhodri had hardly touched the edge of dreams when he felt Melanor flapping and woke to hear voices just below him.

"Where the hell can they have got to?"

It was the men from that afternoon, leading their horses by the reins. The speaker had a strong Welsh accent and Rhodri thought he had heard one of their voices somewhere before.

"I'm sure he came this way," said another, "I saw prints back there."

"Well, he can't have gone that far in the darkness. And when we catch him, he won't be going nowhere again."

"Why didn't we just take him on the road?"

"Too dangerous in the daylight. But there was something about him, too, something about his eyes. I didn't care for the look of that bird, neither, or that sword. It had seen some action all right, and the lad looked as if he had, too."

"But it's the bird we want?"

"It's worth a small fortune, by the look of it. You know how fine folk love their falconing. He must be a Norman lad. That sword'll fetch a pretty penny, too. If we sell them both, we'll eat like kings at the coming Christ mass. The forests belong to us now."

"Hey, look. He came this way all right."

One of the men had stooped to pick up something. It was Rhodri's antler dagger, which had fallen from his belt as he climbed the tree. Rhodri's heart was in his mouth as he feared they might look up, but the man thrust it into his belt and the voices passed away.

The young man lay there against the branch, shaking and frightened, but deeply relieved that he had climbed the tree. He knew that although he had a sword, he hadn't a chance against three grown men and he suddenly wished that his father were at his side. Then he remembered Owen's hand across his face and grew so lonely and angry that he felt like a child again, lost at the fair.

Rhodri wrapped his arms tight around the bark and felt the moss soft and comforting against his cheek. The rock falcon stirred, and from the forest the voice of a lone wolf rose, piercing and dangerous and hungry in the night.

"Oh, Melanor," said the young man sadly, "when my quest is over we'll be safe and home again with Mother and Father."

• • •

After an uncomfortable night in the tree, Rhodri stirred earlier than sunrise, for he knew that the robbers would have had to camp nearby and he wanted to use the first faint light before dawn to find his way around them. He didn't see the villains anywhere, and by sunup he was feeling cheerful and confident again.

He and Melanor had left the path behind them. It was midday when they came upon another track in the forest and a sight that made Rhodri wary again. The men coming down the path through the trees were all heavily armed. It took a moment for Rhodri to realize that it was just a train of ordinary travelers. There must have been forty of them, some on horse, and others in carriages, still more on foot. It was a colorful sight, so many folk in the wood, and Rhodri was pleased not to be alone.

"Good day to you," cried one, as he passed Rhodri on the edge of the path. He was a fat, jolly man with a ruddy face, a little like the pardoner's at St. Martin's Day, and speaking in a Saxon accent. The fellow stopped and looked admiringly at Melanor, though warily, too.

"You're bold to travel alone in the wood in such times," said the Englishman, "or foolhardy. Many would envy such a splendid hawk."

Rhodri didn't correct the fellow.

"With so much trouble in the country, this train has come together for safety in the forests, and I for one am glad to be part of it."

"What path do you take?" asked Rhodri.

"We all have our own paths," answered the man, "some to their villages, others to the castle below. Most go into the West. Why don't you step in with us?"

Since they indeed appeared to be going southwest like Rhodri intended himself, he nodded and fell in gladly beside the man. He was called Gothric and seemed friendly enough. He didn't ask too many questions, either, and Rhodri was greatly relieved to have left the cutthroats behind them. But as they walked, Rhodri found Gothric was beginning to limp and was soon dropping behind.

"It's the gout," the fat man puffed, touching his thigh as he noticed Rhodri looking at his leg. "It troubles me greatly, lad. Too much beer and sac, I suppose. If such a thing's possible. The pleasures they bring are great, but so, too, is the price the body must pay."

They were at the back of the train now, or almost at the back, because behind them and traveling as if not part of the group at all, was a battered old cart, drawn by a single dappled horse. A little old man was seated in it as it lurched along, and he was dressed in the strangest manner Rhodri had ever seen, for his white hair was curled in little ringlets that fell all about his face and his robe was black like a priest. On the top of his head he wore a little leather cap, which he adjusted now, and next to him in the cart sat a girl of sixteen or seventeen.

"Why don't they catch up with us, Gothric?" asked Rhodri, as they walked along.

"Because they're not welcome in this train, I suppose," answered

Gothric, shrugging, and his voice dropping to almost a whisper. "The others call them Christ killers, boy. They're Jews."

Rhodri shivered, but now he found himself looking back constantly, wondering about something as exotic as a Jew.

"I'd welcome them right enough," said Gothric cheerfully, "but it doesn't do to go against the crowd these days."

Apart from the strange attire, to Rhodri they seemed ordinary enough and although he couldn't see her fully, the girl looked pretty, with a thin, proud profile and long dark hair.

Rhodri set his mind on the road ahead, but close to evening there was a cursing and a dreadful splintering noise behind them. The Jews' cart had skewed to one side and was leaning over badly. The cart had hit a large stone in the path and the left wheel had come off its axle. The old Jew climbed down and began struggling with it, cursing and spitting as he did so. It was plain that he would never manage to mend the thing on his own, but although a few had stopped to look back, the train of travelers seemed little interested in the commotion and kept on their march.

"We should help them," said Rhodri.

"Well I would," said Gothric, "but the leader of the train is a God-fearing Christian and he wouldn't really like . . ."

Rhodri remembered Tantallon's words, and the blind old man struggling with his burden of wood.

"Well, I'll help, damn it. Here, Gothric, hold Melanor for me."

Gothric stepped back, but Rhodri had already placed Melanor on his arm, and Gothric froze, quaking and puffing out his cheeks as the rock falcon flapped its wings.

"I can't stay here," spluttered Gothric. "The train will move on without us and it's nearly dinnertime."

"Then go with them, Gothric," grunted Rhodri. "I'll catch up with you later."

"But what of your hawk?"

Rhodri smiled. "Calm yourself and your breathing and he'll learn to trust you, perhaps. Take him on ahead. And don't fear. We understand each other. He'll not fly away."

Rhodri hurried off toward the cart. The old man was bending in the mud as he approached. The boy smiled at the girl, but as soon as he did Rhodri stopped in amazement. It couldn't be. It was the same face he had seen in the Telling Pool, with those beautiful, sad eyes and straight black hair. He had seen the future.

Rhodri said nothing and instead leaned down and tried to help the old man lift the wheel. He looked up in surprise, but his sour, suspicious expression did not change.

"What are you wanting here?"

The man's voice was heavy and thick, for the language of England was not the tongue of his youth and Rhodri thought the man sounded almost like Homeira.

"To help, sir."

"Thieve from us, more like," snapped the Jew, "or slit our throats, and worse."

"No," said Rhodri indignantly.

"You're being a Christian, no?" said the old man coldly.

"Yes, I suppose I am."

"And when have I heard of the gentile helping one of our race? Never, that's when. Do you expect me to be believing in miracles?"

"No," answered Rhodri, "I just wanted to offer you . . ."

"I need nothing from your kind," said the old man angrily. "I'm taking nothing and ask nothing in return. Is that not the only way to walk the world in peace? Leave us be, Christian."

The horse had been startled by the accident, and now she began to stamp.

"Hush, Jezamel," cried the Jew.

Rhodri stepped up to Jezamel and began to stroke her throat and the animal grew calmer immediately at his touch.

"Leave us be," said the Jew gruffly.

As he spoke again the girl jumped down next to Rhodri. The way she looked at him, not so much at his eyes but at his forehead, as if she herself were searching with something other than her eyes, reminded him of his first meeting with Tantallon in the smithy and he remembered, too, Tantallon's words about recognizing a friend on the road.

"Father, please. This young man is only trying to help us."

"Hush your tongue, Rebecca."

"But, Father, you'll never manage that wheel alone."

Rebecca smiled at Rhodri gratefully, and he liked her voice, for it was soft and gentle and very pleasant to listen to.

"Then you'll be helping your father, Daughter, before you make us our dinner. We take nothing from Christians. I've told you a thousand times."

Rhodri felt insulted that this old man should so scorn his offer of help, and in front of the pretty girl, his pride suddenly rallied.

"Well, sir," he said indignantly, "if you don't want my aid, I won't force it on you. I meant you no harm, but it seems there is no trust in the forests."

"Father, please."

Rhodri turned and strode away, but he heard the old man's voice behind him. It had grown calmer and Rhodri fancied there was a grudging humility in it.

"Very well, then. If you'll be aiding us, this once I will accept. It'll be night soon and my daughter and I travel alone, with none to protect us."

At first, Rhodri had no intention of helping the unpleasant old man, but as he turned and looked back, he saw that the girl was gazing at him imploringly. Rhodri knew he had to help her, and with a shrug he walked back to them.

"Don't be expecting any payment, mind," said the Jew coldly, "but my thanks. I have no coins."

Rhodri nodded and they lifted the wheel together. The young man felt another rush of pride as Rebecca watched him shoulder the wheel back onto its axle. As they replaced it, he noticed that near the axle an odd plank of wood had been nailed to the cart, and he wondered what it was for. As the old man saw him staring at it, he seemed to grow agitated and shoved the wheel even harder. Rhodri helped him hammer it back into place, and then the Jew grunted and got back into his seat on the cart. He looked at Rhodri for a moment and, nodding curtly, flicked the reins and the cart rattled away.

Rhodri was furious that the Jew had not said thank you properly, and now he was all alone again, far behind the other travelers. All because he had offered to help. Rhodri was shaking his head and wondering how far off Gothric and Melanor were, when he saw the cart stop. Rebecca jumped down and came running back to him.

"Please forgive my father," she said in that gentle voice, touching

Rhodri's arm. "He has rough manners perhaps, and trusts few. He's grateful in his heart. Father says that you may ride with us and eat with us tonight, too. If you're not frightened of what your own kind will think."

Rhodri smiled, and together the young people ran back to the cart. They clambered up beside the old man and rattled away.

"Well then," the Jew grunted, as they sat there, "I'm known as Isaac and this my daughter, Rebecca. Tell us your name, gentile, and what you do traveling alone in these forests, in such wicked days."

"They call me Rhodri Falcon, Sir. I'm . . . I journey southwest. To seek . . . to seek my way in the world."

Rhodri felt uncomfortable at the lie.

"And have you no parents?"

"Yes indeed," answered Rhodri, wondering how far he had come now and what was happening at the farm. He suddenly felt very worried for his mother.

Isaac grunted. "A good son should be tending to them, if you're asking me, not going off for adventures, or to seek his fortune."

Rhodri smiled resignedly and Rebecca noticed the look.

"Hush, father," she said. "Is it polite to talk to a stranger so?"

"Perhaps not, girl, but they have odd ways indeed, these Christians," said the old man, looking warily at Rhodri's sword. "So keen to fight and kill in the name of their Savior, but so careless of love in their hearts and the duty they owe their elders."

Rhodri wanted to defend himself, but he could hardly tell them where he was really going or why, so he just sat there in silence, resenting this strange old man more and more.

"And how many years have you, boy?" asked Isaac rudely.

For some reason, as he sat next to Rebecca, Rhodri chose to lie again. "Seventeen."

"Old enough," grunted the Jew. "And how do you plan to make your way in such a dark world?"

"I've skills," answered the young man proudly, "and I'm trained in falconry. One day I hope to be a master falconer, like my father. My bird's up ahead."

The old man sucked the air into his mouth and made a strange clicking sound. He looked impressed.

"Falconry? And not a bad way to make coin and serve a lord. Even a Christian lord."

"You talk of Christians as if you hated us all," said Rhodri.

"And so I do," snapped Isaac. "You're young still and know nothing of the real world, boy."

Rhodri thought with a smile of all he had already seen in the Telling Pool.

"You helped us and I thank you for it. Perhaps your home has taught you other ways, compared to many men. But why should I be feeling any love for the Christians? The Christians who treat the Jews like animals. Who herd us into ghettos. Who allow us to raise gold for them on the edge of their towns and then scourge us as moneylenders and usurers."

Rhodri reddened.

"Who hunt us and kill us when it suits them. The Lionheart was not bad to us it is true, but now he's gone, his brother John schemes with your Church and we Jews pay a heavy price."

As Rhodri listened to the angry old man, pictures of far-off places and of other lives were forming in his head, just like the images he had seen in the Telling Pool.

Isaac pulled hard on the reins.

"I'm tired, Rebecca," he grunted, "and will sleep a time. Wake me, Daughter, when we're nearing the train again. It will be safer to camp near them, even if they are Christians."

"Yes, Father."

Isaac got up and pulled back the curtain behind them. Rhodri got a glimpse into the cart. All around the two rough beds were hung rich cloths, and in a shelf sat a number of beautiful books, like the Bible Rhodri had opened in church. On a little table in the center of the caravan stood an odd candlestick, with seven arms to it and next to it a fine patterned wooden box. Isaac scowled at Rhodri as he saw him peering into the cart inquisitively and he pulled the curtain angrily shut behind him. As Rhodri turned back Rebecca was taking up the reins. He smiled and stopped her.

"Here, Rebecca, let me."

"No, thank you. I can do it."

She shook the reins firmly and the cart rolled on, as the two young people sat there side by side and Rhodri grew more and more glad of such pretty company.

"You must forgive Father's talk, Rhodri," the girl said softly, after a while, "but we've seen much suffering on our road. We came into your lands but six years ago, and last year my mother . . ."

Rhodri saw her face grow sad.

"My mother died of fever. They'd been together, side by side, for thirty years and he misses her deeply. I'm all he has now, but sometimes the loss eats at his heart."

Rhodri felt sorry for the old man, but then his thoughts turned to his own mother and father, and Homeira, squeezing her hand tighter and tighter in the cave.

"You look so sad, Rhodri," said Rebecca. "There's something troubling you. Is it your journey?"

Rhodri straightened. "No."

"But I know there's something."

"Know?" the young man said. "How do you know?"

Rebecca smiled softly.

"Men talk and rule in the world," she answered, laughing, "and think women stupid, as we do the work. But in the shadows we learn much, too. Above all I've learned to watch and listen before speaking, and to read what the eyes and the body tell me. For words cover up as much as they reveal."

Rhodri wanted to trust this girl and to tell her all that was in his heart, of his desperate quest, but something held him back still.

"There's something special about you, Rhodri Falcon," said Rebecca. "I noticed it as soon as you came over. Something about your manner and your eyes. As though you've seen far more than your years. And some secret, I think."

Still Rhodri said nothing, though once again he was thinking of her face in the Telling Pool. There was something about Rebecca, too.

"My mother," the girl said, since Rhodri didn't answer, "she always taught me to look for that in people, Rhodri Falcon. Whether Christian or Jew, Moselman or Barbarian. To look at all of a person, before judging them. And to seek their third eye."

"Third eye?"

"Here," said Rebecca, touching her hand to her forehead, "the inner eye. That sees more than outward things. That can see what is truly inside a person. But don't tell Father I said this," she added cheerfully. "He'd probably beat me if he heard me speak thus, for it is against our faith and Father is very devout."

Rhodri smiled, impressed with the girl for talking so openly like this about her own father.

"You honor him though?" he asked.

"Of course I honor him," answered Rebecca, "and more than that, I love him. But that doesn't mean that he's always right, or that I must believe all he says."

No, thought Rhodri, I suppose it doesn't. He thought of Owen again, striking him that terrible day and demanding a respect he couldn't give. With that the cart rounded the bend and they came to a clearing where the rest of the train had drawn up and begun to make their encampment for the night. But rather than drive the cart straight toward them, Rebecca guided it to the edge of the clearing, on its own. Fires were flickering everywhere, and from the ring of branch and leaf the sound of voices and musical instruments echoed hauntingly through the forest. Raucous laughter burst from a group of travelers, and over an open flame, three men were spit-roasting a whole pig, filling the air with the scent of charcoal and sizzling meat.

Once the cart stopped, Rebecca went inside to stir her father and begin the supper, and Rhodri jumped down and looked around. On the edge of the train he noticed Gothric sitting among a group of other travelers and holding up a heavy leather wine bag in his fat hands. They were talking together, and as Rhodri drew closer he was relieved to see Melanor tethered safely in a tree.

"They never took back the Holy City," one of the travelers was saying, "so what use were their blessed wars anyway?"

"Well, maybe not, but they took the city of Acre and slaughtered enough damned heathen on the road for a lifetime," said another, "and ten thousand papal indulgences."

"Perhaps. But meanwhile King Richard rots in prison and seeks in vain to raise a king's ransom. A quarter of each man's wages is being asked, and they say it'll take the rest of the year. One hundred and fifty thousand marks."

One of the travelers whistled. "The king is in the East?" he asked.

"No. They say the Austrian duke caught him and handed him over to the German king, Henry. Someone betrayed Richard's whereabouts and Henry ransoms him now. But if Richard's brother John has anything to do with it, that will never happen. The king will rot in his cell and die there, too, and then what'll become of Albion?"

"Enough of politics," said another man. "Tell us a tale."

Rhodri wanted to sit down by the fire and listen to a good yarn, as he had done as a boy, but he needed to journey on in the night. He had so little time to complete his quest.

Gothric looked up and smiled at Rhodri, but one of the others, a brute of a man with oily brown hair, kicked the fire with his foot, sending up a shower of sparks, and glared at him and spat. They were all looking angrily at the cart now, set off among the trees. Rhodri turned to Gothric for some kind of help, but the jolly fellow simply dropped his eyes and was silent in front of the others. Rhodri felt deeply ashamed of him.

Without saying anything, he lifted Melanor from his perch and, not even acknowledging Gothric, turned his back on the men and returned to the cart. He felt that anger burning inside him again. The young man was so ready to trust the world. To share in its magic and life and adventure. But all he had met on the way so far was distrust and villainy and hate.

Rebecca had lit a fire behind the cart and set a great pot over it. A delicious smell of bubbling stew was coming from the pot, and the girl was singing a melancholy song as she stirred it. She looked even lovelier in the dancing flames, but Rhodri's heart was dull. He knelt down with Melanor and sat quietly watching the fire.

"It's a fine bird, Rhodri," said Rebecca. "What is it?"

"A rock falcon, Rebecca. I trained him myself."

She put down the spoon and walked over to them. "May I stroke his head?"

"Be careful. He can peck."

"Why does he wear that hood?" the girl asked as she gently tickled his neck feathers.

"To keep him calm. Sometimes what he sees makes him wild."

"I'd like to see his face."

Rhodri reached up and lifted the braided hood. Now Melanor's huge eyes were looking about, and Rebecca reached forward to stroke his little feathered head. The bird neither screeched in surprise nor opened its wings, but just sat there calmly, thoroughly enjoying the attention.

"He likes you, Rebecca. He must trust you, too."

"And I him," she whispered warmly. "Perhaps we may be friends. He's very tame."

"Oh, no," laughed Rhodri, "Melanor's wild. Like all birds of prey. Friends you may be, if he trusts you, but you may never truly own a wild falcon, for they stay with you only as they please."

"I'd like to see you hunt him, Rhodri."

From within the cart Rhodri heard a strange sound. Isaac was speaking, but in no tongue the young man had ever heard before, and as he listened, he realized he must be praying. As the chant came it sounded full of longing and mourning and Rhodri thought how beautiful it was.

Yet as the rough, cheerful voices of Christian travelers came from the train, too, speaking both in Saxon and in Norman French, Rhodri felt a confusion he had never known before. The young man thought of all he had heard in the church of Jews, and he felt a little guilty that he was sitting here with these strangers. Yet there was nothing about Rebecca that seemed wicked or evil, and the men by the fire had looked so cruelly toward the old man and his daughter, without even knowing the truth of it, that he felt ashamed of his own kind. Rhodri felt a kind of tearing ache in his stomach, for something in him wanted to be part of the group, of his own, yet he was angry at what the others had said and he did not want to be untrue to that anger, either.

"You must go your own way in life, Rhodri Falcon," said Rebecca suddenly. "We'll understand if you wish to sup with your own people."

Rhodri was amazed that this girl seemed to have read his very thoughts, and it made him think of Tantallon again.

"No," he said quietly, "we'll eat with you, Rebecca."

"Be careful, Rhodri," said the girl softly and she smiled warmly at him, "for an open heart such as yours can bring you much trouble in a troubled world. There are easier ways to be safe in life. Father and I will think none the less of you if you go over to the others, for the longer you stay with us, the more they will talk and hate you."

"Hate me?" asked Rhodri.

"I've known their hate all my life," said Rebecca, looking straight into his hazel eyes. "Sometimes, when we travel through towns, they throw stones at the cart, or laugh at Father's clothes, or try to steal our coin and books."

She shook her head with sorrow.

"When some look out on the world, all they see is ugliness. But you have to see better than that."

"Well," said Rhodri, though he had no confidence that he could be of any use, "Melanor and I will keep watch tonight, I'll leave his hood off. Nothing will happen to you, I promise. But tell me Rebecca, where are you going?"

The girl looked embarrassed.

"We travel to a town on a river in the English lands," she whispered. "Where some of our people journeyed years ago."

"Where you'll be safe again, with your own kind?"

"I suppose so," she answered, and a look of deep distress crept into her face again, the same distress Rhodri had seen in the Telling Pool. She bowed her head.

"What's wrong, Rebecca?"

"Oh, Rhodri. Perhaps I can tell you. My father's arranged for me to be married there. To one of our faith. But I know nothing of him. What he's like. If he's kind or cruel, stupid or foolish. And I'm too young to be married yet."

Rhodri felt desperately sorry for the thoughtful girl, and he wondered at the power that parents had over their own.

With that, the curtain at the back of the cart was pulled open and there stood Isaac, looking warily all about him. Again he looked sullenly at Rhodri, although his eyes seemed impressed with Melanor and especially the little braided hood that Rhodri was holding.

The old man said nothing as he stepped down and shuffled over to the fire. Rebecca had already gone back to it to ladle out some of the stew into wooden bowls, and she handed her father one. It steamed deliciously as he took up his spoon and began to gobble it down, the thick, beefy gravy staining his knotted beard.

Rebecca gave Rhodri a bowl of stew, too, and he drew closer to the warm fire to eat. Isaac looked at the young man rather resentfully as he ate their food, but Rhodri was too famished to notice much, or to care, either.

"That's better, Daughter," said Isaac, smacking his lips as he finished. "You'll make a fine wife, my girl, and a good wife should always know the way to her husband's stomach."

Rebecca was looking at Rhodri, and the wily old man noticed it immediately.

"Mind your eyes, girl."

Rebecca dropped her gaze obediently, but her slender mouth was set hard and defiant as she toyed with the stew in her bowl.

"You're a willful girl, Rebecca," grunted Isaac, "and I know the secrets of your heart, child. You resent your father because you think it unfair I should tell you what to do. So it is with all children. But children do not know the world and its wicked ways. You'll be happy once it's finished and the man you go to marry has gold, too, which'll help your father to some comfort in his old age."

"Yes, Father."

Rhodri kicked out his foot. He wanted to argue with the old man, yet he did not think it his place. Instead he picked up a piece of meat and gave it to Melanor, but Isaac had seen his look, too.

"Too many people," he growled, "especially Christians with their courtly ways, think that love is the path to happiness. But love and passion fade like the fire on a hearth, and then what is left to warm you, but the rugs and clothes you have in your home?"

"But, Father," said Rebecca imploringly, "I don't even know this boy I'm to marry. Not even you have met him."

Rebecca's voice was indignant and her eyes flaring, but she blushed, too, in front of Rhodri.

"Tush, girl," said Isaac. "Silly fears, of a silly foolish heart. You'll thank me one day soon, and from all I've heard, he's not that unhandsome. You'll grow to like him, to love him even, and I'll live with you both in your house."

"But, Father," said the girl pleadingly, "you loved mother. And she you. You chose each other."

A look of such deep sorrow crept into Isaac's eyes that Rhodri felt sad for him, too, but when he spoke his old voice was still angry. "And you think you're so rich that you've many to choose of our race in Albion?" said Isaac. "Or perhaps you'd roam elsewhere with that wild, lawless heart of yours . . ."

Rebecca blushed again. "Please, Father, don't speak like—"

"The rabbi shall hear of it, girl," snapped Isaac, "and you'll say your prayers to him and beg forgiveness for such wicked thoughts. Now go, and fetch me my heavy coat and my book."

Rebecca got up and did as she was told. When she returned, even though she was still angry, she put the coat very carefully around her father's shoulders and then handed him a large leather book, which the old man opened and began to read from. After a time, he noticed Rhodri was watching him.

"You've such books in your home?" asked Isaac.

Rhodri felt bitterly ashamed that he could not read. "No, sir."

"Hmmm. Well, this is a work of very great learning. The first part is on geometry and the movements of the stars. I was given it by my father, who bought it from a Moselman of the East. It's by a famous Moselman writer named Al Raza."

"A Moselman writer?" asked Rhodri, looking at it warily.

The old Jew smiled.

"You Christians," he grunted, "so full of pride and self righteousness. You think that the heathen have not learning equal to yours? Far greater than yours. The Moselmen have great thinkers among them. And more civilization than any of your Christian knights. They've more kindness, too, for under their rule in the Holy Lands, were not all faiths tolerated, and Jew and Christian allowed to live amongst the men and women of Islam in peace? As people of the Book."

Rhodri said nothing, but he was remembering what Homeira had shown his father in the lava pool, of the Christian knight who had chosen to live among his enemy.

"Until the murderous Christians," said Isaac, "hungry for land and power and plunder, came surging from the West like jackals."

Rhodri felt dizzy with all he was hearing, and the world seemed such a complex place he hardly cared to understand it at all. He just wanted his journey over and his father's heart returned. He wanted to be safely home again with his parents.

"The second part of the book," said Isaac, turning over one of the pages, "is on the nature of the body. Of the secrets of dissection and the organs of life. It answers great questions, that thinkers have debated over the years. What makes a man live and where in the body the soul of a person really resides."

Rhodri thought of the heart locked in that terrible box and those souls in the cave. The sands of time were running down on his quest, with each guilty moment he delayed. But Isaac yawned and got up and, putting the book under his arm, wished the boy a curt good night. Rebecca had gone inside to fetch Rhodri a blanket, and now she came over to him.

"Here. To keep you warm tonight."

"Thank you, Rebecca."

"I'm sorry, Rhodri, for embarrassing you earlier."

"You didn't," said Rhodri, "but Rebecca, if you're so unhappy, isn't there one thing you could do?"

"What's that, Rhodri Falcon?" asked Rebecca nervously.

"Run away."

She was silent for a while, but then she smiled sadly.

"And leave my father alone? No. I love life and my freedom, but I love him, too."

Rhodri fell silent. He was thinking of his own parents, and his heart ached with care. But the feeling was not as clear as it had been before. He felt as though this thing he had set out to defeat was a terrible burden, and he suddenly longed to know who he really was. But as he dropped his eyes, Rebecca smiled at him.

"That's a fine amulet," she said, looking at the heirloom around his neck. "I was looking at in the firelight earlier. Sometimes the shape, it reminds me of a wild deer."

Rhodri looked up at her in astonishment. Words came back to him, and the memory of Guinevere in the pool and her strange cloak. The Path of the Deer. He had seen Rebecca herself in the water. Was she somehow meant to tell him this? Rhodri was trembling now. Rebecca stepped closer and reached out to touch his hand.

"Thank you for what you did for us today, Rhodri."

The girl was dipping her head. She kissed him lightly on the lips. Rhodri felt a tingling throughout his whole body and blushed so deeply his face seemed as hot as the fire. For a moment he was terrified that Rebecca might laugh at him for it, but when he looked into her dark, soft eyes, she held his gaze openly, looking at him admiringly and squeezing his hand. Then she kissed him again.

Rhodri felt as if his whole body were blending with hers. He suddenly wasn't himself anymore. He was something much bigger. Much greater. It was like plunging his head into the Telling Pool and becoming a part of the whole world. As Rhodri opened his eyes, it seemed to him that Rebecca's beautiful face had changed, that she was something other that the girl in the cart. As if she had become pure spirit, and in the corner of his eye he thought he saw the silhouette of two shapes among the trees, watching him.

"Good night, Rhodri Falcon. Sleep well," Rebecca whispered, as she pulled back. "And good night, Melanor."

She went inside the cart where her father lay. The young man stood there, and it was as if all the cares of the past months, of nearly three long years since his father had set out for the Holy Lands, were lifted from him. His body felt strong and alive, and he realized that he was aware of everything about him. The scent of wood smoke and meat, of leaf and branch, came powerfully to the young man. He could feel the air on his skin and the breeze whispering in the wood, and he felt as tall as a tree. He looked up, and above his head, through the canopy of the forest, he saw the stars, like a jeweler's casket flung across the giant heavens. In that moment he remembered Tantallon.

"The Miracle," whispered Rhodri.

13 ❖ RHODRI'S DILEMMA

'Courage!' he said, and pointed toward the land
Alfred, Lord Tennyson, "The Lotos-Eaters"

For eleven more days they traveled together, and all Rhodri wished was to draw closer to the witch and push time on before him and his quest. What Rebecca had said of his amulet had set grave questions in Rhodri's mind, too, and made him think again of the voices and his dreams. Several times Rhodri thought of telling Rebecca of his journey. Of telling her, too, that he had seen her before in the water and that somehow their destinies were intertwined.

But each time, Rhodri remembered that he had promised Tantallon to keep it all secret. He had broken his word once, and now he held his peace. It pained him, for Isaac kept grumbling on about the thanklessness and ingratitude of children, and what duty they owed their parents. Isaac was aware, too, that something had passed between his daughter and the stranger, and he always kept an eye on them, never once letting them out of his sight.

Meanwhile Rhodri had begun to think more deeply of Mythirion, and although the very thought of finding it thrilled through his being, he had no idea at all where it might lie. He thought of the story of the stone, and as they rode, he kept looking about hopefully at the rocks and boulders in the forest, as if it might suddenly appear to him, as his visions had appeared in the water. But the young man knew it was boyish foolishness.

It was a Sunday when they reached a crossroads in the forest and Isaac turned the cart directly to the south, away from the western train.

"You can come with us, lad, if you wish it," Isaac grunted. "You'd do better in a town. Your skill could bring a freeman much prestige."

Rhodri looked sadly at Rebecca and Isaac, but he shook his head.

"No, sir. The train goes on southwest and I must follow them."

He climbed down with Melanor on his arm.

"I'd like to come," he said. "Perhaps one day I'll tell you why I may not."

Isaac shrugged, but Rebecca dipped inside the cart. When she reappeared, she jumped down and ran boldly up to Rhodri.

"Take this," she said warmly, holding out her hand. She opened her palm and there was a little colored stone, almost in the shape of a heart.

"It's of no real value, Rhodri," she said, "but perhaps it'll remind you of our friendship and of me. I know that you go to face something dark, so be careful."

Rebecca leaned forward, even though Isaac was watching, but this time she kissed Rhodri on the cheek.

"What about you, Rebecca?" whispered Rhodri, wishing to stay with the lovely girl. "What about your . . . your marriage."

"I'll be all right," she answered, as cheerfully as she could, though her eyes showed she was lying. "Mother always said that the world is full of strange weaves and patterns of fate. Perhaps this man I go to marry has changed his mind, or a sickness has carried him off already. Life is uncertain, Rhodri Falcon, and who knows what we'll all meet on the road. And what we may learn from those meetings."

Again Rhodri felt how wise and grown-up Rebecca was. As she climbed back onto the cart, he knew it was time. "Farewell then, Rebecca."

Isaac flicked the reins, and the Jew and his daughter rattled away. Rebecca kept looking back over her shoulder at Rhodri and Melanor, until they were out of sight.

Rhodri felt a deep ache in his heart. The train had disappeared around the bend in the track, and Rhodri, putting his hand behind him first to check his sword, set purposefully on the road again. A dreadful loneliness surrounded him once more.

It was a few hours before he caught up with the others, and the young man felt very somber as he fell in line with some of the stragglers at the back. There was no sign of Gothric, or the men by the fire, and the walkers seemed to accept him and Melanor easily enough. In fact they hardly seemed to notice their presence at all. It was already twilight, when Rhodri heard two of them talking urgently together.

"I thought you go south, Edmund," said one. "I expected you to leave us at the crossroads."

"Didn't you hear what that traveler said?" whispered the man called Edmund, in the coming shadows. "That road's closed. A band of outlaws have been taking horse and gold. There's no safety anymore for an honest man."

"Is there ever?"

Rhodri drew closer to listen.

"But that old Jew and his daughter," said another of the travelers, "they took that way. Alone."

"Then good luck to 'em," said Edmund and he smiled, "and to the outlaws, too. If it's true what they say of so many Jews, then they should have rich pickings indeed."

"And that girl," said the man who had spoken first, "she's a fruit I'd like to pluck, all right. As ripe and pretty as a peach."

"Then why don't you help them?" cried Rhodri angrily. "Instead of talking."

The men turned in astonishment.

"Don't be foolish, lad," Edmund grunted.

"But they might be killed."

"Help them yourself, Waelas. You've a sword, haven't you?"

They all laughed and Rhodri, furious, dropped behind them. The train had come a long way from the crossroads, and Rebecca and Isaac were in a carriage that could travel perhaps four times as fast as a man on foot. They would already be too far off to catch. But guilt gripped Rhodri and he started to walk back down the track. He stopped again and turned round. It would take time to reach them, and time he did not have if he was to complete his quest.

An image flashed into Rhodri's mind. An image of his mother sobbing at their hearth, and then of Homeira laughing as she squeezed his father's bleeding heart. If Rhodri tried to help Rebecca and Isaac and something happened to him, then his father would never be free, let alone the knights in the cave. No, thought Rhodri, I cannot help them, and besides, Rhodri told himself, perhaps nothing would happen to Rebecca and Isaac at all. Isaac had hardly filled him with the sense that men helped each other much in the world either. He started walking after the train again.

He camped near the men who had spoken of the outlaws and, after eating some food, tethered Melanor on a branch and fell asleep. But immediately Rhodri found himself dreaming of Rebecca, and when he woke in the night, he felt so guilty that it was as if a kind of sickness had entered him. He couldn't just leave the girl and her father to be robbed or killed. A bitter choice faced Rhodri Falcon.

He told himself that more likely than not nothing had happened to them at all and that, anyway, if he hadn't overheard the men talking, he would have been none the wiser. Yet that was like what it might have been not to have looked into the Telling Pool at all. Then where would Rhodri be? Back, safe at home perhaps, but with his father growing angrier and angrier and with no knowledge of why or how to help him. The truth was that Rhodri did know there was danger for his friends on the road, just as he had looked into the Telling Pool and seen the truth of the cave and his father and the curse. That knowledge bound him to a different journey.

Rhodri fell asleep again and had a terrible dream. He had seen a bird in the forest, a bird that had changed into a man. The man had beckoned to him and then led him to a clearing at the other side of which stood a woman, robed in black. The air was thick with smoke, and all about the clearing lay bodies. The knights were all dead and their limbs had been hacked off. Arms and legs hung from the trees, and on a stone nearby were a row of human heads.

"Morgana," whispered the man as he approached the woman, "what have you done? What curse have you brought on us all?"

She turned. It was Homeira.

Rhodri woke with a jolt to the first fingers of dawn stretching through the trees. There was the new vigor of daylight in the air, and he got up and lifted Melanor from his perch. He didn't take the path back to the crossroads though. Instead he set out quickly through the forest, planning to cut across open country and meet up with the southern track wherever he could. Rhodri felt doubt immediately, as he realized he was traveling away from Homeira and his quest. But the image of Rebecca's lovely, trusting face was so clear in his mind that it kept him going.

The forest was full of threat now, with the imaginings that were crowding Rhodri's mind, and as he walked, and sometimes even broke into a run, lifting Melanor high to cushion the movement, sounds and shapes came to startle the young man. Here a bird flew up from a thick tangle of undergrowth, and something that might have been a boar flashed in the distance.

Rhodri kept moving and seemed to have traveled for miles when twilight came again, although he had not reached any track. He tethered Melanor and slept in the bowl of an oak tree, among the hard-knotted roots. He woke with the dawn. He was still blaming himself for turning aside from the quest, but by the time the sun above the forest reached midday, he was frantically worried for Rebecca, too, for still he had come on no track and he was beginning to be disoriented.

It was close to twilight again when Rhodri slumped down exhausted against another tree. He was completely lost and utterly dispirited, and he was beginning to realize he would never find his friends like this.

"Oh, Melanor," he said bitterly, "I'm such a damed fool. Father and Mother need our help and now look at us. Lost in a wood."

But as the young man sat there, Melanor screeched and flapped his wings, and Rhodri looked down in astonishment. A strange light was spilling out of his tunic. Rhodri reached a hand inside and pulled out the vial Tantallon had given him. There, inside the glass bottle, pictures appeared in the water. They were faint and tiny through the glass, but Rhodri could see himself and Melanor sitting there in the forest. It was as if he were looking into a mirror. But the vision swung round, and now Rhodri was looking on the forest ahead, and like a bird taking flight, the picture began to move down the slope. Trees and branches flashed past, and then, in the deepening gloom, the young man could see a wide clearing and beyond it the road through the wood. Rhodri's heart began to pound furiously as he caught sight of the battered old cart in the vial, Isaac and Rebecca's cart.

It was mired in a ditch and the canopy was torn away. Isaac's books were strewn everywhere, and the box that had sat on the table was upended on the grass. But nearby, against the bark of a birch tree, stood Isaac himself. The poor old man was bound fast against the tree with rope. His face was bruised and his black robes torn. The little cap that had sat on his head was stuffed into his mouth. Rhodri recognized the two men standing around Isaac immediately. They were two of the thieves that he had first met on the road.

The picture faded, and once more the vial contained clear water. Rhodri sprang to his feet and thrust the thing back in his tunic.

"Melanor," he cried, lifting the bird from his perch, "they're close. And in terrible danger."

Rhodri began to run, as fast as his legs would go, in the direction the bottle had shown him. At last they came to a rise of a hill where the forest opened, and through the trees Rhodri found he was looking down on a kind of valley. There it was, cutting through the forest, the road traveling directly south. Rhodri could see no one moving along the road though, but then he spotted it, a little banner of smoke trailing up from among the trees.

"There, Melanor," said Rhodri, with a surging hope. "Rebecca and Isaac must be there."

Rhodri made for the fire as fast as he could. It was a while still before he stopped again. He could hear voices up ahead now, but not Isaac's or Rebecca's. These were mens' voices and their accents were Welsh. The outlaws. Rhodri tethered Melanor quickly to a low branch and crouched down.

"Melanor," he whispered, "now you must be still and quiet while I get closer."

Very slowly Rhodri reached round, drew the sword over his head, and pulled it from its sheath. He began to creep stealthily through the undergrowth toward the voices. Loud and angry now, they thrilled through his nerves and body as he advanced, and he found himself sweating terribly. All Rhodri's instincts were on fire, and like a wild animal he fell to his knees and crawled across the ground toward a large tree. He peered round. There was the clearing, the scene exactly as the vial had shown him.

The outlaws stood around the bound Isaac, and from the trees came the third, pushing Rebecca before him. Rhodri's hand grasped the hilt tighter. She seemed unharmed, though her hands were bound behind her. The third thief gave her a shove and she fell to the ground before her father. Rhodri's whole body braced with fury.

"Take the gag off the old devil," cried the third thief.

One of the men walked up to Isaac and pulled the cap roughly from his mouth.

"So then, you miserable old Jew," he grunted, "are you going to tell us or not where it is?"

There was blood on Isaac's bruised and swollen lips.

"But I've told you, sir," whimpered Isaac. "We've no gold. We've only what you see. Please, you must be believing what I say."

The leader walked straight up to Isaac and struck the old man in the face.

"Liar."

It was as shocking to Rhodri as it had been seeing Hellard's head cleaved from his body in the Telling Pool. Yet there was something different about this sight, too. Rhodri had been unable to affect anything he had seen in the battle, and yet he was here, now, with a real sword. If he shouted or cried out, perhaps he could help the old man.

But a terrible feeling gripped Rhodri and he could hardly breathe. He pulled back behind the tree and found himself pressing himself against the bark. He wanted to disappear, to vanish inside the tree itself. His face was dripping with sweat, and his whole body was quivering uncontrollably. Rhodri was terrified.

Yet in that moment another emotion seized the young man, so strongly it was like being scolded by the priest in church. It was shame. Whenever Rhodri had dreamt of battle or warfare or of the fight in the Holy Lands, he had imagined himself marching out like the Lionheart or a Templar Knight, strong and brave and true, and with the force of his body and the courage of his heart, striking down all with the temerity to oppose him. But now that Rhodri was here in this real place, and his friends were in terrible danger, he found himself little more than a boy, frightened and alone and wishing that he were miles away.

Rhodri looked up. The outlaws were talking again.

"You expect us to believe that a miserable old sinner like you hasn't spent a life stealing coin from good Christian folk, see?" The outlaw grunted.

Rhodri tried to relax and calm his breathing. He looked at Melanor and thought of the certainty he himself had always given the bird with his own trust, when it sat on his hand. The certainty of calmness and strength and courage. *Don't be afraid, Rhodri Falcon*, he told himself. Rhodri leaned forward again to look.

"Please, sir," pleaded Isaac, in the clearing, "why would I lie? I'm no fool and you've searched our cart already."

The outlaw turned and walked over to Rebecca. He pulled her roughly to her feet and held her by the back of her neck. Rhodri thought of his father grabbing him in the same way.

"Very well," said the outlaw, "if a beating won't loosen your tongue, perhaps there's something more precious than your own skin to barter with now."

"What do you mean?" whispered Isaac.

"You Jews. You stick to your own kind all right. Is there nothing more terrible for a girl of your race, than to lie with a hated Christian?"

Isaac strained against his bonds.

"And not just one, but all. We like to share, don't we, boys? That's the way of the outlaw nowadays, if it's true what they say in the forest of the kindness and generosity of the Hood."

The outlaws all laughed at the mention of this other outlaw, whose fame was spreading everywhere.

"So tell us, Jew."

"Please, sir."

The leader reached out and tore at Rebecca's clothes. The arm of her dress ripped, but Rebecca stood there coldly and unafraid. The old man had let out a terrible, high-pitched scream. He sounded like a wounded bird.

"Sir. I beg of you, sir. Not my daughter. She's all I have."

"Then tell us, Jew."

"Look," said Isaac, and there were tears in his frightened old eyes, "my books, take my books."

"You think we can read books, you old fool?"

One of the other outlaws laughed and spat on the ground.

"That does not matter," said Isaac desperately. "What does is that they are very valuable, if you find the right buyer. Take them."

For a moment the idea made the outlaws pause, but then the leader spoke.

"I'm tired of this," he cried. "If there's no gold, let's take our pleasure and be done with it, see."

Rhodri had been thinking all the while of some plan, something to distract the men perhaps, or a sudden rush at them that he hoped would delay them long enough for Rebecca at least to get away. Yet now the moment was here, Rhodri could do nothing at all. He looked up to see Melanor watching, and for a moment he fancied there was disapproval in that face.

In the clearing the third outlaw was grinning as he held Rebecca, but then the second spoke. "Hush, what's that?"

Rhodri's heart lurched. He thought they had heard him behind the tree.

"Horses," hissed the leader, "on the road."

He had already pushed Rebecca to her knees again and was crouching, too, as the second outlaw walked straight up to Isaac and thrust the gag back in his mouth. They were all crouched down, watching the road. Four riders came cantering by, from the north. The clearing was set far back and the cart obscured by bracken. The riders did not even look in their direction as they passed. For a moment Rhodri thought of crying out to them, but they were riding too fast.

"The wind's really up them," said the leader, as they went by. "Perhaps they've heard of our work."

He was already moving toward their horses.

"What are you doing?" grunted the second.

"Hywel, come with me. They looked well heeled, and if we can catch them, see, perhaps we'll make up for time lost on this old skinflint. Steal some more horses, too."

A look of hope, or at least relief, had crept into Isaac's eyes.

"And you," said the lead outlaw to the third man, "stay here and guard them till we get back. But don't touch the prize, or you'll have me to answer to."

The two mounted their horses and galloped away, straight onto the track and after their prey. Rhodri's breathing deepened as he sat back against the tree. He knew he hadn't much time before the two men came back. Now the odds were in his favor. The third outlaw pulled Rebecca to her feet and shoved her roughly toward the cart. Then he stooped to pick up a bottle of wine and a leather beaker lying on the ground. He poured some wine and drank. As Rhodri saw him do it, he had a thought. The vial. If he could somehow get closer and pour the fatal water into the man's wine.

"Why are you looking so pleased?" the outlaw grunted at Isaac. "They'll be back soon enough. And then you can watch as we teach your daughter to love three Christian men. Before we kill her. But perhaps I should clean that smile from your face first."

"Leave my father alone. He's just an old man."

As soon as Rhodri heard Rebecca's voice, he knew that she should not have spoken. The outlaw swung back toward her and dashed his beaker to the ground.

"At last the Jewess crows," he cried, "and such a pretty crow."

The man was grinning evilly as he walked toward her.

"You think you're safe, girl, because he told me not to touch you. But I'm a freeman, who takes no orders from him. It won't hurt to sample the goods a little. Come, give us a kiss."

Rebecca backed against the cart, and now her voice shook proudly. "You can't touch me," she cried, "whatever you do to me. You can't touch my heart and soul."

Rebecca's brave words just enflamed the outlaw even more.

"But it's not your heart and soul I want," he cried scornfully.

Isaac was wrestling and kicking against the tree, grunting against the gag. But the old man's eyes opened in amazement. Rhodri was only dimly aware of his look. Of the trees all about him, too, as he stepped forward into the clearing, his grandfather's sword held out in front of him, aiming the point straight at the outlaw's back. Closer Rhodri came, and so stealthily did he move, it was as though he was floating across the ground in a dream. Perhaps it was Isaac's silence as he saw Rhodri preparing to strike that made the outlaw turn, or perhaps the snap of a twig on the ground, but turn he did.

"You," he cried, and in an instant he had drawn the dagger at his belt. Rhodri's own dagger. The young man's arm was shaking and the sword felt as heavy as lead. His mind had closed in and his body felt frozen like winter wood. He just kept walking forward, holding up the shaking sword in front of him, and realizing how scared he was and unused to real fighting. Suddenly the outlaw began to laugh and his dagger arm came up, too.

It happened so quickly that Rhodri was hardly aware of anything at all. There was a screech and the flap of swooping wings. Melanor had broken free of his tether. The outlaw lifted his arm to deflect the falcon's vicious attack, and as the movement shifted his head behind him, Rebecca suddenly caught sight of her friend. With a cry of fury, she threw herself forward at the outlaw. Rhodri saw the surprise in the man's face as he was hurtled forward, and saw the surprise turn to pain and incomprehension as his stomach met the tip of Rhodri's blade. Rhodri felt his own arm brace against something hard and then the hardness became soft and Rhodri pushed. Then Rhodri was falling, falling backward to the ground and the outlaw was falling on top of him. The outlaw's own weight impaled him. The sword passed deep into his stomach and right through his back.

Rhodri felt a jolt of satisfaction, but it turned to horror as the outlaw's face drew nearer and nearer. He could see the sweat and stubble on his weather-beaten skin, could smell the wine on his breath and see the broken yellowed teeth in his mouth. Above all, Rhodri could see the fury and amazement in his startled eyes. It was like a flame at the center of a fire, like the swirling waters of the Telling Pool, or the glow of the lava well.

Even as Rhodri looked and the man pressed down on him, he felt the outlaw's body shake with a terrible sigh. A little bubble of blood formed on his lips and the light went out of those eyes altogether. But Rhodri felt another feeling, one of astonishment. That face. It was one of the men who had attacked Wolfrin. The dead man slumped on top of him and rolled to the side. Rhodri was still holding onto the hilt of his father's sword, and he turned, too, as though he and the outlaw had become one being.

"Rhodri, let go, Rhodri."

From some dark and distant place Rebecca's sweet voice came startling Rhodri back into reality.

"Quickly, Rhodri. Before they come back. The man's dagger."

Rhodri looked about him stupidly.

"In his hand, Rhodri."

Rebecca's voice was so strong and clear it seemed to be guiding him through the darkness. He got up and then leaned down again to pull his own antler dagger out of that dead hand. The outlaw lay there, his eyes still opened accusingly, and Rhodri remembered the skull on Homeira's table and he shivered.

"Rhodri, my ropes. Cut my ropes. Quickly."

Rebecca had turned her back, and Rhodri began to cut at the ropes that bound her aching wrists. In an instant Rebecca was free, and Rhodri hardly noticed as she took the blade from him and ran over to release her father, too.

Rhodri looked down at the dead body, skewered by his grandfather's sword but now he felt little of the triumph he'd expected he would at going into battle. He was glad the man was dead, it was true, and he thought how easily he himself might have been lying there in his place, or even worse, Rebecca. But it had not been a heroic thing at all, feeling that body go cold, and all Rhodri was aware of now, as Isaac hugged his daughter, was how frightened he was still.

Isaac began to gather up his books and their possessions and Rebecca was busy with the cart.

"Rhodri. If they come back and find us . . ." she said.

Fear at the thought cleared Rhodri's head again and he felt stronger. He pushed the outlaw with his foot and felt the body roll, and then, taking hold of the hilt of his sword, he pulled the blade out.

He sheathed the sword without even cleaning it, and turned.

Rebecca was trying to calm their horse, Jezamel, and Melanor was flapping in a tree. Rhodri ran up to help Rebecca. The horse stamped and snorted even more fearfully as Rhodri came close, but by stroking the animal, the boy managed to calm him down again and then urge him to pull the cart out of the ditch. Then Rhodri took charge.

"Into the cart, Rebecca," he cried. "Hurry."

She obeyed, helping her father onto the seat and hopping onto it herself. Rhodri rushed over to fetch Melanor and then jumped up, too. He gave Rebecca the bird, and as he shook the reins the cart lurched away. Rhodri turned the horse to the track and then left, toward the North and away from the outlaws. He kept shouting and shaking the reins as they went, spurring the horse faster and faster.

It was more than an hour before Rhodri slowed the cart again, for Jezamel was exhausted. The young man was still desperately worried though, for he knew how easily the outlaws could catch them. Then up ahead they saw five horsemen. They were soldiers, heavily armed and bearing the livery of some lord local to these woods. The soldiers approached the cart and one of them addressed the boy, with the gruffness of a soldier's purpose, rather than any threat.

"We're searching the forest," he cried, "to keep the roads clear. Have you seen anyone on the path, boy?"

Rhodri was about to answer, when Rebecca spoke for him.

"Yes, sir. Three horses. A way back. They were armed."

"They gave you no trouble?"

Rhodri felt something flutter in his throat. He could not tell them about the dead man. That he had killed him.

"None, sir," said Rebecca, casting Rhodri a look to silence him, "but they seemed dangerous and there were other riders. They were chasing them."

"Very well. Keep going. There's an encampment up ahead where you'll be safe enough."

Rhodri flicked the horse on through the darkness. Beside him Rebecca was still clutching the hand of her father, who sat stunned into silence by all that had happened. Melanor was perched on her arm. But as they rattled on through the cold shadows, Rebecca released her father's hand and reached out and touched Rhodri's. Very gently she squeezed it.

"Thank you again, Rhodri Falcon," Rebecca whispered warmly. "With all my heart."

The young man felt his fists tighten proudly on the reins, but his body was still like a bird on a tether and he felt something scalding his eyes. The young man was crying.

14 ⋄ A WANDERING KNIGHT

O what can ail thee knight at arms,
Alone and palely loitering?
The sedge has withered from the lake
And no birds sing!
—John Keats, "La belle dame sans merci"

Where are you really going, Rhodri? What is it that you seek?"
For three days they had been camped where the soldiers had
suggested, slightly apart from another group of travelers, and Rhodri
was aching to renew his quest once more. Rhodri and Rebecca sat
together by the fire as the girl spoke. Isaac's attitude toward Rhodri

had changed completely, and he had fussed and clucked about the lad like an old woman. He could see, too, that what had happened had forged an even deeper bond between the youngsters, but this time the old man had not tried to stop them from talking, and on several occasions he had even left them alone together.

Rhodri peered into the firelight. He hardly knew what it was that he sought: Mythirion, or his father's heart? Or was it the truth about himself that Rebecca had hinted at when she had talked of the shape of his amulet? The Path of the Deer. Everything he had seen in the Telling Pool was somehow connected to him.

As he sat there, he remembered the outlaw's eyes. He had killed a man, but it did not make Rhodri feel more grown-up at all.

"I'll tell you what I seek, Rebecca," he answered quietly, "if you promise not to interrupt or laugh at me."

"I promise, Rhodri Falcon."

Rhodri began falteringly, and when he finished telling his extraordinary tale by the fire, Rebecca sat there in silent astonishment, shaking her head.

"You believe me, don't you, Rebecca? In my quest."

The girl's eyes shimmered. "I . . . Yes, Rhodri. I believe you."

Rhodri could see the doubt that lingered in her pretty face. She wanted to believe him, yet is seemed so impossible.

"Wait," cried Rhodri, reaching into his tunic. "Of course. You don't have to take it on faith, Rebecca. Look."

Rhodri was holding up the vial. Rebecca leaned forward wonderingly, but as they looked no pictures came.

"Put it away," said Rebecca quietly. "It's all right, Rhodri. I know you speak the truth."

Rhodri smiled gratefully. "Perhaps I shouldn't have told you," the young man said, "but it's been a heavy burden and I know I can trust you."

Rebecca smiled. "Thank you. What is she like, this woman in the cave?"

"Like a queen," answered Rhodri. "The most beautiful . . ." He paused. "But her eyes, Rebecca, they've such anger in them. Such fury and cunning."

"And you fear her?"

If one of the children of the village had asked him such a question, Rhodri would have answered differently, but he could not lie to Rebecca. Since his dream about the butchered knights in the forest, their arms and legs hanging from trees, he feared Homeira more than ever.

"Yes. The casket and the knights in the cave. Her magic is strong. I dream of her sometimes, too. Then I can hardly breathe."

"Then you are brave."

Rhodri looked up from the fire. He shivered, despite the heat.

"Brave," he said bitterly. "In the clearing, when you were nearly . . ."

Rebecca dropped her eyes.

"I didn't feel brave then, right enough," said Rhodri sadly. "I could hardly move, Rebecca, hardly think about anything at all."

"But you did move. As did Melanor. That's what matters."

Rhodri looked up at Melanor. The bird was hooded but pecking at his feathers to clean them.

"Perhaps." Rhodri said more cheerfully, "And when this is over, I promise you this. I'll learn to use a sword properly."

"Mythirion," said Rebecca wonderingly. "In my lands we talk of a similar sword. We call it Azkezal. You think it really exists?"

"The Lady Guinevere told me to find it. Tantallon said it protected all who wield it."

"But how will you find it, Rhodri Falcon?"

"That I still don't know. Once it was lodged in the great stone Bethganoth, but now who knows where it lies? But I fear I must not approach Homeira without it. And her magic has something to do with the king, too, the Lionheart and all that happens in the land. A terrible curse is at work and I believe we are all in peril."

"But Rhodri," said Rebecca, "what about you?"

"What do you mean, Rebecca?"

"You love your parents and have seen something of what happens in Albion. But even when your quest is over, whether you succeed or fail in this task, one day your parents will be gone, too. As Mother left my father. What then?"

Rhodri blinked in the firelight. He had often worried about his parents, and had been terrified when his mother, Megan, lay sick in her bed. But the thought of their death, of their really leaving him, was so distant and unreal to the young man it was like an image from the Telling Pool. Rhodri had no feelings or experience to attach to it, nothing at all except a sudden and terrible sadness.

"I don't know," he whispered gloomily. "I suppose I'll become a falconer, Rebecca. I'm skillful at that at least. Perhaps serve Lord De Brackenois's son, William, as a master falconer like my father."

Now the thought of bending his knee to his friend William seemed less irksome.

"And marry?" Rebecca looked away as she asked.

"I suppose so, Rebecca."

"And live in your home?"

Rhodri paused. For so long he had wanted to journey out and see the world. But he remembered the outlaw and all he had seen so far, and suddenly he thought of his father, sitting by the hearth, telling them of what a dangerous and wicked place the world out there was, and how the only way to find real contentment was at home, sealed away from it all. But even as he thought of Owen, he frowned. His pa had always been a hero to him, but he had been tempted by Homeira and now she held his heart like a slave.

"What's wrong, Rhodri?"

"He shouldn't have done it, Rebecca. He betrayed my mother. Just as . . ."

Rhodri stopped and Rebecca smiled sadly to herself and her face took on a look far beyond her years.

"He's only a man," she said. "Can't you forgive him?"

Rhodri was so startled by the question that he sat up straight.

"Forgive him? What do you mean?"

"You're angry with your father."

The young man remembered that hand, striking out at him, striking out in anger and fury. It was as if the hate his father had felt, wherever it had come from, had passed into him with that blow. As if it was inside him like some subtle poison that was eating at the young man's loving heart. Rhodri felt a terrible weakness inside him.

"My mother," said Rebecca softly, "she saw much of the world and suffered much, too, Rhodri, not only at the hand of men. But she always told me to remember that whatever men are, we are all like animals, who need to eat and sleep and live. Perhaps your father, when he reached Homeira's cave, perhaps he had already been wounded. Perhaps that made it easier for the enchantress."

Rhodri thought of the terrible scar on Owen's chest and then the memories he had seen in the Telling Pool, when Homeira had gripped his heart, the images of pain and death that Owen had witnessed in the Holy Lands. His own hurt memories. Some dim understanding seemed to dawn in the boy, and compassion, too, and he remembered what Tantallon had said of Lancelot and Guinevere. How they were not evil, but what they had done had brought a curse to the land. Rhodri felt sorry for his father again, and proud that his quest might help him.

"And Mother said that some come into the world like soldiers," Rebecca continued, looking hard at Rhodri, "to fight and kill and conquer. But others come to heal. Which are you, Rhodri Falcon?"

The young man did not answer. He did not know. But he was thinking of Tantallon again and of Excalibur, the sword that brings only peace, when Rebecca pointed at the vial.

"There, Rhodri," she gasped.

Before the two young people the vial had begun to glow, casting a beautiful golden light over their raptured faces. Now both of them could see a picture. A young man and a woman were walking past a church.

"She's lovely," whispered Rebecca. "Who is she?"

"Sarah," answered Rhodri, blushing deeply, "and William De Brackenois."

In the glass, William reached out and took Sarah's hand, and Rhodri felt an anguish in his gut and his hand closed tighter on the vial. The picture faded again.

"This picture hurts you, Rhodri Falcon." said Rebecca kindly, studying his face. "I think you care for her. But for him, too."

"I . . ." Rhodri dropped his gaze.

"Jealousy is natural," said the girl, looking a little sad herself, "but never let it eat at your heart. We cannot choose where we love, I think."

Rhodri looked up, and there was something so lovely and kind in Rebecca's smile that the young man's heart opened to her again, and in that moment he was glad for William and Sarah. Sarah was pretty and gentle and he missed her, but Rebecca had something that Sarah had not, a kind of fire in her that made her more like Rhodri himself.

"And tell me," said Rebecca more cheerfully, "now you have proved your tale to me, how can I help you? Father and I owe you our lives."

Rhodri put the vial back in his tunic.

"Some food for the journey, perhaps," he answered, thinking that his friend had already helped him greatly. "But I must hurry now. The year comes to a close and all too soon the bargain will be up. A year and a day. I've not even found Mythirion yet."

"Rhodri. May I come with you?"

Rhodri smiled, but shook his head firmly.

"No. You must care for your own father. This burden is mine alone."

"Then you must travel swiftly," cried Rebecca, jumping to her feet, "and you must no longer travel on foot, Rhodri. You need a swift horse now and you shall have one. That will buy back the time you have lost."

Rebecca ran over to the carriage near Jezamel, and for a moment Rhodri thought she meant to give him their steed.

"But you can't," he cried. "How will you and your father . . ."

Rebecca had not begun to unhitch Jezamel at all. Instead she was leaning down under the cart. She pulled away the odd bit of wood that Rhodri had seen when he helped Isaac fix the wheel, and drew something out. Rhodri saw that it was like a little hidden drawer, and inside was a string purse. When Rebecca opened it, the young man was amazed to see that it was filled with gold coin. Very carefully the girl counted four pieces of gold into her palm and held them out to Rhodri.

"One will buy you a good, strong horse from the traders in camp," said Rebecca, "and the others are for the road. I'm sorry I can't spare more, but Father will beat me as it is, when he finds these are gone."

As Rhodri's hand closed on the hard, gold coins he felt confused and angry. Isaac had known that he and his daughter were in mortal danger, yet still he had refused to reveal the whereabouts of his hidden treasure.

"But your father, then he did . . ."

Rebecca smiled sadly.

"Perhaps with the years," she said, "people can become what others accuse them wrongly of being."

Rhodri found a horse the very next day, a large bay pony called Dusk. He asked the man to stable him for a while, so Isaac would not question him as to how he had bought the steed. That night he ate with the old man and his daughter for the last time. The soldiers had cleared the way and the road was open again. Rhodri tried to be as cheerful as he could, but he and Rebecca kept watching each other through the firelight. There was a compact between them that made Isaac very nervous.

Rhodri rose before sunup and Rebecca followed him to his horse through the coming light. Fires smoldered everywhere, and about the encampment men and beasts were stirring sleepily as Rhodri prepared Dusk. He had placed Melanor behind him in the saddle and tied his jesses.

"Good-bye, Rhodri," whispered Rebecca. "And may your God speed you on your quest."

Rhodri turned and Rebecca stepped forward. Once again they kissed, and Rhodri felt as if his heart might take to the air. But he mounted his horse swiftly.

"And good-bye, Melanor. Look after your master as he looks after you."

Rhodri kicked his horse beneath him and began to trot away.

"Rhodri."

The young man turned in his saddle.

"You fight to help your father and these knights, Rhodri. To face this strange curse. You go to find the fabled Excalibur and have sat where a high king once sat. As Tantallon said, this witch will try to enchant you, too. But remember something, Rhodri. Your heart. It is yours alone."

Rhodri smiled and nodded and turned away. He did not want to leave Rebecca at all, but he had delayed too long and he let Dusk's excitement bear him onward. It was good to feel the animal beneath him, to feel its trust and energy, and soon Rhodri's heart was lighter as he rode through the forest on his quest once more. The mighty sun had risen high and begun to fall once more when Rhodri reached the crossroads where he had first bid Rebecca and Isaac farewell.

Dusk and Melanor felt it immediately. Like something unwholesome on the air. Rhodri pulled up in horror, then jumped down and walked up to the old tree. There, dangling from a low bow was the leader of the outlaws. The soldiers must have caught him and put him summarily to death. His throat had been cut and his tongue lolled from his mouth.

It wasn't this that made Rhodri shudder to his bones. They had hanged him upside down, by one leg, as a warning to others. Rhodri remembered the fair and an old woman with her pack of cards. It was like the card. So it was all coming true. The Hermit and the Enchantress. The Lovers and now the Hanged Man. What next, thought the young man fearfully—Death?

• • •

The days and nights passed. Days and nights of wet and cold and hardship. Now, as he hurried on his quest, Rhodri's thoughts were turned more and more toward Mythirion, but he could find no clues to its whereabouts. Again and again he looked into the vial, but it would show him nothing. Only once did it glow, to reveal a weary and battered face covered in scars, but Rhodri did not know what it meant.

In a small town, Rhodri exchanged one of his golden coins for provisions to pile on his horse and rested awhile in an inn with soft beds and good beer. There he began to ask questions. Questions about the old tales of Arthur and Merlin, and above all of Excalibur. But every time he did so, he was either laughed at, or a tale would begin that was so fanciful or so long that Rhodri knew he was wasting his time.

On he raced, crossing rivers and streams, and came to hills and wide-open plains. He reached a strange circle of standing stones where a band of traveling gypsies entertained Rhodri for the evening with stories and dance and song, but lifted a ham from his saddlebag, too, and another of Rebecca's gold coins from his pocket in his sleep.

Many people Rhodri met on the way. A serving girl in the inn took a shine to his dark, rich locks and so embarrassed the young man by staring at him all evening, that the whole tavern soon noticed him and began to laugh at his blushes. Shepherds he met taking a flock to market told him of the barren moors to the west where they sometimes grazed, and the strange caves there where people had lived since ancient times.

Rhodri was often lonely as he traveled, and more and more, as he felt himself drawing closer to the fearful enchantress, he began to dream of hearth and home. He missed his little room, even if he had outgrown his cot. He missed the stream and the otters and the old oak tree he had climbed to look out on the manor. He missed Sarah and William, too, even though the thought of them also made him sad. But above all, he missed sitting with his parents and listening to stories and playing at domino. But his dreams were mixed with strange visions, too. Of kings and knights, of lords and ladies. Always now that voice came to him, also.

"Find it. Find it for me. For all of us."

But it was the thought of his father's heart locked in the witch's casket that sustained Rhodri in every trial. Sometimes, when he thought of it and the enchantress squeezing it in her hand, he would draw his father's sword and, pretending it was Mythirion itself, hold its hard edge up to the sunlight and let the memory of the witch turn his heart toward anger.

But often when he did so, he thought of the outlaw, too, dying on the blade, and it made him sick. Then another image would come that sustained Rhodri in his journey: Rebecca's pretty face, smiling at him.

He would take out the heart-shaped stone she had given him and hold it in his palm. When he did so, he felt it warm to his touch and he knew she was thinking of him.

One day, riding through a small village Rhodri stopped by a tree on the green and saw a sad sight. A man in stocks. His clothes were soaking wet and his face bruised and bloody. About him on the ground were rotten vegetables, eggs, and rocks that any passing villager was allowed to hurl at him, without fear of the law. He looked on the edge of death.

"Friend," he whispered faintly at Rhodri, as he rode by. "Water, friend."

The man's hands were locked in the wooden slatting round either side of his head. Rhodri had nothing to fear from him, and he pulled up Dusk and dismounted. There was no one else about, for it was only just past dawn. Rhodri saw a pail of water and a wooden scoop nearby. He ladled some into the man's lips, and as he did so he gasped.

"You."

It was the same battered face he had seen in the vial. But the man was too weary and bewildered to know what Rhodri was talking about.

"Thank you, boy."

"What did you do, sir?" Rhodri asked. "to deserve this?"

"Followed my own faith," answered the man bitterly, in a weary Saxon voice, "the Wiccan faith. With the great wars and the king gone, none are safe from the wrath of the Church. But they caught me thieving, also," added the man and he grinned like a child.

"How long have you been here?"

"Three days," answered the man, moving his hands painfully, "and I will stay two more. If I last that long. I fear I'll die first."

"I wish I could help you."

"If you do, I'll show my gratitude, all right."

He was looking at Rhodri's back.

"That's a fine enough sword, boy. But I've a finer for you."

Rhodri jolted. Could it really be? Rhodri had the feeling that everything that was happening to him now was part of some deeper destiny, a destiny that perhaps he had to learn to trust.

"A sword?" he whispered.

"It's old, but it keeps its metal. There's power in it."

Rhodri looked at him hard. "What may I do, sir?"

"There. Undo the bolts there and I'll take you to it."

Rhodri began to work the bolts. With great effort he managed to free them and lifted the top of the stocks from the man's arms and head.

"Thank you, my friend," the man said, stretching painfully, "But we must be away from here."

He led Rhodri into the forests on the edge of the village and they walked for nearly half a day together. Somehow Rhodri knew now that this journey, too, was part of the quest. He was desperately excited by the time they reached the man's home, where his wife ran out to hug him. But Rhodri was clearly in a hurry, and the man embraced his wife briefly and led the young man straight toward his stables.

"I keep it in here, boy. Robbers might ransack my house, but they'll not find it here."

Rhodri's heart was pounding. Could it really be Mythirion?

The man pushed open the door and went straight over to the wall of the stables and pulled back a panel of wood. Rhodri was trembling as the man reached inside the recess and drew the blade forth. But Rhodri's heart sank. It was a fine sword indeed, which flashed as the man held it up proudly, but the blade was curved in the manner of the East.

"A Saracen scimitar, from the Holy Wars," he cried. "I bought it at last month's fair. Take it, lad. It's yours."

Rhodri smiled sadly and shook his head.

"Keep it, sir," he answered softly. "I've a sword already, and if they come for you again, you may need it."

The man and his wife thanked Rhodri warmly as he set off again through the forest. Toward midday he stopped to camp. He tethered Dusk and Melanor and lay down to rest in a deep bed of dry leaves. He was hungry and tired and he closed his eyes to dream. Rhodri woke and sat up and looked around. But his heart jolted when he turned to Melanor's perch. The falcon had vanished.

"Melanor."

His voice echoed through the wood as he began to search for his bird. He had left Dusk tethered safely and he walked for a good while, but as he walked that strange sensation came over Rhodri, that feeling of being watched. Rhodri had come to a clearing at the edge of a lake and he gasped as he heard a little bell and saw his rock falcon. Melanor was perched on a man's gauntleted arm, his little head turning this way and that, as they stood by the water. The stranger was dressed as one of the knights in the Holy Army, although his face was visored. All about the water floated wild reeds and Rhodri wondered what on earth the knight could be doing here. He put his hand to his sword.

"You've no need to fear me, boy," said the knight. "Your falcon already knows it. As animals always know the true secrets."

Rhodri drew closer.

"Who are you, sir? Do you return from the wars?"

The knight nodded.

"And I'm luckier than many," he answered gravely. "I wander alone, as I have for years, but it is better to be in a forest is it not, than sealed in stone?"

Rhodri looked at the knight in amazement. His voice was strangely muffled behind the metal.

"You know of it? The witch's cave."

"And of ancient enchantments. The place you seek is not far now. Keep faith."

"Then you know of my journey, too?"

"Yes, boy. And of the courage in your heart. I know that you walk the Path of the Deer."

Rhodri stepped back. "The Path of the Deer? What is that, sir? It has something to do with the Lady Guinevere and with Arthur, doesn't it?"

"Indeed it does. And the ancient curse. The deer was her emblem."

"Her emblem? Of course, that cloak I saw her wearing in the pool. The emblem of the deer. But how do you know these things?"

"Are there not many ways of seeing in the world?" answered the strange knight. "In fire or water, and on the currents of the air. There are memories, too. Lodged deep inside us and in all things."

He raised his gauntleted hand and lifted Melanor. He was tall in the wood as the bird opened its beautiful, living wings.

"And there are stones, too, from which one may see," he said. "Stones that reach to the core of the world."

"Bethganoth," whispered Rhodri.

"Its power is even greater than the fabled Telling Pool," said the knight, "for when you stand on it, you can see all things. Life and death. Past and future. From there you can see into the very heart of the Miracle. There young Arthur came, as he did once to the Telling Pool, among many knights, and because it was meant to be, he drew forth Mythirion."

"Excalibur," cried Rhodri.

"The fabled blade," said the knight, nodding his visored head, "forged to bring only peace. It took great skill and magic to make it in the Forge of Mythirion. As it does to make a man worthy of holding it."

"Is the sword there?" said Rhodri. "Inside the stone Bethganoth once more?"

The knight shook his head.

"Then the lake, sir?"

"No, boy. But you must find it again. For all of us."

"But how?" said Rhodri bitterly. "I've been searching. Questing. But always it proves futile. Tell me where it is."

"Mythirion is always close," answered the knight softly, "and with it alone may you pierce a heart of stone and break a curse."

Rhodri grew pale.

"But now you must hurry again. The winter is on us and your father's bargain is almost up. It's only twenty days now to the mass of the Christ's birth. Take that path through the wood. Travel for several days and you will come to the moor. You've seen the place before. Good luck, Falcon."

The mysterious knight threw up his arm and Melanor took wing toward his young master. As Rhodri took the rock falcon's weight, he saw that the knight had turned and was walking quickly away toward the trees.

"Wait," called the young man. "Who are you, sir?"

The knight had already vanished into the wood though, and only the echo of his voice remained on the chilly air.

"And who are you, Rhodri Falcon?"

Rhodri turned with Melanor toward Dusk, but as he did so he heard the beating of wings. Rhodri looked up and high above he saw a bird. It was already a little speck, but for a moment Rhodri couldn't believe his eyes. He was almost sure that it was the merlin.

There was no time to delay, and once more he set off. As Rhodri felt the air on his skin, he knew that it had grown colder and that the Savior's birthing day was drawing close indeed. Only twenty days, thought Rhodri desperately.

On the road now the weather began to change again. The cold came quickly and the young man wrapped his cloak tighter for warmth. Soon Dusk's hooves clattered on the hard earth, and the air began to freeze, and then the first snows fell. The clouds opened, and the great crystal flakes of white came sailing down from the heavens.

Rhodri was counting now as he quested, counting the rise and fall of the sun, and it was twelve days later when he and Melanor came to the edge of the moor, robed in white. Its unearthly beauty was magnified by the snow, and as the young man looked out from his horse, he knew immediately that this was the place where he would find Homeira's cave. But the thought only made Rhodri terrified, for he had not yet found Mythrion. It was close to twilight when the young man came on the wild lake he had seen in the Telling Pool. He shivered, for he knew the place straightaway, and his memories carried him up toward the edge of the forest.

There it was. The corral of horses and the break in the trees. Then the cave. The thick grass sward was now a blanket of white, and great spikes of ice hung down from the stalactites where water had dripped and frozen solid, so that the entrance to the cave was barred like a prison. There was the raven again, too, waiting at the entrance and as Rhodri approached, he saw that it was pecking at something on the ground. It was the carcass of a baby lamb, and its eyes had been plucked out. The scavenging bird cawed angrily as Rhodri dismounted and, tethering Dusk to a tree, drew his grandfather's sword.

With a cry and the flapping of wings, Melanor had taken to the air. The raven screeched in terror, and as Melanor made his attack, it flew straight inside the cave mouth. But though he missed, Melanor did not follow it. Instead the falcon hovered for a moment at the cave mouth as if unable to enter it. Rhodri knew something had changed in the moment, and he whistled. But the falcon soared upward, high above the cave, then turned and began to fly away.

"Melanor," cried Rhodri, "Don't be afraid. Come back."

But as he watched his friend, the bird was soon nothing but a tiny speck in the clouds that quickly vanished. Rhodri remembered his father's words about the wildness of the falcon, and he sighed. Now the young man was entirely alone.

He looked nervously toward the cave and again thought how it looked like the entrance to another world. He had nothing but an old sword and the vial in his tunic with which to defend himself against the mighty witch. But Rhodri steeled himself, and lifting his grandfather's blade, he marched on. The bars of ice at the cave entrance broke off with hardly a wave of Rhodri's arm and tinkled to the ground, and the boy found himself standing exactly where his father had been. He was struck first by the narrowness of the tunnel and the beauty of the gems and stones embedded in its walls. But Rhodri did not touch the cave walls. His breath steamed in the freezing air, and deep in his nostrils, he scented the thick, heady smell of incense. It was like a curtain of smoke before him. As the young man came closer, he remembered what Homeira had snarled at his father. "The smoke veil at the mouth of the cave would blind you and make you choke with its poison."

15 ❖ HOMEIRA

I had a dream, which was not all a dream.

— George Gordon, Lord Byron, "Darkness"

Rhodri thought of his mother weeping on the floor of his home and he stepped forward. His eyes began to water and he felt faint and dizzy, but the smoke parted, as it had done for his father. He passed through, and suddenly he was standing inside Homeira's cave.

The chamber was exactly as it had been in the Telling Pool. Everywhere, candles flickered and shadows wavered around the walls, so that the forms and faces and bodies in the stone seemed to move. There stood the table, and perched at its end the skull. There stood those great carved chairs in which Homeira and Owen had sat. In the corner was the silken bed, too. But Rhodri's wide hazelnut eyes were locked now on the center of the oaken table. In the middle of it was the magic casket.

As Rhodri drew closer, its extraordinary beauty and fineness made him gasp. He had not been able to see its intricacy in the Telling Pool. He shuddered as he stepped up to it, for through that colored crystal lay—shut inside—his father's beating heart. Rhodri saw it moving and pumping within, and he reached out his hand. He touched the box, but when he tried to lift the lid, nothing happened. The casket was locked fast.

"You cannot open it, young Falcon."

The young man swung round at her voice.

Homeira was even lovelier in person than she had been in the pool. Her jet-black eyes were cold and strong, but her lips were smiling sweetly, with a slight curve of scorn at their edges. She turned her head, and her curling black locks fell over her shoulder as she came forward. She was dressed all in purple, as she had been when she had first encountered Owen, but the robe was much finer, with delicate embroidery, like the cushions about the cave. Rhodri stepped backward against the table and jogged the casket.

"You. You know my name?"

The enchantress laughed.

"If I could see a king, or your father in the fire," she said softly, "do you not think I have the magic to see his brave son, too?"

"Then you know why I'm here, Homeira?" said the young man coldly.

Homeira smiled.

"I know why you think you are here, Rhodri Falcon," whispered the enchantress. "To win back your father's heart."

Rhodri took a step toward her.

"Yes," he cried angrily, "and to break your foul enchantments. So give it to me."

The enchantress threw back her head and laughed so loudly it echoed through the cave and seemed to make the candles flicker.

"So young and fierce," she cried, "but so very foolish. What did that dolt Tantallon tell you? To be true and loving and pure? Did he spin a story for babes and children?"

"Tantallon," whispered Rhodri in amazement. "You know of Tantallon?"

Homeira's face took on a strange, almost haunted look.

"I know that meddler and his power well," she answered coldly. "And I felt your eyes on me, even as you gazed from the Seeing Place into the deep, dark waters of the Telling Pool. "

"But it can't be," said Rhodri, feeling that in some way his friend had betrayed him and that he had nothing to defend himself with at all, not even the secret of the pool. "Tantallon would have told me."

"A man like Tantallon," said Homeira, not without admiration in her eyes, "has many secret ways, and many ways to pursue the Law. Just as he has many names."

"The Law?" said Rhodri. "Of the God and Goddess. Of moon and water, forest and mountain. The most ancient power."

"A power so deep that everything is made of it. But should I not be disappointed that he sends a mere child to confront me?"

The young man blushed to the roots of his hair. But he remembered what he had seen in the water. Homeira kissing his father, taking him away from their home, from his mother, and he felt a fury bubbling up inside him that gave him courage.

"I'm no child, Homeira," cried Rhodri. "I've seen much and have killed a man already."

The witch just laughed at him.

"Bravely spoken," she hissed. She looked at him slyly. "And now would you kill a woman to make yourself a brave, young man?"

He dropped his eyes. "No. But give me back my pa's heart."

Again Homeira's dark, black eyes sparkled at the boy. "Take it," she shrugged. "What use is the thing to me?"

Rhodri looked up at her in amazement. "What use?" he cried angrily. "But you stole it. Because you love him . . . You love my father and want him with you forever as your slave. Like the knights you have sealed inside the walls."

Homeira tilted her head and again she laughed. There was something so cold and cruel in the sound that the boy felt as if his veins were freezing, even in the heat of the cave.

"You saw many things in the Telling Pool," she whispered, "but are you certain you looked with the right eyes? Are you certain you understood what you saw?"

"The key," cried Rhodri angrily, "the key to your casket, give it to me."

"That I will not do."

The young man looked down at the casket, and in his mind he saw those icy bars at the mouth of the cave shattering before him. The casket glinted and Rhodri swung his sword high above his head.

Homeira did not try to stop him. He brought the blade down so hard on the box that it would have sliced a log of wood in two like butter. It struck the glass, and Rhodri's arms shuddered with the impact. There was a terrible sound, but the casket did not shatter. It did not even crack. Instead a piece of metal lay at Rhodri's feet. His father's sword had broken in two, and still inside the box lay Owen Falcon's beating heart.

"You see," said Homeira, "the finest things are the hardest to break."

She stepped closer and put her hand on Rhodri's shoulder. It felt like his mother's touch, but there was something else in it, too. Something familiar that reminded him of walking with Sarah, and of kissing Rebecca in the forest.

"But you're angry, Rhodri Falcon. And your anger weakens you."

The young man blinked at her helplessly.

"Come," Homeira said, "let us talk like friends. You're hungry and thirsty, no, after your long quest? Far longer than you know."

What could she mean, far longer than he knew? Her voice had become so sweet and conciliating, so soft and kind and gentle that Rhodri felt some of the anger and wariness go out of his body. But he pulled away.

"No. His heart. My father's heart."

"You shall have the heart, Rhodri," said the witch, "all in good time. You've traveled far already to win it and suffered much. How could I deny one so courageous and filled with so much love? But first, talk with me awhile."

She walked over to the table and lifted a goblet and the great silver decanter. The wine sparkled as she poured a cup and held it out to Rhodri.

"Drink. You'll taste nothing so sweet in your entire life, I promise you."

Rhodri shook his head.

"Come," said Homeira, smiling knowingly, "you've the stars in your eyes, Rhodri Falcon. Like any young man, you ache for knowledge and experience, just as you ache to travel the world. Well, let this be your first taste of the real world. And your sweetest."

Rhodri put the broken sword down on the table. His lips felt dry, and his throat parched with thirst and fear, but though he did indeed want to taste the wine, still he held back and remembered Tantallon's warning: "Miss nothing. Your life and soul may depend on it."

"Perhaps you think I try to poison you," said Homeira. "Well, see."

The dark-haired beauty lifted the cup to her lips and drank. Then she laughed again, but this time the laughter was pleasant to the young man's ears. She held out the cup again. "There."

Rhodri stepped forward and took the goblet. He saw the ring on the woman's finger, but it was sealed shut and he was reassured. He had missed nothing. Rhodri lifted the cup to his mouth, and as he did so he noticed that the red paint on Homeira's lips had stained the goblet at its edge.

Rhodri had never tasted anything so wonderful in his whole life before. The draft was not sharp like beer at all, but as sweet as nectar, and he felt a heat and vigor flow through his body, as if it were rising from the tips of his toes up to his head. Rhodri drank again, even deeper, and the enchantress smiled approvingly as he wiped his mouth on his sleeve.

"That's better, isn't it? And now I'll bring food for you and serve you. Then tend to you, as your mother tended to you at home, before she grew ill."

"My mother? Don't you talk of my—"

"Peace, Rhodri Falcon. I've always longed for a son, and you have misjudged me, young man. I'm not wicked as you think. I can be kind, too. So kind. I'm a woman, after all. Will you not give me a chance?"

Rhodri was feeling dizzy, and the jewels in the walls of the cave were beginning to spark and flash in the candlelight. But it was not an unpleasant feeling at all, and he was tempted to believe this beautiful woman. He was tired and frightened, and starving, too, and the thought of food was almost too much to resist.

"Sit then, Rhodri Falcon. Sit at the head of the table. Like a high king."

Rhodri sat down where his father had sat, and Homeira disappeared into the back of the cave. When she returned, she began to place plates before the boy of silver and gold, piled with foods that, if anything, were even more wonderful than the feast he had beheld in the Telling Pool. Homeira sat opposite him at the head of the table, as the young man began to help himself. He tasted of the fig. He ate wild boar, roasted in honey, and venison and quail. He tried sweetmeats and pheasant and apples, fried with cherries. All the things he had longed to taste.

"There," whispered Homeira, as he ate ravenously, "you've a taste for the finer things, Rhodri Falcon. Like your dear father."

Rhodri looked at her guiltily, his mouth full of food. The heady feeling and the strength in his limbs seemed to have faded to a kind of leaden dullness. Rhodri could hardly lift his arms now.

"My father," he said, looking toward the casket.

"You think I stole his heart," said Homeira, "but it is not so simple. Nothing is so simple in life. He gave me his heart, because he gave me his love. Just as one in this very cave gave her heart to a brave and beautiful knight long ago. To her husband's and her king's most loyal friend."

"Guinevere," said Rhodri, looking round in astonishment.

"Yes. The Lady Guinevere. For it is here they lay together that dark, ancient eve. Guinevere and Lancelot. On a wild night, long ago. This is where they betrayed Arthur."

"Here?"

Rhodri gasped, but as he thought of his own father's betrayal of his mother, he looked down.

"That is what makes you truly angry, isn't it," said Homeira, "that you know the truth of it already? That your father was tempted by me long before I plucked his heart from his chest. As you are now. It was his own desire that really enslaved him, was it not, as Lancelot's and Guinevere's enslaved them, too, and brought forth an ancient curse? A curse that still grips this land."

Rhodri felt ashamed, but still he could hardly move. Yet in his mind's eye he saw Rebecca's face, and his strength and will rallied.

"Liar," the young man said, stirring angrily. "I don't know the truth of the old stories, but I saw what you did. You tricked him, Homeira. He was just a man and was tired and hurt and alone. But you cheated and enchanted him."

Homeira's eyes flashed at the boy. "Just as I have enchanted you, Rhodri Falcon."

"Me?" said Rhodri faintly.

"Can you not feel it now, working through your veins? My magic potion."

The young man's limbs were growing heavier and heavier.

"But how?" whispered Rhodri faintly. "Your ring's sealed and the wine, you tried the wine yourself."

Homeira touched a finger to her mouth and smiled cunningly.

"So you saw the secret of my ring in the spying Pool. But not the red pigment I use on my lips, Rhodri Falcon. I've worn it too long for it to affect me, but when I left some on the cup it mingled with the wine and entered your veins and body."

Homeira got up and swept toward him. The young man tried to move, but now his limbs were as heavy as his father's sword. The witch came closer and suddenly she looked down at his tunic, to where the vial lay concealed.

"It is fair, is it not, to drug one who thought to poison me."

Homeira lifted her hand and brought the palm down against his chest, striking the hidden vial. Rhodri felt it shatter within his tunic, and the water running down his skin, and as the witch pressed, he felt the pieces of glass cutting into his flesh.

"Foolish boy," hissed the witch. "You think I did not see his gift, too. But now nothing may help you."

As the pain cut across his chest, Homeira lifter her hand and stroked his face and kissed him gently on the lips. Rhodri felt the anger trying to break from his body, and the revulsion at her touch, but it was as if he had been imprisoned in stone. Beads of sweat had begun to break from his forehead.

"Such dark hair," said Homeira tenderly, "such fine, noble eyes. Such a true and loving heart. Like one of the heroes of old."

She laughed and turned to the table. She picked up a fig and bit into it, sucking at its flesh as she sat on the edge of the table, smiling at the helpless young man.

"But what use are such things in this world?" she cried, "For all you've learned as a boy on your farm, of courage and honor, of truth and a pure heart—they are the real lies. Fables to keep children tame and well behaved, as their parents conceal the bitter truth of life and death in their own lying, frightened hearts. But you've seen something of the real world now, have you not? In the Telling Pool and on your journey, too? You've seen how cold and cruel it is."

Again Rhodri dropped his eyes. He could not argue.

"And to survive in this world," Homeira almost hissed, "it is not love or faith or goodness that's needed. Like those foolish knights that set out long ago on their pointless quest, for a grail that does not exist. It is cunning and craft, strength and knowledge. These gifts of food and wealth and power, they can only come to those you have the courage and strength to take them."

Homeira lifted her hand, and half of the fig lay in it. She squeezed her palm tight shut on the fruit, as she had squeezed Owen's heart.

"To grasp what you want in life and hold it forever," she cried.

Rhodri felt as if he was in a nightmare.

"No," the young man muttered. "Mother, Father. They need me. They . . ."

Homeira smiled coldly.

"Your father," she said. "You come to fight for him like a dutiful son. But somewhere inside you hate and resent him, too. For did he not grasp you by the neck like a slave? Did he not strike you to the ground? Where was his love for you then?"

The young man shuddered, not only with the anger and pain that the memory brought him, but because this woman seemed to know all about him. And something of her words was true. Rhodri was completely defenseless, and yet something else stirred in his gut. What business was it of hers what he felt for his family or his friends?

"And hate is as natural as love," said Homeira, smiling. "So hate well, Rhodri Falcon."

"No," said the young man. "My pa, he did those things because of you. Because you tricked him."

Homeira opened her palm. Her skin looked bruised with the juice of the crushed fruit.

"Grow up, boy," she snapped. "When I hold your father's heart and squeeze it, then Owen remembers, that's all. Remembers what he saw and did in the Holy Wars. What he experienced and felt in my cave, too. But those memories, and the desire and anger and hate inside him, they're his alone. We must take responsibility for what we see. For what we are."

Rhodri was shaking his head, but he knew that this, too, was true.

"Tell me," said the enchantress, "when in the lava I saw you slay that outlaw, did it not feel good to press the sword through his belly? To kill him mercilessly, as a falcon kills the lesser birds on the wing."

Rhodri was silent. Somewhere it had felt good.

"So you, too, are beginning to see what it is like to be a man and that life is not a fairy tale for little children," said Homeira, "One day you'll be a man, too. You are almost one now. But when that time comes, you'll find you have a choice. To live as a man or to hide away on your farm, safe and ignorant of the world. Good and pious in your frightened heart, but seeing nothing more than the stream and the field and your parents growing old and dying, and yourself in their failing image. Is that a fate for one such as you? I think not."

She turned away and her hair swept out behind her. Rhodri noticed the grace of her movements and the flow of the dress against her body, and he suddenly recalled Rebecca touching his lips with her own.

"I don't understand," he said, "why you talk to me like this, Homeira. What do you want from me?"

The enchantress swung round, and her eyes looked at Rhodri so intently it was as if they were piercing to his very being.

"Want from you? Your heart, of course. Your heart and soul."

"Mine?" gasped Rhodri, in amazement. "But it's my father's heart you stole, like the knights in this cave. Him you love."

"Love." Homeira laughed. "I offered him love and power, but he scorned me. Just as in my land, another . . ."

Homeira's eyes were like burning coals.

"And before that . . . long, long ago."

Her voice was faint and wistful, as if she was trying to remember something.

"I have Owen's heart now," she said. "That's enough for my pleasure. He's growing old already, and what triumph is there in taking a heart already tainted by the world? But you. You're pure still. Your whole life is ahead of you. You I can teach of the true power and glory."

She walked back and pulled a single feather from a bird whose body lay unplucked on the table, its neck broken. She turned and, laughing, put it in Rhodri's hair and stroked his cheek.

"You look, Rhodri Falcon, but do you not see the truth yet? It's you

I've wanted all along, not your father. And you who have fallen so easily into my trap."

"Trap?" said Rhodri. "What trap? Who are you?"

Homeira turned away again and walked back into the shadows.
She was wreathed in candlelight now and spoke to him in a voice that
was transformed.

"Come, boy. Come and look. You want to know your fortune
though, don't ye? We all want to know our fortune. Come, boy, don't
be frightened."

The young man sat bolt upright. A fear seized him. *"You."*

Rhodri realized what that feather in his hair meant now, and an
image flashed into his mind, of another card on a table. The Fool. As
Rhodri looked on, Homeira and the candlelight shimmered in the
cave like water, for an instant, an instant so brief he might have imagined it in the dancing shadows, those beautiful features were transformed into a toothless, grinning old hag.

"The fortune-teller," gasped Rhodri in horror.

There was Homeira again, beautiful and young and smiling down
at him.

"Then the cards foresaw everything?"

"Foresaw?" she said. "I planned everything."

"It can't be," said Rhodri, trying to shake the heaviness off him and
the sense that he was really dreaming. "Who are you? At the fair you
were old, but now you're young again."

The witch walked up to the skull and, lifting it, turned the grinning horror in her hand and looked calmly, almost affectionately, into
its ghastly face.

"Age, Rhodri Falcon, and death." she said. "Are these not things for those who do not know the secrets of the Law? For most the body is a prison that they shall never escape. As my casket imprisons your father's heart. As my cave seals the knights in stone."

Rhodri blanched.

"But if you can command the powers of the Goddess and the God, then who knows what is possible? Did Arthur die, or does he just sleep? As all the heroes sleep of old. Guinevere and Lancelot. Merlin and Morgana. Their battles go on throughout eternity, if we truly believe."

Rhodri remembered Tantallon at the edge of the Telling Pool. The thing he had seen in the coming morning. That change in his face when Tantallon had suddenly looked so much younger. Perhaps Rhodri hadn't imagined the change after all. But then what of Tantallon? And Homeira. That dream he had had of a woman surrounded by mutilated knights. Could Homeira really be the fabled Morgana Le Fey? Then who was Tantallon? No, whispered Rhodri's frightened, confused mind, Homeira had come from the East. From far away.

"I was there when Jerusalem fell to your Christian knights," said Homeira, "and I have lived in this cave for a hundred and twenty of your years. And waited."

"Waited?" said Rhodri, shuddering at the thought of all the long years.

The witch's eyes flickered. "Long ago I came into your lands," she said, "and found this fabled cave again. But with time my powers began to fail me. That's why I was old when you saw me at the fair. When I saw that amulet and knew you immediately."

Rhodri clutched the talisman at his throat. His amulet. "Knew me?"

Homeira smiled. "Knew your true destiny, boy. Knew you walked the Path of the Deer. Knew that you were of her line. The Lady Guinevere's."

"Her line?" said the young man. "I am of her line."

"Of course. Here, in this cave, when they betrayed Arthur that night and lay together, a child was conceived, conceived of Guinevere and Lancelot's love. Arthur could not love it, but he could not kill it, either. So the boy was sent deep into the Welsh lands. Where he grew and lived, to sire children. Your father's forefathers."

Rhodri was looking at the witch in astonishment. His amulet. Now he knew what it really meant. It bore not only the shape of a deer's head, like that on Guinevere's cloak, but the Celtic Cross, too, that he had seen Lancelot kneeling before in the Telling Pool. They were joined.

"Then the call came to Holy War, as I foretold," said Homeira, "for men love war above all. And I knew my time would come again. That the curse had come once more, or never really left. For quickly the land began to suffer and darkness ate at each man's heart. That is what opened them to me. The returning knights. For the things they had seen and done in the Holy Lands had weakened them. So I took them, one by one, and sealed them in stone, and each time I did so, I grew younger again."

As Homeira's huge shadow swayed around the cave in the candlelight. a moan seemed to come from the walls and Rhodri saw shapes moving in the stone.

"Help us."

"Many came to pay court to me," cried Homeira, looking scornfully at that weaponry, "but though I have been lonely, none were good enough. And none escaped. Their lifeblood sustains the enchantments of my cave and gives me youth."

Rhodri shuddered.

"But sleep now," whispered the witch, "and you'll understand all of it in time. And you must grow strong and clearheaded. For your poor father did understand one thing. No bargain is truly made by enchantment."

"Bargain?" said Rhodri faintly.

"Your father's heart," said the witch. "I'll open my casket, open it and free him, Rhodri Falcon, free him like a bird, if you'll promise to stay with me. To listen and learn from me, with your whole heart and being. And then . . ."

Rhodri just looked at her. Homeira was offering him his father's heart in return for his own. If it was the only way to save his parents, how could the young man refuse such a bargain? And yet. What of him? To become Homeira's slave.

"When you wake, we'll talk again," said the enchantress, "and you'll taste more of the wonders of my cave. So dream, Rhodri Falcon, as you dreamt in your room as a little boy . . ."

Homeira's voice had become like music, soft and lilting, and the young man found his eyes growing heavier and heavier. It was as if he was sinking downward, as he had as a child, wrapped in those fronds and weeds that grew in the stream. He was plunged into dreams, and his father was before him and crying out. "Help me, Rhodri, please help me." Then his ma was standing over the hearth sobbing. There were soldiers there, too, cutting and killing, and Rhodri felt as though his soul were lost and wandering through a world of shadows.

"You know now who you are," came another voice in his dreams, "but can you truly wake, wake and grasp your destiny?"

Suddenly Rhodri was standing in a big field, but the world was not alive with wonder and mystery, as it had been when he was a boy. The forest around him was a violent, dangerous thing, and even the grass he stood on seemed to hold a threat. Rhodri was looking up and calling, calling to Melanor wheeling high above in the skies. But Rhodri knew that his falcon could no longer hear him and that its circles were taking it farther and farther away.

16 ✷ MYTHIRION

My spirit is too weak—mortality
Weighs heavily on me like unwilling sleep
—John Keats, "On seeing the Elgin Marbles"

The sharp clanking of metal woke Rhodri. He was still seated in the chair and as he opened his eyes he saw Homeira before him, standing at the strange fire in that bowl of lava. It was blazing now, and as she rotated something in its flame, she struck at it with a hammer and a great shower of sparks flew up. She turned. She was holding up Owen's sword. It had been reforged in the lava, and it glowed now with the liquid translucence of hot metal.

"A sign," said the witch softly, "that we're not enemies, Rhodri Falcon. For every brave young warrior needs a sword, does he not?" She laughed.

Homeira had changed and was dressed in a heavy, embroidered gown. She placed the sword at the edge of the lava pool. As she did so the glowing metal began to cool and then it shone silver once more. Rhodri stirred in his chair and found that he could move again.

In front of Rhodri, the table was laid richly once more, and in its very center sat the magic casket. The candlelight played against its glittering edges, and the beating heart inside looked redder and more livid than before. He rubbed his eyes and wondered what time and what day it was. He felt as if he had been in the cave for an eternity already, but as he counted back he relaxed a little. It had been eight days before the eve of the Christ's mass when he had reached the cave, and he had not been there more than a single night. The bargain had time to run yet.

But Rhodri looked sadly at the casket, too. Homeira had offered him a bargain, and if he did not do this thing, his father's heart would be locked inside forever. The young man felt a sharp sting of resentment and almost wished that he had never met Tantallon that day and never looked into the Telling Pool at all. But then Rhodri remembered Tantallon's words, too. "You must not blame the Telling Pool, or a foolish old man, for showing you the truth."

It was true. The things that had happened had happened and Rhodri could not alter that fact. He recalled something else his friend had said, about change. Everything changed, and he could no more stop it than dam up the waters of a river with pebbles. Or stop himself growing up, or growing old and dying.

"Your story," said Rhodri, raising his chin, "go on with your story, Homeira."

The beautiful enchantress smiled and came forward. "As I said, Rhodri, the knights came to me and I grew strong and waited, until Owen arrived, as I saw he would. Then I knew that I could bring you, too. As I had planned when I first found you at the fair. Did I not warn you that you both had a part to play?"

Rhodri jumped up. "But what do you really want from me?"

"From you?" said the enchantress. "Nothing. Wealth and power and knowledge you shall have, from me. All the secrets of the world will be revealed to your eyes, Rhodri Falcon. And if you accept, then I'll give you the greatest prize." She turned and walked toward her fire pool and looked down. Rhodri drew closer.

"The greatest prize?"

"Still you do not understand. Well, come then. And see."

He walked over to the fire pool, and as he looked down he gasped in utter amazement. There it lay at last, deep in the heart of the fire, just as Rhodri had seen it in the Telling Pool. The fabled sword seemed to be floating on the lava, deep within the well. Its hilt was glowing and its blade flashed with fire.

"Mythirion." The young man gasped. "It's here. Excalibur's been here all along."

The image changed and a great hammer was being lifted into the air. A man was holding it who looked as Tantallon must have as a young man, and he brought it down on a blade with a flash of glittering sparks. He was in Homeira's cave, on the edge of the lava pool, and the whole place seemed have become a smithy or a forge, flaring with flame and fire so violent it seemed hotter than the sun, or the heart of hell itself. The man was dressed in a simple black robe, and all about him the air was thick with smoke and steam.

"The forge of Mythirion," cried Homeira, "where Merlin first made the sword."

Suddenly Merlin lifted the blade, and there it was before Rhodri's eyes again. Mythirion. The runes along Excalibur's blade were flickering with living fire themselves, and the golden hilt blinded the young man. Once more the picture changed, and Excalibur lay still in the lava pool. As if waiting.

"So long I've waited to draw it from the pool once more," said Homeira hungrily. "For I saw it when I found the cave and knew what it was immediately. It was here, in the heart of the sacred mountain, that it was forged and here where that fool Merlin placed it again after Arthur's death, to keep it safe from . . ." Homeira paused. "From the wicked enchantress Morgana Le Fey," she said and smiled.

"Excalibur was never returned to the lake. It has been here for all those long, long centuries. In the forge of Mythirion, where it was first made. Though even Merlin forgot the forge's whereabouts when the curse came."

The great sword looked so close that Rhodri thought he could reach out and touch it.

"When the land is in danger again," whispered Rhodri, "then it shall return to save a king."

"To save a king?" Homeira laughed. "That fool the Lionheart is in the German lands, trying to raise a ransom and wash away the blood he spilt in the Holy Lands. His brother John seeks the throne, and hate and greed swamp the forests. But are not such cursed times when my kind may thrive? And with the sword in my hand, my power shall be irresistible."

"But Excalibur," said Rhodri, "brings only peace."

"Peace," spat Homeira. "What foolish lies. Is Mythirion not also known as the blade of Ten Thousand Tears? Tears that men shall shed like a sea, for what they did to me."

"Why didn't you draw it from the pool yourself, Homeira? Why don't you draw it from the fire now?"

Her eyes glinted and she looked down longingly at Excalibur.

"I cannot," she answered bitterly, "for the lava would burn me up like a twig. You know the story of how Arthur became high king. Of how Merlin sealed Excalibur within the rock Bethganoth. Only one with courage and truth and love in his heart could draw it from the stone then, and only such a one may do it now. But only one of their line. Of the bloodline of the ancient ones, who comes to believe again. You, Rhodri Falcon."

Believe, thought Rhodri. He no longer knew what he believed.

"For an age I wandered, even though I was growing old, looking for her last descendent. And I knew you as soon as I saw you and your father at the fair. It's why I laid my trap. Why I brought you both here."

Rhodri felt like a fool. Like Hellard, just a pawn in a king's army.

Mythirion was so wonderful, though, that Rhodri wanted to touch it. He lifted his young hand toward it, but immediately he felt the burning fiery heat of the lava pool and Homeira grasped his hand and pulled it back.

"Not yet," she said. "You have not made the pact."

"Pact?"

"To serve me. You must make the bargain freely. Besides, it is not yet time. Now it would burn even you. No. Though made in a world of older faiths, its coming is always marked by great signs, and so it must be drawn on the day of the Savior's birth. Then, then you may pull forth Excalibur. One of her line, with innocence and purity, may draw it, but one with cunning and wisdom shall wield it again."

The image of Excalibur in the lava began to fade, and a face appeared there. At first the boy thought it was King Richard, but the man was younger and not dressed as a soldier at all.

"Who is he, Homeira?" asked Rhodri, thinking that he must be one of the knights of old. Homeira hardly seemed to care.

"That idiot, John."

"John," said Rhodri, "the Lionheart's brother?"

"Of course," said the witch. "Even now he dreams of sitting on the English throne, and the curse grows strong in men's hearts. Even now he plots with the French King Philip. And his lust shall grow stronger and stronger, for in his dreams I visit him and fill his thoughts with greed and betrayal and ambition. And this is your first lesson. Use the ties of family to betray."

Rhodri felt sick.

"And I visit poor Richard, too, while he rots in his cell," said the witch cruelly, "tormenting him with memories of his failures in the Holy Land and his dreams of salvation, with all that happens at home, and with visions of war. But it is because of me that he is a prisoner."

"Because of you?" said Rhodri in amazement. Homeira's evil seemed to be spreading everywhere.

"When he crossed from Venice, he planned to journey home in secret, but I saw his route in my pool and so I sent dreams to the Austrian prince, whose lands Richard journeyed through, telling him of the presence of the English king. They swooped down on him like a plump little partridge and snatched him up."

Rhodri shook is head. But there was a sound, a voice, from the lava itself.

"Cease your evil, Homeira."

Rhodri's heart leapt at that voice. He knew it immediately. The witch leaned over the fire pool. John had vanished, and there in the fire was Tantallon. He was robed in gray and standing on a great rock, mossed with ivy and lichen in the heart of a forest.

"You," hissed Homeira savagely, "you old meddler."

The old man's lined face was strong and angry, and he was looking straight out of the fire at the witch. His eyes did not flinch, and for a moment Rhodri thought he was not blind at all.

"Let the lad go, Homeira. Let them all go. There has been enough suffering."

Homeira gripped the edges of the stone well as she glared back at Tantallon.

"What do you want here? Foolish old man."

"You call me old so hatefully, Homeira," came Tantallon's voice calmly, "because you fear death. But you know the truth of it. You're young again, perhaps, feeding on men's strength and power and lifeblood. But I knew you at the fair Homeira and what you sought. How you would try to get the sword. So I've guarded the boy all his life. I got to him first and his heart is true."

"And now you send him to fight me," hissed Homeira scornfully, "with nothing to aid him."

"Nothing?" said Tantallon. "Nothing but his heart. For I did not send him, Homeira. He came to help his father and the knights, because of the love and faith in him. That's his strength and his alone. As the power and love was the Savior's, and Arthur's, too."

"He fell into my trap," said the witch softly. "That's the foolishness of an ignorant boy. Remember, Tantallon. He's of her line, is he not? And Guinevere's line is marked by betrayal. But I shall teach the boy a greater wisdom. Not to be ashamed of where he comes from, and how to fulfill the power of a curse, not deny it. Then I shall share with him the true secrets."

"Secrets," said Tantallon coldly. "You'd teach him nothing but hate of humans and of the world. I see that cruelty is still strong in you, Homeira, as it always was. As it was when you blinded me, with that burning poker . . . blinded your own lover as I slept."

Rhodri gasped. The scar across Tantallon's eyes. This man and woman had been lovers.

"It is hate alone that makes you abuse the Law, with your caskets and your lies, Homeira."

"The Law," mocked Homeira, "the Law that keeps you growing old, Tantallon, while I grow young and beautiful again. That makes you hide in the forest away from mortal men, mumbling on of goodness and kindness and healing. Staring into your pool with your sightless eyes and touching only dreams and memories and longing. Because you fear the real power. Life."

Suddenly Tantallon stood up on the strange rock and lifted the hood of his robe. There was something so changed in him and so fearsome that Homeira and Rhodri stepped back from the flames.

"The Law of the God and Goddess," cried Tantallon's booming voice, and the air seemed to tremble with threat. "The Law that made me and the boy, you and the cave. That forged Mythirion itself. None may break the sacred Law, not even you, woman."

Tantallon leaned forward, and when he spoke again his voice was gentler.

"Have you forgotten, Homeira?" said the blind old man softly, reaching out his hand sadly. "Have you forgotten us? Our touch. Our love. Are you so blind?"

As Rhodri watched, he felt the oddest thing he had ever felt in his life. It was a pang of jealousy for this beautiful, evil woman.

"I've forgotten nothing, Tantallon," answered Homeira, drawing closer.

"Open your heart again, and touch the true power. Especially on the eve of the Savior's birth."

Rhodri started. What was Tantallon saying? The eve of Christ's mass. It couldn't be.

"Together," said Tantallon, "together we'll use the power well."

Homeira laughed.

"It is power that I shall use, always," she cried, "Power that you never had the courage to grasp. When I wield it once more."

"Mythirion," said Tantallon angrily. "You could no more wield it than rule a kingdom. And it must stay safe where it lies, Homeira. For it is too powerful for them to understand. That's why it was placed in the fire."

"And forgotten about."

Homeira spun around and picked up the goblet of wine on the edge of the fire pool.

"Be gone, you old fool," she cried furiously, casting the wine into the flames. There was a great hissing and Tantallon vanished. But as the image turned back to boiling lava, a voice rose out of the steam, a voice that echoed through the whole cave.

"Know this, Rhodri Falcon. Homeira's magic is powerful indeed. But with courage and faith and love you may pierce a heart of stone."

Homeira and the young man were left alone again, and Homeira turned and smiled softly.

"Don't heed him, Rhodri, my dear. Because of his age he's full of hate and jealousy. Full of lies."

"But who is he?" asked Rhodri. "You know each other well?"

"Well indeed," answered Homeira, "and he, too, loved me once, as I loved him. But that is a story that you need not know, for it was over long ago. His power was strong once. But it is nothing now. Nothing more than dreams and feeble memories."

"But what Tantallon said. He said it's the eve of the Christ's mass."

Homeira's eyes sparked. "And so it is."

"But it can't be . . . how long have I . . ."

"You slept in the chair for seven days."

"A week?" cried Rhodri in horror, feeling as if he were losing himself entirely. "Then . . ."

"The bargain is almost up. Tomorrow, when . . . when the raven calls, it must be done. Now I must be gone awhile. So think, Rhodri Falcon. There's food and drink and you are free to wander my cave.

But do not try to leave it, for the poison smoke will surely kill you this time."

Homeira walked up to Rhodri and stroked his face again, before turning and sweeping out of the cave, straight through the smoke curtain. It closed behind her and the young man stood wondering why she had left him alone.

He walked gloomily back to the table. The casket was there and he tried to open it, but once more nothing would move the lid. Rhodri had a thought. Why not take the heart from the cave within its box? But as soon as he tried to pick it up he was amazed, for the thing was so heavy he could hardly move it at all. He struggled with it, managing to lift it two fingers' width and no more, and then dropped it back in its alcove with a bitter sigh. His own heart felt just as heavy.

Rhodri decided to explore. He was nervous at first, but soon the young man grew delighted by the richness and fineness of the things he found in there. The carved wooden statuettes, the silks and cushions, the rare boxes and caskets, the wooden globes and astrolabes.

Nearby he found an array of strange glass bottles, too, filled with powders and herbs, liquids and potions, and then beyond he saw that a part of the cave had been turned into a kind of library. The books were wonderfully fine, bound in leather, but inlaid with gilding and strange markings. As he turned them over in his eager hands, Rhodri thought how delighted Isaac would have been to see these things and found himself longing to be able to read the secrets written there.

Indeed, as the young man explored that magical place, so great was his fascination and so inquisitive his mind, that he found himself wishing more and more that Homeira would indeed teach him all her secrets. Just as Tantallon had begun to. She had knowledge and magic and power, too, which a mere Falconer's son could never in a thousand years hope to aspire to. How different this place was to the simplicities of his humble home, or Tantallon's hovel. Rhodri found himself smiling as he wondered what William or Aelfric or Sarah would think of it all, if they could see him now. Or if they would believe any of it.

What had Homeira said about the world? Rhodri had already seen things well beyond his years in the Telling Pool and on the road, but little he had seen had made him anything but angry. His father had taught him so much. Yet he had never taught him this about the souls of men.

Rhodri wandered back over to the table and gazed at the casket. He felt strangely contemptuous of that heart locked inside. But as soon as he did so, he felt a heat arise from the lava in the recess behind him. Rhodri turned toward the lava pool to look once more on Mythirion. As he peered into the flames, thinking once more of the beautiful sword, the images came. Not of Mythirion though. The pictures were of somewhere in the land of Persia. A ring of fire had leapt up around the bubbling pool, and there Rhodri saw Homeira herself. She looked no more than a girl, about Sarah's age, or only slightly older, dressed in a simple white robe that made her thick locks of hair look even blacker.

Homeira was surrounded by men, bearded and dressed as soldiers, with their curved swords drawn. A stern old man was before her, his beard grizzled with gray and he was smiling as he spoke. At first he talked in a foreign tongue, but as Rhodri listened intently, he realized that he could understand him.

"You think you may steal my son, Homeira?" he growled. "You, the daughter of a common servant."

Homeira lifted her head proudly in the fire. "But he loves me," she declared from the flames.

"Fool," shouted the old man. "He has the blood of the caliphs in his veins. He was born to rule, and you think a peasant may steal his heart? You are clay of the poorest bazaar, nothing more, Homeira. And now we shall shatter you like clay."

Homeira's eyes blazed and Rhodri thought how similar were the laws of Persia to his own land. The men had started to advance on her, and suddenly Homeira ran forward. She had grabbed a curved dagger from one of their belts and leapt back into the center of the circle.

"You'd defile me," hissed the young girl. "To you I'm nothing but a servant and a slave. A feeble woman. But I'm far more than that. Such dreams and visions I have had. I have the strength and power of my ancient ancestors in me. The strength of flame."

Rhodri shuddered, but he thought how magnificent Homeira looked now.

"Defile you?" muttered the old man. "No. You've loved my son and though it is a grave crime, for that at least I shall spare your blushes and your life. But you shall be marked. To warn all such as you to know their place, before we sell you into slavery in the marketplace."

Homeira screamed and spat at the old man and lashed out at another with the dagger, but there were too many of them. One of the soldiers had come up behind her and grabbed her arms. She screamed again and kicked and bit into his hand. But it was useless.

Another figure had appeared in the lava, moving toward the helpless girl. He carried a fire poker, and the circle of metal at its tip was glowing red hot. They tore her dress to expose her shoulder and then the poker was moving toward her, searing into her burning flesh. As Rhodri felt the heat from the lava pool, he could feel her pain. Homeira screamed a third time, and Rhodri felt a surge of pity and fury as she collapsed onto the ground and the pictures faded.

"You see," said a voice sadly, "I, too, have loved, Rhodri Falcon. As your father loved. As Guinevere and Lancelot once loved, too, and so gave birth to the future. But what use is love?"

Homeira was standing amid the smoke at the mouth of the cave. There were plants and berries in her hands and her black hair was wet with snow. Again he felt closer to her. This strange woman who had stolen his father's heart had suffered, too, as Owen had suffered in the wars. As everything suffered.

"I once dreamed of a home and fine children," said Homeira. "But that was long ago and in another place."

"Tell me," said the young man softly.

"He was handsome and strong," said Homeira. "As dark and strong as a river, and with eyes filled with moonlight. For a year and a day we were lovers. But he would not take me as his bride, for he was of noble birth and I—just a child of the town."

Homeira reached up and pulled the edge of her robe from her shoulder. There, scored into her lovely skin, was the circle the branding iron had made. It was of a crescent moon.

"So they marked me with a hot iron," she said, "and tried to sell me into slavery. But I escaped and fled. It was in my own journeying that I swore never to be at the mercy of men again."

She smiled at Rhodri. "Or such men at least. And I learned something of the arts that you have beheld here. Knowledge usually denied to mere women. Then I came into Christendom and met Tantallon. And he . . . he taught me, reminded me of even deeper secrets. Even older truths."

Something had come into Homeira's eyes, as if she were again touching a long forgotten memory, but she placed her harvest on the table and filled up a goblet with wine.

"I've tended to your horse again, as I have over the days," she said. "Will you drink with me now?"

"Homeira," said Rhodri quietly, "give me my father's heart. Will you not release him? If you felt anything for him? I know you did."

"And our bargain?"

The young man sighed and bowed his head.

"I'll stay with you," he whispered.

"And you will forget all the foolishness you learned as a boy? Of your room and the stream. Of the farm and your falcon. Will you truly walk the deer's path?"

"Yes. I swear it."

"And when we have Mythirion, I shall teach you to wield it, too," cried Homeira delightedly, and she seemed even younger and even more girlish. "You'll study and read and grow and look into the lava. The wisdom of a true king shall be yours. You're waking to your true destiny."

"How shall we seal this bargain?" asked Rhodri.

"Tell me," answered the witch, "of all your hopes, what is the thing you have longed for most in your heart?"

Rhodri thought then of Melanor, of Rebecca in the wood, of Mythirion and going to war to win the glories of a king. But Rhodri knew well what it really was he had longed for most.

"To read," he answered simply. "To read and write."

"Very well, then we shall write it down together on parchment. Tomorrow we will make the pact when we dine together. But first you must sleep."

Homeira was pointing across the cave to the silken bed this time.

"I want your mind clear and refreshed when you make the pact, Rhodri, and you'll need to be strong to draw the sword. Then I'll open the casket and your father shall be as free as a bird. I swear it."

17 ❖ THE RAVEN'S CALL

The Eternal Female groand! it was heard all over the Earth:
Albions coast is sick silent
—William Blake, "A Song of Liberty"

When Rhodri woke a second time in Homeira's cave, he saw a dark shadow, like beating wings, move across the floor for an instant then disappear. The young man blinked and saw that the witch was standing at the back of the cave looking into the lava. Its flames were flickering against those strange, ribbed walls. He raised himself.

"Soon," she whispered, "soon you shall be in my hand, Mythirion."

The witch had become aware of Rhodri. As she turned, he saw that she was holding a goblet of wine in her hand.

"Good," cried Homeira, smiling sweetly. "You've slept. Now come and see some of the things I shall teach you."

He stepped forward and Homeira waved her hands over the bubbling fire. Such beautiful visions Rhodri saw there of the wide world, that his heart began to pound as he thought of all the secrets they would learn together. At the thought of holding Mythirion, too. So they passed several hours until Homeira, putting her hand tenderly on his shoulder as the pool became fire once more, said, "Now let us feast and make our pact."

Rhodri followed the witch toward the table, and watched as Homeira stroked the casket. The price he was about to pay weighed heavily on him again.

"Smile, Rhodri," said Homeira, "for you cannot imagine what gifts I am granting you."

Rhodri smiled weakly and lifted his cup to drink. So they ate together and the wine warmed him, and once more Homeira began to speak of the lands of Persia. The candles in the cave were burning low when she rose to walk over to the lava. Rhodri looked deep into his goblet, and heard a cawing cry. It seemed to be in the cave with them. A shadow moved against the walls and the boy turned to the witch.

"It's time," said Homeira. "The raven calls and the moon is high. It's almost twelve of the clock. The day of the Christ's mass is nearly done with. A year and a day is up."

Homeira walked over to that library now, and from among the tomes she pulled out a role of parchment. She took an inkwell and a quill pen and laid them before Rhodri. As she began to write, Rhodri noticed a pack of cards sitting on the table. The pack she had used at the fair. The Tarot.

"Of my own free will I make this bargain, to serve Homeira," said the witch as she wrote, "in return for my father's heart and the souls of Christian knights in her cave."

Rhodri had a memory of a pardoner on a horse with his scrolls. Indulgences for the soul, the forgiveness of sin.

"Come, Rhodri. Now you. Sign our pact."

Rhodri felt ashamed again.

"I can't write yet, Homeira," the young man whispered hoarsely, and he dropped his eyes. "I don't know how, Homeira."

She swept toward him and stroked his cheek.

"For now, your mark is enough."

He took the quill in his right hand and Homeira raised her goblet. "I drink to you, Rhodri. To your future. A new Arthur indeed. But not a fool to be betrayed by those he loved. One stronger and far more cunning. One better advised."

Rhodri stepped up toward the parchment, and Homeira picked up the playing cards and began to shuffle them.

"Hurry, for the world turns and night tips toward the day. Soon it will be too late for your father's heart. And so for all that love it."

The young man dipped the quill, and its end beaded with ink, like droplets of blood. His hand was shaking so badly, he had to steady it. He was so close now. A cross on a page, his mark, and his father and the knights would be free. All his father had seen, all he had suffered in the Holy Wars, the pain would be over and his father's heart would be restored. The land, too, would be healed. Because of his own faith and courage. Then, in the pool. Mythirion.

But in that moment Rhodri moved his leg and felt Rebecca's stone in his pocket and remembered all that had happened to him, and all that had happened to Owen. He remembered the terrible images of death and pain in the Telling Pool and his own journey through the forest. He was proud at what he was doing, that his quest was almost over, yet still something held him back. Then Rhodri recalled that morning at the well, when his pa had struck him, and the anguish it brought him drew his hand closer to the page to sign. But then, in his mind's eye, the young man could see Rebecca and hear her whispering to him. "But what of you, Rhodri Falcon?"

What indeed, thought Rhodri bitterly.

"This witch will try to enchant you, too," came Rebecca's dear voice in his mind. "But remember something, Rhodri. Your heart. It is yours alone."

If his father could see his son now in the Telling Pool, would he want his boy to do this thing—to sacrifice himself, as the Savior had sacrificed himself for the love of all? Surely it would break his heart, and his mother's heart, too. Then Rhodri could not do it. Because of their love for him.

All his life, Rhodri had longed to help his parents and he loved his father, but he was not his father. Rhodri's other hand had strayed to his pocket and clasped Rebecca's stone.

"No," he cried, slamming down his hand on the page. Rather than leaving his mark it left a gash in the parchment. "I won't, Homeira, because . . . because I refuse it. I, myself."

Homeira looked back at Rhodri and suddenly she started to laugh. The scorn shook out of her body.

"Foolish boy. Then your father's heart will be lost forever. And these souls in the cave, too. You shall have betrayed everything. Yourself, your family, your own dreams."

"No," said Rhodri. "I'll find another way to help them. But I'll not give you my heart."

The witch lifted her hand from her robes, and she was holding up the dagger she had used to cut out Owen's heart. She smiled.

"Then your fate shall be nothing but to die yourself, beyond enchantments, to die alone and in a ditch."

"So this is your kindness," said Rhodri, "your love? You pretend you're full of love, but Tantallon is right, you're nothing but cruel. Cruel enough to blind your lover. And what of Mythirion? You shall never hold it."

Fury contorted Homeira's face, but she controlled herself and it passed. She put the dagger back in her robes.

"Your heart is true and strong indeed," she said, looking at Rhodri almost proudly. "You are the one. Her descendent. The one to draw the sword from the fire. The fire that would destroy me."

Behind them the forge of Mythirion blazed quite of its own accord. Homeira ran over to it and looked down.

"I knew it," she cried exultantly. "Now it comes. Quickly, Rhodri Falcon."

"But the casket. Our bargain."

"There's no time. Come now."

Rhodri could not resist. There was Mythirion once more, as he drew close, gleaming brilliantly in the moving fire pool. Excalibur looked even closer to the surface and more solid. Its wonderful golden yellow hilt was turned toward Rhodri.

"Quickly," hissed Homeira. "The Savior's birth is here. Before the raven calls again, draw the sword."

"No."

"Do it, boy, or it will be lost to the world."

Rhodri raised a hand and was amazed that he could feel no heat from the lava at all.

"Yes," cried Homeira. "Your hand, Rhodri, plunge it into the pool. Then you shall have everything you seek. I swear it."

Rhodri was trembling as he held his hand there over the burning forge.

"Courage, it takes courage. But this was meant to be."

He closed his eyes and plunged his hands into the lava. He felt a terrible heat all about him, but it did not burn him. Rhodri was reaching down, reaching down toward the fabled sword.

"Yes. It doesn't burn you. Take Mythirion."

Rhodri remembered what he had seen in the Telling Pool of the wars in the Holy Land. A searing pain gripped his hand and the boy cried out in agony.

"No."

"Love," said Homeira almost tenderly, "it takes love, too, and a pure heart. Arthur's heart. Yours, too. Think of your parents and what you do for them. You have the spirit of a king, born of Guinevere's line. This is your destiny."

The pain was passing and Rhodri closed his hand around the hilt. He felt a jolt pass through his whole body, like a wave of fire. An image flashed into his head of a rock, in a wood long ago, and a young man drawing forth a sword from a stone. Rhodri gave a great sigh, and suddenly he was pulling his hand up, up, and out of the lava. Mythirion rose from the forge in a flurry of flaming droplets that dripped from the magical blade. The runes along the blade rippled, and its mighty tip flashed in the shadows. Its light seemed to illuminate the whole cave.

"Excalibur," cried Homeira triumphantly, her eyes as greedy as the raven's, "You have it, Rhodri Falcon. You've drawn the sword once more."

Homeira had stepped back almost fearfully from the fabled blade.

Rhodri's entire arm was shaking, but as he held up Mythirion he felt like a king himself. The sword was light to hold and he knew he could use it easily. He also felt a lightness in his body, but a strength and a peace, too, as if the presence of Excalibur indeed protected him from all harm. But as he looked about, the changes to the cave amazed Rhodri. Those forms in the walls were moving. It was if they were struggling to get out of the stone. Homeira was looking up, too.

"Magic," she cried. "Now the power truly comes. They try to fight it, but it is useless."

Homeira turned and walked back into the hall, toward the casket on the table, laughing to herself.

"Homeira," said Rhodri softly, holding Mythirion behind her, "my father's heart. Return it to me now."

The witch spun round. "Give me the sword first."

"No. Open your casket. Give me my father's heart."

Homeira looked slyly at the young man. "Very well," she whispered. "Bring me the key, Rhodri. It's there, on the shelf above my books."

Homeira was pointing at the books, and as Rhodri turned to look, the witch pushed him toward the cave wall. He was falling backward, back toward the walls of the cave, and Mythirion had dropped from his grasp. As soon as he struck the cave wall, Rhodri felt it. It was as if great hands had seized hold of him and he could not move. He looked down in horror. Folds of stone were wrapping about him. He was sinking into the cave itself.

"No!"

"Foolish boy," hissed Homeira savagely, "you think you may defeat my enchantments? And save your father's heart, too. But the bargain was already up."

Rhodri tried to struggle against the stone, but it was no good. He was becoming part of the rock, and Homeira stepped even closer.

"Now I'll have you both," she cried, "and Mythirion, too. You'll live in my cave, alone and friendless. Cursed."

"Help me."

"Did it not feel good to hold the sword?" said Homeira. "Did you, too, not want to be a king? To feel the power of a king. And my food and wine, it pleased you. You are just like your father. Just like Lancelot and the knights. Weak and greedy, like all men. The betrayal in your blood runs deep. And so you shall live, without love, without anyone. You shall live with a heart of stone."

"Rhodri."

The voice had come from the entrance to the cave. Rhodri could not believe his eyes.

"Rebecca."

Somehow the girl had passed through the veil of smoke and was standing there. Somehow its poison had not been able to touch her. She looked dirty and travel-weary, and was staring in horror at Rhodri seized in the wall of the cave.

"What is happening?"

"Who are you?" said the witch, spinning round.

"A true friend, Homeira," cried Rebecca, "and one who owes a debt of love. Let him go."

"You dare," cried Homeira. "Children dare to come to fight one such as I. Nothing can save him now. His heart shall become as stone. He shall forget everything in the walls of my cave. Everything he loves. Everything he is."

Rebecca's defiant eyes were flashing and she pulled something from her robe. It was Rhodri's antler-handled dagger. She still had it from the clearing. Homeira saw it glitter, and now the witch was moving, moving toward Mythirion. She grabbed hold of the mighty sword and swung round toward Rebecca, but even as she held it Homeira gave a terrible, bloodcurdling screech. *"Aaaagh."*

The witch opened her hand in agony, and Mythirion dropped from her grasp and clattered across the floor. Homeira was looking down at her hand in horror. Her palm was burned and blistered with fire. She had been branded once more.

"No!"

"Help me," whispered Rhodri. He felt a terrible leaden emptiness inside his chest and could hardly see Homeira or Rebecca now. "What's happening to me, Rebecca?"

"Rhodri," cried Rebecca. "Fight it. Remember. Your family and your friends."

As he heard her voice, the young man felt strengh in him and could move his hands again.

"Rebecca. Is that really you?"

"Yes, Rhodri. Fight it. For your father. For all of us. For me, Rhodri Falcon. But above all for yourself."

"Oh, Rebecca. I've been so sad."

And then Rhodri was moving forward, released from the stone. The boy stepped clear of the rock and back into the cave.

"Rhodri," said Rebecca delightedly, running over to him and folding him in her arms. The young man and woman clasped each other tight, and they were kissing each other.

"But how?" stammered Rhodri. "How did you find me?"

"Melanor found me and led me here. We both answered your call."

"Melanor . . ." Rhodri whispered in wonder.

Homeira had moved to the tablet and was pouring wine over her blistered hand. Rhodri picked up Mythirion again. He advanced on the witch.

"Now, Homeira," he said, "your tricks and lies are over. Open the damned casket."

Homeira swung round. Her face was contorted with loathing and rage.

"Never," she hissed. "If I cannot wield Mythirion, then none shall and none shall be free. You father will be mine forever and your mother shall suffer always, as I squeeze his feeble heart."

"Then I will kill you, Homeira," Rhodri said.

The young man could feel that old fury bubbling up inside him. With one strike Mythirion could cut the woman's head clean from her shoulders. It was as if Homeira had read his thought.

"If you strike me down, what will become of your father's heart then?"

"He'll be free."

"He'll never be free. The bargain is up and the casket was forged in the fire, like Mythirion. It is part of the Miracle, too. Nothing can end that."

"I'll find another way, another way to help my pa."

"Go on, then," said Homeira, between smiling lips, "do it. Put the blade through my belly. Kill me and be a man, if you have the guts for it."

It was as if the witch were goading Rhodri on, tempting him to do it. Be a man, he thought, and he remembered his old ache to go to war in the Holy Lands. He remembered, too, the horrors of war and the outlaw and that terrible feeling that had come on him after the other man's body had gone cold.

"You're frightened," laughed Homeira, "like a boy. Frightened to hurt me, as I hurt him every day, squeezing his heart and making him suffer. As I torture the knights."

Another moan came from the cave walls, and Rhodri raised Mythirion.

"Yes," cried Homeira.

Rhodri was about to swing. Even then he remembered Homeira in the lava and that terrible branding iron. He had felt pity for her then. She was hard and cruel, but it was because of all that she had suffered, because of the man who had betrayed her, because of the hate that was locked inside her, as his father's poor heart was locked inside that casket and the knights were sealed in stone.

He could not kill her, he would not. Rhodri lowered Mythirion again.

"I pity you, Homeira," he said. "Excalibur is the sword that brings peace."

Homeira's eyes flashed with hate, but even as they did so Rhodri felt at peace within himself, and then he remembered the last card on the table, of a woman holding up a sword—Justice. There was the most extraordinary sound. It came from the lava pool. It was like a groan, or a sigh, a low boom that flew from the fire and echoed through the cave. Homeira screamed and Rhodri heard a sharp crack.

To his amazement he saw that a great splinter had gone running through the very center of the glass casket. Then it shattered. Splinters of glass and wood flew across the table, and when it was done, there, where his father's heart had been, there was nothing at all. The bleeding, fluttering heart had vanished into thin air.

"My father," cried Rhodri triumphantly, "he's free."

Homeira was looking at the glass shards in astonishment.

"Perhaps," she said, "but I have many others to torture. And first I shall kill her."

Homeira had dashed for the table and picked up the long silver needle she had used to sew up Owen's chest. She was advancing on Rebecca.

"No!" shouted Rhodri.

He remembered something he had heard in the church then. They were the words of the Savior himself, words that he had always wondered about. "I come not with peace, but a sword." Rhodri had spared Homeira, had learned the lesson of love. He could not let her touch Rebecca. The world was a hard place indeed, full of dark and difficult paradoxes, and now he had to act.

Rhodri leapt across her path and plunged Mythirion into Homeira's chest. He held the fabled blade there and turned the hilt. The terrible witch was still standing though, and no blood flowed from her body at all. Homeira threw back her head. She was laughing, as Rhodri withdrew Mythirion and blinked stupidly at her.

"Fool," she cried. "You think you may harm me? If I can steal your father's heart, may I not also hide my own, safe from any harm?"

"Excalibur," said Homeira, dropping the needle. "You shall wield it for me, Falcon."

"Never."

"You cannot resist my will," coaxed Homeira. "For you have been inside the stone. So use Mythirion. The girl does not care for you. She's like all the others. Kill her and step beyond your childhood, to the true glories of the world. A true freedom."

Rhodri swung round and saw Rebecca trembling by the bookshelf. It was as if a great darkness had come over his mind, and his heart felt cold as stone. He stepped toward Rebecca.

"What are you doing, Rhodri?"

"I . . ."

"Strike," screamed Homeira behind them. "Kill the Jewess and we shall be one."

Rhodri could no longer control himself. He was moving toward Rebecca, moving under Homeira's will.

"A heart of stone," he said, as if in a dream.

With an effort that seemed superhuman, Rhodri wrenched his will from Homeira's grasp and turned toward the forge.

"No, boy, don't." Homeira thought that he meant to throw the sword back into the pool. Even Rebecca felt doubt as Rhodri lifted Mythirion. Yet the young man did not cast it into the lava forge. Instead, he plunged Excalibur into the cave wall. As soon as its tip hit rock, it slid straight into the stone. It went into the rock up to its hilt, and as it did so Homeira screamed terribly and fell to the floor. There was a great moan, not one of anguish or pain but one of release, and around them all a voice seemed to whisper one word.

"Arthyre."

The moving walls, the faces there, seemed to sigh as one and suddenly they stopped moving. The cave was restored to bare rock. All about the children stood knights. Homeira shrank back in horror. Her victims seemed in a dream, too, like pale ghosts, and picking up their weapons one by one, they turned and began to walk silently from the cave. As they went the blood seemed to rush into their cheeks and make them real again.

Rhodri felt a presence at his side.

"It is finished, Rebecca," he said. "The ancient curse is broken."

"Look, Rhodri," gasped Rebecca.

Rhodri looked down. There in his hand, where Mythirion had been, was nothing more than his father's humble broadsword.

"How?"

Rebecca shook her head. "Come, Rhodri. We must be gone from this terrible place."

They stared down at the witch and saw that Homeira's jet-black hair was streaked with white. Her left hand was open, and from it the pack of cards had gone spilling across the stone floor. The old woman was sobbing quietly to herself. Homeira looked up, her wrinkled cheeks stained with tears.

"Kill me, Falcon, for you may do it now you have found the secret of my heart. Kill me, but do not leave me alone here. I cannot be alone again."

Rebecca put her hand on Rhodri's arm, but Rhodri was already speaking. "I cannot kill you," he said softly, "for I do not hate you, Homeira. I feel . . . I feel nothing for you. And your enchantments are broken. The curse is done."

"Then go," hissed Homeira. "The magic is ended, too. Mythirion will not be drawn again. Run back to your parents, like a foolish child, and hide away from the world. From the dreams and ambitions of kings and queens. Leave me to die in peace."

Rhodri nodded, and lifting the scabbard, he sheathed his father's sword and slung it across his back. Then he took Tantallon's bag from the table, though he did not need it anymore. At the mouth of the cave the tapers had burned out and there was no smoke to bar their way.

Rhodri and Rebecca walked quickly, without looking back, wanting to leave this place behind them as fast as they could, wanting to forget all about the cave. Even as Rhodri saw those shattered icicles on the floor, and the harsh white arms of winter before him, he remembered his home again and the poverty that had come on his poor family. He thought of Rebecca's father and his fear of the world and suddenly Rhodri turned to the girl.

"My dagger, Rebecca," he said, "may I have it for a moment?"

"What are you doing, Rhodri?" asked Rebecca, giving him the antler knife.

Rhodri opened Tantallon's bag, and quickly he began to pick at the wall of the cave. Diamonds and sapphires he pulled away, rubies and emeralds, and when the little bag was full, Rhodri took Rebecca's hand and turned and strode into the night. As they went, they heard a bitter shriek from within. It was the cry of a raven.

Outside there was no sign of Melanor. Dusk was still tethered to the tree, and next to him stood Jezamel. The horses whinnied delightedly as they saw the young man and woman. Quickly Rhodri and Rebecca untied them and mounted. In the distance, all about the moor, the once corralled horses were carrying their masters back to their homes and peace.

Rhodri and Rebecca kicked their own horses hard and soon they were galloping, galloping as fast as the surging animals would bear them. The wind scoured their young faces and Rhodri's dark hair streamed in the air. Again there were tears in his eyes, but this time they were the tears of hope and release, and Rhodri remembered that other name for Mythrion that Tantallon had spoken in the forge—Tintallor, the Hope Bringer. Rhodri Falcon felt prouder than he had ever felt in his life.

18 ❖ HOME

Dear native brook! wild streamlet of the West!
How many various-fated years have passed
—Samuel Taylor Coleridge, "Sonnet: To the River Otter"

For a whole week, Rhodri and Rebecca rode together, hardly stopping. They spent the nights comforting and holding each other, and by day watched as the sights of Rhodri's journey to the cave swept by in a dream. They came to the stocks where Rhodri had seen that poor villain. They came to the tavern where the serving girl had embarrassed him, and now as he entered with Rebecca at his side and ordered a tankard of ale, he looked at the serving girl calmly and simply smiled. They rode on and entered the forest, but Rhodri felt little fear of the outlaws they might encounter on the road, for he knew he had his wits and his courage to guard him.

It was only when they came to that crossroads and the hanging tree that Rhodri pulled Dusk up and dismounted. The great tree stood there, unadorned by its human fruit now, and it looked strong and fine. Rhodri went up to it and put his hand on the bark and then he turned.

"Rebecca, this path leads to my home. You'll come with me, won't you?"

Rebecca's beautiful face was grave and deeply sorrowful. "Rhodri, I cannot. When Melanor found us, my father was sickening. I must return to him quickly and help him to heal."

Rhodri looked sadly at Rebecca, too, but after all he had done to help his own father he could not argue with his friend.

"I'll miss you, Rebecca. Cannot we . . ."

"Hush, Rhodri," said Rebecca softly. "We are of different worlds, you and I. Worlds kept apart by the hatred and foolishness of men. But perhaps we shall meet again. In happier times."

Rhodri smiled bitterly, but he knew the truth.

"Yes, Rebecca."

"Melanor," said Rebecca, "he led me to you. I'm sorry he was gone when we left the cave. I would like to think of you with a friend. Though I know you shall find many."

Rhodri smiled. "He's wild, Rebecca. He helped me before he left for a different aerie."

"He helped us both. Good-bye, Rhodri Falcon."

There were tears in Rebecca's dark eyes as she spurred Jezamel, but Rhodri cried out.

"Wait, Rebecca."

Rhodri ran over to Dusk and, taking Tantallon's bag, pulled out some of the gems.

"Here," he cried, thrusting them into her hand, "take these. They'll help you and Isaac."

"Thank you."

Rhodri stood watch as Rebecca disappeared into the forest, and then he mounted. Though his heart felt a pain, he knew that he was on the right road now and that it would not be too long before he would be in sight of his home. The casket that Homeira's wickedness had made in the Forge of Mythirion had shattered, and Owen's heart had been released, but Rhodri did not know now if his parents were well. He ached to see them again, and stroking Dusk's head, he spurred on his horse.

It was snowing again when Rhodri reached the ford. The waters were swollen with snowmelt, and as the young man crossed that little border, he knew his quest was over. That he had come home. Yet something strange came on him as he trotted along. A kind of sadness. Sometimes as a boy Rhodri had played by the ford, trying to dam it up with stones like the stream, or imagining it was a mighty river that he had to cross, or defending it against outlaws and invaders.

But now, even swollen as it was, so that the waters would have touched the bottom of any cart, it seemed a little thing indeed. The old ash tree was there, except that the low branch had broken off, leaving a scar in the bark. It was as if, as Rhodri rode and looked about him at all the familiar sights, the boy didn't know this place at all. As if some-thing almost imperceptible had changed. Rhodri couldn't work out if it was the covering of white, or something deep within himself, and he touched his amulet.

All the adventures he had had as a child, all the acts of heroism he had done in his dreams, they seemed such slight and silly things now. Rhodri had seen so much, in the lava and the Telling Pool and in Homeira's cave, and he had held the fabled Excalibur. He knew so much more of the wide world, which all his life he had longed to see. But the things he had seen, all the things that lay out there still, made Rhodri feel as if he had been banished. As if he could never go back home at all.

He kept on riding. Yet rather than approach the house from the front, he pulled the horse up and tied it to a tree. He set off across the field. In no time at all, Rhodri was standing by the big oak. He looked up, and the height to the first branch seemed simple to climb. He began to pull himself up. It was not with the same urgency as he had climbed so many times as a boy. Now he measured his pace, and soon he was up high and looking all about him.

There was the barn and the yard and his home, the same as ever. A plume of white smoke rose from the chimney, and Rhodri wondered where Melanor was and if the other birds were still locked in their cage, or if they had survived the snows. He turned on the branch to survey the manor. It also seemed smaller than it had before, and now as Rhodri peered toward the stables, he felt none of the fear or won-der he had once felt. He thought of Wolfrin and his son, Aelfric, prob-ably snoring somewhere inside, and as he remembered the groom's secret that he had seen in the Telling Pool, a kind of cold contempt crept over him.

As Rhodri clambered down again and made for the house, he saw the door open and he stopped dead in the snow. There was his father, stretching in the morning air. Rhodri did not call to him though, or run forward. Instead he crept toward Owen as his father walked toward the well, and crouched down by the low wall to watch him. Owen drew up the bucket quickly and then took off his shirt to wash. Rhodri's heart was thundering, but in his mind he was willing his father to turn.

Owen's head lifted as he caught the feeling, and he swiveled round. Owen did not see his son, but Rhodri saw his father. He saw his chest bared to the day, and that scar still marking his body with the shape of a sword. Of a kind of cross. It looked fainter and less livid than it had before, but it was still there. Rhodri's stomach tightened, and though an ancient curse was broken, he wondered suddenly if all he had hoped for and all he had done had really been in vain. Owen shivered with cold, and lifting his shirt, he wrapped it about him and Rhodri felt a desperate surge of pity for this man who had suffered so much. Then Rhodri heard a familiar voice that made him happy.

"Owen, my love, come in before you catch cold and I'll make our breakfast."

Megan was in the doorway, and as soon as he saw his mother's face Rhodri knew that his quest had not been fruitless at all. That Owen's strong, loving heart was returned to her. Her eyes were glittering, and Owen smiled as she stepped toward him, and then he opened his arms and folded her tight within them.

"It's been far too long. I should set out today, *cariad*," said Owen softly, "to look for the boy."

Megan smiled and shook her head.

"No need, my husband. He'll be back soon. Rhodri promised. And he is no longer a boy."

Owen paused, but he nodded.

"Yes, my darling. And then we'll all be together again."

Megan tilted back her head and kissed Owen, then slipped from his embrace and went inside. Owen was about to follow her, but he stopped and looked round once more. He was not looking toward Rhodri, but out over the fields and the forest and the mountains. Just for a moment Rhodri fancied his father's brow had darkened and a familiar look had come into his eyes, like the look when he remembered Homeira. It passed as soon as it had come, and the master falconer smiled. He turned again and went straight into the house to Megan.

Rhodri found himself walking now, but not after his father. Instead he walked up and out across the fields. He plunged into the forest and after searching for a long while began to call, as he came close to the clearing.

"Tantallon. Where are you, Tantallon?"

As the young man reached Tantallon's hovel, he gasped. The door was broken in and the rowan tree had been cut down. Rhodri ran down toward the Telling Pool, and everywhere he noticed deep footprints in the ground. Soldiers had been here. Rhodri raced down the steps. When he reached the pool, he was horrified. There it lay, but the stone that formed the Seeing Place, where he and the high king had sat, had been rolled into the water, and logs and stones had been cast into the pool.

"They came in the night," said a voice behind him.

There among the trees stood Tantallon. He was dressed in that simple gray robe, but the hood was down and he seemed less stooped. As Rhodri drew closer, he noticed Tantallon's face and hair. The lines had gone around those old eyes, and that gray was flecked with gold. The scar across his eyelids seemed to have faded, too.

"The riders," whispered Tantallon, his eyes hugging the ground, "they were led by that groom up at the manor."

"Wolfrin," said Rhodri angrily.

"And his cruel boy, Aelfric. They didn't find me, but they stole the golden hat, and in their fear and ignorance, they tried to destroy the pool. As all try to destroy what they cannot understand."

"I'm sorry," whispered Rhodri. "It was because of me, Tantallon. I broke my promise not to tell of it. Aelfric must have heard."

Rhodri looked down among the rocks and logs, but even as he did so the waters began to ripple.

"It is all right, Rhodri," said Tantallon, "for nothing may truly harm the Miracle."

Rhodri could see a man in the water, riding through an English wood. It was the Lionheart. King Richard.

"The king," cried Rhodri. "The king comes home, too."

"The ransom was raised and the anguish is ended," said Tantallon softly. "Your knights return to their manors. We shall have peace, for a while at least. For the Lionheart is very fond of war, and he has his lands in France to fight for."

Rhodri nodded. He knew now that it took much to be a king.

"It is good to see you again, Rhodri. You've come home, too. And become a man."

Tantallon's voice was changed, too. It sounded younger and more powerful. Rhodri thought of Homeira on the floor of the cave, an old woman once more. He felt a jolt of anger, as he recalled how much Tantallon had kept from him.

"Why didn't you warn me, Tantallon? Of who I am? That you knew Homeira. That she wanted to trap me, so I would draw the sword from the Forge of Mythirion."

Tantallon smiled. "Because, Rhodri, you needed to discover your path for yourself. And you needed to set out for your own reasons, not anyone else's."

"But in the cave, I was nearly lost. But for Rebecca."

"And your own heart."

"You could have helped me," said Rhodri, "to fight her."

"No, boy," said Tantallon calmly, "for your greatest ally was the courage and faith and love you carry inside you. That alone let you use Mythirion to break the casket and her enchantments. That alone taught you how to wield the sword that brings only peace, like a man. Like a king."

"But Excalibur," said Rhodri, "it vanished."

"For it had done its work once more," said Tantallon. "But Excalibur waits. Waits always. As the stories of old wait in our dreams, to aid us. Excalibur is always close, if we keep faith."

Rhodri felt his father's sword at his back.

"Homeira," said Rhodri, "you knew and loved her. But there's something else about her. Who is she really? On my journey, I saw strange things. A smith making Mythrion, Merlin, and I dreamt of the sorceress Morgana Le Fey. I thought it was her and that you . . ."

"Do not ask too many questions," whispered Tantallon, though his smile was suddenly sad, "for the Miracle goes very deep. But how do you feel, young man?"

Rhodri sighed. "Strange, Tantallon. I held Mythirion, but in the end it was not like winning a battle at all. And when I saw my pa, I know his heart is no longer locked away, but that scar is still on his chest."

"For men and women must bear the real marks of the world," said Tantallon. "The hurt and pain it can bring, too. Just as they must bear their memories. And one day both your parents will be gone. That, too, is the Law."

Rhodri blinked. They were the same words Rebecca had used in the forest, yet this time Rhodri did not feel so terribly sad. In the Telling Pool he saw another face. That face that had spoken to him from the fire. King Arthur. Arthur smiled at Rhodri, and another face was beside his. Guinevere. The queen with the star on her forehead looked kindly, almost lovingly at Rhodri. As if she were looking on her own lost son. Guinevere turned to Arthur in the water and gently took his hand. Then both of those ancient faces faded away.

Rhodri wanted to shout with happiness. He'd done it.

As he turned away from the water and walked joyfully with Tantallon back through the forest, his thoughts gradually turned to home and the confused feelings he'd had when he'd first seen it again. He knew his old friend could help explain them.

"I don't understand why everything feels so different, Tantallon. The manor and my home, they all seem so much smaller somehow."

"Perhaps you're learning the greatest secret then," said the hermit.

"That there's something bigger even than the love of hearth and home, and all that was once so dear to you as a boy. There's a world out there and you are part of it, Rhodri, as we are all a part of the Miracle. None may escape their destiny, without harm."

"And though much is dark and cruel, Tantallon," said Rhodri, "much is beautiful and noble, too. And it doesn't frighten me so much now."

"Then you've won something just as important as the knights' freedom or your father's heart," said Tantallon, looking proudly at the young man, "as important perhaps as peace for the land, or breaking a curse."

"Won something?"

"You've won your own heart in the world."

Rhodri felt a shiver run up his spine.

"But it's time," said Tantallon, "to say farewell once more. Don't worry, we shall meet again, Rhodri."

Tantallon stepped forward and put out his hand. The young man clasped it warmly.

"Thank you."

Tantallon looked up and smiled, and Rhodri almost jumped back as he looked at him.

"Tantallon," he cried. "You can see me."

Tantallon's clever eyes shimmered joyfully.

"Yes, Rhodri. Thanks to you. For the curse had harmed me, too, but your faith helped restore a foolish old man."

Rhodri was overjoyed.

Tantallon smiled at the young man one last time and turned away.

"Wait," said Rhodri, wondering when he would see his friend again. "I've something for you. It can't replace what they stole, but . . ."

Rhodri dipped his head and pulled his amulet over it. Tantallon took it and clenched it tight in his fist. With that, Tantallon turned again and walked slowly away. His shape was silent in the snowy wood as his form moved through the trees.

"Tantallon," cried Rhodri, as the old man vanished among the branches. "Who are you really? Are you . . ."

A branch snapped underfoot, and a voice came back to him through the trees, like an echo fading across time itself, a voice he had heard before.

"And who are you, Rhodri Falcon, who are you?"

Rhodri walked back up the steps and crossed the forest. Then down through the field in the snow. He cut through the branches and found Dusk waiting there patiently.

"Well, my friend," said Rhodri cheerfully, as he untied him, "I bet you're cold and hungry, right enough. They'll be some hay in the barn, see, and a warm bed tonight. And now we've a horse and gems to help my family."

Dusk whinnied. Rhodri heard hooves on the track. William De Brackenois, Wolfrin, and Aelfric were riding toward him. They pulled up in surprise as soon as they saw him.

"Where've you been, Falcon?" snorted Aelfric. "Trying to escape your bonded duty perhaps? Or looking into that evil pool. When the priest knows of it . . ."

"I've been on a journey, Aelfric," said Rhodri coldly; then he turned and smiled at William. "But now I'm home. And any who speaks of the pool as evil is a liar."

Aelfric grunted.

"And what did you see, Aelfric, when you looked into the water?" asked Rhodri scornfully. "Perhaps your own foolish reflection?"

Aelfric flushed, for he had indeed seen nothing.

Wolfrin pushed his horse toward Rhodri.

"You speak to my boy so?" he growled. "And call him a liar."

Rhodri glared at Wolfrin but he didn't flinch or back away. He put his hand to his sword.

"Yes, Wolfrin. As I call you a liar."

"You dare, Waelas."

"And what use are lies, Wolfrin?" said Rhodri. "Except perhaps tales of robbers to prove our courage, or the truth of a dagger in the neck to hide our cowardice and trickery and betrayal."

Wolfrin blanched so white he looked like death, and Rhodri thought of how the bandits had been punished. A fear had come into Wolfrin's eyes, and his son and William were now looking at the groom strangely. William pushed forward on his horse and dismounted.

"Rhodri," the young noble cried, "it's good to have you back. I'd hear more of this. There has been much foolishness since you left."

"Yes," said Rhodri, "but now it's over."

Rhodri, too, jumped down and, taking the sword from his back, offered William the hilt and bent his knee.

"My lord," said the young man, "you've been good to my family and I honor you for it. I do not think it right to do so to all men, just for a fact of birth, but to you it is a privilege. So I offer you my loyalty and my fealty, as my father once honored yours."

William De Brackenois blushed proudly. It was as if some of Rhodri's new strength and courage passed to the young lord with his pledge.

"Thank you, Rhodri Falcon. And this oath I accept as a bond made not only of duty, but of true friendship."

"But, my lord," said Wolfrin angrily, "the priest's warning and the lad's stories . . ."

"Silence, Wolfrin," cried William, looking a little surprised at his own words. "Do you forget that you are nothing more than my groom? I've listened to you long enough. There'll be changes at the manor now. Rhodri Falcon, come up to the manor next sunup."

Rhodri smiled and nodded.

"And don't worry what they say of the pool," said William as they mounted. "The soldiers saw nothing, and how can they burn you for looking into water?"

William turned to ride away and the others followed meekly, but the young lord suddenly swung his horse round.

"And Rhodri," he said, as he rode back, "go and see Sarah soon. She misses you, you know. She'll be overjoyed you're back."

The young men smiled openly at each other, and once more William rode away. Rhodri felt proud of himself and William as he drew Dusk on toward the house. He stopped for a moment as he came round the bend. He had heard a cry, high up in the winter blue. It was strong and clear and piercing and the young man knew immediately what it meant.

"Melanor."

Rhodri lifted his head and gave a long, low whistle. Melanor's screech came again, and then Rhodri saw him wheeling in the frosty sky. He was a speck at first as he circled high overhead, but then his shape grew clearer and clearer. Then two more birds were at his side,

Glindor and Breeze, and as the hunting birds turned and dived and wheeled around one another, Rhodri's heart could have burst with joy. Their wings looked so graceful on the invisible currents of the sky, and their plunges so wild and reckless, that Rhodri's heart soared with their newfound freedom. The young man felt a great rush of triumph and exhilaration.

Then another bird was there in the skies, too. It came like a spirit and joined them only for an instant, before turning and wheeling away. It was the merlin. Rhodri's pace quickened, and he lifted his strong arm and called. Melanor stooped from the others, and like a master falconer, Rhodri showed his arm to catch the falling bird. Then Rhodri dropped Dusk's tether and, with Melanor on his fist, the falconer was running, running back toward his home and his parents.

ABOUT THE AUTHOR

David Clement-Davies is the author of such highly regarded novels as *Fell*, *The Sight*, and *Fire Bringer*, which *Booklist* called "a masterpiece of animal fantasy" in a starred review and which Richard Adams, author of *Watership Down*, hailed as "one of the best anthropomorphic fantasies known to me." Both books were named *Booklist* Books of the Year and Book Sense 76 selections. David is also a travel writer, and his wide-ranging journeys are often inspiration for his vividly set stories. He is a graduate of the University of Edinburgh, where he studied English literature and history, and now lives in London.

This book was designed by Jay Colvin and art directed by Becky Terhune. It is set in Caslon, which was created by the eighteenth-century type designer William Caslon. The chapter titles are set in Zoroaster.

Enjoy this sneak peek at
David Clement-Davies's epic animal fantasy

Fell

sequel to *The Sight*

The girl went sailing backwards and, to her horror, found that she was falling, not towards the drop, but towards the wolf. Her body struck Fell's, and with a furious snarl, he turned and sprang at her, as she landed on her back on the ice.

His jaws were open, and Alina didn't feel fear as such, just a kind of grim resignation, yet as the wolf stood over her, something new stirred in her too, the anger of a fighter. Her eyes blazed.

In that moment Fell remembered the powers of the Sight to control wills. Could he control this human? His thoughts, directed by the Sight, began to reach out towards her consciousness, as they had once reached out to the Balkar.

"Give in, Drappa," whispered his angry mind. "Obey me. I, who have been darkness. I, who shared the vision with Larka and all the Lera. The secret of what man is and what sorrow he can bring. I command you."

As Fell wrestled there, he realised that it was as if, in all his journeying, he had reached the borders of a strange new land, and that no curse or blessing would ever let him pass. He could not reach Alina's will. Fell felt strangely foolish.

They both sensed the energy though in each other's being, moving through their bodies like a secret language, and as their eyes locked again, so close this time it was as if they might meld into each other, Alina saw the strange sliver of green in Fell's right eye and the wolf the green splinter in Alina's left.

It brought something like wonder and recognition to them, and although all Fell's wild instincts were telling him to strike, he couldn't attack this Drappa. The wolf remembered wrestling long ago with his sister Larka in the Red Meadow, the field of spirits that lies before the journey beyond, and the words about destiny and a Guardian, and then the ache in his head came again. Suddenly Fell was thrown sideways in the cave.

Alina had not moved, or done anything at all. It was like the force that two lodestones make when brought together, that men in later days would call a magnetic field, and somehow both the girl and the wolf knew then they could not harm each other. Ever.

A voice came sounding and echoing through their heads, as if from the cave itself. "What is happening to us?"

The wolf and the girl looked at each other in utter amazement, and suddenly they were talking. Not in words or in growls, but with their thoughts.

"You are Fell, are you not?" asked Alina's frightened, wondering mind. "The lone black wolf."

"A Kerl, my kind call it, man cub. And you are Alina, I think. I've dreamt of you, with that mark on your arm. Though I thought you a Dragga."

"But how can this be? Are the shepherd's stories of werewolves and transformations true? How are we talking like this? Is there really such magic in the world?"

Alina thought of goblins and sprites and fairies. This was far more miraculous.

"It's the Sight, child. The gift that comes through the forehead. Only a very few possess it. My sister Larka looked into the mind of the Man Varg once. The Man Wolf. It brought the animals a terrible vision of the past and future. And I have the power too. The power to look into minds and control wills entered the world when my aunt Morgra summoned the spectres from one of the worlds beyond, with her Summoning Howl."

"But what do you want of me, Fell?"

Fell remembered that voice in the cave, the voice he had tried to resist.

"I don't know. To aid you perhaps? To learn from you and understand? Before I met you, my dead sister told me to help you, I think. Told me you may have a great destiny, child."

Keep reading! If you liked this book, check out these other titles.

Fell
By David Clement-Davies
978-0-8109-1185-7 $19.95 hardcover

The Lighthouse Land
By Adrian McKinty
978-0-8109-5480-9 $16.95 hardcove
978-0-8109-9361-7 $7.95 paperback

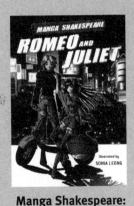

**Manga Shakespeare:
Romeo and Juliet**
By William Shakespeare
Adapted by Richard Appignanesi
Illustrated by Sonia Leong
978-0-8109-9325-9 $9.95 paperback

Visit www.amuletbooks.com to download screen savers and ring tones, to find out where authors will be appearing, and to send e-cards.